RECKLESS
COVENANT

TWISTED LEGENDS COLLECTION

LILITH ROMAN

Reckless Covenant
Copyright © 2022 Lilith Roman. All rights reserved.
First Edition | August 2022

This is a work of fiction. References to real people, places, organizations, events, and products are intended to provide a sense of authenticity and are used fictitiously. All characters, incidents, and dialogue are drawn from the author's imagination and not to be construed as real.

Editing by Mackenzie Letson
www.nicegirlnaughtyedits.com
Proofreading by Zoejayne Knight
Formatting & Cover Design by Raven Designs

ISBN 9781916888951 (eBook Edition)
ISBN 9781916888968 (Paperback Edition)

Author's
NOTE

Thank you for choosing Reckless Covenant as your next read. This is my first mafia story and also my first second chance one, and I've had so much fun diving into the plot of it. It was a different experience than my other stories, so many more characters to play with, so many more layers to add, and I'm holding my fingers crossed that you will enjoy it too.

Happy Reading!

Love,
Lilith

CONTENT WARNING

WEBSITE: lilithromanauthor.com

Welcome...

Ten authors invite you to join us in the
Twisted Legends Collection.

These stories are a dark, twisted reimagining of
infamous legends well-known throughout the
world. Some are retellings, others are nods to those
stories that cause a chill to run down your spine.

Each book may be a standalone, but they're
all connected by the lure of a legend.

We invite you to venture into the unknown,
and delve into the darkness with us,
one book at a time.

The
COLLECTION

Dedication

To all of us who are too independent for our own good…
sometimes it's okay to let yourself be the damsel in
distress for the right person.

Prologue

8 years ago

THE UNMISTAKABLE CRACK OF BONES TWISTS THE SOUND waves, gripping my muscles in a wince, my teeth clenching as a sharp vibration taints the air. We watch as he grabs onto his jaw on a pain-filled bellow, but the enraged curses she spits at him almost shadow it.

His screams fuel her, her eyes filling with a familiar madness, yet... so much richer than what looks back at me in the mirror. She's a fucking tornado of punches, hits and kicks, as her small body shoves him in a frenzied attack.

It's goddamn mesmerizing... Even Madds just stands there, admiring the image with starry eyes.

And he never admires anything...

But when she throws herself on top of the kid, her knee digging in his stomach, as she leans onto the forearm she's locked onto his throat, it's time to stop her.

I step forward, sliding my hands under her armpits to pull her off the guy who's at the brink of tears, his nose a bleeding mess, but she pushes me back with more force than should reside in her slim frame.

Madds replaces me just as she pulls back her elbow, grabbing her before that small fist lands in the asshole's face once again. He yanks her back as she kicks her legs, screeching at the intrusion, but he doesn't flinch, lifting her small body to his tall one, wrapping a strong arm around her as she hits his chest to let her go. He doesn't. He lets her get it all out as I stalk toward the mangled piece of crap lying on the floor.

"I'm gonna fucking ruin y'all! Send your asses to jail, fucking white trash!" He spits blood onto the tiled floor, the words slurred through the pain in his jaw, as he pushes his broken body to get up. My foot lands on his throat in the next second and something in my gaze makes him pause, his eyes growing wider as his body stills and tenses.

There's fear in those dilating pupils, and it takes one glimpse at my reflection in the window before me, to realize what he sees there—it's the sort of malice that makes angels fall, villains rise, and summons armies.

Our army has been assembling for a while, and he's exactly the type of person that would be a target. Only this pathetic pussy right here poses no advantage to our less than charitable cause. His daddy though, yeah… we could entice him with a deal he definitely couldn't refuse, since he holds some information we could exploit. But maybe his kid is not that useless after all…

"I wonder what your daddy would think if we threatened to expose his only son, the future of his name, the heir of his business, as a rapist…" I press a little harder on his trachea as those words spill calmly off my tongue, and when his hands grab onto my leg, I increase the pressure. "Get your filthy hands off me," I bite out in a low, guttural voice.

His mouth moves and some gurgling sounds come out just as he taps his palm on the floor.

"Give him a chance, Vin." Madds laughs in the background, the girl's screeches now having quieted.

I shrug and take my foot off his throat, his following coughs getting a bit boring after a few seconds.

"Spit it the fuck out!" I rasp, enjoying the wince that crumples his face.

"I didn't ra..." He all but whispers as he rolls onto his front, pushing his aching body on all fours so he can get up.

"Speak up, motherfucker!"

"I didn't rape her." He spits blood onto the floor, rising and sitting on his heels.

"Who the fuck do you think you're playing?! I got one word for you: Rose." The seconds stretch as his shoulders tense and he slowly turns his head toward me. "She couldn't go to the police. There wouldn't be enough evidence for them, but there's more than enough for her father and us, motherfucker. We were coming for you, catching you on Lover's Lane, with your tiny dick in your hand as you were about to force yourself on yet another girl, who was clearly refusing you... was just our motherfucking luck, and you..."

But I don't get a chance to finish...

"I'll fucking kill you, motherfucker! I'll chop off your dick and shove it up your ass, you goddamn son of a bitch!" the girl shrieks in her sharp, angry voice, the words making me cringe, but I resist the urge to cup my own dick at the disturbing thought.

She escapes Madds' hold, rushing to the guy. Her foot lands on his back, pushing him to the floor, and it's followed by a strong kick between his legs, just as he curls into a fetal position.

I reach over, my hands on her waist attempting

4

to pull her back, and in the next second, my ear is ringing, the shock of the hit knocking me backward a couple of steps, before I realize the back of her elbow collided with the side of my face.

"Jesus fuck!" I rasp, ready to haul her ass over my shoulder and leave before she kills the guy. But I pause… trapped in her gaze, the fury so fucking pretty in her green eyes. There's no trace of remorse looking back at me. It's in this moment, before she lands one last punch in the guy's ribs, with her gaze on me the whole time, that something far more shattering hits me. Only it doesn't land on my flesh, nor on my bones, but in my fucking heart and soul, and I know… I'm ruined.

One

MORRIGAN

Present Day

I FELT THE AIR SHIFT BEFORE MY EYES CAUGHT ON TO THE silent disturbance. The skin of my back prickled with an uncomfortable chill, even in this sticky humidity. It's spreading up my spine, onto my shoulders and grips my neck, forcing my body to turn, as one by one, the people around me change their tune, either to silence or whispers, just as my gaze slowly lands on *them*.

It's almost impossible to think of the men as individuals at this moment, or any other—they almost present as one entity, yet the shift in the air would make one feel they are a legion, commanding the attention of all who are around.

They are not from the same family, yet somehow cut from the same cloth, moving in unison like they share blood, muscles, bones, and DNA. Their arms sway at the same time, their feet gliding in a matching beat on the moonlit asphalt, and fuck me if it doesn't feel like time slows down, allowing everyone to take in the creatures making the air tense into compliance.

Only they are no creatures at all… just people.

People forming one very important faction— The Sanctum.

Our southern city is big enough that we don't all know each other, yet wherever they make an appearance, the world stands still. Rulers over these lands. Only it's not fear holding you still, it's *power*. Fear is simply a byproduct. It stems from the rumors swerving about them—violence, sex, secrets, murder—and no matter which you've heard, they add on to one thing and one thing only… *danger*.

I guess this is what happens when you deal with The Serpent… the devil that sneaks out of its kingdom and offers you the forbidden fruit. No one knows how many of these rumors are true, yet there has never been any denial, and their presence alone is enough to make you believe all of them and more.

There's no denying life is much more intriguing like this, when all fear you, bow to you, and you are predictable in a completely unpredictable way.

It is a red carpet weaved with fear and blood, and no one dares cross the velvet rope. Not when they think they know the terror waiting on the other side. Their brand of organized crime is different from any other I've known.

I remember them as teenagers; it's hard not to. They were a force of fucking nature, and no matter what, you somehow craved to throw yourself in the middle of that storm, chase the tornado and let it consume you. As adults… their attacks are silent, like a rising tsunami, silently gathering its strength, and when it roars… it's too late to save yourself.

Their affairs aren't common knowledge, they exist in an underworld they created, and normal people simply don't have access to something like that. One thing I personally know for sure—they deal in secrets. Prey on them. Harness them and keep them safe. Until the time comes and their trade is beneficial. Information is power and power is worth more than money.

The Serpent should know. The only one of The Sanctum who didn't come from money. The one who can trap even your shivers with just one look. His black eyes pierce you, opening gates into your mind you don't know exist until he's there, until all your deepest cravings want to burst through and suddenly… you can't recognize yourself.

He *is* power. He doesn't need *old money*. The

world would bow at his feet with his pockets empty.

Very few men have that talent. The one sitting next to me right now would kill for that particular skill. It's not a thought I would have had about him six months ago… but things change, so many things changed.

As they walk on the sidewalk, past the old-time cinema, slow and determined, past Mrs Dawn's pretty flower shop, looking like they are gliding over the concrete, they pass one of Queenscove's fanciest restaurants, then slowly shift directions to the dark alley next to it. There are rumors of a speakeasy nestled in plain sight somewhere in the middle of the city, around here. Only rumors, because the ones who know of it, which building, which door, or how to gain access, do not speak of it. And considering The Sanctum lurks there, I don't think they would risk saying a word.

I watch as the first one dips into the shadows, then the second one, their black suit covered bodies absorbed by the darkness.

After the third man disappears, The Serpent takes one more step and stops.

I swear time slows down just for him, his body turning ever so slightly, his eyes closed as he moves to look over his shoulder. And then they open… not wide, but the slits of a snake who found its next meal—and I am it.

What happens when you gaze upon the devil...
and he catches you?

When his eyes land on yours and he marks you
as a target?

What happens when the devil doesn't look like
a devil at all?

Dozens of people sit at the tables of this street-
side bar terrace... yet his gaze landed straight on
mine. Saliva pools in my mouth, but swallowing
means moving and somehow moving seems to be
the wrong action right now.

He's fixed on me, unnaturally still, but the alley's
shadows seem to swallow him, as if the darkness is
part of him, a coat he wears well.

Around me, whispers break out in unison, and
one by one the other patrons turn toward me, each
pair of eyes burning more holes in my skin as their
interest peaks. The moment the members of The
Sanctum stepped out of their SUV, all eyes were on
them, so hiding this silent, yet powerful exchange is
impossible.

Moments pass, the night breeze unhelpful as
my eyes begin to burn with the need to blink. Only I
have a fucking point to prove—I am not submitting
to him, I will not break eye contact first.

"Darling?"

Shut the fuck up, Ryan.

"Morrigan?!" His tone commanding now.

Suddenly, The Serpent's gaze turns even darker, a gentle scowl forming between his eyebrows, yet I'm sure no one else notices but me. I'm also sure it isn't meant for me either, but for…

A hand waves in front of my eyes, breaking the connection.

Goddamnit, Ryan!

When his hand vacates my line of sight, The Serpent is gone… the alley empty.

Turning to Ryan, the ruckus of the terrace patrons fills the night again. Stealing a glance around myself, I can see them all, watching me from the corner of their eyes, even if their conversations are not about me.

"Yes, Ryan." My eyes land on him before my face fully turns.

There isn't much more I can take from our relationship, even though I do kind of care about him. I think I loved him once, but I've been ready to leave for a while… ever since it all started to change. When *he* started to change.

However, our families seem just as involved in our relationship as we are, well… more than I am, and leaving him seems like breaking a treaty between two nations. They always insist on meeting, pushing us together, forcing us to dinners and events. Every encounter breaks the confidence I've been trying to build. And it's just as hard for me to break away from my own family.

"What the hell was that?!"

I finally turn to him fully, and the exasperated look in my eyes is harder to sustain when I take in his expression, one eyebrow cocked and lips arched downwards.

"I don't know." I shrug.

I'm lying. It was hate. Betrayal.

This city is big, so I managed to avoid The Serpent unintentionally over the years. We've rarely crossed paths and I like it this way. It must have been months since the last time I saw him... God, I'm fucking fooling myself. Five months, three weeks, and... two days—my mother's 50th fucking birthday. The fucking elite were invited. The Sanctum were too. I was sure it was either a power move, to show some sort of alliance, or my parents begging for a business deal.

Five fucking months and that night still haunts me.

If only it was the only one...

I focus on Ryan's eyes. Brown, like a marsh, with hints of green... swampy. Nothing special sparks in them anymore.

"He was just staring at you."

I blink and turn my gaze back toward the dark alley.

Yes, he was.

Maybe that night stuck with him too. Maybe I left a scar on his taut skin. I hope I did.

The Sanctum... they are fearless, seemingly indestructible, and my parents did business with them, or maybe just tried to.

For five months, I've been trying to figure out what was happening with my family. They were dysfunctional in their normal state, but lately things have shifted further. It feels different. Like we're sitting at the edge of a cliff and any moment now, a storm will tip us over. I wish I wouldn't think about *us*... I wish I wouldn't be involved in this, but somehow I'm being pulled into it, whatever the fuck it is. But in this game of chess, I'm no Queen, not even a Knight... I'm a pawn. Not that I was ever anything more to my parents, to my father. I was never as important as my older brother. He is the future of this family, the one to take over whatever businesses father has, the one to take the O'Rourke name further, carry it deeper into our fucked up history.

Even our ancestors were fucked up sons of bitches. Some worse than others.

I'm not implying I'm a saint; I know where I belong, but it doesn't mean my place is with them. As long as I'm careful, they won't know I'm trying to get away from all of them until it's too late to stop me. And if they do try to stop me, they will find out exactly what this family bred.

Ryan used to be my escape from them, long ago. Not anymore, not since he realized he couldn't quite tame me, when his views started aligning with his father's... and mine. His exertion of control these days runs deeper than I would care to admit.

His time will come though, and he will pay too.

"I think I'm ready to go home now."

"Alone?" A scowl forms ridges on his forehead.

But I mentally roll my eyes. *As if I'm ever alone.* There are constant eyes on me, especially as of late. Since Ryan's father passed away, he is slowly taking over the family business and accepting his place as the head of it. Something is brewing, and I'm not in the inner circle. All I know is that our families, before the passing of Jonah Holt, were working on something, a business deal, an alliance.

Have the terms changed now?

"Alone. I have things to do."

"Things?" He spits the word out like the lack of respect he has toward my work isn't already very well known. Just because I work online, it doesn't mean it's not work.

I get up before he can say anything else, dip down and give him a peck on the lips, as I know he won't let me leave without the faked affection. But he catches my upper arm just as I'm almost standing, and pulls me back down, his lips crashing onto mine, in a much deeper kiss.

Some sort of claim on me, for everyone around us to see…

After The Serpent's earlier display, such a rare one, I'm sure he feels the need to piss all over me, to make sure everyone knows who I belong to.

I allow the kiss for a similar reason. My own survival.

I have to play nice…

Hopefully not for long.

Two
MORRIGAN

I STEP INTO MY CAR, EAGER TO START THE AC AND ESCAPE the humidity, shutting the door as the engine roars to life. The busy street drowns the noise of it, but it's not like people didn't already turn their heads as I sat in it. They probably think it's my boyfriend's or daddy's car, as most do. Technically, they wouldn't be wrong.

As I was finishing university last year, my parents suddenly decided moving about in taxis wasn't safe for their daughter anymore. They insisted they buy me a car, even though I didn't want to be tied to their money, and the only way to escape their flashy choice, which would have ensured I would flaunt their wealth around the city, was to concede. After some negotiation, I managed to sway them from the same mid-life crisis red Ferrari my father has, toward this black beauty, a Dodge Challenger GT.

I love this car, but it's a constant reminder of their control over me, and I fucking pray for the day I can just drop the keys on their fucking table and buy my own, the day I'll be able to afford to move out and escape their damn clutches. Ryan's too... but it's been just over two months since his father died, and I'm still trying to find the right time to leave him. The courage to...

Luckily, my parents wanted to raise good *stock*, and the best uni took me 400 miles away from them, up North, even as they protested it was too far. The freedom allowed me to have a part-time job without them knowing. I saved every penny, along with most of my allowance since I was fifteen, and began to understand that my family's values, their view of me or women in general, are much different from most, and I had to plan my way out. But all my savings are tied up in my first business venture in which I'm a silent partner. There's no way I can let my family, or anyone else, know just yet, that I'm involved. Lulu and I worked too hard for it.

I pull away from the curb just as my dashboard flashes with a phone call, Lulu's name popping on the screen. I turn the volume down and answer.

"Give me a sec, let me put my AirPods in. I'm in

17

the car." These days, I'm careful we're not overheard, especially when it's about business.

I fiddle with them and switch the connection on my phone as I stop at the traffic lights.

"You good?" I hear her sweet, soft voice on the other line. It's deceiving. The woman may sound sweet, but she's vicious. Calm… but vicious.

"Yeah, all good. I was just thinking of you. What's up?"

"I'm just having a little trouble making a decision and I wanted to ask if you can come in and help me out." I hear her long nails tap one by one on a solid surface. She sounds impatient.

"Yeah, give me ten, or actually fifteen minutes. I need to…"

"I know," she interrupts. She knows my life all too well, including the regression of my relationship. I need to lose my tail, if there is one, since I told Ryan I'm going home. Her location or my friendship with her isn't a secret, but I would rather have a head start anyway.

The four-story pre-war building looms, the beautiful details of the facade hiding many secrets beyond it. On the top floor Lulu lives with her boyfriend, the two floors below unused, and on the ground floor, Lulu opened a quirky bar, which brings her constant income.

I look around before I leave the car, a habit

that has become second nature now, but I wasn't followed. Before walking into the bar, I glance briefly at the windows of the floor under Lulu's apartment, the one she insisted I should have. I didn't want to bring my fucked up life so close to her, but her love is the only unconditional one I know, and in the end I accepted her offer.

This place was an inheritance from her late grandmother, who had it from her own mother, and it's been rotting since the 50s, stuck in time. Lulu started renovating it, she finished the restructuring, part of the ground floor, and her apartment, but when our business idea fully formed, all the financial efforts shifted. The works on my apartment halted before they properly began. It doesn't even have a floor right now, just some bare beams that used to hold the rotting parquet.

I step into the bar, so ingeniously placed in the space that the bar itself is at the front of the space, and all the tables are behind it, away from the windows, away from the road. She started from a small front, slowly extending it toward the back once it became more popular. But it's still small, narrow, as the rest of the ground floor and the basement is being turned into something much, much more exciting.

"Hey, sugar!" I greet the bartender as I walk past, toward the back door hidden nicely from the view of the street. The location for our business is

19

perfect because even if someone was following me, going to see my best friend is nothing unusual.

After punching in a code, I step into the well-lit short corridor surveyed by two cameras, arriving at two other doors. Both lead to a different secure foyer, one at the front of the building, where the access to the apartments is, and the second one, where I'm punching in yet another code to get in, leads to the back of the building.

As I make my way inside, a dim gold light bathes the space where a black 3D diamond pattern covers most of the walls, the decadent glow reflecting off of some of the faces of the shapes, and I think I'm in a bit of disbelief, as this space wasn't finished the last time I was here. To my left, double doors lead to the entrance hallway at the back of the building where there is a private courtyard and parking lot. To my right sits what will be a staffed wardrobe, and right in front of me, in the middle of the wall stretching the entire length of the space, sits the pièce of resistance—the black marble and dark wood, semi-circle shaped reception desk.

I step closer, in awe at the beauty our artist created on the black velvet covered wall, bas-reliefs of naked bodies protruding out of the flat surface, the gold light absorbed by their sinful positions. On either side of the desk, five feet away, two entrance ways interrupt the wall, and this is where their beauty lies. On the left-hand side of the reception desk, on his hands and knees, there is a bas-relief of a man with a leash clearly wrapped around his neck, held by a woman standing on the inside of the reception desk, her legs spread in an imposing stance. On the right-hand side, outside of the reception desk, sits a woman, ass on her heels, palms on her thighs, a leash held by a man standing on the inside of the desk, wrapped around her throat. And in-between these two scenes, centered on the wall behind the desk, is my favorite—a beast of a man, standing tall, one hand wrapped in the hair of the woman before him, holding her head, neck bent back uncomfortably, while his other hand is lost in the relief, between them, where their hips join.

They are so beautifully sculpted behind the soft fabric, so enchanting and mildly hypnotic.

I continue through the entrance on the left, into a wide corridor with a couple of sitting areas, the doors to a set of toilets and dressing rooms on the opposite wall, but my attention is caught somewhere else. Against the same wall as the reception on the other side, the stairs lead down into our club, and right above them, one word written in large brushed-gold letters, tells you exactly where you're going and what awaits you while you're there— METAMORPHOSIS.

It shines discreetly against the black velvet, and

21

its meaning is as much tied to our own evolution as it is to the experience of the people who will join us here.

As I walk down those steps, gold spotlights illuminating each thread, my soul feels freer, here beneath the ground, as a sultry rebel blues song floods my ears. The moment the block heels of my knee-high boots hit the floor, as my eyes sweep over the space before me, I clutch the handrail so hard my bones ache.

"It's ready…" I whisper to myself.

"Tadaaaa!" Lulu startles me as she jumps from behind the bar sitting against the right wall, fairly close to the stairs. We wanted to give people this proximity, as some could be overwhelmed when they first step into the fetish club. Even in normal clubs, most people run to the bar first. It's a comfort thing.

Her icy blond ponytail whips around as she dips behind the black marble-topped bar, and the music quiets. I walk toward her, but my eyes are gazing anywhere but in her direction, mesmerized by the reality of this finished space. I'm in awe, speechless at how insane the finished product looks. I mean, I'd seen it only a week ago, and it wasn't far from this stage, yet… it still shocks me. The implication of it being finished, more than the look of it.

"I can't believe it's finished…" I almost whisper.

"Is it really?" I whip my head to Lulu, my excitement seeping through.

"It is! I was dying to tell you we would be done today, but I wanted to surprise you! It's fucking beautiful, isn't it?" She clutches her fists to her chest, an emotional look in her eyes as she looks around the space.

I rest my back against the bar, facing the center of the room where a large circular stage stands, two stripper poles on it because as much as it is a fetish club, everyone loves seeing some good dancing skills on them. It's funny, actually, Lulu insisted on them, and I still think she did because she knows how much I enjoy pole dancing, and how hard I shy away from being seen doing it. I reckon this is her way of kicking my confidence into gear. Either way, the stripping, the dancing, it will provide amazing background entertainment when the stage isn't used for its main purpose—shows. We're taking our inspiration from the club in our university city, Rosston, where experienced couples or groups booked the stage for various activities, either actual play or instructional sessions. Watching those shows will certainly be… intriguing. The rest of the space is filled with booths and tables, with enough space around to still dance.

"I can't believe we're three weeks ahead of schedule." I push away from the bar and walk around the counter, my gaze set on the bottle and glasses stashed behind it. The bar isn't stocked yet, but we kept a bottle of Bourbon here for tough times. There's just under a third left... there have been quite a few tough times so far.

I pour two fingers into each glass and hand one over to Lulu, clinking with her.

"Congratulations, Miss Dietrich."

"Congratulations to you too, Miss O'Rourke." I take a large sip, then head toward the right, the opposite side of the room from the stairs, where a corridor splits the wall, each side covered by large windows from wall to wall and two doors, each leading to separate playrooms. They're special double windows, so from inside you can choose if you want the small crowd to watch you, or turn it into a mirror. Or you could just pull the curtains and have private playtime instead.

I drag my free hand over the dark wood paneling covering the wall, admiring the equipment sitting beautifully behind the windows—benches, St Andrews crosses, toys, crops, tables, and just simple chairs. The main reason this place cost us pretty much all our savings is because we made sure all the equipment is of excellent quality, comfortable, a lot of it handmade by a great local carpenter and tanner we found. One of the things the club in Rosston was lacking was quality equipment. We're new to the business world, and we wanted everything about this club to scream excellence and taste, last thing we need is to give someone an excuse to tell us we're not serious about this venture, especially since our market research showed us there's enough elite in this city seeking this kind of place somewhere else. Safe to say, after making all these for us, the carpenter/tanner decided he will be our first member, and we can't wait to welcome him.

"We're keeping the same opening date, right?" We reach the end of the corridor, which opens into a small hallway, to the right heading toward the bathrooms, a security desk and the fire exit, and toward the left, where we're heading right now, is our office and private bathroom. Lulu walks in, sits at the desk, leaning back and propping her legs up on it.

"I think it's a clever idea." I follow suit, sinking into the sofa and propping my legs up on the coffee table. "It gives us time to reach our member goal, but we could potentially hold a pre-opening party for the ones who have signed up so far. There's enough there for a good one, and I'm almost done with their background checks. We can invite a few guests to play, put up a show, create a great atmosphere, and offer an incentive at the party for the current members, if they recommend another potential member."

"It's a great idea! We can ask Rose and Jasmine if they are available to entertain earlier than planned. Maybe talk to a few people from the club in Rosston to come and play."

"Are you gonna play?" I ask Lulu as she downs the rest of her drink. We want to give members the comfort of feeling free, without people recognizing them, or seeing that they are in the presence of someone they know personally. Of course, it's impossible to promise true anonymity since it depends more on them than us, especially when tattoos are involved, but the least we can do for them, and our staff as well, is to make masks mandatory; simple carnival style, or on the tasteful horror side, it doesn't matter.

"I'm sure Luke would enjoy that, but the party is too important, and it will be hard enough to keep myself focused, so I don't need to get involved as well." She smiles, but I don't miss the slight roll in her eyes.

"Yeah, you're right," I agree. I pop my glass on the coffee table and lay all the way down on the sofa. Damn, it's comfortable... I would rather sleep here than go to my parents'.

Lulu actually met Luke in the fetish club up in Rosston, and they clicked from the start. After uni, he pretty much followed her here, not that it was a big move, as his hometown is about 200 miles up

North from here, close to Venator. However, who wouldn't want to be here on this Topaz coast, close to the light blue waters and white sands it got its name from. It feels almost tropical without most of the discomforts of a tropical climate, although we still have the humidity and stickiness.

This place attracts a healthy number of tourists, but our mayor has limited the number of hotels that can be built, by local ordinance, to avoid ruining the landscape and infrastructure. Every single local agreed. That number was reached a few years ago, so even as a tourist town, it's fairly exclusive. And not many people move in, since most don't want to leave, and the real estate is through the roof expensive.

Queenscove is a corner of paradise.

It's one of the reasons why I knew I couldn't refuse Lulu for long. Getting this apartment from her was a godsend! It was also a godsend that her grandmother left her this place, along with some money. Her parents and older sister got an equal share of inheritance, but none received real estate as big as this, not as dilapidated either. Her grandmother knew she was the right person to take care of this beautiful old building properly. Long before our time, it was a small hotel which Lulu's great-great-grandmother owned, only she decided she would make each floor its own apartment instead.

"You alright?" She pulls me out of my thoughts. "You wanna crash at mine?"

"Nah, you and Luke need your space. Besides… I don't wanna give my parents, or Ryan, any other reason to be suspicious of me." I get up and down the rest of the drink. I really want more, but I have to drive back.

"We have enough for you too, but I understand."

I know she does, but Luke is kind of weird about his privacy. He was the same in university when he came to our apartment. I like him, but there is something about him that makes me feel… unwanted.

"Thanks, honey."

"You found out anything else?" She settles back into the chair, the expression on her face suddenly serious.

"Let's not do this. We need to enjoy this huge victory. Our club is ready… *fuck*! It's incredible! My family and darling boyfriend can wait for another time."

I don't miss the silent sigh as her chest slowly deflates.

"Come on. I want to show you something else." She gets up and walks out without waiting for me to agree, and all I can do is scramble to rush after her.

What the fuck?!

I follow her through the corridor, the club, up the stairs, passing through the reception, back into the small corridor I came through from the bar, but she takes the door leading to the foyer for the apartments.

"Babe, I don't want to disturb Luke… maybe he's…"

"We're not going there." I follow her into the elevator, watching as she presses the 'No. 2' button, the floor of my future apartment.

I turn my head to her, confusion straining my features, but I'm met with a mischievous expression.

When the elevator stops and the doors open, she flips a switch of a faint dangling light, and my mouth falls open. Way down. And I have to force myself to close it because I'm in complete shock.

"You… how? Where did you… Fuck…"

She laughs as she excitedly grabs my wrist and yanks me inside, onto the dirty, bare concrete floor.

"I made some calculations some time ago and realized I have some spare money to start the renovations slowly. Build some bones."

Lulu has money to live, tied up in investments and bonds, but not necessarily spare cash to make a no-return investment, as in my apartment. We're investing together, although she argued it's her building so most of the investment has to be hers, but since our priorities changed to the club, there's

29

barely anything left for this place. We decided to trickle club profit in here to help us out. But it seems the vixen found some money already, and I'm not sure what's stopping me from screaming in joy and jumping all over the damn place! Maybe the memories of the rotten, broken floor that was such a hazard. Only now, it's completely gone.

"Fucking hell... Oh my God!" It's all I can express right now, and the wide smile on her face makes me wanna fucking kiss her!

The walls are cleaned and scrapped back to the brick, and the mold which riddled every surface is gone. Even the wood frames for the walls are built, electric cables already weaving through some of them.

Fuck, this is amazing!

"The electrics will be done in about a week, maximum two, and the walls will be rebuilt after. It will take a bit of time. We'll see what position we are in by then." She walks straight ahead toward the very tall windows on the opposite side of the room, the soft moonlight shining through them, filling the space with a deep blue shade, giving me a strong urge to steal some money, just so I can get this place done quicker and move in.

"Wouldn't you want this space when it's ready?" I watch her standing by one of the windows, looking toward the sea, the view clear between two rows of buildings, the sea only a five, maybe ten-minute walk away.

"Nah…" She turns to me. "I love the apartment above. I built it exactly as I want it. What's the point in copying and pasting it here, since I wouldn't change a thing about it."

I shrug. She's right.

"This is amazing, Lu! It speeds up this process so much!"

She nods and pulls me into a brief hug. She knows my situation all too well. If I wish to get out of my parents' control, simply moving out and renting an apartment won't do it. They have enough influence to tell a landlord to fuck off and refuse me. Only they cannot treat Lulu as any other landlord. No one tells a Dietrich what to do. Her family might not be part of The Sanctum, but they still have a reputation you wouldn't want to mess with.

When I returned from university, they insisted I live with them. It was either that or live with Ryan, but he wasn't even a choice in my mind. And it wasn't hard for them to notice. Either way, I was naive, thinking they were taking me in out of the goodness of their hearts.

No matter, I'm a step closer to freedom now.

Three
VINCENT

"**W**HERE IS HE?!" MY VOICE BOOMS, BOUNCING OFF the concrete of the basement surrounding us. "Where the fuck is he?!"

"Boseman?"

"Don't fucking play with me, Finn!" I rasp at the same time I stop walking, pointing to him as I turn around. "I will not fucking hesitate!"

"Jesus, man... calm down." He raises his hands in front of his chest like a shield.

"I swear to God, Finn." I can feel that vein pulsing in my temple, my throat strained with pain as I grit my teeth.

"I don't know..." He drops his arms, shoving his hands in his jeans' pockets.

I sigh as I go deeper through the concrete

corridor of the basement. Although, it has the feel of a nuclear bunker instead. Good too, since the thickness of the walls and the depth of the spaces is necessary to ensure no noise escapes to the surface. The light reflects off the glossy walls, every step on the shiny floor taking me closer to the son of a bitch who will pay for this. I even have a fucking hole already dug up for the motherfucker. He's not leaving this place... but parts of him will.

That thought brings me a bit of peace and a muscle twitches in the corner of my lip. There's something about this finality, the moment the pain slowly seeps out of their eyes and a wicked serenity replaces it for a second or two... then they're gone. Their light goes out, and in that moment, mine shines brighter.

I don't feel anything in particular about the actual killing process, not that I hate unloading the weight off my shoulders on someone's internal organs, but it's only a tool taking me to the ecstasy that makes me feel the most... death.

"Serpent..." The piece of shit hisses through bloody teeth the moment I open the heavy metal door to the room, which has seen more death than the cemetery downtown.

But this is not the same piece of shit I wanted to see in here. He's connected enough that he could be useful. He's tied to a metal chair bolted to the floor, on the opposite side of the door, the only in and out of this concrete box. Carter and Madds stand next to the only other piece of furniture in this space, a metal table holding a few… instruments.

"Mr Crowley, pleasure to meet you in person." I peel off the suit jacket and hang it on the hook on the door, pulling on one of the long, clear plastic robes from there. I don't plan to burn these clothes later, so this is a smart choice. I do take off my shoes, though. I like them.

As the slapping sound of my bare feet on the finished floor resonates through the room, Crowley's eyes grow bigger. He knows what this means… the robe covering my clothes.

And with my last step, my fist connects with the side of his face with a force that makes his neck crack, blood spouting out of his mouth and straight onto Carter's shoes, seven feet away.

"Oh, come on! They're new fucking shoes!" He walks toward us and lands another punch to the other side of Crowley's face, the blood now staining the bottom off my trousers where the robe doesn't reach, and my bare feet.

"Happy?" I look up at him from under the shadow of my eyebrows.

"Quite, yes." Carter turns and goes back next to Madds, pulling a handkerchief out of his waistcoat pocket and wiping his shoes. Sometimes I wonder about him, he loves that… the style of another era, another century. The brogues, the waistcoats, the handkerchief, even the pocket watch. But the son of a bitch pulls all of them off.

"You can kill me now. I have nothing to say to you." Crowley draws my attention back to him, before he spits blood on me.

I can't help the rumble vibrating from my chest, through my throat, coming out in a menacing laugh.

"I'm not entirely sure why you believe that the moment you die is a decision you make. No, Mr Crowley, we have exactly"—I lift my left hand to look at the simple Vacheron watch wrapped around my wrist—"thirty-four minutes until I have to get ready to go out to dinner. So, ten, maybe fifteen minutes, seems like a good amount of time for you to share where the fuck Boseman is. I seem to remember a deal we made, when a certain transgression of yours was suddenly forgotten by the police. You have not delivered on your end of that." I shove both hands in my pockets, my back slumped slightly, head cocked as I regard the fat man before me.

It's interesting, sometimes just silence makes people talk. A look is enough, and the constant unbroken eye contact makes them squirm. Their pupils dilate, they shift uncomfortably in the metal chair, their throats bob as they swallow invisible lumps. The anticipation of pain is sometimes painful enough, and they think they can avoid the physical pain by spilling their secrets.

It's more time-consuming for sure, but... so much more satisfying.

Mr Crowley is already starting, his eyes shaking from left to right as my gaze makes him feel increasingly uncomfortable, but he fights the urge to submit... nothing like Miss Morrigan O'Rourke yesterday.

Morrigan... I narrow my eyes as that intrusive thought of the fiery redhead penetrates my mind. *What the fuck?!* No, I don't have time for this. I slam my fist into the man's gut, somehow with more anger than I needed to exert, but her image invading my mind triggered it.

"Joanne. Fifteen Harrigan Road. She's home right now, cooking dinner. I believe it was beef roast, your favorite." Crowley flinches, his pupils dilating for a split second as he regards my words about his wife.

I walk to the table, running my fingers over the few, but effective items we hold here—the disposal instruments, some chains, a couple of pliers, a cleaver, then right at the end, two knives, one serrated and one smooth. I pick the smooth one and head back to the man with his wrists tied, palms up. He can turn them face down if he really wants to, but the rope burn will be a bitch if he tries.

Clasping his left hand in a handshake, I bring the blade to the side of his wrist, sinking it into his skin. He holds in a scream, and grips me hard… at first, but as I slice deeper, moving toward the other side, splitting open veins and tendons, his fingers give out, and his tongue too, screaming through gritted teeth, as he spits out blood and saliva.

His teeth are no longer clenched as his screams fill the room when I repeat the process on the other wrist. I like doing this; it's a guide mark on the skin for where to cut later when we remove the hands completely. After all, we need to ensure we get rid of the fingerprints.

"I guess the thought of us killing your wife doesn't move you." I smirk. "Figures."

His breaths stagger as he fights through pain and blood loss, but I carry on. One by one I slice the skin between each of his fingers, using his pleas to stop as motivation. This is what a lot of them fail to understand—they do not make the decisions here. Even if they are ready to talk, it only matters if we are ready to listen.

When I'm done and I raise my eyes to him, his mouth is tightly closed, fury and fear staining his eyes, blood vessels broken as red spreads through the white.

"Scott is there too," I say as I bring my blade to the left corner of his mouth and sink it in before slowly dragging it into a half smile as tears mix with the blood pouring out with his swallowed screams. His close-mouthed cries are strong as blood pours out of his fat cheek. He leans his head over his shoulder, forcing his mouth to stay closed, his light blue shirt turning purple fast, as his whimpers begin to bore me.

"Please... please stop." Defeated sobs scrape my ears, as he tries to speak with his mouth barely open.

"I lied..." He spits the blood pooling into his mouth, ready to talk now his son is being threatened. Not his wife, though. From what I hear, he would throw his wife to the wolves in exchange for much less than his own son. Not because there's something wrong with her. His misogynistic, abusive ass doesn't need a reason, and from what we've heard... his son has learned a lot from him.

"I don't know where Boseman is. I thought I could find out before you came to collect. I lied... I just wanted to get out." I can barely understand what he's saying, gurgling blood.

"And here we were, thinking you knew who you were dealing with. Who we are!" My patience is wearing even thinner. "We are the fucking Sanctum! Do you think that if it would have been that easy to find this motherfucker, we would have had any need for you?!" I land a fist so hard in his cheek, the slice opening farther, and I could have sworn I felt teeth dislodge under my knuckles.

His cries bounce off the concrete walls, and somewhere deep in my soul, I do feel a little bit of pity for him.

But he deceived us; and unfortunately for him…
it negates that tinge of pity.

"Holt," he groans.

My eyes flicker to Carter and Madds, who
suddenly turn their heads slightly toward the man.

"Holt is dead." I hear Finn behind me.

"Mhm… son."

"You're saying his son knows where Boseman
is?" I take a step back, the guy bleeding all over the
fucking place.

"Maybe. At a party a few months ago, I heard
him say this name to someone as I was walking
behind them." He spits another mouthful of blood
on the floor. "I tried to get him to tell me about this
guy, but he said he has no clue who I'm talking
about. He was lying. I know he was."

"And Holt is now going into business with
O'Rourke too…"

Motherfucking O'Rourke!

These sons of bitches are playing mafia now.

Turning around, I stalk toward the door where
Finn still stands, and he hands me some wet wipes
to quickly clean my feet. I discard the robe in the bin
sitting next to the door, annoyed that I'll have to get
rid of these trousers too when I get home.

I look at my watch, then at the heaving man.
"Thank you, Mr Crowley. You've been helpful, but
it should have never reached this point. I'm afraid I

will not have the pleasure of taking your life today, as I have my dinner to prepare for. Good evening." His eyes go wide, brightening at my words, filling with hope, even as the blood dripping out of his wrists drains him of life.

As I turn to Finn, I hand over the knife, and the bastard's eyes fill with a menace that scares me sometimes. I can't help but grin, because menace looks good on his pretty boy face. It turns his soft, bright blue eyes into ice.

Opening the door, I look at Crowley over my shoulder. "Finn is going to finish carving that smile. I hear you put one of our girls into hospital, then claimed *the whore deserved it*. Our girls are anything but whores, Mr Crowley, and Finn sure does hate it when they're called that." The hope falls from his face, his mangled mouth falling open, either from surprise that the girl works for us, or shock that he's not leaving this room alive. I nod to Carter and Madds before I close the door behind me, drowning out a scream so excruciating, it makes my muscles tingle.

"We all pay for our sins eventually…" I whisper as I walk back the way I came.

MORRIGAN

"You always were a dirty liar. I can never believe a word you tell me." Ryan's tone is grave as he fixes me with a disgusted stare, even as he sips his white wine.

He lets that silence linger long enough that it allows too many scenarios to run through my head, since nowadays almost everything I tell him is a lie meant to protect me. But I grab my glass of dry red and sip as I force myself to hold his gaze.

"Please, do tell me what you believe I lied about." My snippy attitude hides my dishonesty, but as much as I practiced it, my insides tremble. Not because of the fear that he could find out about the club or the apartment, but... because of the constant threats, the constant abuse, even if he never touched me further than holding my arm too tight, or pushing me aside.

He insists on teaching me that physical violence is not always more effective than the psychological one.

Sighing, he joins his hands, and I can't help but notice that the cold, sharp look in his eyes has now taken permanent residence there. When we got together, almost two years ago, he was a different man, or maybe I just fucking missed all the red flags. But no... he just hid them very well behind

41

that fucking mask. I still hold hope for the man he used to be, for my sake more than his, because I'm stubborn and refuse to believe I was this fucking blind to who he really is. I've known this man since school... how could I have been so stupid?!

"Jesus, you think you're such a smart fucking bitch. I think it's time to tighten that leash."

What the fuck?

"You're out of line, Ryan, and we're in a damn restaurant." I look around the fancy space, the most expensive restaurant in the city, and I'm not sure why he brought us here if his plan was to make a scene.

But then again, nowadays he rarely misses an opportunity to *put me in my place* publicly, even if it is only calling me a derogatory term or stating some sort of failure he believes I have achieved. Even the clothes I wear... they never fit me well, always showing my fat belly... my thick thighs... my big ass.

"You didn't go home yesterday, after you left."

"So?"

"Don't fucking play with me," he seethes. "You see too much of that Lulu. When you say you're going home, you're going the fuck home."

"Are you fucking kidding me? What is wrong with you? What the hell happened to you?!" I've withstood a lot, mostly since his father died, and I honestly thought for a while that it was grief which turned him into this abusive fucking bastard. Only as it persisted, I realized the signs were there before his death, he's just unleashing now.

"You have such a filthy, spoiled mouth! For just once, act like a fucking woman, or just keep that disgusting mouth shut!"

Oh, hell no!

"Listen to me, Ryan." I lean just a little closer, my heart thumping in my chest, my hands shaking. I'm so close to making a scene. "You don't get to tell me what to do, who to see, and when to do it. You don't fucking own me. No one does!"

"You're mine, Morrigan. You always have been, and even your parents know it now. And friends… you don't need friends, you have me. There's nowhere for you to go, and your future is decided. Soon you will learn that." He grabs my wrist under the table table in a bruising grip.

"Fuck you," I spit through clenched teeth. What the hell is he talking about? *Soon I will learn that…* those are not just words thrown at me for the sake of it. That smirk on his lips tells me that much.

"I plan to." My eyes go wide for a split second. I've done a decent job at avoiding sex with him in the last couple of months. Except for one occasion… But I'm not sure how much I can avoid it before it's going to get violent. I'm not a fearful woman, but

43

something about him... it fucking scares me. The grip on my wrist tightens even more, and this time I can't hold the wince as I feel a pop in my bones.

I open my mouth to rasp at him...

"Good evening. How nice to see you here." That fucking voice! That low, slithering, cold voice which makes people bow their heads in fear and submission, I would recognize anywhere. Only it fills me with a need for goddamn blood. It makes me want to unleash whatever creature hides deep beneath my skin, the one that comes out once in a while and destroys everything in sight. One of these days, I really hope it will be him.

That thought makes a part of me tingle... a part I wish would mind its own fucking business.

Ryan releases my wrist, and I resist the urge to rub it.

"Hello. Nice to see you too." Ryan shakes his hand, and I can't help but notice the veins under The Serpent's skin, menacing, like his grip could shatter bones.

I wonder if he could shatter Ryan's bones?
He turns his gaze to me and nods briefly. I got about a second and a half of his attention... Fucking hell, what does a woman have to do to get some respect around here?!

"Are we going to see you next week?" he continues.

"Yes, I'm quite looking forward to it. The others too. This time of year can get a little… dull." The Serpent's eyes flash to me for another split second, but not to my eyes… but under the table, where I'm rubbing my aching wrist.

Did he see what Ryan was doing?

"I couldn't agree more. This one is definitely going to be entertaining, talk of the season for sure." Ryan has a peculiar expression in his eyes and on his lips, and the fact that I have no clue what they are talking about makes me uneasy. I don't have a good feeling about this. "And with the demand of the business, I could definitely use the entertainment."

"Business takeover is going well, I gather? My condolences for your father." The Serpent's politeness is borderline deranged, yet so natural, which makes it even worse. Not that I expect him to be some rude thug lashing out at people, but his interaction is so polite, it makes one question his reputation as a terrifying organized crime boss. Wait, is he the boss? When it comes to The Sanctum, it's hard to tell. Somehow they all seem to be in charge of their mafia empire.

"Very well, the changes I'm making are quite… fruitful."

The conversation continues and since no one is paying attention to me, all I can do is observe. It's strange. I didn't know these two knew each other by name, or at least that The Serpent knows of Ryan—everyone knows who the black-eyed snake is.

He's dressed in all black, the suit jacket, the shirt, the tie, fitted so well over those wide, round shoulders, his six foot-something frame… I can even see the trace of his pecs under the soft fibers. I snap out of it, realizing I have no fucking business drooling over this asshole's pecs, swiping my gaze around to see if anyone noticed. Only my eyes stop on his square jaw, along the sharp line of it, covered in a permanent dark stubble, then on his straight nose, apart from a small bump on one side of the bridge, and those damn thick black lashes that would make any woman jealous.

Fuck!!! Pull yourself together, Morrigan O'Rourke!

I can't deny the asshole is attractive, but he better walk away to be attractive somewhere else, because I have a damn date to escape from.

"I will see you then. Enjoy the rest of the evening." Their conversation appears to have ended, and he turns to me, nodding yet again, only this time his gaze lingers for a moment longer in the direction of my hands, and the look in those dark pits is… grave.

He knows… Was The Serpent's interruption on purpose?

"What was that about?" I turn to Ryan.

"Nothing you need to know of yet."

46

"Why do you do this? What happened to you to have changed you so much? This shift... you were never this person, never talked to me this way."

He watches me as if I'm a problem and he's brainstorming a solution. Does he even care anymore? Only a deviant grin spreads over his lips, a mad look in his eyes.

"I did not change." Four words, only four words he speaks and they're enough to shake my soul. They imply too much, they change my view of him, our relationship, our past, they change everything...

Even my future.

Four

VINCENT

"Tell me again why we're here?" Finn asks beside me, as we stand in the grand doorway of the Rosenberg Hotel ballroom, the aroma of fresh flowers and vanilla assaulting me as I watch the Queenscove's elite stealing glances at us, as they're socializing.

I wish I could tell him the real reason I insisted on being here, why I can't fathom being anywhere else, because I want to make sure she fucking looks me in the eyes when they tell the world why we're truly here. The sadist in me needs to kill them all and burn this fucking place to the ground, but the masochist seems unable to save my fucking heart from breaking all over again. I thought I had time... I really thought I had more time.

"Holt. No one but us could get information out of him. Plus, he's going into business with O'Rourke, and if he knows the information too, then we need to be here." I don't turn as I reply, my eyes running through the crowd, registering as many people as possible. I would say I'm scanning for enemies... but in reality, there aren't any allies here.

"Can't we just tie them to a chair and extract it the old-fashioned way?" Madds chuckles next to me. I don't need to look to know that chuckle hasn't registered on his grave features. I don't quite remember the last time the man's face contorted into a smile. Not even sure it can do that anymore.

"We all know the answer." I would love to, and we will eventually because O'Rourke, that goddamn son of a bitch, deserves my fucking fury tenfold, and Ryan... I'm starting to believe he may deserve just as much.

I take a step in, and I don't miss the communal twitch in the crowd's flesh at the movement. Like a pack of gazelles that noticed the lions moving toward them.

"So we're socializing." Finn sighs.

"We are. O'Rourke is desperate to get into business with us, and by association, Holt is too. If we play our cards right, we'll find out not only what we need to know about Boseman, but why they're so desperate too. He is involved somehow...

us." As we walk through the middle of the crowded space, people don't fail to make room, most keeping their gazes away, and I see O'Rourke and his wife noticing us.

No daughter... Considering her permanently pristine look, she's probably in the back somewhere, making sure there's no thread loose on her dress, any bit of makeup out of place, or loose strand of hair. I stopped the internal eye roll from reaching my face a bit too late. I don't remember her ever being so... anal about her looks, but I guess a long time has passed. I would much prefer to see her disheveled, runny makeup, wild hair... tangled limbs between my sheets.

"I'm struggling to figure out what the connection between Holt and Boseman is... How would they know each other, or *of* each other?" Finn continues, pulling my thoughts from that dangerous direction.

"Well, that's why we're here. This whole thing gives me a really bad vibe, and we need to get our foot in it. These sons of bitches can't move without us knowing about it." Madds finishes just as we approach O'Rourke.

"Gentlemen, thank you so much for joining us!" His enthusiasm appears to be genuine, and I resist the urge to cock an eyebrow.

If I didn't know any better, I would say he

completely forgot our past, what she did, or maybe he thinks I did. No, he's just feigning ignorance since he now has something to gain from me, from us; no one forgets something like that. I think the party we were invited to about five months ago was to test the waters, to observe my reaction to him, and now he's diving all the way in.

One by one, he shakes our hands, pulling Finn's attention from some blond in a skimpy skirt, which seems to have momentarily distracted him. We all nod to his wife, a woman in her early fifties, wearing a form-fitted dark blue dress that's just… too much. Too sparkly, too overfilled with lace details, too flashy and most likely an intentional choice. They're the type of people who have this burning need to stand out at all times. What definitely stands out is the look O'Rourke gives her every time she touches that high neckline, which could definitely do with a little tucking down to give her some room to breathe.

"Thank you for inviting us, and congratulations to you both." At those words, Mrs O'Rourke winces and internally I do as well. It stung to say it. Her husband though, he tries to keep a straight face.

"Thank you." He nods, the movement a bit staggered.

It's a power move. He needs to understand that no matter how small or insignificant the information, we will find it. This particular information though, left a far too bitter of a taste on my tongue. It lingers... heavily.

"Sheila will take you to your table." He nods toward his wife, and she scrambles into compliance. "I do hope we can have a... drink together later. Enjoy your evening, gentlemen."

The tables are all round and of various sizes, from four to ten seats, and luckily, we are led to one which sits four. *Good.* Mrs O'Rourke moves away shyly after we thank her, and I can't help but wonder what the woman's life is like at home. There's something too familiar about the dynamic between her and her husband.

Gripping the wooden frame of the chair, I pull it away and freeze. I see her red, silky hair first, flowing in large waves around her alabaster skin, bouncing with each slow step. The tips of her strands touch the V-neckline that plunges low between her breasts, the black satin dress held only by two thin straps, covering just enough that you want to beg for more. The smooth fabric of the knee-length dress clings to her curves without being tight, and in proper Morrigan fashion, instead of the pumps the women around us wear, the high slit reveals the end of thigh-high leather boots.

Never in my life have I noticed all these details in the way a woman dresses... yet I always do with her. And I was right... perfect. No hair out of place, pristine.

Someone clears their throat, pulling me out of that enticing distraction, and when I look to the left, Finn has a stupid grin plastered on his face. Maddox glances at her, but his expression never changes, and Carter sits down, one eyebrow raised, aimed at me.

"She's off limits, man. Especially now," Finn whispers as we all take our seats.

There are no limits when it comes to Morrigan O'Rourke.

I swipe my gaze back to the redhead, her steps light as she heads toward her parents, arm curled around Holt's, her green eyes stern. Only the look in them shifts in an instant the moment they fall on me. Surprise flickers for a split second, before irritation takes permanent residence, and I hold it. I hold that gaze because I know it's a challenge. She would rip her eyes out before she would submit to me. And isn't that fucking fun.

Her nostrils flare when she approaches her parents and has no choice but to look away, and I can feel a tinge of a grin on my lips.

"Jesus, she looked like she could gut you right here, right now." Finn smirks.

"Knowing her… she probably would," Madds continues as he takes the Bourbon bottle from the waiter that intended to only fill his glass.

"Excuse me. *Knowing* her?!" Finn slides his

empty glass toward Madds, who regards me from under his eyebrows.

He is the only one that knows exactly who Morrigan was to me back then. Carter had his nose far too deep in computers, and Finn in university pussy. Madds and I were still here... putting the bases down for what was going to become our empire. The other two knew of her, knew we hung out a few times, but... it ended before they came home, before it could become more... so I never told them everything. There was no point.

"*Knew* her. Enough. She was hard not to notice, a firecracker. We watched her beat the shit out of this guy once, she broke his jaw... put him in hospital." He nods his head in appreciation. If Madds appreciates anything, it's a good fight.

"*Watched* her? You didn't intervene?" Carter asks.

"I didn't need to. She was doing fine on her own." He shrugs.

"That's not what I... fucking hell, man."

Finn's laugh booms through the music that's getting louder now and a few heads turn to us. Our presence is rarely seen at cocktail parties or private events like this one, and when we do make an appearance, it makes a statement. I guess O'Rourke and Holt want a statement—"we have The Sanctum on our side"—so any investors will know that they're either in for big money, or they stay away completely. We're letting them have their moment until we get what we need.

My sweet tooth led me to the dessert table stacked with multi-level ornate cake stands, filled with macarons, meringues, fruit next to a decadent chocolate fountain, and dozens of different mini cakes in all the colors of the fucking rainbow. Now I understand why the crowd gathered around it the whole evening. Just as the person that stands next to me begins to move away, I lean over and reach for a mini chocolate eclair, when my hand bumps a bit hard into another, sending the tips of their fingers straight into the chocolate stream of the fountain.

"Fucking hell!!!" She curses loud enough that the person that stood between us is gone in a split second.

I swallow my apology, when I realize whose voice that is before I even look up—Morrigan.

"You!" she seethes when her eyes land on me.

"Hello." I take a second to take in those piercing green eyes, the brick red waves framing that soft skin dusted with freckles, spilling down her slender shoulders, her chest, and down her naked arms.

"I don't get it. What the fuck are my parents

playing at? Why are you here? All of you?" That's one way of saying hello back... I guess.

She notices her fingers dripping chocolate on the white tablecloth, and she does the goddamn fucking unthinkable. One by one, she slides those fingers into her mouth, and I know the way she does it, the way she intends it as well, is nowhere near sexual... but I could have fucking sworn that time slowed down, because I'm mesmerized, following those lips as they suck every drop of chocolate, leaving a faint red lipstick ring on them. This woman... this goddamn woman.

The blood flow shifts from my brain to my cock, and I yank her fingers to me, hand wrapped tight around her slim wrist, stopping it inches from my face. She parts her lips to spit her protest, but her jaw locks as her eyes fix onto mine. I don't know if it's hunger she sees in my eyes, or the stern aversion for a clearly ungracious gesture considering the occasion.

I turn to find a stack of napkins farther down the table, grabbing a few and putting them in her trapped hand, releasing it before I do anything more stupid than that.

I can feel eyes on me... which I usually don't. I got used to them over the years, but it's the situation... Morrigan.

She wipes her fingers, not that there's anything

left on them but the red trace of her lipstick, then looks at me as if she's about to stab me with a dessert knife. Better than a steak one, I guess.

"You're welcome," I scold, as she shoots me the most defiant gaze she can muster.

"I'm serious, Serpent. What the hell are my parents involved in? Or getting involved in? It has to be fucking atrocious if it's with you." Her eyes flash around us, making sure no one's listening.

She really doesn't like us... or me. But she's not exactly a fucking angel, not with goddamn Ryan-fucking-Holt on her arm. Not with the man who now controls half the docks, his late father's business... and from the sounds of it, the trafficking business has been growing since his death. She doesn't have a moral leg to stand on when she's involved with him.

"Atrocious... okay." I reach over once again, grab an eclair, shove it in my mouth, and lean back against the table, watching the crowd dance to a cheerful song I don't recognize.

"You're not answering my goddamn questions!" Her words pour like lava, burning their way through the loud music, drawing my eyes back to the emerald of hers.

"Nothing you need to concern yourself with." Oh, she didn't like that response, but I do. I fucking love seeing that fire take over. She's beautiful on a normal day, but she's fucking gorgeous when she's

57

in flames.

"Concern myself… motherfucker! Am I just a fucking doorknob to you people? Just fucking grab me and turn me whatever direction you want as long as it's the one that is advantageous to you! Like"— she leans in ever so slightly, her tone lowering almost to a whisper—"I don't know the rules of the fight club, the right way to do laundry, the fastest way to take one's breath away, or the fastest route to take when… escorting someone." There's a grin in her eyes; it cracks the skin at the edges, pupils dilating in mischief, but that grin barely touches her lips.

She just listed almost all our businesses… the fight club, the money laundering, the killings, but the one that strikes me the most… is the escort business. There is almost no trail back to us. Yes, we meet once in a while if direct instructions are needed, if Ekaterina can't liaise for us, but even when we do that, it's nothing more than a normal meet up for dinner or drinks, usually in our bar. How the fuck did Morrigan know about it? She doesn't even have access to the bar.

"I'm gonna go ahead and take your silence and slightly parted lips as shock and pat myself on the back for a job well done." I focus back on her and notice that the grin is now nicely plastered all over her pretty red lips. She leans back against the table, facing the crowds as the music fades out, coming to an end. We both watch as her father, mother, and boyfriend stop in front of the stage, waiting as everyone brings their attention to them, and she stiffens.

"So that's it, then. You think you're so much better than me, than us? I've seen you get high on X and fucking rescued you when some shithead was forcing himself on you, then I watched you shatter that guy's jaw, and you weren't even legal yet. Fuck knows what else you've done since. Especially considering your... association with Holt." I spit out that last sentence and her eyes return to mine, the grin long gone. Not sure if it's that particular memory from the past that caused it, or the fact that I remember it.

"Ladies and gentlemen!" Liam O'Rourke's voice booms through the ballroom and the party goes quiet, only she's still looking at me. *"We are sorry to interrupt your dancing, but we would like to tell you the whole reason for this celebration, so we can fully enjoy this evening."*

"Get off your fucking moral high horse, baby, because you missed a few entries in that list you're so proud of putting together..." I hold her gaze as she shoots daggers at mine, that fire pretty in her eyes as she grows increasingly more frustrated.

"I am pleased to announce..." Holt's voice replaces her father's, building a tension in the moment, and

59

in her as well. I don't miss the way the muscles in her shoulders tense, and she crosses her arms as her eyes flicker around us.

My tone is low, and when I lean in sideways, close enough that our shoulders touch, I finish. "And some of those you might just have to learn more about, since it will be your family's business, *Mrs Holt*."

Her brows furrow in an annoyed confusion, but that emotion doesn't have time to settle in her features.

"*...that Morrigan O'Rourke and I are getting married!*" Holt finishes his short speech, and it's in that moment, when chaos erupts around us, the crowd bursting in applause, cheers and laughter, that I see a shattering fear cracking her eyes with emotions that she forces herself to suppress.

I watch her suddenly begin to blink way too fast. She looks as if... she's in *actual* shock. Her head slowly turns toward the crowd that gathers and cheers her on, and we're split apart when a few people come close and pull her into a hug.

That fear in her eyes, like her soul shattered in an instant, tells me one thing's for certain: what I witnessed wasn't a fiancé revealing this important piece of news too soon.

I catch a glimpse of her between hugs and kisses, and for a moment there, the desperation in her eyes hits me like goddamn lightning.

She didn't know.

Five

MORRIGAN

A LUMP FORMS IN MY THROAT. IT GROWS BIGGER AND bigger with every *congratulations* I hear from the faceless people that hug me, or squeeze my shoulders, or kiss my cheeks. I don't know where The Serpent went, but I suddenly feel the need to disappear along with him.

He knew… he knew even before I did.

I thought I had the upper hand tonight, but it seems that I'm just a pawn in a game I'm not privy to. What is happening? How is it possible for even The Serpent to know an arrangement as this one, even before me?

My family, my fucking family planned this! They all fucking sold me. Passed me on like some piece of goddamn meat!

And Ryan… goddamn motherfucking Ryan! He thinks he can just force me to marry him? Is this the nail in the coffin? The apex of all his lovely treatment? This is his ultimate display of control over me…

The problem is that at this very moment, my imagination is running wild with the despicable things I would love to do to him, but nothing seems to translate to the outside. My body won't budge. I can't seem to make a move… any move.

Goddamnit! Do something!
That lump is impossibly big now, stuck right at the base of my tongue, and breathing is increasingly harder. But my emotions are well masked behind fake ones that mar my face.

My body begins to tremble as I force myself to look around for an escape, something, anything, to pull me out of this fucking nightmare. But the crowd turns quiet, as a familiar song begins to cover the ruckus of debilitating congratulatory chatter.

Every breath you take… seeps into the room.

I catch his eyes through the crowd, a special evil residing in them as he walks toward me.

The next verse of the iconic song gains new meaning in my soul.

A few more steps and my heart beats so hard it shakes my flesh. I'm frantic on the inside, searching for something that could indicate I'm not awake right now. It's only a nightmare... this is not my life. It cannot be.

I look away from him, hoping to catch a glimpse of Lulu. Someone to fucking ground me right now before I implode.

But the song continues with every step he makes toward me.

The crowd parts, all the ones that were congratulating me move away, clutching their hands on their chests, sweet emotions plastered over their faces for the *happy couple*, and I want to vomit.

Right here, right now.

But not even my stomach seems to want to make a move. What is wrong with me?

The chorus ends with it ominous verse that seems to cripple me, because I know he'll be watching me too.

Then he's here, his hands around me, his lips on mine, and I'm forced to move with him as he pulls me deeper into the center of the ballroom.

Every single muscle in my body is tense to the

point of pain, that lump stuck so well in my throat that I'm not entirely sure how I'm managing to breathe. By the time he releases me from the kiss, he pulls my hand in his, and leads me into a dance to the disturbingly suggestive cover song.

"You belong to me..." Ryan whispers into my ear, at the same time as the song, the hand clutching mine a little bit harder than necessary, the grip on my waist firm, and if I wasn't at the edge of a panic attack, instead of holding his shoulder, I would hold him by the fucking throat. Until he choked on his Adam's apple.

I'm not looking at him, I'm looking over his shoulder as he spins me, trying to find something to ground my soul, an object, a face, a fucking piece of food, I don't give a shit. I just need to learn to breathe again.

I used to have some love for the famous song The Police graced us with, but it's all gone now... its meaning tainted.

And when it slows, so do his steps, and through the blurred faces, I finally see her. Lulu clutches Luke's bicep, completely still, looking at me with a shocked expression that does nothing to settle me. No... it makes me even more uneasy, because I see on her face exactly what I feel... *no escape.*

But as Ryan spins me farther, I catch another face through the sea of blurred ones, it's fixed on me in a way that no one else in the room is, none of the ones that watch us right now. He pulls me in, commanding my attention with those black eyes that feel almost hypnotic—The Serpent. Those dark pits of tar make me sink deeper and deeper, pulling me into the denseness of them, a deeply satisfying pressure on my soul. My throat softens, the lumps shrink slightly. I come out of that hypnosis and actually look at him—there's no joy, no pity, no excitement, no shock in his features, only this calm severity, one that somehow cheers me on. A silent urge to focus, driving me toward the right path, as my muscles slowly relax and that lump in my throat shrinks enough that I can control my breathing again.

I don't know what this was, but it worked.

However, I do know that I'm going to have a little chat with The Serpent again soon.

"What the fuck did you do, Ryan?" I pull my head back, facing him. A grin spreads over his lips and suddenly that bile rises in my throat once more and I have to swallow too many times to push it back down.

"You think I didn't know you've been planning to break up with me?" I attempt to pull away, but he presses his palm on the small of my back and pulls me hard against him as the rhythm of the song increases. "You're not fucking going anywhere. You. Belong. To me." He finishes that sentence with a crooked quirk of his lips, muddy eyes rabid with victory.

"You think that just because you made a fucking scene, and put me in this situation..." The son of a bitch knew exactly what he was doing, he knew how much it would fucking hurt my soul not to lash out and rip his goddamn throat out when he did this. So he did in front of half the fucking city, at a party that apparently he planned with my parents. "...You think I'll go through with it?! Marry you against my damn will?! What the hell makes you think I will hesitate to leave you the moment this dance is over?"

There's a strange sort of madness in his eyes. It's been infusing his features for a little while now and I'm not sure what to make of it. I don't know how to handle it or how to make it fucking go away. Because it's true madness, seeping in his words and actions, making him do stupid shit like announcing a fucking fictional marriage that will never take place.

"Try." Too many promises and threats lie in that one word, and I know for a fact that the man I knew is gone. I see no traces of him in the muddy eyes staring back at me. This man right here would throw me to the fucking alligators in the delta at the edge of the city, without thinking twice about it.

He spins me with a little bit more force than necessary, but at this point more couples have joined us on the dance floor and the move goes unnoticed. I think. I'm not sure, because my spine tingles with that feeling you get when someone's watching you.

"You see your parents dancing next to the Chief of Police?"

I follow his gaze, but when I don't respond, he squeezes my hand until I wince.

"Yes," I spit.

"They signed you off t o m e." T hose words carry an amusement that I want to fucking strangle. "They're not going to support you if you do something stupid. Not when you are a price they paid."

I turn my head to him fast enough that my hair whips around me, wrapping around my throat, slowly falling against my chest as my gaze settles on him.

"I'm not goddamn currency, Ryan! You've gone insane!"

"Maybe. But I'm not about to reject the insanity when the prospect of it is so entertaining. And you have to understand something... You're mine,

Morrigan. I fought hard to make you mine, to make you love me when I loved you for so long. And I'll have you forever."

"This is not love! This is madness, pure fucking madness! I'm a possession to you, not a partner, not a girlfriend. I am nothing to you and I cannot figure out why the hell you want me. Why would you want a woman that doesn't love you anymore?" My tone grows just a little bit louder.

"Shh…" He puckers his lips. "Why do I want you? Because your freedom becomes mine, and isn't that just a lovely, lovely thing to own. Freedom is all we are, it holds our wants and needs, our soul, our mind… our personality. It holds it all, a little crystal ball, so full of wonder…" He pauses enough that my eyes burn from the need to blink. "…So easy to shatter." He bursts into maniacal laughter, one that the couple around us seem to have mistaken for joy as they throw at us the sweetest smiles they can muster.

He's gone, he's completely gone.

"You can't have me. I'm not yours. I haven't been for a long time, Ryan. And you know it." My voice cracks a hint.

"I worked too hard not to have you, Morrigan. Breaking up is not an option. It's either no one else has you, or you're mine forever. And I chose the former."

"I will not marry you. This will not happen." I shake my head and fail to hold his gaze for long.

"Oh, but it will, because"—he points toward my family, waving at them, and they respond with big smiles in their eyes. Then he turns us slightly, just as the song ends on a high note, waving at my brother who dances with some random girl and nods back to him—"if you don't, they all die."

And just like that, the song ends...

The dance ends...

My freedom ends with it...

VINCENT

We all follow Liam O'Rourke, who disappears through a wide corridor at the other end of the ballroom. He waited to see us until the main wave of people came to congratulate him for marrying off his daughter... Funny, the things people celebrate nowadays.

I catch Morrigan's eyes following me as she stands beside her future husband, accepting even more congratulations from people ecstatic for her tragedy.

"Something's off, isn't it." Madds watches the same person I am.

Both Finn and Carter turn their heads slightly to glance at us as they walk in front, humming their approval in unison.

"She didn't know," I tell them, but look at Madds most of all. I think he had a soft spot for her back in the day. Or at least I always thought so, but the bastard hides feelings all too well, and I never allowed myself to talk about her, after... after our abrupt demise. Somehow, because of all I know of him, I never felt enough jealousy to ask about it either. I would have just been happy to know he cares for something.

Judging by the look in his eyes now, he definitely had a soft spot for her. Maybe still does. Under his olive skin, around his temple and forehead, there are some veins that look like they could burst every time he fixes on someone. It's the most anger he tends to show outside the ring. Even the times we've been attacked, or been in any precarious situations, his composure is eerie when he smashes someone's face in with his fists alone. He simmers that anger in his veins, debating the most efficient move, and I have seen many adversaries that backed out before the first punch was thrown, just because of that grim expression and those throbbing veins. It does help that he's stacked with muscles like a fucking bull, and tall enough that he looks down at pretty much everyone around him.

His amber eyes flash from her to me and I know he's already calculating his next strike.

"We need to see what her father wants." I steady him, as Finn and Carter quirk their eyebrows at us over their shoulders.

He doesn't respond, but shifts his gaze to the end of the corridor where Liam waits with his son, and that's the most confirmation I'll get from him.

"Gentlemen, please, have a seat." We're led into a private room with its own bar and we take a seat on the ornate sofa and armchair. Only Madds chooses to stand. He usually does. "I'm not sure if you've been introduced to my son, Cillian." He nods to his son, curly red hair trapped in one of those buns at the back of his head, thick wiry beard more muted in color than the rest of his hair. "Cillian, this is Vincent Sinclair, Finn Hennessey, Maddox Severin, and Carter Pierce."

We all nod, but Finn speaks.

"Yes, many years ago. I had the pleasure of breaking his nose with my knee."

Liam quirks an eyebrow, a hint of that protective father figure peeking through, but his son doesn't smile, doesn't even blink, his thin lips completely straight behind his mustache, only his nostrils flare ever so slightly as he looks at Finn.

"After I dislocated your shoulder in that legendary tackle." The redhead walks behind the stocked bar and grabs a bottle of Bourbon, as I catch a hint of a smirk in his green eyes that match his sister's.

His father passes around some glasses to each of us, and it's at that moment the wooden door opens and Holt walks in, leaving it to close behind him as he regards each and every one of us, one by one. He doesn't linger on me, and why would he, he doesn't know how much I want to cave his face in right now. No matter how much I don't have a right to do so, but I saw the way he acted with her in that restaurant... It's enough to tell me what kind of man he is. And the announcement tonight... that just tipped the fucking scale.

I have no right to be protective of her; she doesn't belong to me, and I've been repeating this to myself too many times in the last few months, but I can't seem to be convincing enough. She was mine once, and I've been telling myself she was too young to count it as real... we weren't deep enough to warrant what lingered after. Either way, it doesn't make *this* right, forced marriage or whatever the fuck this is!

It's staying with me, the petrified look in her eyes as he led her onto the dance floor, the way she fixed on me, desperate for a lifeline, and no amount of hate for me could have swayed her away. Desperation. Fear. Rage. It darkened her gaze, but

I held her there, without blinking I willed her not to move away, whispering in my mind the same words I chant when shit is about to go down—*death is freedom, but my life is their demise.*

It worked.

I watched as she blinked through the heaviness that weighed on her, as she sorted through the amalgam of confusing emotions, taking some sort of fucking life force from me, and leaving me with a gaping hole. It didn't feel like a loss, it somehow belonged to her already...

Madds shuffles slightly behind me, his boots scraping the old wooden floor, and Holt's gaze lingers on him. I'm not going to look up to figure out why, but I can't help but wonder if those veins, or the sinew in his throat, have made an appearance.

"Congratulations on your... engagement." Finn's tone holds his usual charm, but I know even without looking that the usual blue of his eyes has turned to ice.

"Thank you. We're looking forward to having a wedding as soon as possible." He sits in the last empty armchair across from me.

We...

None of us say any more on that subject.

"Look, gentlemen, I'm going to go straight to business. I am looking to branch out my import business, and Mr Holt and I are joining forces on that. However, we find that we need more... room to grow."

Okay, so he's not skirting at the edge of the law anymore, he wants to dive straight to the other side—smuggling.

"Only, the one person that has the ability to give me more room at the seaside is... a Ghost. All I have is a name, no face, no contact, and it's not enough to get in touch with the man." Liam flickers his eyes to his son before he comes back to me, then Madds.

Jonathan Rees. He controls the other half of the docks that Ryan doesn't have access to.

"We would also like to make a deal on transport, as we heard he holds the rails as well. It would be a long-term business. Profitable for... all parts." Holt swipes his gaze between all of us.

The cargo trains are controlled by him as well. That means that these two are looking to expand beyond Queenscove. What exactly do they plan to smuggle in?

"What's the cargo?" I finally ask.

"That's none of your business, *snake*," Holt all but spits at me and in unison all three of us rise, Madds is behind him in three steps, and I in front of him in two, my hand at his throat. The air in the room shifts, the lights appear dimmer, and the asshole's body twitches, as he forces himself to stand straight. He can't move, not with the beast behind him and a fucking venomous *snake* in front of him.

"You're a motherfucking cub in this jungle, Holt. You haven't learned the rules, haven't lived here long enough, and definitely haven't earned your fucking place." I wouldn't usually get quite this heated, but it's a combination of what happened out in the ballroom and the motherfucker's insolence. "I don't fucking tolerate insults."

"Ryan, shit... gentlemen, my apologies..." O'Rourke says, but I don't turn. I'm not sure where he found his balls, but he better shove them back in their hiding spot before we rip them off and shove them up his fucking ass.

"Maybe... this was premature," Carter speaks as a matter of fact.

"It is definitely premature for Ryan to speak before thinking." His tone is cold and stern.

"No," Carter interrupts. "Maybe this meeting was premature."

I step back, looking at the old man. Holt may hold more dirty business than him, putting him in our field, but he's never controlled any of that shit until now. O'Rourke though, he's skirted the law for long enough to know how the game is played. The only reason he hasn't jumped fully to our side until now is because he's been aware of how to play the system to his favor. His mafia is a different brand from ours, but it's still mafia. He knows how to treat people to his benefit.

From the corner of my eye, I can see Madds grab Holt's shoulder hard enough that he winces, but this time around, he keeps his mouth shut. *Snake* is not far away from *Serpent*, but one is a derogatory term and the other a title.

I am no snake. I have never deceived, never cheated in the life games we play. People fear us because they know exactly who we are and what we are capable of. And one of our tricks is to never allow them to believe that we give second chances, especially when we are disrespected. Either they repent, they die, or they simply cease to exist in our line of sight. In this situation, dying is not yet an option, as we need something from them, from Holt.

As Finn and Carter step closer toward the door, we hear a grunt. We turn and find Cillian looking straight at his future brother-in-law, a scowl deepening every wrinkle of his freckled forehead. There's something about that man, a brand of madness that I've only ever recognized in his sister. And I've had the pleasure of seeing what she's capable of.

"I spoke without thinking." The asshole finally opens his mouth. I can see how much it hurts him to submit. I revel in it. We all do. "I apologize."

I turn straight to O'Rourke.

"You need to make a deal for access to the docks

and the lines. What are you moving, when do you want to start, how often, and how many? No one will even acknowledge a meeting without knowing the reason for it. Not that I can guarantee a meeting, or that I can reach him."

I can reach him.

"Rounds and dust. In about three months. The pattern will change, between one and two weeks. Two to four containers at a time. To start off with. We just need to make sure we spread them thinly first. Test the territory," Liam responds without hesitation, and I make a mental note.

"We'll be in touch." I nod, before I turn and walk toward the door behind the others.

"Wait. You haven't named your price."

I turn just enough that I can see him when I look over my shoulder. "I'll tell you the terms of the pact once I am assured I can grant your request. Have a nice evening." I walk away, the door slamming on its own behind me.

I don't miss his booming voice through the thin walls.

"Boy, you will learn your fucking lesson too soon and it will be too harsh if this is how you think business is done! We fucking need them if you want this shit to work! You have no fucking leg to stand on! Your business may be old, but you're goddamn new and you suddenly think you're the big kahuna?! Sit in your fucking place

and learn how it's done!"

"*Old man…*" Holt says something else, but he's not loud enough for any of us to hear. Safe to say, from the way Cillian just rasped his name, it wasn't good.

We walk away, back into the ballroom where the lights have dimmed, turning into a nice party. We absorb the gazes everyone gives us as we head toward the exit, willing one in particular to hit my skin.

It doesn't.

She's not here anymore.

Good.

Six

MORRIGAN

THE SOFT LIGHT REFLECTS OFF THE LEATHER THAT BARELY covers my body and the five chains wrapped over it. I've been staring at myself in the mirror for too long now, and here, in Lulu's apartment, dressed this way, surrounded by the smell of jasmine that always seems to gravitate around Lulu herself, I feel more like myself than I have in months. Disregarding the couple of weeks since... *the announcement*.

That's how we refer to it now, Lulu and I—*the announcement*. Impersonal. Cold. It allows me to detach from it, like it has nothing to do with me.

I check the wig again, making sure it's unmovable, the bobby pins tight. I chose to cover my easily recognizable ginger with sleek black, such a contrast against my pale, freckly skin. Not that it will matter much in the gold light of the club.

I love black. It somehow gives me a confidence I seem to have lost in the last few months. And since blonds are more memorable, I would rather live in the shadows, as the silent partner that I am. I can just blend in as any other employee.

I slide my fingers over the leather of the two extra decorative thin straps that meet between my breasts, down two of the four that meet from the underside, to a two-inch gold ring that sits in the middle of my torso. From there, four more straps spread to the edge of my leather panties. The five gold chains are connected to this ring as well, two over the straps that meet between my breasts, two around my waist, and one straight between my legs, up my ass, until it connects to the same point as the waist chain. A thin, see-through, long lapel jacket covers the minimal ensemble, a subtle gold sheen catching the light, and the thigh-high velvet boots make me feel less naked.

"Going to the toilet is gonna be a bitch in that thing." I turn to Lulu, and it takes a bit too much effort to reassure myself that I'm straight.

"Fucking hell, woman!" She wears a floor-length leather skirt that would be tight if not for the two slits on the front of each leg, right up to the velvet waistband, which clinches her waist. A velvet bra covers the rest of her, with straps wrapped around her neck, and the bottom band wraps behind her back before coming around to the front, where it's tied into a cute bow. It's simple, but damn… every man in that club will want to see what's behind those slits that make her legs look as though they go on for miles. "You look incredible, Lu!"

"You too, love. Look at you… those straps. You're gonna fucking kill it tonight." She comes next to me, and we both turn to the full-length mirror, admiring our work.

"I'm nervous," I confess.

"Because of the party, or the dance?" She tucks her icy blond hair behind her ears.

"Both." I exhale as I pick up the mask from the side table next to the mirror.

"Yeah…" Lulu nods and picks up hers, and we help each other strap them on.

We chose venetian inspired masks, with black and gold details, from the same collection. It's not as if we wouldn't recognize each other in the club, but it made us feel better that even though I will be pretending to be a random member of staff, we're actually on the same level. My mask comes to a point at the tip of my nose and, from its lowest point between my eyebrows, it curves upwards above each one, to a sharp point in my hairline. Lu's is the opposite, curving down her cheeks and raising into one sharp point just above the middle of her forehead, close to the hairline.

They fit.

We fit.

She smiles at me, and I feel like I'm swallowing my heart. This is it... months of work have come down to this moment.

"I think it's time to go."

My heels fall heavy on the hard floor, slow steps taken between the small crowds that stand in front of the wall-to-wall windows, so deeply enthralled by the couples that put up shows in the playrooms, that no one is talking to each other.

Some sway to the lascivious music, some couples rub on each other, some are simply lost. Lost in the images they witness, in the way the flesh trembles and the skin reddens when the leather paddle hits, the way the arm muscles tighten as they pull on the straps of the St Andrews cross, the way eyes roll to the back of the head as the orgasm shakes the body, the way a cock spasms at the pull of his balls when his mistress denies his own. Each and every spectator is either lost in themselves or the beautiful acts they see, and two of the rooms aren't even occupied by the people we specifically invited. *That* is a success.

I step into the main club, the bar to my left

surprisingly not as busy as the rest of the floor. I was expecting people to huddle there, however everyone seems to be relaxed, enthralled by the show one couple we met in Rosston is putting on up on the main stage. Others are joined in intimate dances between the busy tables, and at the back of the space, the opposite side from the bar, the shadowed tables seem to be full, most likely with people enjoying more private exhibitionism.

The whole atmosphere is loose, comfortable and enticing—so much better than we hoped this night would be.

"I can't believe how incredible this is!" Lulu comes out from behind some people she was engaging with, grabbing my hand and pulling me toward the bar, leaning in so I can hear her over the music. "Everyone came! I checked with the door a few times, and every single member that signed up was scanned in!"

Fuck!

I didn't think *he* would too…

I turn my head slightly, swiping my eyes over the crowds, forcing myself to figure out which one he is. It's impossible, though… I can tell who he is not, by the various body shapes, but that's about it.

"Morri?! Are you okay?"

"Yes, sorry, I was just… observing. It is incredible, such a fucking success, and people are engaging! Two of the playrooms are occupied by actual members!" I grab her forearms, shaking her lightly with girly enthusiasm.

"No way! I have to go watch!" she squeals. We worked so hard on this club, so fucking hard, and we have so much to be proud of. And this party, the atmosphere... it's perfect, fuck it... it's beyond perfect.

"Jaz told me that she and Richie are coming back!" she all but yells at me.

"But they live so far away..."

"They don't care. They said this doesn't compare with the club back home. The equipment, the quality, the intimate decor... I'm not fucking complaining! They put on such an amazing fucking show, I mean... look at them." She points to the stage where Jaz weeps from pain and ecstasy as Richie canes her red ass, finger fucking her in between hits. "And they're perfect for BDSM education as well. We would be lucky to have them."

"Yeah, I wonder how we can convince them to move here." I laugh as I watch the middle-aged couple absolutely killing it on stage.

We met at the club in Rosston and fell in love with them, their interactions, their connection. It was incredible to see how he could read her, in even the tenseness of her muscles or the pitch of her voice, he can tell when it's wrong. One of the best moments we've seen was when Jaz was so completely caught in the play, exhausted, slightly delirious from too much pleasure and a little too much pain, that her safe word, the same one she's had for years, completely skipped her mind. But Richie… it took him a few seconds to realize something was not right and stopped immediately, swooping her in his arms and dropping to the floor, her curled up between his legs as he cradled and whispered sweet nothings in her ear, until she came out of it.

The whole crowd watched in silence, some were cuddling each other as they witnessed the love, the understanding, that bond… we all had a lot to learn that night.

It was them that encouraged us to build Metamorphosis when we told them about our idea. It didn't come from our passion to practice, but a different kind of desire… the ability to offer people a safe, comfortable, and high-quality place where they could be themselves. We wanted to offer them a freedom they don't have in their real lives, freedom to be themselves, freedom to indulge, freedom to push their limits, even if only for a few hours.

There's nothing more important than freedom.

"I have to go up there in a bit." I nod toward the stage.

"How do you feel?"

"Anxious, but a good kind of anxious. Do you

think they will be disappointed that I won't actually strip?" I tuck my hair behind my right ear, the hair of the wig a bit too silky for my liking, and nod to one of the bartenders. Rachel knows who I am, but not necessarily that I'm her boss. Everyone is on a need-to-know basis, so at the moment, I'm simply Lulu's friend. She grabs a bottle of tequila and a bowl of lemon wedges on her way to us, then fills two shot glasses, before she pulls a saltshaker out from behind the bar.

I'm about to open my mouth to speak, to thank her, when my skin tingles, soft goosebumps bursting between my shoulder blades, to the back of my neck, wrapping around to the right, until they sizzle right behind my ear, where a cold breath brushes my skin. I want to turn, but my head is suddenly filled with voices screaming at me not to move, to stay put, to not meet the devil's eyes.

Yet, self-preservation has no place under my masochistic skin.

So I turn, swiping my gaze slowly over the crowd, my eyes unable to hit anything that stands out.

"Do you think he'll be watching you?" Lulu leans in, pushing a shot glass along as well.

"You said all members came..." Vincent *The Serpent* Sinclair... his name showed up in the membership applications and I had half a mind to reject it. I really fucking wanted to. But wouldn't that have caused a goddamn stir? I didn't want to cause any issues for Lulu, but then again, I had no reason to reject him, no real one beyond the flashes of memories from eons ago. I was just a kid, and he was establishing an empire... then he was gone, and I... I changed my life forever.

Fuck... He brings out a different anger in me, a vicious desire to break bones, to crush hearts with my bare hands, and destroy goddamn empires. Sometimes, I would rather pull out his black eyes, than see him watching me as if he forgot who I was, who he was... what *we* were.

Only he hasn't really forgotten who I was, has he? As he reminded me before *the announcement*, he remembers very well how I smashed Johnny Bray's jaw, and here I was thinking that if it wasn't for my parents, he probably wouldn't even remember my last name.

I'm not fucking in love with him or some shit, he just brings out parts of me that have no business being on the surface. I have enough reasons to be angry, without him.

"But in all fairness, he could just be in one of the rooms already." Lulu taps me on the shoulder in reassurance, and I realize... I don't care. I don't care if he's in the playrooms, or at the bar, or dancing, or right in front of the stage watching Jaz and Richie's

88

show end.

I don't care!

Even though I can't get those dark pits out of my head, the way they pinned me when Ryan was holding me in that uncomfortable dance. Even though somehow it was enough to pull me out the shock and momentary terror. Even though it was him that calmed me with only a gaze...

I lick the skin between my index finger and thumb, sprinkle salt, swipe my tongue over it, and down the shot after cheering with Lulu.

Rachel returns, Tequila bottle clutched as she pours another one, and I down it this time without bothering with the salt. Hell, I didn't even bother with the lemon after the first shot. I tap my glass on the bar before she gets to move away, and she pours a third, Lulu watching me with interest. I know that under that mask there's a quirked eyebrow.

"Just... don't fall off the fucking stage." She pushes the shot glass away from me, then downs hers before gripping a lemon wedge with her teeth. "Are you ready?" she asks after she swallows the zesty juice.

I nod and adjust my outfit, ensure my wig is secure and rub my hands together against my chest, watching Lulu disappear through the crowd, before she jumps on stage. She's been up there a few times already, first to welcome members and start the party, and a few times after to introduce the dancers, or various guests, like Jaz and Richie.

The crowd quiets down after clapping enthusiastically for the couple, and before they leave the stage, Lulu thanks them, then addresses the crowd, just as two assistants show up to clean.

"The next one will be more casual. Another person I met in uni." I laugh at that, making a mental note to thank her later for that cover. "Someone who discovered pole dancing whilst there. I know, our expensive education has certainly taught us some useful skills, right?"

The crowd laughs and I can't help but admire how nonchalant she is in front of an audience.

"So, she's a good girl. She won't show you the goods, but she has the body of a goddess and she'll make you wish you're that pole. So please... enjoy the show."

As I walk toward the stage, the light begins to dim, hiding me in a darkness that I welcome. My inhibitions begin to dissipate with each step that gets me closer, and Lulu gives my hand a reassuring squeeze when I pass by her. When my foot hits the first step up to the stage, *God Be You* by Nostalghia pours from the speakers, filling the atmosphere and my veins. My muscles respond to the slow, sultry beat, tingles spreading under my skin as I take my first step onto the stage, but they're good tingles. Like

90

the ones you get before your first kiss with someone new, or the first touch in just the right place, or the anticipation of a cock slamming into you that first time.

The red spotlight hits only one pole, and as I force the rest of my nerves away, I dare a look toward the crowd, breathing out in surprise—I can't see anyone. The whole place is bathed in darkness, apart from the dim light under the shelves at the back of the bar, and the fire exit signs, making me feel... alone. The good kind of alone. It'll allow me to sway my hips on the rhythm of the music, to undulate them as I drop lower and lower to the floor, to step slowly toward the pole as I run my hands from my throat, down my breasts and to my waist, untying the see-through jacket and dropping it to the floor, my leather strapped body on full display.

And when I'm a couple of steps away from the pole, I throw my body into a handstand right next to it, swinging my legs around the metal on a collective gasp from the hidden crowd. I don't get up right away... no, I grasp the pole behind me, letting it spin as I tighten the tops of my thighs around it, legs falling almost parallel to the ground, my ass rolling against the metal. At this point I forget there's a crowd... the music floods me, the ecstasy takes over, filling me with lust as I raise my upper body, gripping the pole and opening my legs as wide as they allow.

I release the blocks in my mind, dancing against the metal bar, rubbing, splitting, dropping to the floor in moves that I would make for a lover only, feeling tingles touch my skin like a sharp gaze that wants more than to look. So I move for that look, I touch myself for it, roll my hips for it, lick my lips and suck my fingers for it, hook one foot at the bottom of the pole and the other above my head for it, opening my legs in splits that make my muscles ache and tendons burn. And goddamnit, it's so satisfying.

Before the last few seconds of the song sound through the speakers, my hands are above my head, the metal bar between my breasts, squeezed together, my legs rising, heels under my ass, and on that last note, my kneeling body hits the floor, legs open wide toward the shadowed crowd, palms on my thighs.

The club bursts into cheers and applause, so loud the next song is completely covered by their enthusiasm, and I can't help but blush. I've only ever done this a few times. Yes, I go to a pole dancing club, since I don't have one in my home, but actually dancing on stage, I've only ever done three times. And that first time doesn't count, as I would rather not remember it. I laugh at myself as I rise to my feet, my muscles aching as the hired dancers come back to the stage to keep the atmosphere going in the background.

"You smashed it! You fucking smashed it! To the point that a few couples had to retire into the playrooms and the back tables, you were so fucking hot!" Lulu pulls me into a big hug as I step off the stairs, and as the lights lower to a dim level again, I can't help but notice all the heads that turn to me as we walk back to the bar—men and women. Yet when I reach our earlier spot and grab the shot that Rachel already poured for me, I feel that cold breath again, those tingles wrapping around my throat in such a possessive way that it makes me want to drop my head back and let it choke me. As invisible as it is.

I swipe my gaze around the crowd yet again, and just as before, not one person stands out, but there are definitely more eyes on me now.

Yet this feeling, it becomes as uneasy as it is intriguing.

Seven

VINCENT

"ARE YOU SURE HE'S COMING TODAY?" FINN ASKS AS he sits next to me on the leather sofa.

"A password was requested, so I'm going to assume he is." I pull out the little cup of Absinthe that I've been patiently waiting to be ready, the sugar now dissolved, and take that first satisfying sip that burns straight down my throat.

We run Midnight, a speakeasy in the center of the city, a very useful place when you want to have control over the people present in your bar, but it's also very different from a normal bar. It was Carter's idea. He loves this old-time shit, not sure whether it makes him feel distinguished or not, but the bar is filled with low lights, leather and wood, antique furniture and decor pieces, expensive and rare drinks, and signature cocktails that even Madds touches once in a while.

But this Absinthe… he got me with this. I didn't know how to drink it properly until we opened this place and Carter found the right bartender to show me.

I crack my neck, impatient, even though we didn't exactly set a meeting, waiting for Jonathan Rees to come in. He is truly a Ghost. He has a very peculiar way of doing business; very few people outside his faction know his face, or even his real name. We do, mostly because of Carter, not because of our business with him, and over time he has become a frequent customer of our speakeasy. And the man, even if he rules with an iron fist, is nothing as most expect.

"Even I'm not sure if he's going to be down for this deal." Carter comes from the bar, dropping into the wingback armchair to my left.

"He will. He listened to our terms, took his time doing his own research on the matter. And just the speculations around why O'Rourke and Holt want in on his territory are enough to make him want to be in."

"And for the right kind of money…" Finn smirks.

"The Ghost won't give a shit about the money. But it's a perk of course." Carter shrugs.

"Yeah... how lucky of Holt, marrying O'Rourke's daughter, getting into business with him, just at the right time." What Carter and his hacker team found was most enlightening. Turns out, old man Holt wasn't that smart with money.

Carter's gaze snaps to the entrance, and I turn to see Jonathan and his husband walking through, gazing inconspicuously around the locale, as they make their way toward an empty table.

"Give them a few minutes." Carter picks up his drink and sips, his eyes not hitting the couple even once. "So how was the other night? You tried the new fetish club in town, didn't you? Was it worth it?"

"I signed up," Finn replies quickly. "I've had five people already recommending me and only three of them are women. That told me enough."

"Yeah, that you attract both men and women."

But Finn winks at Carter in response, unaffected by the comment. "I know you're jealous, baby, but it's okay, you can join too."

"You should. The official opening is in a few days." I turn to Carter as he laughs and shakes his head at Finn's crazy confidence. But I don't doubt that if Finn would try a little harder, he could probably get any of us in bed. The man is too pretty for his own good. "It was much, much better than I expected. The owner did a pretty fucking good job.

Even if you just go to enjoy the shows, it's still worth it."

"Remind me who the owner is?" Finn cocks his head.

"Loreley Dietrich. You should really pay more attention to this shit man." I answer.

"Or Lulu. She's O'Rourke's best friend." Madds shows up out of nowhere, dropping his bulky frame on the sofa next to me, and I can't help but notice the scraped, bruised hands. He fought bare-knuckled again... fucking idiot.

"Liam's?!" Finn gasps.

"Morrigan, you idiot."

"Oh. Yeah, I remember her from the party... she was holding on to this guy for dear life. I think she was just as shocked as Morrigan was. She looked terrified..." Finn lays back in his seat as Madds hums his distaste for that entire situation.

"I think it's time." Carter nods toward Jonathan, and we watch as the bartender leaves their table after delivering their drinks.

I get up, grabbing my drink, and walk toward the man that can make or break our whole plan.

MORRIGAN

I burst through the front door of a house that hasn't felt like home since a month ago, when my parents all but sold me off to the highest fucking bidder. And my mother, my goddamn mother, should have known better, because she's one of two people I told that I wanted to break it off for real with Ryan. One of two people that I had the guts to admit why. Now I know why she was insistent on me holding off.

"I didn't love your father when I married him. Our parents worked in the same business, and back then... you wanted to strengthen your legacy, uniting two fronts was the best thing. I learned to love him. I would never take it back."

Fucking liar. She gave me that speech the last time I talked to her about this. I wasn't even the one to open the subject and now I can't help but wonder if she discussed it with my father and he pushed her to talk to me.

"Have you lost your goddamn mind?" I storm through the house, straight to the living room, where I know she sits reading her magazine, as she always does at this time. "You're seriously going ahead with this charade? I just got a fucking call about a cake tasting."

"Language!" She barely raises her head from the magazine, her eyes flashing to me briefly before they return to whatever she was reading.

"Don't you dare. I can't do this, you know, bend to your will like I'm still that kid that took your word as law, depended on you, and thought she wanted the same things as you, just because that's what you told her. I'm not marrying him. I'm not as stupid as you to ruin my life."

I'm fucking seething. Since the moment that bakery called me, I've felt the need to smash everything around me. But I was in the office at the club, and I worked too hard on that place to destroy it.

My mother watches me, her eyes cold, emotionless in a way that makes me wonder if she's always seen me as a puppet, if my only purpose here is for the strings attached to my limbs to be pulled to the will of its master. She cocks her head ever so slightly, her gaze deepening with the movement, my spine urging my body to straighten.

"Are you done?" That eerie calmness transfers to her tone of voice as well, and I wish her words would surprise me. Yet they only disappoint.

I nod.

"For some strange, unknown to me, and useless reason," my father's deep, threatening voice booms behind me and I stiffen, "you seem to believe that you have a choice." I watch my mother's reaction to the man behind me and one thing becomes clear: I'm not the only puppet here.

I don't turn to him, my body completely still as I stand in the middle of the large living room of our... *their* house. They insisted so much on me coming back here after university. I foolishly thought for a long time, that it was their low-key love or some protective parental instinct to help me out while I saved my own money to buy a place. But it was just as I always feared... all about control, and now they're refusing to let me move, unless it's to Ryan's house.

What a fucking idiot I was.

That was never the case. And I'm not sure if I feel betrayed, disappointed, or just... broken.

My father appears to my right, walking toward the gaudy, floral sofa, where my mother sits, without sparing me a glance.

When did they become this? Or was I that blind?

"I'm not your slave, of course I have a choice." My tone grows urgent, but I don't yell, don't raise my voice too high, which is a feat in and of itself since I can feel that all too familiar simmer under my skin.

My father sits down on the sofa, and I swear the grandfather clock at the end of the hallway has slowed down its ticking for effect.

"Mmm... true. You're not a slave, and you do have a choice. Many, actually." He speaks in a low, far too calm tone, and I'm just about to smile, victorious, thankful for some fatherly instinct, but then he carries on. "You have the choice between Coveview Estate or Ruthford Hotel for the reception."

My grin falters.

"You have your choice of lavish wedding dresses, flowers, jewelry, decorations, everything you want for your inevitable wedding to Ryan Holt." He leans forward as if he wants to make sure I hear him, his hazel eyes darkening at the movement.

"No!" My self-control is but a memory now, as my tone heightens.

"You have a duty toward this family!" My father's voice follows mine, an octave higher, enough for my feet to feel the urge to take a step back.

"Marrying a man I don't even want to be with is not a fucking duty! What Cillian is doing, training to take over your business, that's fucking duty! This is a forced union, a marriage of convenience, and it's not *my* goddamn convenience!"

"Not yours? So all we ever gave you, all we've provided, the troubles we got you out of, the protection, the studies, the money, the car, the roof over your head... and the simple fact that you never had or have to work a day in your life, even though you keep fucking insisting on it, is not convenience enough?"

Now I do step back, just as he rises from the sofa. I've played this game before with him, and I know exactly what's coming. It's in these moments that the fiery attitude I'm known for sizzles out, my body shutting down from years of this... this displaced dominance, the emotional distress that a father… or a boyfriend, should never cause. As my eyes flicker to my mother, I can see that she knows what's coming as well.

"I didn't realize that there were conditions attached to parenting. I didn't know there was a price to pay for being your daughter!" I guess I have nothing more to lose.

His brows furrow, but the deranged smirk on his lips screams *peril* as he rushes toward me, his steps falling heavy on the parquet floor. I back up quickly, and the moment my shoulder blades hit the wall, his heavy hand slams against the left side of my face. My head whips to the side in a flash of pain, and the metallic taste of blood flows over my tongue.

"There's always a price to pay, girl! Just be thankful that at least you like Ryan."

"I don't," I say quietly, licking the cut on my inner cheek, resisting the urge to rub my hot skin, or my aching jaw. But I've shown enough weakness to this man, and I'm not about to fuel his abusive ego further.

I catch my mother's eyes as she turns toward the window, a flicker of sadness in them. But it's gone as fast as it appeared. *She's fucking useless.*

"You will marry him, you will have his children, you will do your duty to this family." He steps back and I refuse to bow to him, so I step forward.

"Why… why are you so desperate to unite our families? Or whatever is left of his," I ask.

"You always ask too many questions that don't concern you, wanting answers you couldn't begin to understand." He raises a busy eyebrow at me.

"So that's how it is. Fine." I smirk. It's not a pissing game, and I don't plan to prove myself to him. "If you care about me at all, don't send me to the man that wants to break me."

He blinks slowly over hazel irises, and it's in that gaze, beyond those colors, that the terrible truth lies. He doesn't even bother to hide it.

"I'm nothing to you…" I whisper, moving a little closer. "I'm a tool, the right kind of currency for you to pave your way down the fucking lawless rabbit hole you're digging… I'm nothing."

He doesn't speak, just shifts a little closer to me.

"Did you ever care? Was I ever anything else but a trade commodity?" My voice cracks, disappointment, fear, rage, all mixing together.

He's so still, blinking in boredom like he can't fucking wait for me to just stop existing in his universe.

"You fucking bastard!" I slam the side of my fists on his chest. "I'm your fucking daughter, goddamnit! Your fucking daughter, and you're selling me without a fucking second thought!" I'm screaming now, a guttural sound that scrapes my throat. "You can take back all your shit! You can take my goddamn business diploma, my clothes, my room, take it all! You're stealing my fucking life away! Well, goddamn take back the price I paid and just leave me alone!"

I don't see the next move coming. The moment his palm slams across the side of my face again, I'm thrown straight to the ground, my ribs hitting the side of an end-table, all air leaving my lungs on a hitched breath.

I swallow the sharp pain, because I refuse to show him any more weakness.

"You're not going anywhere. You're not giving anything back. It will simply go to waste, so it might as well stay with you. And you're not getting out of this. This is your forever."

I get up on a strained exhale then, pushing the ache away, and without blinking, I slap my father so hard across his cheek, his glasses fly off.

"You're no fucking father, not to me anyway. Not anymore."

I catch that stunned, furious look in his eyes for a moment, before I turn on my heel and storm out. I rip open the front door and almost run into my brother, who was just about to come in.

"Wow. What are you...?" He stops, narrowing his eyes and cocking his head as he takes me in further.

"Don't. Just fucking don't. Unless the next words out of your mouth are '*Morrigan, I'm your brother, I care about you and I will help you get out of this bullshit,*' don't speak to me."

"I can't..."

"Yeah, I fucking thought so. And to think you're taking over this fucking circus when the old man croaks. Nice to know you'll carry on his legacy. Just do me a favor. Don't ever have fucking kids."

I push him aside and storm past, skipping down the front steps, then stop at the bottom, turning to him.

"I thought more of you, brother. So much more..."

Eight
MORRIGAN

I DRIVE LIKE A MADWOMAN, SWERVING THROUGH THE easing traffic, dinnertime clearing the roads enough that I can overtake left and right as an angry song from a random playlist on my phone reverberates through my speakers. I weave around the cars that honk, a blur of lights around me, my mind too far gone. Heaving breaths make my throat sore, as I blink through the tears of frustration that threaten to cloud my vision.

More honking sounds around me, as tires screech on the asphalt, the sun now a trace of decadent lavender in the sky, the clouds angry on shades of burnt orange. The streets are clearer now, the roads bumpier. I avoid potholes rather than cars, the edge of the city much harsher than the rest. But I don't care, I just… drive.

The playlist changes. A harsh voice singing in moody modern Blues soothes my ears, but anything beyond that is too far gone. My soul is in flames, my heart broken, and my mind… my mind struggles to find reasons why I should hold back anymore.

Why… why in God's name am I holding back?

No one but Lulu cares… no one! My fucking parents, my goddamn fucking parents, care only as far as my auction value. If I wouldn't have met Ryan, if my father wouldn't have had dealings, or attempts at, with his family, who would I have belonged to now? Who would he have given me to? Sold me to?

"Aaah!!!" My screams get louder as my foot pushes deeper onto the gas pedal, the engine roaring just as angrily as I am. But it's beyond that… I'm fucking hurt!

Suddenly, the music stops and my phone rings, pulling me out of my rage. As I finally acknowledge my surroundings beyond driving on autopilot, I realize the sun's traces are almost gone from the sky. *Shit…* must have been driving for at least an hour. The phone keeps ringing and Ryan's name flashes on the car screen.

I would let it ring out, but I'm a sucker for pain.

"Yes," I finally answer.

"Why the fuck aren't you answering your

texts?!" Jesus, he sounds furious.

"Why are you calling me?"

"Excuse me?! You're my future wife, my *fiancée*!" Fucking hell, that last word doesn't spill off his tongue, no… it scrapes its way out of his throat, spits out at me like a medieval weapon only designed for torture. "I don't need to justify my call. Where are you?!"

"Out."

"Where?"

"Driving."

"Get the fuck home, right now," he seethes.

"No."

"You fucking bitch, I said get home now, or I swear to God…"

"What? What are you going to do, Ryan?"

"Do not test me. I don't have time for this. Move your goddamn ass to my house right now."

"Your house is not my home. And you… *you* don't fucking own me."

But what follows chills my bones. A maniacal laugh, one that is so familiar it even makes me picture the look in his eyes when those sounds work their way up from deep within his chest. The madness is most visible in these moments, and no matter how clear the vision of him is, I'm glad I'm not there.

"Oh, silly woman, it is your home, no, your house of course. There will be nothing in your name. I'll make sure the prenup is solid. But more importantly, I own you, all that you are belongs to me, and once we are married... I will have so much more." His laugh booms through my car, and I swear I can hear unspoken words, secrets... he's plotting something. "There's no escape for you."

"Fuck you!" I spit.

Only he continues like he didn't hear me. "I am trying to be a bit more courteous, keeping the leash loose while I'm busy reorganizing the business. But make no mistake, if you push me, I'll lock you in a spare room. Push me even harder and I'll be the only person you will ever see, and my only use for you will be your tight cunt. But careful, there's better pussy than yours out there, prettier women, skinnier, more attractive... I might just use that leash like a noose if you don't behave."

These men in my life... they only know betrayal. Cunning double-faced cunts, showing their true faces. His words cut in strange ways, different from my father's, and just as the road before me sinks into darkness, my soul does too. I can see the color of it now—fury.

I can't describe its shade, but this is it...

Fury.

"You seem so sure that this plan of yours will work. Father too. You confuse confidence for brains. This alliance is between you and him, not me. I shook no hand, signed no contract, I'm not yours. I'm not anyone's. Strap your leash on someone else, because I'm not your fucking bitch."

My headlights light up the road out of town, the dense forest surrounding me as Ryan's unhinged laugh vibrates through my speakers, and suddenly his tone turns grave.

"You're so brave over the phone. But we both know you crumble in front of me. It took a while to break you... but I think I'm there. Just in time."

A shiver runs up my spine at those words. Months of little digs that turned into more than that... I can't even describe how it happened, but it did. Always putting me down, criticizing, humiliating me, pressuring me... controlling me.

"Tell me. Which version of yourself will you be when my gun will be aimed at your father's head?"

The shadows of the forest seem to come down at me, swallowing the glow of the headlights.

"How about when your mother looks down that barrel?"

Shit! He was fucking serious... *"If you don't, they all die."*

"What about your brother? Will you be as brave? Or will you crumble and beg at my feet to let them live?"

Goddamnit!

I slam my finger on the mute button and

violently pound my hand against the steering wheel, the car swerving dangerously on angry curses.

"Son of a fucking bitch!!! He's blackmailing me with my family's lives?!" Another series of curses make my throat raw, but I unmute the phone before he starts believing I caved.

"They sold me off to you. What makes you think I fucking give a shit about them?!" I finally reply to him.

"Because you might fool everyone else with that harsh exterior of yours, but you don't fool me. You still believe they'll come around…"

I truly don't.

"And…" he continues, "you wouldn't want your brother to die, would you?"

I lied. Secretly, I do think he will come around. He's my brother…

"Go ahead, motherfucker! We both know your threats of violence and death are as empty as your fucking skull. You won't touch them, not now, not until you've set up whatever fucking business you have with them. We both know you can't do shit right now." I finish in a low tone, and the grunt I hear on the other side is answer enough.

So I hang up, floor the gas once more, the music returning to full blast as my pulse speeds on anxious beats.

"Fuck!"

I can feel the rush of blood in my veins, the pressure in my temples rising, my breathing staggered, my grip painful on the steering wheel.

"Goddamnit!!!"

I think… *shit*… I slow down the car and spot a forest road to the right, so I take the turn, the car making cruel noises on the uneven terrain. I press one hand on my chest, the pressure painful in my lungs, air not quite filling them.

I think… *fuck*, is this a panic attack or something? But I push through that uneasiness, dropping the beam of my headlights, the adrenaline rising when the visibility drops.

I drive deeper into the woods, my headlights the only light here, a slow modern Blues song beginning to blare through the speakers, and those notes… they do something to me. They reach somewhere deep under my skin, brushing softly over my muscles, and they begin to relax.

My tires skid on the gravelly road as I follow the turns through the forest, and I know… I'm gonna get lost. But fuck if I care, I need to be lost… I need to lose myself.

My body begins to rock in the car seat, fingers tapping nervously on the steering wheel, and I'm running out of fucking air!

"I need to get out!" I need ground under my feet.

My brain… it feels like it's on fire.

I slam my foot on the break, tightening my grip on the wheel to keep it from skidding as it comes to a stop. Before me, in the glare of the headlights, surrounded by grass and wildflowers, lies a crossroads.

Right here, in the middle of the forest, where I decided to stop, two roads cross, with four directions to choose from…

Before my mind can sink further into the panic of my hypothetical road ahead, I turn the music as loud as it'll go, rip open the door, and rush out to the middle of this crossroads. The wave of panic slams into me from the inside out, and I fall to my knees, slamming my fist into the ground on a painful bellow. It bleeds from the pits of my lungs, shrieking until my throat burns, until the desperation that taints it eases.

They betrayed me… they all betrayed me.

I take a deep breath that finally fills my lungs enough that it cools the burn in my brain, and slow drum beats fill my ears as they echo through the forest around me. The song coming from my car lulls my nerves, guiding my body to stand. My feet respond too, my hips follow, the music carries me… it always does. I don't know the moment my whole body listened to the song, but I'm dancing like there is nothing but me in this entire world. Mad southern sounds guiding me as I sway and spin, arms up in the air, hips rolling on every beat, the panic dissipating with every movement.

The damp smell of moss and wildflowers comforts my senses, as a breeze makes its way through the branches of the trees, their leaves rustling almost on the bass of the song. And I feel like I'm dancing with them, with the hypnotizing sweet scents of the forest, the breeze that wraps around my bare stomach guiding my direction, the softness of the soil beneath my feet, my mind losing itself in the heathen beats that echo through the forest. But the only heathen here is me. Wild and... free.

Here... I am free.

But am I alone?

VINCENT

It was the bass of the music vibrating through the trees that called to me, but her scream, the pain and desperation... that's what summoned me. The last thing I expected to see when I found the source was the blur of wild red hair, whipping around as she moved freely to the dark music, the dipped headlights bathing her in a strange light.

Morrigan O'Rourke.

Those red locks I would recognize anywhere, but I certainly didn't expect to see them on my run tonight.

I stand in the shadow of the trees, hidden from the headlights. Even if she looks in this direction, she cannot see me. And I don't want her to.

She sways her hips, then rolls her body to a low bass, moving on light steps as she spins over and over in a hypnotic dance. I stalk through the shadows until I'm almost behind the car, my eyes glued to her luscious body swaying, every roll an exquisite shock to my cock, but I force myself to focus on the recklessness of this woman. Christ, anyone coming from behind those headlights is invisible to her. They could attack her. What the fuck is she thinking?!

But my mind is drawn back to that scream... *She's not thinking of that, she doesn't care. Something happened.*

I move behind the trees again and stop as her fingers run through her hair, pulling it up as her short t-shirt exposes the soft flesh of her belly, her body undulating on the heathen notes of the song.

I can't help it, she lures me in. My steps crunch on the gravel as I come out into the light, slowly walking in a wide circle around her, close to the line of trees.

With my next step, as the song quiets, her muscles tense all at once, and her eyes dart open straight onto mine. I expect to see panic or fear in them, but I feel more like prey than the predator, with the fury so vividly painted on her features.

"Serpent..." she hisses, her shoulders falling when she realizes it's me. The fury stays put.

Interesting.

I continue walking around her, taking slow steps as she turns my way, keeping me in her line of sight. No words exchanged. Not yet. She drags her gaze over me, head to toe, assessing my state, but she's blinded once I'm in front of the car. I stand between the headlights, and the stubborn woman still forces herself to look in my direction, as with wild animals, dropping one's gaze means submission. And that just won't do for Morrigan O'Rourke. I can't help but grin, because the fire in her eyes burns just as bright as her hair right now.

There's something bugging me, though; she's stubborn as a mule, strong and feisty to the point of self-destruction, yet she's submitting to this arrangement her father made with her... fiancé.

It just doesn't fit. There's a story here, and I need to hear it.

A dark and moody guitar fills the forest in slow tones as I step toward her.

"What happened?" Finally, I speak, and she flinches.

"Don't pretend to give a shit. It doesn't look

good on you."

"Why are you here?" I ignore her faint insult.

"It's none of your fucking business, Serpent!" She crosses her arms, tight against her chest. "We both know you don't concern yourself with feelings, so don't pretend to give a shit now."

Damn, I'm a fool, thinking that she has moved on from the shit I had to pull all those years ago. How many have passed now? Eight? Judging by the look in her eyes, even if twenty went by, her disdain toward me would be just as vivid.

I hurt her…

"What did he do?" I can't lie and say her situation doesn't bother me. It does. A lot.

I don't miss the hitch in her shoulders.

"Who?" She feigns ignorance.

Stopping a few feet away from her, I cock my head and watch. I won't entertain that question with a response.

She sighs, long and loud, exasperation in her tone, but her eyes tell a much more painful story as she concedes. "I can't get out of it…"

"Why? What's holding you?"

"I can achieve many things on my own, but this…" She shakes her head, and for a moment, she looks away in the distance, taking a deep breath before continuing. "It's bigger than I am, and I don't know how big. I'm some sort of card in an unknown

117

game and I don't know how many players are involved. I need an ally at the table."

I nod. She's caught in the middle of the game I'm already inserting myself into. I suspect somehow this was meant to be.

"You want to get away from Holt."

"I have for a while now." She sighs again.

Oh. Interesting.

I shove my hands in my pockets, narrowing my eyes on her. "But do you want out of the game?"

She blinks once, twice, cocking an eyebrow as her eyes defocus from me. I cock my head and the light that pours from behind me hits her pale face. Only it's not as pale as it should be... not with the angry reddening on the side of it. The other side doesn't look intact either now that I'm observing more clearly.

"He hit you." My hands come out of my pockets, rolling into tight fists as I fight a growl.

She shakes her head, her eyes honest.

"My father. Ryan is more creative with his pain."

Motherfucking O'Rourke! But I'm confused again. What the hell is she saying?! That fire in her eyes falters for a second.

"What do *you* want?"

She debates telling me for a moment too long.

"I want to be free. Free of him. Of them. I can't marry him."

118

"Run, then." I know it's a useless thing to say, yet I said it anyway.

"Never!" she seethes. "That son-of-a-bitch took one thing too many away from me. He doesn't get to chase me out of my home too, my damn future! He has to pay. I *will* make him pay!" She spits every single word, hate vibrating in her throat.

"How?"

She stands there, cocking her head and watching me intensely for a moment longer than I'm comfortable.

"You." She drags out those letters, like a spell she's mouthing under the light of the moon.

And I'm thoroughly enthralled, taking a step closer.

They say the serpent tricked Eve out of Eden, tempted her with promises of power and desire. But I think he was merely answering a call, an obscured need to escape the oppression of the man that didn't want her to have a stray thought beyond serving him. Eve craved more, she had an appetite for the wicked, she wanted to be free, so the serpent freed her.

As I look into Morrigan's eyes, I see it... I may be wicked, but she's just like Eve, a heathen in disguise.

I can't help the slight quirk in the corner of my lips. "You want to make a deal with me. Just like that."

I know she hates me; she doesn't hide the feeling, so this is utterly disturbing. Even through that disdain, she looks at me as if she's about to sign off her soul... and I suppose she's about to do just that. A deal with me is always an exchange, never free.

"Yes. I can do it... but not alone. I... I need help." She sighs yet again, those words like lava that pour from her depths, and they pain her.

I step even closer, and offer my open hand to her. Her brows furrow as she looks between it and my eyes, but caves. The moment her soft skin touches mine, it prickles, like wicked black magic shooting through my body on a silent, hitched breath. She's had a spell on me for a long time... Little Eve. I clasp her small hand, lifting it above her head as I guide her in three slow pirouettes on the dark southern tune, then pull her against me. Her free hand braces on my chest, holding me at a distance, mine on the small of her back, but I don't allow her a moment to rethink the stance, instead I follow the music, leading her in a languid dance on its notes.

After all, pacts need to be sealed somehow.

She's antsy, waiting for a response as she pretends she doesn't enjoy the feel of me against her, but the hand holding me away has softened. I made my decision before she even told me her desire, but I'm enjoying this, her skin electric against mine. Only it makes old memories flash through my mind… her lips on mine, mine on her bare skin… And I really hope it's happening to her too, because this is a whole other brand of torture.

"I will help you."

I spin her in another pirouette, before I bring her back into my body.

"What am I trading for this dangerous pact?"

"What are you willing to give?" I ask, testing her.

But she drops her gaze and turns her head to the side.

"I…"

"You…"

Her gaze whips back to me in an instant, tensing as she regards me like she's about to kick me in the gut, even as she still follows my lead to the music.

"Give me your trust and patience… for now. What I want, I can only get from Holt. I can't get rid of him until I get it."

She narrows her eyes, lips parting, but I interrupt and dip her, leaning over, my lips just next to her ear, breath brushing against it.

"I will give you what you want, you have my word. For now, I only need your trust."

"For now…" she whispers back. "What about later?"

I straighten, pulling her with me as I hold her

121

cunning, green gaze. I want many things from her, but none I'm willing to take unless they're willingly offered.

"Deal."

Fuck.

"I have to warn you, what I want from Holt might not be owned by him alone. Your father is in deep with him now." The flesh between my eyebrows tenses as I await some sort of surprised reaction, only she doesn't move a muscle. I suspect by the end of it all, Holt will not be the only one paying.

"You may be The Serpent, but my choice is between losing everything to them, or losing something to you." She's desperate, agreeing on incomplete conditions, no one in their right mind would make a deal with me without knowing the terms. If I'm her only choice at survival, it says more than it should.

Nodding once, I reluctantly pull my hand away from the small of her back, and spin her one last time, her feet kicking stones through the crossroads. When she stops, her palm is in mine, my index on her quickening pulse, and I keep my gaze on hers as I lightly press my lips on the top of her hand, a faint vibration passing through her tense flesh.

"It's a deal… Little Eve." I flash a faint, wicked grin as she narrows her eyes, and I don't miss the goosebumps that flare on her skin, but I let go of her anyway.

If I'm The Serpent, then this covenant is the forbidden fruit, and this forest is our Eden. How lovely.

I take one last look at the fire in her eyes, then skip back into a jog, leaving her behind as I continue my trail through the dark forest.

Morrigan-fucking-O'Rourke just made a deal with The Serpent, at some crossroads in the middle of the forest.

How fucking poetic.

This must be my lucky day.

Nine

MORRIGAN

"**J**ESUS, YOU SCARED ME, WOMAN. I DON'T THINK
I'll ever get used to you wearing that wig. I
thought you couldn't come tonight." Lulu sits back
in the desk chair, a little rattled from my sudden
presence in the office, as I pull off the mask.

"I managed to escape another grueling, show-
off dinner. He got a call. I'm telling you, it's harder
and harder to get away from him." I crash onto the
sofa, resisting the urge to rub a hand over my freshly
made-up face. I didn't need to draw the inky cat eye
on my lid, or roll the mascara over my eyelashes,
but sometimes the makeup serves as a switch to a
different version of myself. A better one at times. Not
the one that seems to have lost all levels of courage,
or self-respect, in Ryan's presence.

He's scarier nowadays, that madness much more prominent, much harsher on his features.

"Did he do something?" Lulu leans over her desk, a slight tremble in her golden eyes.

"Not really. At this point, I'm sure he has a mistress somewhere. Wait. Is it a mistress if I'm thankful for it?"

"Probably not." She leans back into the chair. "So he didn't…"

"Not more than the usual slimy touches, grabbing my ass, my jaw…" There's more, but I don't burden her with the rest. Luckily, he seems to take any sexual tension he may hold out on someone else. It doesn't make me feel less like a victim, though. And I hate that, so fucking much… the idea of being a victim, even though a little voice in my head tells me I'm not worthy of the title.

I have to hold tight. I know The Serpent is on it, even though I haven't seen the bastard since the crossroads. But I have to trust him, and I know this game is too complex for the results to be immediate.

"I just…" Lulu huffs. "I don't know how you do it, Morri. I don't get it. How can you take it? You're not yourself with him, at least I don't recognize you. Do you? You are a fucking force of nature, yet next to him, you're barely a broken leaf carried around by a breeze. How is he doing it?"

Fuck… I wish I could explain in a way that

125

doesn't make me sound as if I'm wallowing in self-pity. Sometimes I can't make sense of it either. He doesn't really touch me, beyond the occasional grabbing, maybe pushing me against a wall, but it's his words that cut. The threats, the degradation, unworthiness... constant waves of it. Like I'm floating in the middle of the sea and his rough waters bash me, over and over, with no time to breathe. I can't explain, can't make sense of it.

I wish I could confess my suspicion, one that he hasn't confirmed yet, and that would make her look at me so differently. Her, The Sanctum, this club, are the only things keeping me afloat. Everything else is just... internal pain, causing a numbness I cannot shake.

"I don't want you involved, Lu. The less you know, the better. I love you too much to get you involved in this. But it's being handled."

"By The Sanctum." She crosses her arms against her deep cleavage, over the tank top made of thin chain-link she wears, yet I can't tell if there's anything underneath covering her boobs.

"By The Sanctum."

"You made a fucking deal with the devil, Morri, and I fear you've sold your soul to him. I fear he's yet another man taking something from you. The Serpent, The Sanctum, they don't give anything away for free."

126

I laugh, because this is just fitting. "May I remind you that The Serpent is the first man ever to take something from me?"

"You're right. You were such different people back then that somehow I forget it happened. It's quite interesting how he suddenly appeared back into your life… when you needed him most."

Funny… yeah. I've been thinking the same thing. The timing is impeccable.

"I'm not gonna complain, he's useful now. Just… please, as I said before, do not whisper a word of this to Luke. No one can know of my involvement with him. It could ruin everything."

Lulu nods, bracing herself against the desk. "You have my word." She rises and I notice the chain-link is actually a dress, the hem right under her ass.

"Jesus, doesn't your ass hurt when you sit?"

"Not gonna lie, it wasn't meant for sitting. Wanna get a drink? Watch a show?" she asks as she offers me her hand.

"Yes to both."

"Let me see you!" She steps back, running her gaze over the see-through circle dress that covers a lingerie set made more of straps than fabric, the panties rising in a V to my waist, while the biggest piece of fabric of the bra covers my nipples only. "Morri, you look like you want to play tonight!"

I'm quite exposed, I know… fairly unusual for me. Plus, I never wear dresses this short, or this transparent.

"Nah, you know me, I love watching much, much more." I wink at her and she blushes. "If I ever find the right person, maybe I will test out the equipment, but the chances are slim to none. Either way, this club is not for me, it's for them." I nod toward the door.

"Fair enough. Come on, let's find something good to drink, and something better to watch."

We've spent some time observing the patrons, taking care of some business, watching the girls dance and two couples engage up on the stage, and I can't suppress the unbelievable pride I feel when I see how comfortable and at ease our members are. This… this is why I worked my ass off into countless sleepless nights, doing freelance graphic design work, with another part-time job during uni, and this is why I want to fight back at Ryan. This fucking club is our future, and he doesn't get to run me out of town.

A crowd gathered by one of the playroom windows catches my attention, as a moody song fills the air, sending a shiver down my spine. I signal Lulu toward the playrooms, making our way through the crowd, and the sight greeting us behind that window forces me to steady myself on the window frame.

Fuck...

I feel Lulu's gaze on me, the same stunned expression most likely plastered over her face as well, but I can't look away.

A dark green mask covers the eyes of the woman hanging from the ceiling hook, by the restraint that ties her hands together. Her legs are spread wide, heeled feet barely touching the ground as she stands over a narrow bench, maybe a couple of inches in width at the top. These are used for a specific type of pussy teasing, but they usually have a narrower piece laid on top. Only on this one sits a dildo, a very thick, violent looking, monster-type dildo, looking as if it was inspired by hentai porn, and the tip of it has disappeared inside the black-haired woman. Behind her, one of the hottest men I've ever seen, looking like he swims every single fucking day, with his wide shoulders and taught abs and chest, wearing a black mask with glossy thin patterns on it, paddles her ass in controlled hits.

I'm not sure if they chose to see the crowd on the other side of the window, or if it's their reflection staring back at them. But by the look in her eyes, aimed low, probably at the reflection of the girth she squeezes her dripping wet pussy around, I think I can guess it's the mirror.

When the paddle slaps against her skin once more, we can hear the impact through the microphone they turned on inside. His technique is impeccable—he hits hard, but pulls back at the same moment it makes contact, so not to push her over, slapping, rather than hitting. I can actually see the flesh of her perfectly shaved pussy squeezing around the thick toy. I can see the moment it just about pushes her over the edge as she struggles through that ecstasy and pain.

"Remember, do not dare come." We just about hear his deep voice through the microphone, mixing with the music of the club.

"Yes... yes, Sir." I can see the tremble in her flexed thighs, and I realize she's keeping herself from impaling her pussy, not because she fears the monster-dildo, but because she'll come if she does.

I feel a strange energy surround me, tiny prickles on my back, pouring in wave after wave over my skin, and I roll my neck, absorbing it into my body. There's a lot of people around me, so the breath that touches the top of my shoulder as my hair falls to the side doesn't surprise me. Yet it does entice me.

He hits her again, and again... tears fall from under her mask as she bites her lips, my pussy contracting on a long shiver as my fingers dig into the window frame. Again, the slap of the wood on skin makes her grip the rope above her head, and the muscles of her arms flex hard as she struggles to pull herself up. As her legs tremble, my pussy clenches.

The man moves to her side, his back to us as he brings the paddle down on her breasts, her mouth falling open on a silent scream just as she comes down farther onto the dildo. Female voices gasp somewhere behind me, and I whip my head around out of instinct, only it makes me lose my balance, straight onto the man that stands behind me. My shoulders are rested against his chest, and his obviously hard cock right on my ass, as I catch a glimpse of him, and his gaze falls on my profile. He wraps his hand around my upper arm to steady me, and in that moment, the electric contact burns an image in my brain—lightning searing through flesh and muscle, a deep, primal craving fed by the image of the couple behind the glass.

As he steadies me, my ass can't feel his cock anymore, my back no longer touching his front, and I don't dare look up to his mask-covered face. I don't want to. I acknowledge him, and the fact that he has not released my arm yet, then turn my attention back to the playroom.

When the paddle reaches the skin of her ass again, the stranger squeezes my arm ever so slightly, and the woman drops her head to the side, her eyes rolling in the back of her head for a split second before they come back. There's a lost look in them, filled with pleasure and pain, an ecstasy she's lost control of, now held by her lover. He ghosts his palm over her cheek, his thumb swiping over her lips, before it drops to her throat and grips it possessively.

"Look at me."

And she does. In an instant. The look in her eyes is still lost, but he assesses her, rubs his thumb over her pulse, then dips in and touches his lips to her cheek. She smiles, her lips slightly parted, and just like that, his hand goes to one breast, squeezing her nipple before the paddle hits her clit on a sharp note.

I can't help it, a moan escapes my lips as my muscles tense, more aware of the stranger's grip on me. Or maybe he just squeezed harder, I can't tell.

Someone touches my hand and I look over to my right, Lulu signaling me to Luke, who now stands next to her—I almost forgot she was here. She points in the direction of the office, asking me if I'm okay here, and doesn't leave until I smile and nod. Then they're gone and I stand here alone, and a couple takes her place, embracing as they watch the image unfold before them.

But I'm not alone, am I. As that paddle makes contact with one of her breasts, I feel his breath on my shoulder, and I can't help but roll my neck as those goosebumps snake over my skin.

My gaze follows the man as he walks behind her, his eyes on the mirror, watching her, but God... it feels as if he's watching all of us. He reaches in front of her, sliding his fingers through the wetness she drips onto the dildo, before he pulls away, his hand disappearing between them. Her mouth falls open on a hitched breath, eyes wide as her body stills, and suddenly I realize where those fingers disappeared, and I can't help but gasp softly.

I don't notice the stranger's front against my back until his hand grips my hip, steadying me once more as my body leans into him. His grip is firm, tight, but somehow, I know that if I decide to move away, he will let me go. But I'm not moving, too enthralled in the way the man before me denies the woman's orgasm, the way she navigates just on the edge of it, pushing herself to live in that permanent state of torturous ecstasy, without the knowledge of when the denial will end. She cries, she screams, she moans... and I moan right along with her.

The man that holds me pushes a little farther against me, and it is now that I recognize the slight reluctance he held in his body until now. The purpose of his grip on my arm wasn't just to keep me steady, but to keep me away too. Not anymore.

His fingers flex on my hip, with every twitch in my body, on the thrust of the man's fingers in his woman's ass. My head falls against my stranger's shoulder, and his hand glides onto the curve of my ass. The man slaps the paddle against her flesh, finger fucking her as my stranger's hand reaches under my dress, gripping my ass cheek with a firmness that makes me quiver.

I don't stop him.

I don't want to.

I don't even want to look at him.

I'm curious, but why break this spell?

I've never done this before. I played back in Rosston, but it's different here, where most people know me, doing this with someone that might not be a stranger at all. The masks hold an eerie power in a moment like this. He could be anyone.

As his hand kneads my ass, his fingers snaking closer between the cheeks, it makes me want to try this every night. The adrenaline rises through my lungs, just as his palm leaves my ass and tips of his fingers touch that sensitive skin beneath the ass cheeks, brushing slowly toward my center.

The same moment the paddle swats over her pussy once more, as he thrusts into her, my stranger's fingers dip between my legs, slide under my panties, and push inside of me on a brutal thrust, as he presses his free hand on my chest, holding me against him. I can't swallow the moan that sneaked its way out of me, I can only brace myself against the window frame as he continues to thrust in and out of me on the same rhythm as the man before us. I can feel an achy stretch as he pushes another finger inside of me, just as the rhythm picks up. He's harsher now, and my knees grow weaker with each assault, his hand on my chest feeling like fire on my flesh, my eyes fixed on the couple before us.

I have a burning need to push onto his fingers, onto him. I... I want...

"More..." I whisper on a dragged moan.

Just when I think he did not hear me, my pussy stretches as he pushes one more finger inside, my lips curling inward as I bite back a screech. He holds me tighter as my legs shake, the tips of my finger pained as my grip on the window frame is impossibly tight, my body dying to do anything but stand right now. Only he thrusts harder, my body jolting with every brutal movement, and I'm floating on the precipice of a cliff... just there... at the edge... my whole entire being craving to dive into the abyss, into the unknown, into the filthy promise of ecstasy.

"Touch yourself." A whisper brushes against my ear, so soft I'm not even sure if it came from him or from the inside of my mind. But I comply either way, and I don't even gaze around to check if anyone is watching. I slide my hand straight under my short dress, inside my panties, and to that sensitive, swollen bundle of nerves that craves attention.

The moment the pads of my fingers touch that sensitive flesh, it spreads a current through every

135

single part of my body, every single muscle shaking at the contact, and I'm sure that any moment now I'm going to implode.

Suddenly the man before me throws the paddle on the floor, pulls his cock out of his pants, and at the same time he presses his fingers onto her clit, he thrusts into her ass on her wanton moans. He whispers something in her ear, and she smiles through her tears, sliding farther down onto the dildo on a strained moan, and she comes so fucking hard, everything shakes—her body, the bench, the toy, his own body too… And so do I.

I come on the stranger's fingers on shaky legs and swallowed moans, as his fingers slowly drag through my orgasm, and for a moment there, I could have sworn I hear him moan too.

I'm lost… my eyes close, my whole body leans against the stranger, and his hand on my chest glides just under my throat, holding me still when his fingers leave my drenched pussy. I feel that loss much deeper than I should, deep enough that my soul wants it all over again. It needs it. The release, this reality that should be mine in its entirety, not whatever the fuck I'm living outside of this club, but this… this was incredible. Exactly what I needed without even asking for it.

I open my eyes to see the woman before me being released from the man's tight hold, and I don't even know when she left the narrow bench, when she ended up in his arms, but he walks her to the door and as they walk through it, his eyes land straight on me and the man behind me.

I look back to the room, then to him, the woman now out the door too, looking straight at me as well...

Wait...

He nods, and she smiles...

Was the mirror off all along? Were... were they watching us?

I can practically feel my cheeks flush, knowing that I engaged in some sort of fetish without intention. Yes, the people around us could have been watching us too, but I doubt it, since the show behind the glass was far more enthralling. Yet the people putting it on had their eyes on us all along; as he thrust into her ass, as she slid down that dildo, as she cried in ecstasy. Me and her... we came while looking into each other's eyes, and there's something deeply satisfying about that.

As I slowly turn around, the stranger releases me, and moves away, just as I catch a glimpse of his black mask, thin green accents running over it, but I lose him through the darkness.

Jesus... fuck!

Watching a show behind that glass will never be the same.

Ten

VINCENT

THE BUSY RESTAURANT IS FILLED WITH A CONSTANT STREAM of noise—music, chatter, clinking of plates and cutlery—and some days I enjoy this switch, from the ever-calm atmosphere of Midnight.

"Evening." Carter pulls a chair, distracted for a second by the waiter carrying a couple of plates of what smells like a very delicious steak. He sits across from me, taking off his sunglasses, revealing tired eyes.

"Had fun last night?" I smirk, knowing full well the extents of his activities. Except for when they ended.

A shallow grin quirks his lips. "Mmm... so much fun. What about you?" He rests his elbows on the table, intertwining his fingers, as he leans in, that grin deepening.

"It was certainly interesting." I grab the bottle of wine and fill our glasses. Before I continue, I catch movement in the corner of my eye.

"... maybe it's time to collect." Finn's voice reaches me before I turn in his direction. He takes a seat next to Carter, and Madds shows up next to me.

"Collect... what?" I ask.

Finn leans in. "You made a deal with the O'Rourke girl. You didn't consult with us, and we're supposed to save her? We're supposed to get involved between O'Rourke, Holt, the Ghost, and who knows who the fuck else, so she doesn't get married to that asshole? Why? And more importantly... for what?" he rants almost in a whisper.

"Christ, you can hold a grudge. It's been a month. Get over it already." Madds rolls his eyes as he signals the waiter.

"No, because I want to know exactly how this will affect us, our business... our lives. Especially since you bargained for nothing."

Oh, I bargained for something alright, only it's not for The Sanctum's benefit...

"I admit it, this one was more for me than us."

"Our deals are usually much more calculated than this," Finn continues.

"You're right." I turn to Carter, knowing full well why he has not questioned my decisions yet. Being calculated is his thing; the man started writing the formula on the board long before I made the deal with Morrigan, because he doesn't shift unless he knows at least the next three moves. Being calculated is a deep-set need, not just a desire, for him. "That's why we need to shake hands with Holt and O'Rourke on this business."

"What?! That makes no sense. I'm talking about one problem, and your answer is introducing another one." Finn leans back in his chair, dragging a hand over his face.

"It's the only thing that makes sense." Carter shrugs as he drags his gaze between all of us, like that conclusion is the most logical one in the world and he doesn't understand why no one else sees it. "There's a reason O'Rourke was so keen to hand over his daughter to his new business partner. This arrangement is new. It wasn't part of the one he was making with Holt Sr, and we need to find out why. The logical explanation is that Holt has something O'Rourke really wants, or maybe their deal is much more ambitious and needed further payment."

He picks up his glass and takes a polite sip as his eyes drag across the busy restaurant floor.

Finn huffs from his chair, shaking his head. "I hate it when you make so much fucking sense."

"I know." There's no smugness in his eyes, just a logical self-awareness. "They're here, you know."

I hum my acknowledgment. They're sitting on the other side of the restaurant.

"O'Rourke is the type of man that likes the limelight. And he certainly enjoys people knowing that he's associated with us in some way. So I thought we would shake on the deal in public. Give his ego a boost. It will bring him closer to us, and we need him close. Do you all agree?"

They all nod without hesitation.

This is how it works with us, how it's always been. We pick a direction together, we move together, and we lead together. We learned young that we move on the same tune, and we were smart enough to understand that the song shouldn't be disrupted. We don't always agree; we challenge each other, but in the end, it's never one person deciding—always all of us.

Except with her… but then again, she's not a business deal.

"Hello, gentlemen."

"Jasmine, Roxanne. Glad you could join us. Please, sit." Finn points to the empty chair next to me, then makes Carter scoot so Roxanne can sit next to him.

"How are you, darling?" I smile at Jasmine and kiss her cheek.

I don't miss the stolen glances from most of the men from the restaurant, and some of the women.

The girls are gorgeous, and this is the exact reason why. Both brunette, with shiny, wavy hair framing their slim and chiseled cheeks and plump lips, both leaving enough to the imagination in their tight, yet fairly conservative dresses.

"Very well, thank you. Am I your date for the evening?" she asks politely.

"You are." I nod as she gives me her sexiest smile. She plays her role well.

We asked Ekaterina to send two girls, because our plan is to get involved with Holt and O'Rourke from all fronts. We have our team of hackers, our vault of secrets, but most men... they forget themselves around the right women. And we have the right women.

"And whose attention am I catching?" She throws an electric gaze around all the tables.

"You'll see soon."

"Perfect." She holds her glass as I pour some wine and settles into her role.

Our game isn't prostitution, but an escort service, with a set of skills specific to us. Our business deals in information—and so do they. They're high end, intelligent, strong, and their beauty distracts all who can afford hiring them. Ekaterina is incredible at finding and selecting the right ones, with the right skills and desires. She runs and takes care of the girls, but technically, Finn is the one in control of the service. Just as Carter has the hackers and Madds, the fight club.

But Ekaterina knows exactly what goes into training and taking care of them. Her background is so different from ours, brutal, trained as an asset to her country, and her knowledge has been invaluable to our operation and the girls interested in it. They're different, they crave a level of control that normal escorts simply aren't interested in. Their beauty and brains work in tandem, giving them a specific power they wield like an irresistible weapon.

"I want to make something clear. Morrigan O'Rourke—this was not *our* deal." I look at Finn in particular. "It was mine. But as it happens, she's one of the cards in a game we're interested in learning, and she may be useful."

Finn raises his eyebrow, a sly smile in his eyes. I'm going to get the twenty questions soon. "She's here too."

My gaze moves to their table in a heartbeat, struggling to be inconspicuous in front of Finn and the others. Only, that thought leaves me when I meet the surprised gaze of one very beautiful redhead.

That... I did not know.

She struggles to be inconspicuous too. Especially when I feel a slender arm wrap around mine, and some words I can't focus on, whispered in my ear. Morrigan's gaze darkens, frowning as she looks at

143

the woman next to me.

Am I seeing what I think I'm seeing?

My line of sight is quickly cut off. "What may I get you this evening? Would you like to start with an appetizer?"

I curse the waiter mentally, and we order quickly, adding another bottle of wine on the bill.

"I thought you guys wouldn't touch alcohol after last night." Madds regards me and Carter with a grin on his lips.

"Drinking wasn't exactly our main activity. We were quenching our thirst in a much… tastier way." I wink at Carter.

"Much more satisfying." He smirks at me.

"You should come next time. Even just for a drink."

"I'm sure there's a particular blond that wouldn't mind visiting Metamorphosis with you." Roxanne winks as she lazily brushes her long fingernails over Finn's bicep, clearly referring to one of the girls that has a thing for him.

"Maybe. I don't think it's quite my scene." Madds turns his attention back to the O'Rourke table on the far side of the restaurant, dismissing the whole thing. "Should we go give Liam the news?"

"I think it's exactly the scene you need once in a while. Your only hobby these days is fighting in that ring… you need some diversity. And no, not yet."

144

When I look back at the table, O'Rourke looks at me, a different brand of surprise in his eyes. I lift my glass, nodding to him, and he returns the gesture. Holt turns to me too, but I ignore him.

"He knows we're here. He either comes to us himself, or waits for our convenience."

He better wait, because I see a flicker of a red dress on my Eve, and I would very much like to see how it looks on her pale skin. I want to find out if it matches with her hair… if it brings out her eyes.

But most of all, since I left her in the dark since we made the pact, I want to see if she's squirming.

As we walk across the restaurant, some men straighten, nodding their hellos to us, while some women can't bat their eyelids any faster. I glance at Carter who walks next to me, and it's fascinating how oblivious he is to their attention.

He has an old-world vibe, a certain charm, different from Finn who is a blatant player. He's quiet, similar to Madds from that perspective, coming across as broody and hard to get. Only the difference between them is that Madds ignores it, and Carter doesn't actually notice most of the attention from women. He has a special kind of tunnel vision, because the moment someone truly catches his eye, he is so hyper-focused, he becomes relentless.

The neat waves of her red hair fall over the back of her chair, and almost as she feels the air shift in the restaurant, she turns to look over her shoulder, but stalls at the last moment, still for a second longer, before she turns back.

"Good evening. Pleasure to see you here." We swipe our gaze over everyone at the table as we stop right behind Morrigan's chair. I don't miss how her shoulders tensed at the sound of my voice. She doesn't try to look at me though, but when Carter speaks, she leans back slightly to look at him.

"How are you all this evening?" His charm rubs off on Sheila O'Rourke in an instant, her smile shy as she greets us.

They're sitting in a corner booth table, the daughter and wife on this side on chairs, Holt and Cillian O'Rourke on the opposite side, while the head of the family took his rightful place at the head of the table on the sofa.

"Gentlemen. It's been a while…" Oh, he's been waiting for us to come back to him with some news. He knew what he wanted was not easy. That doesn't mean he hasn't been getting impatient. The Ghost told us he's been trying to find other ways to get to him. He ignored them all.

"It has indeed. Work has been keeping us quite… busy." I watch as Carter gives him an insinuating

146

smile. "Some tasks are a bit more time-consuming, so we tend to retire until we are satisfied they are successful."

At those words, Morrigan turns to me for a couple of seconds, the look in her eyes questioning. I slide my hand on the back of the chair, behind her hair, enjoying the way her back muscles flex as she pulls her shoulders back gently. The table is oblivious, as Carter and I flank her, all eyes on him as he continues the conversation. I, however, tune out, my gaze lazily moving between them, wherever I see lips moving, but my focus is solely on the woman before me.

She smells of wildflowers and rain, as if she laid in the rays of the setting sun in the middle of a meadow during a wild summer storm, and I find myself craving to be right there with her. This scent... it awakens a recent memory I can't pinpoint. I can almost taste it, feel the pressure of it on my chest. And damn... it tastes good.

My thumb moves from the backrest of the chair, brushing over the skin of her back that suddenly loses its softness, bursting in goosebumps. She's tense, yet utterly and completely nonchalant, like nothing's happening. Like the devil isn't on her shoulder. Like The Serpent isn't brushing against her skin, enticing her with his touch. I brush my thumb over the goosebumps, a ghost of a touch across her spine, the softness of her hair so pleasant against the back of my hand.

The conversation Carter carries lives somewhere in the back of my mind, because the main sound that fills my ears is one that I can't actually hear. It's what I think the slow brush of my skin against hers sounds like, how I'm imagining it does. Back and forth... a soft abrasion, as I imagine she lies on her stomach in my bed, my head on her shoulder, as I drag a finger across her spine. A minute passes, maybe two, maybe more, and the goosebumps and tenseness in her flesh have been replaced by soft skin and enticing heat, as she all but leans into my touch.

I've been watching the men in the meantime, O'Rourke nodding excessively, Cillian's narrowed eyes turning over each of Carter's words in his head, repeatedly, checking for traps or dishonesty, and when I get to Holt, he's staring right at me.

I've met enough arrogant assholes to recognize even the ones that try to hide it, hell... I'm probably one. Yet this motherfucker before me... his arrogance borderlines so hard on stupidity that I'm not entirely sure if it's already crossed the line. The sheer boredom in his eyes, head leaned back, slumped body, it gives him an air of disrespectful arrogance, clearly believing he's above everyone at this table.

It gives me another reason to wonder what the hell Morrigan saw in him? I'm baffled, but then again, I wasn't there for their beginning. Maybe whatever she saw disappeared in the meantime.

I've certainly heard that story before. And it hits close to home.

I look at Carter in time to catch his gaze flicker down to the back of the chair, his expression utterly unchanged. He doesn't give anything away, to anyone else but me—that second his pupils shrunk told me he knows exactly where my fingers lie.

"Yes." His eyes return to Mr O'Rourke. "As expected, some negotiations will be in order, however the terms have been agreed."

"We are ready to move to the next phase asap." I drag my stern gaze over all the men, as a grin forms on each of their faces. Satisfied. *Good.*

"We should return to our table. Our guests are waiting for us." A faint smirk quirks Carter's lips, and as he begins shaking hands with the men, Morrigan snaps her head to me, her eyes boring holes when they latch onto mine, but she returns it to her plate a moment later.

The bastard did it on purpose, mentioning *our guests*, and she reacted. How very interesting.

"It was *very* good seeing you. Enjoy the rest of your evening." O'Rourke smiles as I slide my hand slowly from his daughter's skin, immediately missing the feel of it on the tips of my fingers.

I move away before they extend their hands to

shake mine too. I don't want their touch to taint the memory of her on me.

I wonder if her family, her fiancé, consider this behavior of hers normal, or if her distaste is giving us away. I wonder how she behaves with them. I wonder how she would behave with me at dinner. I wonder if she chose herself to wear that sleek red dress tonight. I wonder what she ate. Are garlic fries and a simple burger with far too many layers of pickles still her favorite foods?

I wonder how she's changed in all these years.

Eleven
MORRIGAN

*H*AVE *I BEEN HOLDING MY BREATH THE WHOLE TIME?* My lungs spasm, burning as I force my breathing to stay even. And with that burn, I crave more. That touch ghosting over my skin, *left, right, left, right,* moving like a pendulum, hypnotic as I forced myself to keep a straight face. Especially with Ryan in front of me.

Torture—it's the only way I can describe it— torture. Because I never thought I would refer to his touch as that.

Ever again.

It came out of nowhere, disrupted my balance and perfectly crafted stoicism. It felt as if it was the first time...

All over again.

"So we're in." The enthusiasm in Ryan's voice makes me want to roll my eyes.

"I believe we are, yes. We'll set up a meeting and discuss all the details. The wait was worth it…" Father's voice sounds somewhere in the background, my mind distracted by the strange prickle running under my skin.

"Especially since none of the other sources amounted to anything… Wasted money, fucking crooks." I swallow a large gulp of wine as my fiancé continues.

The Serpent made a deal with them and is close to delivering. What about me?! Where is his end of the fucking deal? Every day that passes brings me closer to a permanent life with… *him.* Bile rises in my chest as I look at Ryan, slowly burning its way up my throat, and I swallow it down with the rest of the wine.

"Excuse me." Placing the glass on the table, I rise.

"Where?"

You have to be kidding me.

I stare at him, with every intention of not answering. But I cave… "Ladies' room." I always fucking cave. Fucking asshole.

"Don't be long."

"I will be as long as I need to be." Before he can spout anymore bullshit at me, I turn, catching my *dear* brother's gaze. We haven't been close in a while, especially since our four-year age gap separated us quite a bit. I was a kid when he was in high school, then when I got older, he went to uni, and when he came home, it was my time to go away, and we never really synced. Holidays were not enough to maintain a close relationship. Yet, deep down, I hoped that he wasn't cut from the same cloth as my father. I thought he would defend me.

I was wrong.

I head straight to the bathroom as his words to me, from a couple of weeks back, run through my mind. *"We all have our roles to play, this one is yours. And I know you're strong enough to do it."*

Bastard!

I shouldn't have any need to be strong enough to do this! This *role* should not exist, damnit! I shouldn't have to make a deal with The Serpent to save myself! There should not have been a need for any of this! Family, fucking family, should be on my side, not... a stranger.

But he's not really a stranger, is he? His touch lingers on my back. It tickles me still, making this whole night, this situation, just a smidge easier to handle.

The loud clicking of my high heels is absorbed by the background noise and music, as I hurry to the bathroom, my chest visibly heaving now. I step behind the wall that conceals the corridor to the bathrooms, and in that same moment, the air turns cold, the heaving stops. From the other end of the corridor, The Serpent narrows his eyes on me.

My steps falter only for a second before I carry on. And so does he.

I'm not sure if time slows down or we do, the milliseconds stretching between the moment my foot leaves the ground and the next one finds it again. My gaze is on that bathroom door, walking on the left as a lump forms in my throat, one I need to swallow badly. The fabric of the flowy knee-length dress brushes against my skin, spreading goosebumps all over, my nipples pained by the bra against them.

My palms dampen as he gets closer, his body slowly passing mine, the breeze his movement creates making my hair and dress flow and graze against my skin. But that's not what makes my whole body shiver… it's the ghost of a touch as the backs of our hands brush against each other.

One simple touch. One of many more before it. Yet somehow… the sizzling energy of it makes it feel new.

I can finally breathe, the pressure in my chest easing, and I pat myself on the back for resisting the urge to look back before I stepped in here. I check all three stalls are empty, and finally manage to swallow that lump in my throat as I brace myself against the cold porcelain sink. But my lungs fill with the excessively perfumed air that somehow reminds me of Ryan and his house, and anger fills my veins. I wish this anger would be more prominent in his presence...

I drag my gaze over my reflection, sighing at its pathetic look.

Who am I with him?

How deep has he crawled under my skin? Bit by bit, he's ripped out pieces of me, then replaced the voids with this unsettling cowardice. No one, absolutely no one, makes me feel so unbelievably meek. The only comfort I have is that I'm only *this* way with him.

As my eyelids begin to burn, the person looking back at me in the mirror becomes even more unrecognizable.

"Who are you?" I whisper at her.

"Vincent *The Serpent* Sinclair."

I flinch, then still, as those words taint the air around me. Yet I inhale deeply, letting them taint me as well. My fingers ache, my grip brutal against the porcelain, and the burn in my eyes is gone. At the sight of him, those feelings from mere moments ago, dissipate, and the woman in the mirror... her shoulders are pulled back, her chin higher. The green in her eyes shines with a feral darkness, and that darkness smiles back at me.

Now her, I recognize.

"You're risking an awful lot, *Serpent*." The man appears in the mirror, the expensive all black suit fitted so well, tight against his pecs and wide shoulders. I bet it's tight against his nice ass too.

Jesus fuck!

But he doesn't answer, a crooked smirk on his lips.

"Someone could walk in. It could be my mother."

I don't know when this man noticed me again. Was it at my mother's party all those months ago? Was it on the street when I was with Ryan at that bar? At my surprise engagement? When did the devil's eyes land on me?

He takes one step forward and I cock my head at his reflection, noting the all too familiar shift in the air, forcing myself to resist that dark gaze in the slits of his eyes, the one that penetrates deep, making most either freeze or tremble at the power the man emanates. Only that's not what I feel right now; but the ghost of the touch out in the corridor, I feel his fingers brushing against my back as I sat at the table, I feel his lips against my ear as he whispered to me in the woods.

He steps behind me, invading my space, his front against my back, barely touching. Deep notes of bergamot and cedar cover the gaudy bathroom perfume, pulling me into a place I desperately wish to escape to. *The forest…*

His eyes trail over my features, following my pulse down my throat, to that soft spot between the neck and shoulder, and as my flesh explodes in an exhilarating shiver, I close my eyes, letting my head fall to the side.

I'm drowning in his proximity, and the moment warm air blows against my shoulder, my eyes dart open and I straighten, the spell so evident.

Fuck, what is this man doing to me?!

"I'm serious, damnit! What are you doing in here?!"

Suddenly he swipes to the side the hair that lays against my neck, the tips of it tickling my skin and sending a betraying shiver down my spine.

"Stop it!" I turn on my heels and slap his hand away. "I don't know what you think you're doing, but I'm not it. This"—I point swiftly between us, finishing with my palm pressed hard against his chest, trying to push him away—"is a business transaction. If you think I'm giving myself in exchange for your help, you're sorely mistaken. I would rather die by my own hands than get trapped by another man again."

"So that's it, then?" He pushes against my hand. "You're going to kill yourself."

"Did you just confirm that you want *me* in exchange?" He better choose his next words carefully, or I swear to God…

I bring the other hand to his chest as well and push him away. I'm heaving as I watch him take no more than two steps back, effortlessly, as if he allowed me to push him, my force barely affecting him.

"No. It was more… hypothetical. It's a bit radical, don't you think? Do I repulse you so much that this idea is so terrible?" He cocks an eyebrow at me, that look on his features melting me in a way that makes me even more furious. More at myself than him, at my inability to suppress my own attraction.

"This wheel doesn't go around, *Serpent*. It's broken. It cannot roll on the road that damaged it that first time…"

There's a flicker in those eyes, that charm cracking for a moment. At least he remembers… now, I don't know if it affects him in any way.

"Broken wheels can be fixed, *Little Eve*, especially when there was no intention behind the damage." He takes a step closer, and I flinch on a hitched breath.

What the fuck is he talking about?!

"No intention? You're taking this metaphor too far and you don't seem to understand the message—I. Don't. Want. You." I straighten my back, crossing my arms against my chest. But as he takes another step, the fabric of his suit brushing against the hairs that stand on my arms, I have to tighten them just a bit more… to hold myself together, to not make a liar out of myself.

"You only want my help." He pushes his hands in his pockets, cocking his head as he looks down on me. He's maybe a head taller, maybe a bit more. But I give him my best disdainful look from under my lashes, refusing to bend my head to look at him.

"I *need* your help."

He nods slowly as he straightens, the implication clear in my words.

His hands leave his pockets, his chest pressing against my crossed arms, pushing my body back as he leans forward and braces his palms against the marble on either side of me.

And I'm out of air.

Entirely out of air, a strange sizzle infiltrating my airways instead. It bends my will and turns my mind into this creature that I secretly wish to be. Because this creature craves him. Not just body, but soul and mind. The man before me bathes in this mysterious obscurity which my soul wants to touch… a delicious abyss it wants to be part of.

As his head dips down, mine turns to the side, and his breath brushes over my shoulder… velvet against my skin.

Until it's more than that…

Skin brushes against mine, and my chest rises on a long, heavy inhale. The air is not the only one sizzling anymore—my whole body is too. His parted lips drag slowly against my shoulder, sensual and enthralling, catching me somewhere between intrigue and protest. He reaches that betraying spot at the base of my throat, and when his tongue touches it, I cannot hide the sharp inhale that escapes me. My protests are trapped in the same throat his tongue drags over, my breasts pained under the pressure of my arms, and I cannot resist the urge to tighten my thighs together, reveling in the faint burst of pleasure. When he reaches my ear, catching the soft lobe between his tongue and teeth, my body shudders on a slow exhale, the treachery seeping deeper into my flesh. Then, he moves away.

He fucking moves away. Leaves me cold, breathless… and furious.

"And you don't *want* me."

Son of a bitch!

I'm caught off-guard.

"I *want* you to honor the pact. Help me get the fuck out of this."

He nods once, but the smirk is not yet wiped off his face, his arrogant ass infuriating me.

"Okay, then… So what's the plan? I see you're keen to shake with my father and… fiancé"—I don't miss the slight scrunch of his nose at that last word—"but not me."

"I thought we already shook."

"Technically, yet it's been a month and I'm still planning a fucking wedding!"

My tone rises and he takes a look at the door.

"We're gonna get caught." I sigh.

He returns his gaze to me, and I catch that subtle way in which he bites his lip, sending another shiver straight down to my fucking pussy.

"I'll send you a text in the next few days with a time and a place. We'll talk then."

With those words, he slips out the door, and I'm left with less knowledge than when I first came in here, if that's even possible. But I have something else. Something better.

Hope.

Twelve
VINCENT

THE UNEASINESS IN HER GREEN EYES IS THE FIRST THING I notice as I rush out of the office at the sound of Madds' booming, urgent voice.

Her presence stops me dead in my tracks. She is standing in the main area of our bar—our *secret* bar. Fortunately, it's currently closed.

I'm certain there's a quicker way for my brain to process what I'm seeing, only I haven't found it yet.

With determined steps I walk toward them, the look in Madds' eyes feral, but it's something more than anger that I see in them, and it concerns me.

"What the fuck?!" Finn rasps as he steps out behind me. "What the hell is she doing here?"

"Careful, brother…" I warn, and I swear I hear him hissing.

Carter rises from the sofa before we get to them, his eyes narrowed ever so slightly on us. There's barely any emotion on his features, but those tensed shoulders as he watches Madds and my Eve are hard to miss.

My… Eve.

When the fuck did that happen?!

The way she manages to shadow that uneasiness from her bones with that cocky attitude that has gotten her into a fair amount of trouble in the past, is fascinating. She's breathless though, cheeks flushed. Has she been running?

"What's going on?!" My tone is low as I look between them.

"Tell him." Madds nods to her.

"My father… I don't know what it means." She swallows, catching her breath. "I don't have your number. It took me too long to find you."

"I found her running through the alleys, trying to find the entrance," Madds explains.

Carter suddenly appears with a glass of water for her. She downs half of it and carries on.

"I don't know what it means. I overheard a phone conversation, maybe it was with Ryan, I don't know. He was angry, he said… umm… *He needs to be put back in his place! He's going after some bitch, Ekaterina or something.*" At that last word, we exchange serious looks, and Finn pulls out his phone immediately.

163

"What else did he say?!" His finger hovers over Ekaterina's contact, eyes wide and lips tense.

"He said…"—she rubs her temples, squeezing her eyes shut for a few moments—"*I don't know who she is, but he thinks she's important to Sinclair, so he wants to mess with him.*" For a split second, she fixes on me. "*This Boseman individual is getting in the way. He'll fucking ruin everything!*"

"Shit," Carter mutters.

"Fucking Boseman… Find Ekaterina, now!" I rasp at Finn, who already has the phone to his ear. "Carter, we need to make sure they are all okay, all accounted for."

"We have to be inconspicuous," Madds interrupts. "We start rushing around now and we'll draw the wrong kind of attention to us… to *them*. At this moment, Boseman, O'Rourke, and Holt think Ekaterina is your woman. We cannot let them know who she truly is to us."

I sigh and nod. Carter agrees too, and Finn paces like a cornered animal, phone to his ear as he curses under his breath, while Morrigan quietly observes it all.

"Ekaterina! Fuck, baby, where are you?! … Fine, I won't call you baby. Where the fuck are you?! … Okay, check in with all of them. When you're done, call me. Lock your doors and windows, grab a gun, and wait for one of us. Okay? … I don't know yet. But… Yeah. Okay. See you soon." He hangs up and rushes to us.

"She's home. She's fine. I'm going to…"

"Madds has a point. We'll attract attention if we start running around town now." I stop him, watching the wheels spinning in his head as his gaze goes from confusion to understanding.

"It should be you." Madds nods toward me. "If Boseman thinks you're with her, it won't look unnatural. Go, bring her here. Take an unusual route, and make sure you're not followed."

"Okay." I turn on my heels and rush back into the direction of the office, but her voice suddenly makes me halt.

"Who's Ekaterina…?" The bar goes silent, still. I look over my shoulder, catching the forest green that looks back at me, strands of red caught on her freckled cheek. "And… Boseman?"

I inhale one deep breath, then continue on my way. I grab my car keys from the office and run to the back entrance.

"Maddox, stay with her!" I yell from the end of the corridor, then push through the door.

The sunset burns in shades of lavender, the humidity high in the air, and I inhale the warmth that lingers.

She came to warn us… even when she didn't know what against.

165

MORRIGAN

If I wasn't already clued in that they own this place, by the rumors and the fact that they're in here while it's closed, the scents of bergamot and cedar, lavender and… something else, something decadent, would definitely clue me in. This whole place smells like *him*.

It maintains an intimacy fitting for a living room. Everything in here is made out of stained wood and vintage leather, from the mismatched chairs, sofas and armchairs, to the coffee and dining tables. Even the low ceilings are split by rough wood beams. But the vintage style bar with the overly thick marble top and brass pump handles ties everything together, wrapping it in an old-world decadence.

The one I know as Carter leans in, placing a glass of something in front of me on the coffee table, only my stern gaze is fixed on him. I may be coming from a point of assertion of my strength, but I'm also enthralled by the man. Everything about the way he looks and moves belongs perfectly in this space. Almost as if it's his world, and his world alone.

"Espresso Martini, with a kick. It will calm your nerves." He speaks in a monotone, gravelly voice.

"My nerves are fine, thank you." I hold his strange gaze, a deeply saturated blue seeping into

166

hazel, shadowed by thick long lashes, and he holds mine. It's a fight for power here, only I can't read the man. He's still, in an eerie kind of way. Different from The Serpent. Almost as if emotions are useless in his world… *Almost.*

"If you say so." Just like this bar, the man has an old-world look about him, with his square, chiseled features, wearing suit trousers, a white textured shirt, and waistcoat. He nods, a slight quirk in his full lips, and I follow it up over the defined hollows of his cheeks, and strong, high cheekbones, to his effortlessly neat undercut, the longer hair on the top of his head slicked back. It's those hollowed, high cheekbones that give me a dejá vu feeling, though.

Carter takes a seat on the sofa, next to a gorgeous specimen of a man—Finn Hennessey. Every girl I knew in school had a crush on him. Hell, every teacher too. He probably fucked half of them as well.

"You came to tell us… I'm surprised," he states, one eyebrow cocked above his beautiful blue eyes, his lips straight.

"Was I supposed to keep the information to myself?" I take a sip of the dark drink, humming in approval as sweet and bitter mix in a delicious way on my tongue. "Damn…"

"You're welcome." Carter watches me, a smirk shining only in his eyes.

"You owe us nothing." Finn ignores him. He's

167

blunt, giving me the impression that he wears his heart on his sleeve. I certainly don't think he bothers hiding what he thinks or feels. I doubt there's any filter between emotions and speech. Nothing like the other three.

"Jesus…" I can't help but sigh and roll my eyes. "You've been cooked up in this world of secrets, sins, and chaos, for long enough that you don't seem to recognize human decency anymore, do you? I'm sure The Serpent told you by now about our little deal. You think I can sit around and watch your world burn to the ground?"

Silence falls upon the room, the only sound is that of drinks being sipped.

"I recognize it just fine, but human decency does not exist in our world." He pauses, letting out a deep sigh. "Thank you."

Well, fuck.

"Who is she?" I ask once more, and I get the same response where all they do is exchange looks. "Okay, who is Boseman?" Once again… nothing. "Oh, for fuck's sake, come on!" I rasp as I rise and look between the three men. "She's one of *the girls*, isn't she?"

There's yet another round of exchanged looks, and considering their expressions, I wonder if The Serpent told them I know of the escort service.

"You think you're the only ones holding your

secrets in your world, but..." Suddenly it hits me like a ton of bricks, and I fall back into the armchair, eyes wide, mouth open, the previous thought gone.

"Morrigan?" Maddox's heavy footsteps move toward me. "What is it?"

"I was wrong..."

"About what?! Morri, talk to me!" The warmth of his large hand wraps around my entire bicep.

"My brother... How did it skip my mind?!" I sigh, bracing my elbows over my knees, mumbling under my breath. "He's not on his side." I focus back on the room, the men impatient as they regard me. "A few months ago, maybe five or so, my mother asked me to take something to my brother's house. When I got there, he wasn't inside, but out in the pool, and I ran into his open laptop. He never leaves that thing unattended, but he wasn't expecting me to walk into his own home with no invite. I managed to read quite a bit before I went to him, and it was all about you—The Sanctum. A roadmap of your businesses, connections. One of them was the escort service, and only now did I make the connection. Ekaterina's name was there—dead center. Only hers. She runs it, doesn't she?"

"Yes," Maddox responds.

"Might as well just give her our laptop passwords." Finn sighs, annoyed.

"No, you don't understand." I shake my head.

169

"My brother knows who Ekaterina is to you all. But my father had no idea over the phone today. None at all."

Then it clicks, for all of them.

"He's not on his side." Maddox finally sits down. "Then whose?"

Cillian's words run through my head. *We all have our roles to play, this one is yours. And I know you're strong enough to do it.*

"Hopefully mine…"

Thirteen
MORRIGAN

"**D**ARLING, THERE YOU ARE." I'M FROZEN, SQUEEZING the cold metal of the door handle, as my heart tries to weigh the consequences of my next move.

Darling. To many, it is a term of endearment. Once, it was one for me too. Not anymore, not coming from this man standing in the middle of my parents' foyer, head cocked as his muddy eyes study me.

"I've come to take you *home.*" My body hasn't moved, but a burst of current splits me in a shudder at those words. *I should have stayed with The Sanctum.* I should have waited for The Serpent to return after he called Finn to tell us Ekaterina was okay, but I couldn't stay too long. I couldn't risk these people knowing I have any dealings with their underworld.

"I am home…" The words crack as they tumble off my tongue.

"Don't be silly, *darling*. We're getting married. It's time you come and live with me."

I still haven't moved. My entire brain activity focused on how to get out of this. It's been a month and a half or so since the surprise, and I managed to avoid his advances. Only I suspect it wasn't due to my own efforts, but with his attention pulled on establishing the new business, he's just been giving me slack. Now, as that shudder lingers, my knees slightly weaker, I'm not sure how to keep him away.

"No." I don't think I can convince anyone with that whisper. I'm definitely not convincing myself.

"What did you say?" He turns his head, ear toward me, one brow cocked.

"N… No." It comes out louder this time, and he draws back.

He takes one determined step in my direction, and I still on a hitched breath.

"What are you doing standing there with the door open? I'm trying to keep the humidity out and this house cool!" I have never been more thankful for my mother's annoying high-pitched scolding voice.

I take the opportunity, shut the door, and step quickly toward the stairs, keeping to the edge of the foyer, away from Ryan.

"Morrigan." My foot pauses just above the first step, fingers digging into the warm wood of the ornate balustrade. "Look at me."

Taking a deep breath, blinking slowly as the air fills my lungs, I turn around and hold his stern gaze.

"This…"

"No!" I interrupt, my mother looking positively shocked at my daring attitude, and I do feel just a little bit sick. Not because of the attitude, that in and of itself is probably my most defining trait, but because I know… he'll use it against me. "You cannot have any more say in what I do with my own life, Ryan Holt. I was yours once… once. Not anymore."

"So you think you can stay here?" That voice sends chills down my spine, as the man that owns it appears in the foyer. "You have a duty to your husband."

I roll my eyes, digging myself a deeper hole. "He's not my husband."

"Yet," Ryan punctuates. "I packed a bag. You're coming with me tonight. You can return tomorrow if you wish."

Wait, what? This is not how it works.

"You're coming for dinner tomorrow anyway." My father fiddles with a letter opener, ripping open an envelope he carries. Who gets letters anymore?

"Of course. Not sure if Morrigan's going to be

doing much eating, though." Ryan runs his eyes slowly over my body, an eyebrow raised, lips pursed, and my throat fills with bile. If my appetite wasn't lost the moment I saw him here, it's lost now. He walks next to the staircase and picks up a weekender bag I didn't notice before. "Shall we, *darling*?"

My parents' gazes on me are enough to drag me down the steps, as Ryan extends his hand to me. What choice do I have? There is no escape for me here, not amongst them. Cillian's words echo through my mind as Ryan's eyes flare at me... *"You're strong enough..."*

Am I? Everything that I am feels trapped in a tsunami, splashing violently around my axis, but when Ryan is around me... it dissipates, and breaks to the ground in an anti-climactic wave.

And I succumb...

"I've been busy, and made your illusion of freedom too real. We'll have to remedy that, won't we? No Holt woman gets so much unsupervised freedom."

Those words have been playing like a broken record in my mind since we came back to the beach mansion that has been in his family for at least three generations. He forced me into his car, since mine offers a freedom he apparently doesn't agree with anymore… for the most part. He said that the freedom he allows is an illusion, but I'm beginning to think that what we once were was one as well.

"I have a surprise for you." His grin curves his top lip in a way that makes him look… sleazy. Has his lip always done that? Am I just noticing this? Or is it another new aspect of his new personality that even Jekyll and Hyde would be envious of?

A surprise? Nah… this version of Ryan doesn't prepare surprises, not good ones anyway.

"Thanks, but I'm good." If he's waiting for my enthusiastic response, he's going to wait forever.

I turn and begin to walk toward the library, the only place in this house that gives me a semblance of comfort. I'm not a huge reader, not of the books that lie on those shelves, but neither he nor his father ever spent time in that space. It's not tainted; it doesn't feel as if it belongs to them.

"It's in *our* bedroom." I've barely made it five steps. I don't turn, though. "Come." I take a deep breath and move forward on a shaky step. "NOW!" His voice changes its tune, booming through the grand space.

"Ryan, Morrigan, you've returned." I'm startled by the sound of his mother's voice, and turn to find her walking toward us from the living room. "Have you eaten? Should I get Pierre to prepare something for you?"

"Hello, Mrs Holt." She hates being called by her first name, and even as a widow, when she should be called Ms, not Mrs, she still rejects it. At least she's always hated me calling her by her first name. I think she just hates me… period.

"No, I've eaten and…" He swipes his eyes over me once more, lingering on my hips, as he does all too often "…Morrigan's not hungry. Dismiss the chef. You can go too."

Her gaze widens as she takes in those words, before she looks between him, the top of the stairs, and I. There's a peculiar, all-knowing look in her eyes. "Very well. Have a good evening." Then the woman looks as if she hesitates to move away. What the fuck is going on?

Involuntarily, I look at the top of the stairs as well, hoping that there would be some sort of indication of that *surprise,* which made even Mrs Holt wary. Suddenly I feel the need to make some excuse and bring her back. She's a good buffer. Only it seems that since her husband's death, she's just another pawn in her son's life. I wonder if she inherited anything from her husband. Somehow, I doubt it.

I know it's not going to work, but I begin walking away again.

"Morrigan! I said… now!" His tone lowers, deepening, and shakes my insides.

I have no choice. I never have a choice with him, not anymore.

Sighing, I turn and walk up the stairs, then toward his bedroom at the end of the hall. At the thought of what could possibly await on the other side, I grip the handle much harder than necessary, the metal digging into my palm.

You can do this. You can do this, Morrigan.

I take a deep breath, attempting to force away a lump that made its way into my throat.

You'll be okay. It will be okay. Just… just relax.

"Open!" His rasp startles me. So I do… I push that door open, ready to face the reality of my situation, the situation I've been trying very hard to avoid for the last two months, maybe. Only the image before me stuns me in a completely unusual way. I'm confused, irritated, shocked, and slightly relieved, all bundled into one emotion I cannot name.

"What the fuck is this?" Against the left wall, on top of a white fur throw that covers the whole of his super king-size bed, lies a naked woman—spread eagle.

"This…" He pushes me into the middle of the room to face the bed, then walks toward it, his eyes meeting hers as she smirks and licks her lips. "…is Jasmine."

She's the woman that was sitting next to The

Serpent in the restaurant. The one attached to him…
The one he kissed on the cheek. Oooh, she's one of
the escorts! Does Ryan know who she belongs to?
No. He can't. Unless Cillian said something… but
I have a feeling this is more about pissing on The
Serpent's territory than anything else, since he saw
them together.

Right? Fuck… too many games are being played
and right now I feel like a pawn in all of them… but
not a player.

He stops near the bed, and she swings her legs
over the edge, then slides off it until she's on her
knees, her ass on her heels and hands on his belt.

"What the hell are you doing, Ryan?" My body
suddenly breaks out of this strange spell, and I rush
toward the door.

"If you dare step out of this room, I'll fucking
cut your head off and deliver it to Loreley myself.
Then I'll fucking cut hers off too."

Shit.

"Come in and shut that door."

The blond kneeling in front of him is not phased
one bit. She continues her task as she looks up at
him, unbuttoning his pants, one hand straight to his
cotton-covered dick, rubbing slowly up and down.

She's definitely a professional.

"Jasmine here is going to do for me what you
refuse to."

I can't help but roll my eyes. "Well, shucks. Am I supposed to be sad about that?"

"Until we're married," he cuts me off. "Until those hips get smaller and that belly flatter. I think the wedding preparations have stressed you out a bit too much and you put a few extra pounds on top of the existing extra ones. Until then, you will sit here and watch." Jasmine has his dick out and in her mouth by the time he finishes that sentence.

I blink more times than I should, forcing away those hot tears that threaten to sear their way out. It's impossible to settle on one feeling, too many running through me, my chest burning as I swallow each and every tear away. I'm not even sure why I'm shedding them. I don't love him anymore…

I *don't* love him anymore.

I don't love him!

Then why the fuck does it hurt? Why does it feel like he's ripping apart even more than he already has? Why does it feel exactly like it's not supposed to?

Because I cared about him… I thought he cared about me too.

"You're sick," I manage to whisper in a shaky voice.

"Maybe. But you're going to stand there and be sick with me." He grins, grabbing the woman's hair and gagging her violently with his dick.

I turn my head toward the window, wondering what the fuck my life has come to, why am I here, why does it hurt, when will it stop...

"Don't you fucking dare take your eyes off. Look at me now!" he rasps as I hear the woman gag yet again.

I do as he says, all thoughts slowly dissipating... one by one, they leave me... until my features are void of feeling, until my muscles are limp, until... I'm but an empty shell.

Or so I wish to be.

I want to be void of any trace of emotion I've ever had for this man. I'm not sure where it hurts. Is it my soul, or my ego? It definitely isn't my heart... I just never thought that his disrespect for me would reach such lows.

Yet, the man threatened to kill my whole family and my best friend if I even dared to leave him. Why am I shocked by what lies before me? Quite literally, as Ryan pulled her up by the hair and laid her on the bed. He flips her over, pulling her ass up, then fists her blond locks while throwing me the sleaziest smile he can muster. Then he impales her on a savage move, and her scream makes me cringe. I can't even tell if it's in pleasure or actual pain.

He does it over, and over, and over again... his eyes on me the whole time, guiding her by the hair so she can look at me too.

I'm forcing myself to control the bile in my throat.

I've watched plenty of people have sex in the club in Rosston, and I fucking own one now, yet this… this is different. It's malice; revenge; evil. This is a man I've been with for almost two years, I've cared about him, we've known each other from school… But he's also the man that at this very moment carries in his gaze the promise that he will do to me exactly what he's doing to her.

Only I will not be willing; and he will not care.

This helps, though. This moment right here… I should thank him for it. It pushes me over the edge, killing off that part of me that still believed there was hope for the old him to return, that this period was only some sort of temporary madness.

It's not. It's just madness.

The man before me doesn't deserve any emotions from me, not even disgust. And I suddenly realize that even most of my reactions to his abusive behavior were tied to my lingering emotions, that lingering hope.

So I carry on as he orders—I watch him. Watch him fuck the woman's brains out. Watch as he grins at me. How she moans her pleasure… or her fake one. I watch it all because he's making every decision I will have to make from this moment on so much easier. Every thrust, every sound as their skin slaps together, every grunt, every way in which he squeezes her flesh, kills another part of the person I am around him.

So I smile. He's just decided his own fate, and he doesn't even know he did.

Fourteen
MORRIGAN

MAYBE I'M ALREADY DEAD, BECAUSE THIS DEFINITELY feels like some sort of hell.

"It's so exciting, isn't it, Morrigan?" My mother's friend sits on the other side of the dining table, trying to smile, but failing miserably. Whoever the fuck injected that Botox into her face should have their license revoked. It looks revolting.

I open my mouth to respond, but my mother cuts me off.

"Oh yes, so very exciting! Organizing the wedding is a dream."

The woman blinks once at me before turning to my mother, but I can't be bothered to be affected in any way, so I just stick my fork in another tomato and shove it into my mouth, chewing through her next question.

"So have you made any arrangements? Did you set a date?"

I chew the rest of that tomato, and again, I'm just about to speak when Ryan's voice booms next to me.

"We've made plenty of arrangements, and we did actually set a date as well. We are very excited." They're really scared I'll open my mouth and out them, aren't they? He grabs my thigh under the table, squeezing hard enough that my back straightens and my body twitches. I slap my hand over his, pulling at one of his fingers to try to get him off.

"But then again, there is no..." I begin.

"Point in waiting." The motherfucker interrupts me again! "We want to do it as soon as we can. We're just waiting for me to settle into the business."

I can feel his threatening gaze on me, but it doesn't have the effect he hoped for. A heavy indifference has made a home in me since last night, and I'm basking in its chill. When his bruising grip tightens farther, I turn my gaze to him, and without hesitation, I dig my fingernails with as much force as I can muster at this moment, until he scrunches his nose and snaps his hand away.

"I agree," my mother continues. "There is no reason for a couple in love to wait too long to get married. Not when you know there's a perfect union

184

already."

I turn my gaze to the woman, an incredulous smile creeping on my lips. She's trying too hard with her deception. Does she think the people around us are blind?

"I'm afraid I'm going to have to excuse myself." Ryan peeks at his phone screen, his brows furrowing slightly, before putting it back on the table, screen down. "I'm putting off fires everywhere nowadays." He laughs at the guests, his gaze fixing longer on my parents.

"It's to be expected. Picking up a new business, it takes a while to adjust and work out all its kinks." My father takes a sip of his red wine as he places his knife and fork on his plate, next to the half-eaten steak. "I'll walk you out."

"Thank you, Liam, but that won't be necessary. Morrigan will walk me out. Sheila, this was delicious. So sorry I couldn't stay any longer. Everyone"—he turns to the rest of the guests—"it was a pleasure."

His politeness just about turns my stomach over, but everyone else at the table swallows the bullshit, smiling and extending their well wishes. Goddamn idiots, all of them... with two exceptions—The Serpent and Maddox, sitting on the far right next to the head of the table. They merely nod at Ryan, in such a slight way you could blink and miss it.

"Morrigan." He's already pulling my chair back

with me in it, forcing me to suddenly drop my cutlery onto the plate with a loud rattle. I would very much like to make a scene right now. Only, after last night, I have little energy, and I would prefer planning my move.

I walk out of the room, the rest of the guests continuing their meal and chatter as we go to the foyer. He grabs his coat, and before he closes the buttons, he pulls a large brown envelope out of it and hands it to me.

"I would advise you don't open it around your parents, or anyone, for that matter." He hands it to me, and I reluctantly reach over for it.

"What is this?" It's on the heavier side, but I can tell there's paper inside.

"I figured that threatening your family's or friend's life might not be enough motivation for you to stop your refusal to marry me. So I'm threatening yours as well."

What the hell?!

I don't have time to react, too consumed by his words, when he grabs the back of my head and pulls me to him, his slimy lips pressing onto mine as I attempt to push him away.

There was a time when kissing him was pleasurable. It feels as if eons have passed… I can't pinpoint anymore the exact moment it all shifted. The memories don't feel like they belong to me anymore.

"By the way, they're not the originals. You can stay at your parents tonight, if you need time to process." His sleazy, mad grin lingers in my memory minutes after he walks out the door.

I want to go open it, but everyone will expect me at the table. *Fuck*.

No one really notices when I walk back into the dining room, all caught in conversation. Except for two penetrating pairs of eyes. They didn't miss the envelope I put away on my lap. I managed to finish dinner with minimal conversation, and even The Serpent and Maddox attempted polite exchanges. Enough not to seem rude, but not enough that it would allude to our current proximity. After all, both my parents are fully aware that we knew each other once. Once...

Now that dinner is over, my parents are inviting the guests to the formal living room on the other side of the house for drinks. And I take the cue to excuse myself.

"What's that?" My mother's voice stops me in my tracks, and I think the hand clutching the envelope is beginning to sweat.

"Something... for the wedding," I improvise. "I just want to go look it over. I'll be back in a while."

"Oh, I should look too if it's about the wedding."
Fuck!

"This is a bit more private—some honeymoon arrangements."

Fire and ice hit my back at the same time, yet somehow, they both burn. I know in my gut which pairs of eyes are doing that to me. I move away before more questions are thrown my way, and the moment I'm out of sight, I all but run upstairs, heading to what used to be my room.

Bursting through the door, I go to the bed, turning on the lamp closest to me, and throw the envelope onto it. It feels like it's staring at me, that rough, brown paper hides something he said threatens my life too. I know it's not possible for it to be what I think… I fucking know it. Yet this man managed to flip a switch on the person he used to be, so he makes me believe in the impossible.

I rake my fingers through my loose hair and finally rip the envelope open. Large photos fall onto the bed. It takes but a second to recognize what I'm looking at, another second for my breath to hitch painfully in my lungs, another one for the shock to reach my heart, and I'm not sure if it stopped beating, but when I press my hand onto it, I can't feel the movement.

"Son of a bitch…"

A slight creak makes me jump and turn to the door. The tall, strong body that fills the doorway looks oh-so-stern in his black ensemble.

His darkness arrives with a rise in the pressure of the air, and as he closes the door behind him and steps into my space, that pressure becomes almost unbearable. Yet somehow strangely satisfying. The type that quickens your heartbeat, that makes you forget to breathe, that makes your knees weak.

I don't move the moment he steps farther in, my back to the photos I try to conceal. His eyes still flicker to the bed, but they don't linger. Instead, he prolongs the torture as he looks around the room, taking in the parts of me that exist here, clearly curious by the insight. He pauses on certain things, only I don't care enough in this moment to figure out which, or what, it could mean. This room has evolved with me over the years, no traces left of the teenager I used to be, the one he used to know.

That teenager died young.

And those photos laid on my bed show the reason why.

When he finally turns to me, in this room that holds secret memories we share, he looks at me as if I'm both good and evil, Heaven and Hell, love and malice, like I'm… everything.

He closes the distance between us, my breasts almost touching his chest, and grips my chin between two fingers, cocking his head as he holds me still.

"Private honeymoon arrangements?" he asks

in his signature calm voice that chills bones. But what shocks me is that he does not hide the blatant jealousy.

I don't have the courage to speak though, not when it means those fingers will leave my skin. Not when the alternative is for him to see how Ryan has just complicated things.

But he lets go anyway, and I sigh as his simmering touch lingers and he steps next to me, picking up one of the photos from the bed.

"What is this?" His tone changes its tune.

He leans over, assessing each photo as I rake my fingers through my hair, grabbing two handfuls, feeding the sting on my scalp as I tighten my grip.

"That's you." He pins me with a stern gaze and throws the evidence onto the bed. "These were taken years ago. Who took them? And who the fuck is the person you're burying?!"

One by one, those images from the night I killed a man imprint in my memory. It's not as if I needed to be reminded I did it, it's not something one forgets, but… I never truly regretted doing it, so I rarely ever think of it. And that's what brings me true guilt.

"Speak!" He raises his voice as high as he can in this room, but I hesitate. Not because I'm afraid to admit what he can clearly see already, but because of how that story could affect him. Or maybe it won't affect him at all, and that scares me more.

My lips part, but I'm interrupted by that slight creak in the door again, and we both turn, shielding the evidence. My heart falls back in its place when I see Maddox entering and quickly shutting the door.

"What?!" He looks between us as he steps closer. "What the hell is thi…" He trails off as recognition hits him, and his wide eyes snap to me. "What the fuck, Morri?! Is this who I think it is?"

The Serpent turns to me and my eyes flash from one man to the other, both waiting for different explanations.

"Yes…" I sigh.

"We don't have much time. You need to tell me what the fuck is going on." The black-eyed devil tenses his shoulders as he regards me.

I pick up one of the photos and stare at it. I'm in the middle of the forest, a flashlight lighting me and the patch of ground before me as I dig the hole, the body of a man laid next to it. Even in this grainy image, you can tell there's no life in that body. Only Ryan could have taken this and the more I look at it, I realize that I know exactly when. All this time, all these years, this son of a bitch had leverage on me. All these fucking years!

"That's Lawson, isn't it?" Maddox asks.

"Wait, is that the guy we caught almost…" The Serpent navigates around that particular piece of memory. "…The one whose jaw you broke?"

"Yes."

"When was this taken? For fuck's sake, just tell us, you know you will! Stop prolonging this."

"There's a goddamn reason for that! Fuck! It was taken not long after we… after you left." After *he left me* out of the blue. "When he noticed you weren't around, and I didn't have your protection anymore, he decided to get his revenge for that night I broke his jaw."

Maddox quickly grabs one of the photos, bringing it closer to his eyes. "Wait… is this *your* blood? Ripped clothes… Morrigan, what the fuck happened?!" He slams his large hand on the bed, on top of the photo, his tone threatening.

Even if he is built like a beast, the scariest one of them all, who much prefers killing a man than showing feelings, I know he cares. In a ruthless, rough around the edges, kind of way.

"In a way, I was lucky, because he came after me alone. Maybe he didn't have the courage to tell any of his friends that it was a girl that broke his face that night." I lean over and gather all the photos back in the envelope. "I still remember the sick grin on his face when he told me that you're not there to save me again…"

"Not that you needed much saving." Maddox becomes a bit uncomfortable with my insinuation, what they saved me from that night. The look in The Serpent's eyes though, is eerily still.

It may have looked to them like I didn't need saving, but it didn't feel the same to me. I was... unhinged, definitely not in control, and only control can give you the confidence to win something like that. I had none of it, I was just... manic.

"Ryan used to be like a puppy after I became single, always following me, always around. Now I wonder if any of that was a normal crush, or if it was just a growing, unnatural obsession. It turns out that he was around that night as well. At least that's my conclusion, because there's no way anyone else would have found us there. And I'm sure Ryan wasn't expecting what he saw when he did."

"What *did* he find?" The Serpent speaks in a different tone now, lower, rougher, each word spilled slowly, punctuated, my skin responding with goosebumps before my brain even registers the need for a reply.

"Lawson knocked me out and put me in his car. I woke up in the forest, not far from Brook Lane, as he was trying to rip my clothes off." I hear the growl coming from Maddox before my eyes land on his fury. But it's the darkness, the possessiveness in The Serpent's eyes that pulls my attention. "He didn't intend to finish what he started. Believe me. He wanted to beat the shit out of me, humiliate me, leave me for dead, naked, for the animals to find me. When I woke up and pushed him off, he got two more kicks in my stomach before I managed to get on my feet. I guess Ryan saw his car at the side of the road and came into the forest. Maybe he thought he was coming to my rescue... only I wasn't the one in need of it."

I pause for a moment, catching my breath.

"I fell into a frenzy. I saw red and no other colors. He screamed... Ryan did, when he saw me bashing Lawson's head in with a thick tree branch. I couldn't stop myself. I'm not even sure I thought of stopping at all. I broke it on his mangled skull..."

"Jesus..." Vincent whispers. But I don't know what to make of that reaction. He stands there, his eyes just a tad wider than normal, enough for that to be a complete shift in his demeanor.

It's strange, but I always think about him as my first kill, and this haunts me more than the memory of his cracking skull. I haven't killed since; he's my one and only, but my brain... I think it already calculated the risks, considering my behavior. Maybe it's just a matter of time. And I wish that would actually scare me.

"Ryan helped me. He left, got shovels and some clothes, while I stayed in the forest. He helped me

194

bury him. He helped me move his car, then took me home. I thought it was done. We never spoke of it ever again." I look at the envelope clutched in my small hands. "Now I understand why."

"So he's the one that took the photos," Maddox states.

"Definitely. I remember there was a point when he said he was going to the car to pick up something, since we had some fingerprints to wipe off Lawson's skin. I was in the middle of digging. I didn't think anything of it. I was broken, exhausted, and that's most likely when he took the photos."

I turn toward the window, watching the clouds move slowly in the night sky, at the same speed as the breeze that moves the branches of the walnut tree that hovers from the right-hand side of the window.

"The world moved on from Lawson. He was so problematic, even his dad thought he ran away. No one even questioned the fact that he disappeared suddenly. More girls were coming out, accusing him of rape or sexual assault. Everyone just thought he ran away to escape a trial. I moved on too... never did I think that it would come back to bite me in the ass this way."

"We need to get all the copies," Maddox speaks as he walks to the door, his ear close to it as he listens for movement. He opens it and peeks through, then walks out without another word.

We should go too. We can't risk my parents even thinking we're friendly any time but in their presence.

"We'll never get the copies. He's not going to tell us anything, you know that." I walk toward the door too, stopping just in front of it, when an arm wraps around my waist from behind, and the other pulls the envelope from my hand. My body hums in awareness, tense as I force myself not to sink into him. The corridor is lit, but here, in my childhood bedroom, we're bathed in the shadows. The same shadows that adore The Serpent so much.

"We'll get all the copies." His breath brushes that sensitive spot under my ear. "Then we'll get him, Little Eve. Then your parents. We'll get them all, pull them in our hell and burn them in your heathen fire."

Each and every syllable slithers around his tongue, dripping from it onto my skin, as he whispers into my ear. Then he kisses the edge of it, sending electric shocks through my whole body with that soft touch of his lips. When he releases me from his hold, my legs almost give out. Almost. And he convinces me… I'm not sure if it's confidence, or just the tone of his voice, but I believe him.

So I walk into the light, carrying his darkness on my skin.

Fifteen
VINCENT

THE SCENT OF HER ROOM BROUGHT BACK MEMORIES THAT
I didn't think touched me anymore.

It was a different life.

One I was ripped out of by the man I just cut a deal with—her goddamn father.

But that scent... her soft red curls, the feel of them against me, the curves that turned that teenager into this goddess, the freckles that seem to sparkle like stars in certain lights, they brought me back to a time where my fury wanted to rip him in two.

Rip him away from life itself.

Only now, I can actually do it.

But before I do, I will make sure to tell him why—*my* reason, not the new one Morrigan gave me.

I followed her car as she drove to her friend's building. For her safety, but my curiosity too. I need to know if Ryan put a tail on her. If we're going to keep meeting, and we certainly will, I need to know if I have to give her instructions, how to take precautions. Only my curiosity was fed in a completely different way.

"Why didn't you tell me that her best friend lives in the same building where Metamorphosis is?"

"I thought Carter would have told you when you went there with him. He did the research before you guys signed up." Maddox sits at our usual table in the bar when I arrive. There's already quite a few people here, yet a bit less than usual at this time. Saturdays tend to be busy nights for Midnight. Everyone needs to let out some steam, only I have a feeling even more are going to go to Metamorphosis.

Carter arrives just as I settle onto the sofa, nodding hello to us both.

"Yes. I followed her last night, after we left her parents' dinner."

"Morrigan? You... followed... her?" Carter raises an eyebrow at me.

"Jesus Christ, get over yourself. I wanted to see if Ryan tracks her. It's to our benefit after all."

"Mhm..." he hums, clearly not convinced in the slightest.

"It's her friend's club. What's so unusual about her living there too?" Maddox shrugs.

True, there shouldn't be anything unusual about it. Only somehow, Morrigan's presence there makes me... think. It's her best friend. That means there's a high chance that she frequents the club too. Which means that I could have seen her there. I haven't caught sight of her signature locks though, the few times I went there.

"I think I'm going to go out tonight." I look at Carter and there's a faint twitch between his eyebrows. He doesn't question me, only nods, but I can see that sneaky sparkle in his eyes.

"I'm waiting for Ekaterina. I need to catch up with her, then I'm going to go look into those photos." Carter signals one of the waitresses, letting her know we're ready to get some drinks. They know not to disturb us until we ask.

"I'm gonna go downstairs."

We both turn to Madds. If he goes downstairs to our fight club... something has to be wrong. This time, I suspect it has something to do with the story Morrigan told us.

When he speaks those words, there is usually one of two looks in his eyes—the fairly placid one that says that he's just supervising, or the one that hides that feral beast scratching its way to the surface. It's the beast we see now, not yet at the surface, and he needs to let it out, de-stress.

"Okay." The corner of my lips quirk. Sometimes it's better for one of us to be there, just in case he goes too far. And he has gone too far, a few times...

"Stop fucking looking at me like that," he spits at Carter. "Call Finn if you want. He can *supervise* me." He leaves the table, his heavy footsteps shaking the floor on the way to the back rooms.

"Shit... What the hell is going on with him?" Carter asks, but the waitress interrupts us, and we send her on her way with our order.

"Morrigan and him, they've always had this... connection. I think what she revealed tonight stirred him." Not that he would ever admit it.

"But I thought that you and Morrigan had... a *connection*." He narrows his eyes on me, and I can't help but roll mine, ignoring the comment.

I wish I could explain what I saw between them. "It was more like a wild beast recognizing its kind and latching onto it. And Madds doesn't latch onto anything, ever. Only us." But her and I... we're a different kind of beast altogether. I don't tell Carter that, though.

He nods, then leans back into his seat.

"Why are you going to Metamorphosis, Vincent?" The man rarely calls me by my name.

The waitress sets our drink order on the table with a soft smile, not lingering once the last glass touches the surface.

"I can't help but wonder about E... Morrigan." *Shit.* Carter quirks an eyebrow, but I cut off that train of thought quickly. "Her best friend owns a fetish club, and she would have supported her, especially now at the start. Which means she was there when we were. But I would have noticed her red hair."

Carter raises an eyebrow, a smile pulling at his lip. "Yes, it's certainly unmissable."

"But... since *it is* her best friend. I can't help but wonder if there's more to it all."

"Interesting. Well, I hope you enjoy your journey finding that out." The bastard smirks and I start laughing.

"I'm sure I will."

The gold details shine in the darkness of the club. Metamorphosis was most definitely built with both style and comfort in mind, and as I sit on the upholstered barstool, sipping a glass of quality Bourbon, I have to give an extra point for that comfort. I didn't think I would enjoy it much. I joined more because The Sanctum has to ensure it has a foot through every door in this city. But the anonymity is refreshing. Exhilarating even.

The music, the atmosphere, the people... it's

immersive.

The song changes, but it's the raise in volume that stops me mid sip, and when the lights dim to the cusp of darkness, it pulls my attention away from the bar. The moment I turn in my chair, a fresh, wild scent envelops me, so different from the one that dominates this space. It submerges me into a visceral, yet untouchable memory, and like a warm summer breeze, it passes by me. Our eyes meet for a brief moment, before she disappears through the crowd. It was too dark to see more than the faint shine of her eyes behind the mask, but her scent lingers, and I don't want to exhale just yet. I don't want to let it go. It brought a strange wave of emotions with it, and they're the good kind.

Suddenly she appears on the stage, the only light in the space aimed at her, but not blinding, just bright enough that it's like an aura around her body. She wears a long skirt, her legs peeking through the high slits, this garment looking more like multiple scarves tied on her waist. The song intensifies just as she sprints the small distance from the steps to the pole, and jumps onto it, clutching the metal between her hands and bare thighs, the long skirt flowing as she throws her head back, eyes closed, spinning around to an ethereal tune. She's pulled everyone's attention, all eyes on the woman that I have seen dance once before. The one I couldn't take my eyes from the first time I stepped in here. The same one that I finger fucked as we watched Carter in one of the playrooms. I recognize the mask, the hair... but mostly, I recognize her scent.

Her shiny, black hair flows in waves as she pole dances, switching positions slowly, following each note of the song. She's treating the pole as her partner, each movement a testament to her passion for dancing, a testament of her sensuality. She moves like she's all alone in this club, and considering the darkness around her, she probably feels as though she is.

I'm caught in this spell and somehow I feel guilty. Have I ever had this sentiment? I'm enthralled by this woman, while actively pursuing another, the one and only...

She lets go of the pole, filling the stage with an elegant, contemporary routine, but it's the borrowed ballet movements that make me drop down from my seat. The moment she flies into the air, doing the splits mid-leap, I head straight toward the stage.

"It's called a Grand Jeté, not jumping splits, Vincent."

I can practically hear her voice in my head, correcting me again. I caught her dancing for the first time... and it was the first time I allowed myself to talk to her.

I catch glimpses of her as I walk between the

people gathered to watch the routine, and by the time I reach the steps, she's back on the pole. Before I get the chance to linger on her swaying curves, the beat drops... and so does she, sliding down the pole until her ass hits the floor at the same time as the bass booms, vibrating under my feet.

I feel it straight in my cock, or maybe what I feel is the effect of the woman herself—the pole is snug between her breasts, as she holds herself by it, arms stretched high above her head, and her legs spread wide, the crowd getting a clear view of her lingerie.

Now this stirs something in me—a jealousy I should have no business feeling, yet that's not the dominant thought, because it stirs pride as well.

Everyone claps and cheers in unison as she rises to her feet, her lips curving into a shy smile as she bows her head gently. She runs off the stage as the light returns to its usual dimness, and her steps falter the moment she takes the first step down and notices me at the bottom. The closer she gets, the better I see behind the shadow of her mask, and her forest green eyes are so much clearer...

My Eve.

She cocks her head, and I wish I could see her expression. But in a split second, her hands shoot to the collar of my black shirt, pulling open the buttons with a clumsy urgency, and I know... I don't need to see her expression. She knows. And I let her get her confirmation.

She pulls away one side of the fabric, and brushes her soft fingers against the scar she left there, on my left peck, a few months before. Her eyes shoot back to mine, and I'm not entirely sure what I see there—anger, shock, annoyance... relief?

I think the music stopped playing because all I can hear are her heavy breaths, echoing somehow, her chest rising and falling slowly, her nostrils flaring, and I feel like I'm waiting for her to strike.

What is the appropriate conversation starter with the woman you thought you last touched years ago, only it turns out it was much more recent than that, under the anonymity of a mask?

I'm thankful for the covering right now. Last thing I want is for the whole of fucking Queenscove that's currently in attendance to see me speechless in front of O'Rourke's daughter.

She moves all of a sudden, shaking her head as she steps around me, and the music and background noise fill the air.

Jesus... what is she doing to me?!

Without bothering to button up my shirt, I follow her, touching the bumpy skin on my chest where she stabbed half a year ago, at her mother's party—the first time I saw her face to face in years.

It was the moment I realized all was not forgotten for her.

I was stupid to think it was—I left her with someone else's lie as the only explanation.

It was also the moment I confirmed without a shadow of a doubt the only reason I accepted the invite to that event—I want her back.

But does she want me?

Sixteen
MORRIGAN

*V*INCENT-*MOTHERFUCKING*-*SINCLAIR!*
Son of a bitch! I'm heaving as I make my way through the crowd, wishing I would be back in the middle of that forest, because God-fucking-damnit! All I want to do right now is smash, destroy something, break some bones, and open this motherfucker's scar with a knife again!

Did he know?

Did The Serpent fucking know that it was me the other night, when he fingered me in the middle of my goddamn club?!

Wait…

My steps falter and I slow down just as I reach the stairs that lead up to the reception.

Does he know it's my club too?

I feel a grip around my wrist, but carry on up the stairs, shaking it off violently. He must be following, but rage slowly makes its way through my bones, like another entity living inside of me, and I know I can't let it take over. I cannot make a scene here.

So I keep going, through the reception, which still has people walking about, unlocking the door that takes me away from it all. Only, I'm not the one pushing open the door. Instead, his hand lands right next to my head, and he does it for me.

"Miss?" We both stop. I turn slowly toward the receptionist. "Everything… okay?" A few more people turn their heads in our direction.

She's seen me walk through here before. Though never followed, or with company.

I take a deep breath, his signature scent suddenly noticeable now that we're away from the crowd.

"All good, darling, see you soon."

She nods, returning to the customers talking to her, and I push through the door he kept ajar as that rage returns too.

"You!" I whip around, pointing at him the moment the door closes behind us. I have no idea what else I want to say to him, but I'm only seeing shades of red.

I go to the closest door to me and punch in another code, pushing it open when it unlocks, but this time around, I stop him as he tries to walk through with me.

"Did you know?!" I have one hand on the edge of the door, the other on the frame, blocking his access. "No, fuck, scratch that. I don't wanna know!"

"Know what, Little Eve?" I catch his grin, shadowed by the mask he wears, the low, even tone of his voice making me even angrier.

"Don't play with me, Serpent."

He places his palm on the door and pushes on it, only I hold it tighter.

"No, you're not coming through here. This is where this ends."

"Where... what... exactly ends?" Stepping forward, barely a foot away, he looks down at me.

"You knew, you fucking bastard, you knew!" The sentence finishes on a dragged-out scream, and I release the door frame, swinging my palm at his handsome face. But he catches my wrist. So I swing the other one too, and the bastard has both in his grip now.

One second passes from the moment he pushes me into the room, turns me, and pins me against the wall at the same moment the door closes next to us.

Our heaving breaths are too loud, mixing together, our bodies too close. He's pinned my wrists above my head, held with just one large hand, his whole front against mine, his free hand gripping my hip.

"I will ask again. Where. *What*. Ends?" His tone is firm, only I can't meet his gaze.

I swing my leg up, ready to knee him where it hurts the most, but he fucking predicts that too, his left leg pushing mine to the side, situating himself between them. *Fuck.*

"Little Eve, do not make me ask again." His tone is lower, menacing, gravelly in a way it's never been like before. Ever. It's not a voice I recognize on him, and my body shudders from my throat, down my chest, my hardening nipples, my belly... through the one spot I really hoped would not react to him anymore, and finally to my toes.

"This," I spit, looking down between us. "You knew it was me, you son of a bitch, in the club when you... It. Ends Now." I push out those last three words, because I somehow feel betrayed. He took advantage of me!

Didn't he...?

"This." He copies me, his eyes dragging down to the point where we are joined, where he can feel my hardened peaks against him. "I wasn't aware it even began. I did *not* know it was you when I played with your tight cunt as Carter and his girl watched."

My mouth falls open, stretching wide while my eyes threaten to pop out of their sockets.

"Carter! Wha... Carter?! Are you shitting me?!" Sweet Jesus. "That was him?! Oh my God! Get the

210

fuck off me!"

Only, I'm pushing against a brick wall.

"I didn't know who put that fucking spell on me with those sinful hips. I. Did. Not. Know." He cocks his head, his eyes dark pits under his mask, his look utterly devilish as no light shines there. No sparkle. All sincerity, and I have to look away.

Because my body doesn't seem to care that much, as it struggles to keep itself from reacting to that delicious tone in his voice.

"I don't believe you!" I snap.

"It's the truth. Want to hear another one?"

My eyebrows furrow, but I stay silent.

"When I left you, wet and satisfied in front of that window, I was dying to know what you tasted like. But you were a stranger… I couldn't put a stranger's cum into my mouth. Only you, your soft body against mine, those lush hips, the feel of your skin under mine… I didn't know if I would see you again." A wicked grin paints his lips as he speaks those words, and with each one, my breathing quickens, already knowing how it will end. "So I tasted you, I brought those fingers to my lips, sinking them beyond… and allowed myself one taste. Just one. Little. Taste." I steal a glance in his direction, and catch him as he licks his lips. I find myself licking mine at the same time. My mouth waters at the image of the mighty Serpent sucking my cum from his fingers.

His eyes flicker between us at the same moment a shiver runs through my breasts, my hard nipples pressing a little harder onto him. He did not miss that.

"I almost came back to you after that one taste... I wanted more. You tasted like I needed it all. So I walked away."

He leans in slowly, our gazes on each other's, the tension rising, the leg nestled between mine pressing on my center, and my God... I feel myself, wet and needy, and I know he'll feel it too.

The moment our noses touch, his grip loosens just enough, and I pull my hands down hard, pushing him off me. I rush to the stairs that lead up to the apartments, because there's no way I'm waiting for the elevator. Taking two at a time, I rush past the first floor, up the next flight, stealing a glance behind me... I can't see him. I keep going, reaching what will be my apartment, punching in the code for the door. No keys yet since it's easier this way with the contractors. I walk into the darkness, pushing the door closed with both hands... and at the last moment, a shiny black shoe wedges in, and the door bursts open, throwing me back a few steps.

"I don't want you." The words fall too fast off my tongue. Too fast for even I to believe them. Because here, in what will be my home, all dressed in his signature black that hugs every inch of his lean body, he looks exactly like what I want.

I walk backwards slowly.

"You don't want my hands on you."

Another step.

"My palms on those soft breasts."

Another one.

"My fingers stretching your pussy."

Another…

"My tongue lapping at your clit."

One more.

"My cock pressing inside of you."

"No," I all but whisper.

He's right in front of me now.

"No…" he repeats.

He reaches up, and as his fingers touch my forehead, I'm afraid to move. Not fearful of him, but of what I might do as the image of him balls deep inside of me haunts my way too vivid imagination.

"You look good in black, but stunning in red, darling Eve." He runs those fingers through the hair of my wig. But I'm not ready to relinquish it.

Suddenly I feel his touch behind my head and my mask drops from my face, hanging by its ribbon in his hand. I feel exposed… But he doesn't stop there. He reaches behind his head and pulls his own mask off.

We're on even ground.

Eve and The Serpent.

I blink once... twice... pushing a hand on his chest again, holding him away enough to catch every flicker in his eyes. Only I think I'm holding myself from sinking in the enticing abyss of them.

"You didn't know it was me." I'll know if he lies.

"I didn't know it was you, in *your* club." No shift, no dilating of the pupils, no hitch in his breath, no change.

I believe him. I've seen the look of a lie in his eyes... even if he's gotten better at it, I think I would still be able to see a flicker of it.

Wait.

"*My* club?" I repeat, an eyebrow raised as I steady my pulse.

He only nods.

"It's not..."

"It is," he interrupts, cocking his head, his eyes boring into me once again.

Is it hotter in here? It feels hotter. I feel hotter. No, no, control yourself, breathe, for the love of God, breathe.

"No." My voice is a little firmer, but not enough to convince him. *Fuck...* I need to practice this. I can't be caught this way by my family, by Ryan.

Only The Serpent is neither of them, is he? He never was...

"It's not my club." Firmer this time, voice louder. I think of the risks, of what I could lose, of

214

what Lulu has built.

"Only The Sanctum will know, no one else." He holds my gaze and I think I lost this battle before it begun. There's no point.

"Listen to me, Serpent! Does anyone else know?! Anyone but you or your precious Sanctum?!" I grip his open shirt, that fear of what could be lost clearer now.

"I haven't even told them yet. You only just confirmed it." The corner of his lips curls in a hint of a smirk. "I just had a hunch."

"You… goddamn son of a bitch! If you're lying to me…" The fabric scratches my fingers as I grip it tighter, pulling him to me as panic and rage fill me at once. "If this information reaches my family, or… or anyone else, from you or The Sanctum, I will fucking kill you myself. I may not be the strongest, the scariest, or the fucking brightest, but I swear it… I'll kill you all."

He nods. That's it. Just a simple nod. And I'm left wondering if he just thinks I'm joking, or if my threat is actually believable.

"How did you know…?"

"'I've connected the dots. But your eyes don't believe your lies, Little Eve. You'll have to get better at that." His hand grips the side of my throat, his thumb swiping over my bottom lip, and I swear he does it so he can feel my quickening pulse on his palm.

"I'm not your Eve…" I find my balance and step back.

"Oh, sweetheart…. You ran to the crossroads, all desperate in your steps, and there you met the devil when you were seeking to escape. Our pact was made in the middle of the forest, but is that so different from a garden? Granted, I didn't offer you an apple, but you sealed a deal with me…"

"I don't remember *sealing* anything." I'm playing with fire now.

"Then I believe it's time." It happens too fast—one short step, and he's against me. He grabs the back of my head and the moment our lips touch, a gate opens. Desire floods through me in waves. Everything I've suppressed when I thought of him over the years, everything I've pushed away since he came back into my life. His soft lips press harder against mine, and I let go of my grip on his shirt, my hands grabbing onto the back of his neck and threading into his hair in the next second.

I thought the devil seals the deal with a kiss… this Serpent… he demands more. So much more.

And in this moment, I'm going to give him everything.

Fuck denial. Fuck Ryan. Fuck my life. Fuck it all. I'm taking that fucking apple and giving into sin in my own Eden.

Our steps fall backwards until my back hits something with a rattle and when I open my eyes, teeth clashing as we bite at each other, tongues swiping our words away, our hands sinking too hard into our flesh, he looks clearer, brighter.

I turn my head, breaking the kiss, to look behind me at the window I'm now pressed against, only catching a brief glimpse of the street below before his hand grips my jaw, turning me back to him. We pant in unison, his dark eyes feral with a matching need, before his lips slam down on mine again, his tongue pushing through, exploring every bit of my soft mouth. I feel his other hand on my shoulder, pulling down the straps of my top and bra, and the brisk air caresses my breast. The moment his hand touches my pebbled nipple, a moan vibrates through his mouth. Mine. And he swallows it whole. Just as the next one. And the next one after that, as he pinches me, playing with me in a way that drives me mad. With lust. With need. Mad with the unknown of what's to come beyond tonight.

Letting go of my jaw, he exposes me fully, my lace bra now uncomfortably tight under my breasts. But I draw on that discomfort as he bites on my bottom lip and pinches my other nipple, reveling in both pleasure and pain.

He releases my mouth and pushes me down, my ass hitting the low windowsill as he kneels before me. I steady myself, gripping the edge of the wood when he pushes my legs apart, situating himself between them. The confusion lasts but a second before he dips down on my breasts, his tongue flicking my nipples before he goes all in, sucking, licking, worshiping... it's the only way I can describe it—worshiping.

"Oh, beautiful Eve... Pleasure looks so fucking stunning in your eyes." He looks up at me and tiny prickles slither onto my cheeks.

"And you look so fucking pretty kneeling at my feet." Oh, I'm definitely playing with fire. And from the look in his eyes... I know I'm gonna get burnt.

But the man smirks, his lips parted, the crinkles at the corners of his eyes deepening as his tongue sweeps over a bit of his top lip, and the moment the dimples appear on his cheeks... I'm done for.

He's so fucking handsome my fucking heart hurts.

Those dimples I used to swipe my tongue over so long ago. That smirk on his lips... sweet Jesus.

He pulls back enough that he can look down at me, quickly finding the small buckle that holds my skirt up, pulling it apart. My lace lingerie covers me, but he doesn't seem to care, as he drags his index finger down my center, carrying with it a shiver that goes through my body, feeling exactly what he does to me. Before I can take that next breath, he swipes his tongue over the lace. The pressure is so delicious, my eyes close as he grips the inside of my thighs, the tips of his fingers digging into my flesh, my head falling back.

"You smell so fucking good…" he hums his approval.

"Good enough to eat?"

VINCENT

The dim light of the moon hits her from the side, the cheeky grin that pulls at the corners of her mouth beautifully lit.

Definitely good enough to eat, lick, suck, stretch, and fuck. More than good enough for it all.

"Don't move." I pull out the knife I hid in the small holster above my ankle, looking up at her, then press the blunt edge on the inside of her thigh.

Her mouth falls open on a hitched breath, filling whatever space we're in right now, but she does as told, as I drag that knife up her thigh until I reach the lace that covers what I crave the most right now. More than I should. I slide the tip under the fabric and drag it along until it falls apart.

Jesus fuck, she's gorgeous.

I tease her and blow on that pretty pink cunt

219

that glistens in the faint moonlight, watching it grip on nothing but air, and her moan makes my dick hurt, constricted under too many layers.

Pressing two fingers on her center, I drag them down as she holds her hips from bucking forward, and open her up to me. I forgot how pretty her pussy is. I flip over the knife and press the slim handle onto her clit, the foreign object making her jump ever so slightly.

"Goddamnit, Serpent... just... fuck me!"

I laugh at her impatience.

"Don't worry, sweetheart... I will."

"Please..." Fucking hell, her begging voice would put me to my knees if I wasn't already here.

Once I holster the knife back in my boot, and with no notice whatsoever, I push two fingers inside her wet cunt, her ass lifting off the windowsill at the same time I press my mouth on her.

I slide them in and out slowly, as I lap at her clit, suck and bite, holding her down with the other hand wrapped around her hip. On a moan, she grips my hair, holding me tight as she almost grinds into me. I up my rhythm, and her walls tighten around my fingers, her moans growing louder, the grip on my head stronger. Fuck... she's going to break me. I just know she will. The moment our lives met after all those years... I knew she would be it.

It was reckless of her to make a pact with me,

because there is no escape, not after the events of our past, and certainly not after today.

This covenant is forever—her soul is mine.

My tongue flicks her clit over and over, my lips pressing, rolling, sucking, as I pump those two digits harder inside of her, over and over and over, feeling the tightness of the muscles in my forearm, loving the burn. As her walls grip me in bursts of contractions, and her legs gently begin to shake, I know…

"I'm coming…" she whispers. "I'm coming!" This time she moans it. "Hoooly fuck!" Her legs convulse, her pussy gripping me even tighter, and I slow my rhythm, allowing her to get down from that high.

"There's nothing holy about this, Little Eve," I say as I get up, lift her from under the armpits, and flip her trembling body around.

"No, there isn't, is there?" the glass steaming with her whisper as she steadies herself against the window frame, just as her back arches when I grip her hip. It's such a pretty sight, her hair wild down her back, her ass perched out for me, with the view of the moonlit sea as a backdrop.

I release myself from my trousers and boxers in record time, gripping my dick way too hard, willing it to calm as her delicious taste lingers on my tongue. I need to last more than ten fucking seconds. But as

I watch her now, still catching her breath from the orgasm, her lush hips, her full ass, that soft skin... I realize I might not last at all.

Fuck!

I fumble quickly with the condom I pulled out of my pocket, giving my dick a final squeeze, the pain doing a good job at keeping me sane. I drag the glistening tip down between her ass cheeks, and her head falls back the moment it reaches her pussy.

Wrapping a hand around her throat, the other around her hip, I slam into her in one long stroke, and the sharp moan that echoes through the dark space is enough to make me come right now.

"Holy fuck!"

"I thought there was nothing holy about this." She laughs.

I pull out and slam right back into her.

"This is as fucking close to it as I'll ever get!" I groan.

The window rattles, the slapping of our skin a cheer, pushing us further and further into this depravity.

"More..." she moans. And I give her exactly that, slamming into her with a force that I'm afraid might break that window. So I pull her up, wrapping my hands around her, and carry on the assault we both so desperately need. It goes past the moment of craving... past the moment of mindless lust... I'm not even sure if it was ever only that.

She protests with a sharp moan as I pull out of her, turning around with fury painted brightly in her eyes. But I grab her face, pressing a bruising kiss on her lips as I push her against the wall next to the window. Then I lean over and hook her knee on my arm, teasing her as I rub the tip of my cock along her wet pussy, insisting just a bit longer on that swollen clit, as she digs her nails into the skin of my back and waist.

"Don't fucking play with me, Serpent. Fuck me or get down on your knees, either way... make me come!"

"Oh, you've got a filthy mouth on you, Little Eve. Is this what you want?" I slam into her, balls deep, her body hitting the wall with a loud thud, knocking the air out of her. As I slide out slowly, her pussy grips every single inch of me. "Or this?" I slam harder and she yelps.

"More!"

So I give her more, with one arm hooked under her knee, holding it up, the other slammed on the wall next to her head, as she digs her sharp fingernails hard enough into my skin that she's gonna draw blood. I fuck that tight cunt of hers, the one I've thought about too many times in the last few months, the one that I've dreamt of a few times since our little dance in the forest.

"More!" she yells louder as I begin feeling the spasms of her core, and I slam my lips onto hers at the same time I take my hand off the wall, pressing my fingers onto her clit, rubbing with enough pressure that she explodes around me in the next moments. And I shatter right along with her, swallowing her moans as she wraps both arms around my neck, holding herself together. My knees begin to shake... the pleasure too much. Everything is too much.

She moans filthy words into my mouth, one more intelligible than the former, and I could have sworn that one of them was my name... not Serpent. My actual name.

We crash onto the floor, her soft body panting as she straddles mine, her head on my chest, her arms still around my neck, and all I can do is hold her. I draw lazy circles on the skin of her back as we come down to earth, and I cannot think of a time when sex was like this, when I needed a minute, not to catch my breath, but for my mind to reel back in too.

Was it ever?

Seventeen

MORRIGAN

"**I** HAVE TO GO," I WHISPER.

"No." That's all—short, firm, no breath wasted.

"I've disappeared for too long." I push myself up, clumsily getting to my feet, pulling on my bra and top. I follow the light of the window to pick up my skirt and after I wrap it around my waist, I realize that this thing is just six wide ribbons of fabric and I have no panties now.

Fuck.

Time to improvise. I grab the fabric right at the front, pass it between my legs and loop it under and over the band of the skirt at the back.

"Do they miss you that much downstairs? I don't think you can dance in that anymore." I turn to find him zipping up his trousers, then covering his scar as he buttons up his shirt.

God, I was so angry that day. It was the first time I'd seen him in years… his voice, his eyes, everything about him made me furious. His sheer presence in my space was an insult. But the worst thing was that it didn't feel any different from all those years before—it felt as if he belonged right there, next to me. I don't even remember what he said, but I was holding that damn knife and I just wanted him to shut up… Well, he did. And the motherfucker smiled as well.

"I'm not dancing anymore, not tonight." I try to look around for our masks, but this darkness is too thick. I know there's a switch next to the unfinished kitchen cabinets, so I fumble my way over. "It's not the club I've disappeared for too long from…" I flip the switch and the open space fills with a soft light, both of us blinking a few times to adjust to it.

"Then who?"

Suddenly, the door flies open.

"Mooorri!" Lulu bursts through, panic in her voice. She stops, panting as she looks between me and The Serpent, confusion slowly narrowing her eyes. But she shakes her head and points to the window. "He's here."

"No, no, no. Fuck!" I flip that switch back off, then rush to the window, slowly peeking down, trying to confirm the bad news. It's him… "I have

226

to go!"

"What the fuck is going on?!" The Serpent's voice booms through the open space.

"It's Ryan, he's downstairs. Security alerted me that there's someone in front of the building, trying to get inside the lobby of the apartments." Lulu's still trying to catch her breath, and I know she probably didn't even wait for the elevator, she just ran up. "Wait… what are *you* doing here? Morri, what is *he* doing here?"

She turns to me, the light of the moon shining on her, bright enough that I can't miss that scolding gaze.

"Just… sealing a deal." I can read the smirk in his voice even if I can't see him. "Why is Holt here?"

"Because I'm not supposed to be. I have to go." I see our masks on the floor and pick them both up, handing one to him and mine to Lulu. I quickly unwrap my wig, flipping my hair over a few times and handing that to her too. "I need a long dress, something I can quickly throw over this. My clothes are downstairs…"

"Come on, quick!" She runs to the door, ripping it open, and it's then that I hear the loud bangs, rattling the metal of the lobby doors, way down on the ground floor.

"Listen to me, goddamnit!" The Serpent yells, his hand wrapping around my upper arm, turning

227

me around to face him. "I can protect you. You don't need to go."

I shake my head, feeling the tears burn their way through my lids, emotions I've never shown to the man before me, slowly seeping through. I'm terrified. Fucking terrified that right now I'm risking exposing our hard work to the man I want to kill. He's threatening everything I am, my family, my brother, my best friend, my goddamn freedom. And I've disappeared for too long... I knew it was a mistake coming to the club. I should have gone anywhere else... but then again, he probably would have come here anyway.

"He can't know. Listen to me, he can't know." The usual dark slits widen for a moment as I say those words. I feel a tear fill each eye, and I blink them away quickly, before they get to fall down my cheeks. "You're the last hope I have to take them all down. I won't risk it. You're my secret weapon, and it's too soon to draw you out."

I pull myself out of his grip and run away, ripping open the door.

"Come on." I keep my tone low and look back, waiting for him. I don't miss the deep sigh before he rushes to me and follows up the stairs.

We reach Lulu's floor at the same time she comes out the door, a long black dress in tow. I quickly pull it on and look between them.

"I'm going to try and talk to him. He knows that sometimes I stay here with you, so this should not be any different. He's gonna be against it, obviously, but… he usually gives in. He claimed I still get some freedom until the knot is tied. I'm gonna try to reason…" I give Lulu a quick peck on the cheek, then take one last look at the man that should have never come back into my life, yet we somehow gravitated toward each other, and run down the stairs.

I have a bad feeling about this, like a sickness filling my insides… But what choice do I have?

VINCENT

"Come with me." Loreley grabs my wrist, displaying no sense of self preservation, no worry that she's bossing the fucking Serpent around. What is it with these two women? Have they no fear?

The moment we're inside the apartment, I pull my hand from her grip and she stops, turning to me. Now, in this closed space, all alone, from the look in her eyes, she finally realizes who stands tall before her. I don't miss the slight shiver running down her body.

"I know who you are." She tightens her shoulders. "I also know who to come to if anything happens to her, because you two made a deal... and I know the terms." She stands tall, unmoving, holding her ground.

"You know... everything?"

She narrows her eyes, but stays silent. Does she know about my past with Morrigan? Or about the guy she murdered? About the leverage Holt has against her?

My bet is she knows what she needs to.

"Come." She finally speaks and runs toward the window, the lights still off, so we're slightly protected from whoever looks from below.

The image before me breaks a part of me I didn't know existed until now, and I grab onto those pieces, holding them tight because I need to put them back together eventually. I'm losing her...

My hands tighten into fists, nostrils flaring, as a painful tension rips through my chest, watching her fight off two guys that grab each of her arms at Holt's orders. The moment Loreley cracks the window slightly, Morrigan's scream splits me in half, my short nails digging into my palms painfully.

"Let me gooo! Damnit, Ryan, let me go, you're better than this! Just..."

Holt takes one step, just one step toward her, and the way her body freezes, the woefully defeated, submissive look in her eyes, pushes me over the fucking edge.

It brings back memories I've buried, of a broken woman at the hands of a controlling, abusive man... But there's no way I'll let this situation get as far as I allowed it with my mother.

That motherfucker is dead. Just as my goddamn sperm-donor will eventually be. Hers too.

His death sentence was signed already, but this might just warrant a more special execution.

A feral growl fills my ears, and when Loreley's head whips in my direction, I realize it was me. But I'm already on the move, a few more steps and I'm out the door, ready to fucking end this right here, right now!

"No! She was right! She was right! You can't do anything now!" That voice is desperate, cracking with a similar pain that rips me apart at this moment. Its familiarity makes me stop.

She whirls around me, gripping my arms, her golden eyes pleading, a lonely tear dropping on her high cheek, before slowly sliding down. That's her best friend out there and her pain... is mine too. Her throat bobs, once, twice, before she swallows her breaths... and another tear falls onto her cheek, then another, and another.

With no notice whatsoever from my brain, I shake off her hands and pull her in, wrapping my arms around her. And she breaks. She cries into my chest, quiet whimpers of fear...

"He will pay for this," I whisper.

She finally pulls away, her lips parting to speak, but at the same time, we hear a commotion through the cracked window and we rush over.

One of the guys is on his knees, clutching his crotch, the other one holding both her hands behind her back, and in the next second, Holt's hand slams against her cheek so hard, the guy behind has to hold her up.

I see fucking red! Crimson rivers of their blood filling these motherfucking streets, and I know one thing for sure—that's not my imagination, it's the fucking future.

"You'll never see your precious bitch Lulu ever again, you'll never step foot here… or anywhere else for that matter, unless you're with me. I hope you enjoyed yourself tonight, because your freedom ends here," Holt spits at her before shoving her in the back of the SUV, and leaning in. *"Oh, and by the way, I moved the wedding date."* He slams the door closed on her screams, and we hide as he turns to look up.

I have to get her back.

"She'll be okay… she'll be okay… my girl is strong. She'll be okay." Loreley repeats those words like a whispered mantra.

She'll be okay.

Tires screech on the asphalt and we both peek out the window—they're gone. She's gone. And this complicates things.

"What are we going to do?"

"*We* are not going to do anything. You will carry on as per usual, take care of your club and whatever else you do. If you need any help with that in *her* absence, you let me know."

"No offense. Morri might be desperate enough to make a pact with you, but... I would rather not." Her chin raises and her gaze is a far cry from only a minute ago when she was sobbing into my chest. Like a switch, she flipped it and whoever she was a minute ago is buried deep. If it's even buried at all... it might just be gone.

Funny, her sweet voice doesn't quite match that stern look in her eyes.

"I'm not making a pact with you. I'm offering support." I take a step forward. Not toward her, but to the door.

"Yeah. You seem to be a very... supportive man. I didn't peg you as the type to hold a crying woman as you did."

I turn my head to her, the muscles of my face slowly relaxing in that usual state that makes people around me uncomfortable, fearful.

"I've never claimed to be heartless, Miss Dietrich." I move away, toward the exit, and stop before I'm out. "But I would still appreciate it if you kept that information to yourself."

"Sure. We wouldn't want people to know that The Serpent has a soft side." I can hear that hint of amusement in her tone.

"Not when his enemies could rip away the reason why he does." And on that slight hitch in her breath... I walk away.

Eighteen
MORRIGAN

THAT VEIL OF HATE HAS FALLEN THICK OVER ME... OVER us, over everything we were, are, and never will be.

Who imagines a relationship ending in a forced beginning? No one... not even me, even knowing I live in this world where the barrier between good and evil is drawn with chalk.

"You brought this on yourself!" he rasps.

I've never seen him this angry, never felt the sting of his palm on my face until today, and I think that shocked me most of all. That fury in his eyes rendered me close to catatonic when we were out on the street, because that type of emotion has never lived in him. I've never witnessed it anyway. It's excessive, it's new, and most importantly, due to the

235

madness that has been dominating him for months now, it's unpredictable. Dangerously so.

"I didn't do anything!" My pitch heightens as my voice splits the atmosphere, clutching the sides of my face, fear and anger mixing in a concoction that makes me erratic in an unmoving kind of way, where my brain can't fucking decide on the next move.

"Oh, of course you did! You made me go out on the fucking streets looking for your trampy ass! Then you made a fucking show out of it all!" He moves toward me, and that fickle bitch called fear makes me shuffle backwards on the bed in an instant.

Then I see it in his eyes, creeping to the corners of his lips, a victorious smirk that brings back those threads of what makes me… *me*. And that fear that confuses me so much, slowly starts to dissipate.

If only it would go away completely.

I take one slow, deep breath that fills my chest with an uncomfortable pressure, hanging on to that marvelous feeling that grin gives me.

You will pay for this. You will pay for it all, and when you do, I will make sure you feel the agony before you receive the kiss of death.

"My trampy ass?! *My* trampy ass?! You fucked a woman in front of me to prove some sort of point that only made sense to you! You've gone mad! You lost yourself in this dark world, in the money it can bring and the power you will never, ever obtain! You delusional motherfucker!" With every statement, my tone catches a bit of strength. And that only triggers him more.

"I found myself! I fucking found myself, and it took me too long to get here! So many fucking hands I rubbed and asses I kissed, including yours! You always thought you were so much goddamn better than me, up there on your high horse, with your rich, clueless family that bailed you out of all the fucking bullshit you've caused. And they don't even know the full extents of it yet; you killed a fucking man before you even left for university!" His arms are all over the place, waving in the air to match his tone and the wild look in his eyes, which engages my fight-or-flight instinct. The former much more. "And even without that knowledge, they still fucking hate you! Enough to sell you to me without a second thought!"

His maniacal laugh echoes off the walls, the creases in his skin bizarre in the dim light of the only lit lamp in the room.

"For so long I waited behind you," he continues. "Waited for you to notice me so I can get my in with you... even in those teenage years when you had eyes for anyone but me. Then I waited for you through fucking university! And I finally got you, fucked and ruined you, and I want more! I want

237

everything you are and everything you have! I want to destroy every fucking piece of you until all you'll be is a shadow under my control!" The veins in his temple and the ones in his throat are bulging, the pulse raging high as his eyes grow so wide they look feral. A cold shiver runs through me, and I don't know where to go from here. So many words, so many thoughts. I'm shocked, confused, weirded out. I can't make sense of it. Of him.

"Why...?" It comes out barely louder than a whisper.

"Because you were my first love, and you said no. I loved you... and you said no. I worshiped you, and you said no! I always knew that we were perfect for each other, and you still fucking said no!!! You only noticed me when the time came for me to help you bury a goddamn body, and it was awful timing for you. Why?! Because betrayal tastes fucking bitter and you filled me with it, eyes only for the snake you had, only for the snake... and that night you gave me exactly what I needed to make sure you will have no escape from me."

"We were goddamn teenagers! Are you being serious right now? You're doing this because of something that happened all those years ago?! Some sort of sick vendetta, even though we did end up together?!" He's insane, Jesus Christ, he's insane! I... I don't know how to deal with this. "This makes no

238

sense, Ryan, we ended up together... who are you taking revenge on?! You keep blaming this on me, but *you* ruined us!"

"We may have been young, but were we not human?! We were! And I loved you and you went to someone else! Either way... after that night, I knew I needed to wait for all the pieces to fall into place, until the time came when my love turned into destruction—yours. And the world shifted, my goals aligned, and I wanted more. I needed more! I watched my father take too little risks, make too many mistakes over the years, and I knew I could do so much better than him. I could bring this business to a greatness that would control this whole fucking city and everything around it!" He raises his arms to the sides, palms up, like he's presenting his victory to me. A megalomaniac in action... "And you fit perfectly in my shift in views, only this time around, you serve a different kind of purpose, my love." I suppress the retching at the endearment. He walks around the bed and I stiffen as he leans over, swiping the backs of his fingers against my cheek. One by one each muscle in my body twitches as it prepares it to flee.

"What's my purpose, then?" After hearing all of that, I wonder what else he could say to surprise me.

"Tsk, tsk, tsk... all in good time."

"I loved you, you know I did... and you shit on

everything." I don't turn, but only look in his eyes.

"Until you didn't and planned to leave me. And I couldn't have that." He leans over more, planting his hands on the bed, and just as he's about to climb up, a ringing blares through the room, making him pause.

He waits, enough to inhale and exhale his irritation, before he rises and pulls the phone from his front pocket.

"What?!" He frowns at the name on the screen. "When?"

I try to listen, hoping I can pick up something from the other line.

"And they want to throw in another dozen? ... Okay, we need the space... In the..." He catches himself, turning to me just before he reveals something I most certainly cannot know. "Yeah, I'll come now." He grins at me and hangs up.

He walks around the bed, back to the middle of the room, and stops. "This is yours." He gestures around the room. "You will not leave unless I allow you to. You will be out for meals downstairs and nothing more. You have essentials here and if anything else is needed... well, you can try asking my mother. You will stay in here until I can trust you with me in my room. It will not change your condition, but you will be allowed more freedom in this house."

240

It's a whirlwind. I'm pulled in directions I cannot even think of anymore. What's up, what's down, what the hell is going on? This night... this night that started so beautifully... it crashed and burned in a way I didn't expect.

All I anticipated was a heated reaction... not a kidnapping.

He rips open the door and before he disappears through it, he turns his head slightly.

"And by the way, there is no question that I will obtain the power I deserve. I will rip it right out of the clutches of the *sanctity* that rules this city." And with that last spit off his tongue, he slams the door behind him, the pictures rattling on the walls in his wake.

The last thing I hear is the click of the locks.

VINCENT

It should not feel the way it does. It should not make me feel like a savage, ready to burn down his fucking castle to claim her back. But it does, goddamnit, it does, and I can't figure out when I fell. When that shadow of obsession shifted forward, the one that always cast its darkness in a deep corner of my soul, noticeable even amidst the crepuscule that already resides there.

She was always there, always.

My little obsession.

The one I was *forced* to let go of all those years ago…

I had to move on. I convinced myself that she was too young for this life anyway, even though it was bullshit. The preconceptions that come with certain ages barely applied to her, and when they did, they gave her a sort of naivety that made her even more desirable, a perfect mold that you could model in the right way, with the right qualities. Not that she needed much modeling, but… I wanted to be the one to teach her about the affliction that lives upon this world, and show her how to corrupt it so it bends at your will. And goddamnit, she had will. That fire that dominated her was ravenous even then, and so goddamn dangerous, it took me too long to stop worrying that she'd end up in fucking jail, or… dead.

Eventually, I had no choice. And I managed to convince myself that this way, she would stay out of this world, my world, and she'd be safer.

Eight, or nine years later, I don't even know anymore, and here we are… magnets that finally turned the right way around and got pulled to each other once again.

"You look rough."

I sigh and look up. Bright blue eyes grin at me, only the moment they actually catch my gaze, they darken.

"What's wrong?!"

You can always tell when Finn gets serious, because that pretty boy face suddenly becomes sharper, his lean, wide shoulders pull back and somehow seem to widen more, his whole stance just shifts, making you feel like you're in the savannah, out in the open, and a cheetah has its eyes on you. You want to run, and even if you do, you know there's no way you're going to be fast enough.

I open my mouth to speak as Madds walks in. "You know, one of these days I'm going to walk into this bar and your faces are not going to look the way they do now. What the fuck happened now?!"

I swipe a palm over my face, then settle my elbows on my knees, clutching my hands together.

"Holt took Morrigan O'Rourke."

"Wait, what do you mean he *took* her? I thought they lived together, future wife and all." Finn sits in the opposite armchair, confused, and I narrow my eyes on him, slits warning him off.

"They didn't. She's stayed at her parents as much as she could, whenever they weren't paying attention enough to send her on her way... Fucking gems they are." Madds crosses his arms, looking a little uneasy.

"I don't get it. Why doesn't she just run away?"

I look at Finn, then at Madds, who knows the answer to that question. It's not our secret to tell, but then again, it's the one we need to, if we're going to help her. And at this point, no matter what, the whole Sanctum is involved, no matter if the pact was made with me.

"Because he helped her bury a dead man, and Holt is blackmailing her." We all turn at the same time, watching Carter walk quickly towards us.

"What the fuck?! How the hell did you know?!"

I agree with Madds. What is going on here?

"We're in. I finally got into his personal computer, but I have limited access. The bastard is not great with technology, so he doesn't back up to clouds or online servers. I only have access when it's actually turned on. One of my guys traced it and got in about an hour ago. We didn't have much time before it got disconnected. We only managed to copy about twenty percent of his drives. And one of the things we copied"—Carter turns his gaze to me—"is an album of photos of a younger Morrigan, digging a hole in the ground and looking over a dead body."

"Is there any way to find out where else he holds this information? If he copied it on an external hard drive?"

"Wait, you know of this?!" Finn leans over, looking between us.

"Yeah... found out the other day, pretty much at the same time as her. She had no idea the bastard took photos and had them this whole time," Madds responds.

"Wait, I understand why Vin would know, but why do *you* know?!"

"Because Holt decided to reveal this to her when we were at the dinner party the other day, the one O'Rourke invited us to. Before he left, he gave her an envelope of photos and we walked in on her after she opened it," I explain, and he rubs his jaw as he listens.

"And... who killed the guy she was burying? Although I think I have an idea what you will say..."

"She did... and it was my fault."

The room goes silent at those last words. Madds is the only one that knows the whole story... almost. Finn and Carter had different interests at the time, and they were away for most of it too. Jesus, I don't want to be a soppy prick and bear my fucking heart out to them; this is not who we are, no matter how tight our bond is. *Shit.* But they have to know something, they need some context.

"Fucking hell..." I swipe a hand over my face, sighing. "Look, Morrigan and I were together. A long time ago. You guys were in uni and I was here... I mean, Madds was here for most of it too. And... yeah, shit happened. We were at that point

245

when all of this"—I point around us, at our bar— "was starting, when we were making our first deals and establishing ourselves. And it ended."

"You're skipping a few parts of that story, brother…" Madds' tone is lower, pinning me from under his eyebrows.

Fuck, I know I'm skipping over a few parts! I'm skipping over the way her green eyes stood out in the crowd of girls that always seemed to notice us in school. I'm skipping over the fact that I always noticed *her*, only her, even when no one else seemed to, and I couldn't believe that wild red hair framing that freckled pale skin and those forest eyes could ever be overlooked. I'm skipping over how I broke up a fight one day between her and some kid that was bullying her, and she was winning. I'm skipping over how I actually stood there and admired the fire in her for a while, before I stopped her from making a big mistake. I'm skipping over how I pulled her away and dragged her behind the maintenance building to calm her rage. I'm skipping over how I felt when her heaving breaths were turning to something else other than rage and I had to step away from her… how she ran to me after I left, jumped into my arms, and pressed her soft lips to mine… Over how pure and wild it felt. I'm skipping over how she smirked at me and ran back to class, but not before telling me…

"I saved that one for you… the first one."

Her first kiss…

I'm skipping over how she left me speechless and confused. How I finished school and moved on. How I found her again a couple of years later, beating up the guy who was forcing himself on her. I'm skipping over how important she became, how deep she crawled under my skin, seeped into my blood and filled every part of my heart.

I'm skipping over how I got to ask her…

"Did you save this first for me as well?"

And she did… and it meant more than I ever thought something like that would. Because it was her. Because everything she was, her mind, her soul, her heart… they fit with mine like perfect puzzle pieces, and it made no sense how it was possible.

I'm skipping over all of this… and more.

"Madds and I saved her from the guy we told you about a while back, the one whose jaw she broke. And we got together not long after, for a few months." I hold myself straight, pulling that shield up, strapping the armor on, the one that contains The Serpent they all know. It's not a mask, this is all me, but that armor protects and conceals those vulnerable parts of me, the softer sides that enjoy their privacy. "When we broke up, that same guy came for her, because he knew she was no longer under my protection, that I was gone and she…

was all alone." I finish off telling them the story she told Madds and I and by the end of it, Finn has a sympathetic look in his eyes, whilst Carter… well, emotions aren't his strong suit, so that analytical look in his doesn't quite surprise me.

"Why did you break up?" The bastard's calm, cocking his head subtly.

"It doesn't matter now." My eyes flicker to Madds for a split second. "What matters is that Morrigan O'Rourke cannot leave. The guy threatened to kill her parents, her brother, and when she seemed not to care that much about that, he threatened her with jail. And there's no way she would get out on self-defense, not after hiding it and burying the guy. He threatened Loreley too… and she cares more about her than she does her own freedom. She's stuck, hence—"

"Why she asked you for help." Carter nods.

"Yeah… well, she asked for my help when it wasn't even quite this bad. I think she still had some hope then. But I've seen how Holt treated her. He kidnapped her from the sidewalk, threatened… slapped her. And there's one more thing that has to stay between us only."

They all nod in unison.

"Metamorphosis is hers too. She's a silent partner."

"Why silent? I mean, it wouldn't be unusual for

248

two friends to go into business together. Look at us."

"Yeah, Finn, but none of us have abusive families and partners that want to destroy us."

Carter clears his throat in an all-knowing way, but I interrupt him.

"You know what I mean."

"Knowing her… she's doing it for Loreley more than for herself. Holt, even her family, would use the club against her." Madds nods in understanding.

"What would they do if they found out we're backing them?"

Finn's words lay heavy in the air and grins form on all of our lips.

"As much as I will love seeing that, we have to hold off until the time is right. No one can know. No one."

Nineteen

VINCENT

"Hello, my darlings." Jonathan, the Ghost, is a lean man, well into his fifties, very well dressed in his tweed suit that Carter is currently admiring. Both men have style, but Jonathan definitely has an edge, always wearing some sort of flashy accessory, something to give him that touch of extravagance, whilst remaining tasteful. This time around, a filigree gold brooch shines on his lapel.

"Jonathan." Carter nods.

He was the one that created this connection with the man. He was Carter's father's friend when they were young, and they connected maybe about five or six years ago, by way of a fortunate accident. It was Jonathan that looked straight into Carter's eyes and saw his father right away. He knew he had died years before, never having had the chance to meet his son as an adult.

"Come, come. Follow me." He leads us quickly inside a warehouse, and we're eagle eyed as we pass large industrial shelves filled with packed boxes of all shapes, sizes, and materials. Some more heavy duty than others. But we don't stop at any of them, instead we go straight to the other end of it, where two of Jonathan's men stand by a huge door.

He stops and turns to us.

"This is one thing I won't work with, and if I'm not mistaken, you won't agree with it either."

His men open the door, only we're looking right at the back of a container, its doors cracked open. I guess this is a clever way of checking contents, without having outside eyes on you, since the access to it is inside the warehouse.

And when the doors to the container open, we're all stuck for words. The stench is horrendous. The image even worse. Girls and boys. In the worst state, dirty and so fucking scared. They don't even dare to say a word to us, completely still, just in case the wrong move would be fatal. Most of them look drugged out of their mind.

"How long have they been in there?!" Finn reacts first.

"The container has been traveling for three days. We fed them and gave them water when we found them, about an hour or so ago. We haven't logged the receipt of the container yet, but I will have to soon."

"Are you telling me that this is O'Rourke's container?!" I take one more step forward, swiping my eyes over the delicate faces that don't dare look at me. They're probably between ten and sixteen, at most.

"And Holt's," he confirms.

"But the deal was for ammunition and fucking cocaine!" When I turn to Madds, he's barely containing himself. One thing he will kill a man for without debating, are crimes against children... especially sex trafficking. Nothing will touch him as much as this does.

"That was indeed the deal. I'm supposed to be discreet too. But one of my guys heard crying when we pulled the container off the ship and set it in the docking area. I won't condone this, Vincent." He looks straight at me, eyes wide, not with shock or fear, but a stern gravity.

"I agree. It needs to stop now." Madds steps forward and walks inside the container. Some of the kids cower instantly, trying to make themselves invisible, and it's fucking hard to keep your heart whole as you witness this.

"We can't stop it now." At my words, everyone freezes. When their predatory gazes turn to me, various levels of outrage and fury meet mine. "If we do, they'll find another way, which means that this operation is going to continue behind our backs. What we need is to end O'Rourke and Holt, and with them… this entire operation."

"Are you fucking saying that we're supposed to close these doors and let them go, wherever the fuck those assholes are taking them?!" Madds' voice booms through the small space of the container and some of the kids start crying.

"We don't have a choice. He can't know we know of this. We need to find out where they're taking them, because this might be bigger than this one container. The hydra has many heads, and we need to cut the root and find all of them." I know I'm making sense, and from the looks I'm getting, it's clear that the wheels are spinning in their brains right now. "Saving just them will not save all the others. If there are any others."

"So we need someone on the inside. But no woman we have would fit in with them… They're too young." Finn sighs, rubbing a hand over his face.

"I'll… I'll do it." We all turn at the same time a girl, maybe the oldest one in there, gets up on very shaky legs, and tries to walk from the back of the container. Madds rushes to her, reaching over to help, but she pulls back quickly. No one speaks, as the girl doesn't need to be spooked more than she already has been. Eventually, she gently places her small hand in Madds' large one and walks forward. We don't miss the way every single soul in that container turns as she walks past. They quite literally look up to her. If she's the eldest, she probably protected them in there.

She steps out into the brighter light of the warehouse and one of Jonathan's men rushes away and quickly comes back with a chair.

"I'll do it. If there's more..." She looks back toward the inside of the container. "...I want to find them. But it has to happen fast... I can't let them... I can't."

"I know... I know." I don't think my current, stern attitude is much comfort to her, but right now I'm blinded by the disgust I have toward this entire situation. "How much time do we have until you have to tell them the container arrived?" I turn to Jonathan.

"An hour, tops."

"Okay. We need a tracker." I look at Carter and he nods, rushing through the warehouse. Seconds later, we hear the car leaving. "We're going to put a tracker on you. It's going to be small. You might have to swallow it or—"

"It's okay. I'll do whatever it takes. Slice me open and put it under my skin, I don't care. Just... help them."

Not us, not me, *them.*

"What's your name?"

"Evelyn." Her voice is calm, not defeated, but composed, as if she's been trying to hold herself together through all of this.

"How old are you?" Finn steps forward, the look in his eyes hard to pinpoint. Somewhere between anger, shock, and heartbreaking sadness.

"Seventeen…" She turns her head toward the container. "My sister is eleven."

"Fucking hell," Finn exclaims.

Everyone in this room right now is broken in some way. I swipe my eyes over all their faces and even the two men I don't actually know, Jonathan's men, they look as if they could cry and kill at the same time.

"We'll get you all out. I promise. But everyone has to be very, very brave." I want to comfort her, place my hand on her shoulder, something to make this better, make what she's about to do better. But I don't think some other stranger touching her will help. Madds stands beside her though, and she seems comfortable with that.

"Will they… Will they get to the children?" She lowers her tone to a whisper, looking at me with big, hazel eyes, broken veins spilled on the white, dark purple circles around them.

"I really hope not. I don't want to lie to you."

Tears slowly fill her eyes, but she doesn't cry, doesn't whimper, she just... lets them pool there until they fill and fall down her cheeks, down to her jaw, some spilling off before she wipes them all.

"I understand..." She turns to the others again, and nods once. A gentle reassurance she doesn't really believe in.

"Where did they take you from?" Finn steps even closer to her.

"Various places. We're not all from the same city, they just brought us all to the same place. My sister and I, they took us when I was picking her up from school after work."

"Work, not school?" Finn squats down in front of her chair, keeping a safe distance, but leveled eye contact.

She shakes her head. "It's only us two." She pauses and inhales deeply, wiping more tears before they find her cheeks. "I can't fail her."

"You won't. We'll get you out before..." Finn promises. But he shouldn't promise that at all.

Not long passes and Carter returns with a small tracker, small enough that he managed to put it in a pill cartridge. I'm not gonna lie, the advances of technology are rather scary.

"It won't dissolve, it's specially made. But it will pass through. Keep it in your mouth for as long as you can. Swallow it only if they try to check your mouth, okay?" Carter hands her the pill and nods.

"We should go." I look toward everyone, and Finn gives her a crooked smile, while Madds squeezes her shoulder, helping her up and back into what's probably going to become her nightmare.

She stops and turns before the container doors close. "I can't have the police know of me and my sister… it's only us. I can't lose her. I'm not of age yet…"

Finn and Madds nod to her. Considering what we're about to do, the police will be the last people to hear of this. Their idea of justice doesn't quite align with ours.

We stand in front of those doors, watching them close as those terrified eyes look upon us, each of us making silent vows and murderous promises.

"Carter?" I turn to him.

"It's already tracking. I spoke with Dani; he's on it, and they'll follow her signal. We'll all go and do the re-con to make sure we take everyone out, without Holt and O'Rourke knowing we're involved. Ekaterina is looking into a safe space to hide them all, and she's bringing a few other girls too. But… we don't know what number to expect."

"It's not going to matter. I think they're just going to be happy to be in a safe space," Finn continues.

"Jonathan, are you staying for the pickup?" I turn to the man.

"No. The less I have to deal with this, the better. For them... and your plan. I have eyes on them, though. Constantly."

We all rush out, apart from Jonathan's guys, who stay to coordinate the pickup. Carter opens a line with one of his hackers, shoving a small pod in his ear to listen to the running commentary, in case it all starts moving before we get to the fight club. It sits deep underneath our bar, with its entrance at the back of the building, and a private one for us through Midnight.

"Follow us, then. We'll meet at Midnight and figure it all out. Actually, meet us in the club, through the back entrance. It's closed tonight."

Besides an outlet this city definitely needs, we use the fight club to move money illicitly obtained or... made. Madds is the one in charge of the operation, but he's a fighter too. One that not many manage to beat. He's been the running champion for a while. But it's not legal, clean boxing. There are very few rules and most of the time, it's a fucking massacre, and some people barely make it out alive. It's their choice to fight though, and some people pay to be in that ring. But we're quite selective about both our clientele and our fighters, just as we are with Midnight.

It's Monday, one of four times a week it's closed, so we'll have privacy. Plus, we have a change of clothes there, ones that would be right for what we're about to do.

And fuck knows exactly what that is.

Twenty
MORRIGAN

T HREE DAYS HAVE PASSED, AND FOR THREE DAYS, ONE thing hasn't left my mind—The Serpent.

I cling to memories of him; they bring me a strange sort of hope and at the same time... anger. We made a pact that he would be the one to help me get out of this bullshit. But these new memories of him, of his touch as he dances me through the forest, of him fucking me against the window he didn't know belongs to me, all of these are infiltrated by that heartbroken teenager that he left behind.

I'm not that girl anymore, but I fear he might just be the same man he was then.

We avoided each other, or better yet, I avoided him for all these years. University and this big city gave me enough space that I didn't run into him much. If I did, it was distant enough that I didn't have to acknowledge him.

Until my mother's party.

As far as I knew, my parents did not navigate in the same world as The Sanctum. I never had to worry about having The Serpent inside my fucking house, and I still remember the moment he walked through the door with the other three guys. The guests stilled and their chatter turned to whispers, but when our eyes met... it was just him and I. No one else... There was no hiding how hard I was trying to look unscathed. How hard he was trying too...

The silverware clacks loudly on the fine china, pulling me back into the grueling present, back into the overly decorated formal dining room of the Holt's house.

My prison.

As I bring back my attention to the sparsely filled plate, I move some bland steamed broccoli around, nothing about this dish appetizing enough to force my empty stomach to accept the nutrients. I'm not entirely sure if I ate today. I think I did. Maybe? The last three days have been a strange blur. A nightmare I've been witnessing through someone else's consciousness. I did try tonight, I took a few bites and bile rose up my throat.

I look up at the row of windows opposite me,

seeking comfort in the burnt orange and deep teal shades of the sunset reflecting on the calm sea. Flashbacks from a few weeks ago spring to mind, when once again Ryan and I fought, and I ran out onto the beach. No theatrics, just escape—anger, that fickle bitch, it seared my insides, but in his presence, it sizzled out before it reached the surface. Again. I remember the feel of the wet sand under my feet as the soft waves danced over it. It usually calmed me. Not that day. Too much pain, fury, frustration... fear, piled up. They riddled my body, a virus tainting my blood, sickening and debilitating.

Then I turned to the beach mansion that was to be my home after the wedding, and a vision flashed, my imagination running rampant. Flames exploded through each and every window, spreading, hugging every wall, every bit of the structure, and a smile crept onto my lips. Relief grew in my chest. And so much goddamn joy flooded me that I couldn't help but be wary of it.

It made my darkness shine and sparkle.

When I blinked, it was all gone. The perfect white mansion unscathed and that dread seeped in once again. Sometimes when I close my eyes, I can still see those flames. They're my happy, yet fake memory, which gives me hope.

It's through that memory that The Serpent snakes through. The same look in his eyes as when we were in my apartment and I told him I had to leave. It spoke words he couldn't fathom to say aloud, and my fucking heart betrayed me in ways I would rather ignore. It's unfortunate that I'm not ignorant enough to believe I can.

Or maybe I'm fooling myself with the desires of that teenager from long ago. The one that dreamed outside of her bounds, foolishly infatuated with the sinful and dangerous older guy she couldn't have. One she crushed on for years, the one that she hoped would fall madly in love with her and make her world a better place.

It was sick love powered by a misfit soul. Young lust, and a darkness that was creeping through my veins, growing with me. That darkness found The Serpent before that was even his name, and recognized the kindred soul. Latched onto it and refused to believe that it could never be. And suddenly… it was. He noticed me too. I couldn't believe it was happening just as none of the popular girls from school who hated me couldn't either, as they all lusted for him too. Only by the time I got used to the idea that it was happening… it was too late. He was gone, and I was left behind, foolishly in love. It ruined me.

Will that ruin find me again, or will it fuel my salvation?

Somewhere in the distance, a rough sound

scratches my ears. Only it's not in the distance at all...
Ryan clears his throat, but I don't bother turning to look at him. I may feel ill, I may feel weak, but that asshole can go fuck himself with barbed wire.

I look down at my plate once again, moving slices of steamed carrot around... that broccoli definitely had enough exercise.

"You better finish that, you're not getting any more." Even his voice sounds wrong. Everything about him is just... wrong. I close my eyes and take a deep breath before I turn to him, those muddy irises holding secrets behind that grin. "We have to make sure you fit into the wedding dress I chose for you. Otherwise, we might have to hire another person just to stuff you and the fat on your hips into it instead."

I ignore the fat comments. I'm used to them by now. God forbid I ever eat a cube of chocolate in front of him. The comments about my *fat* body never stop. At this point, I have no idea if what I see in the mirror is his vision of me or my own. I see softness, I see love handles, I see jiggle when I jump, I see a big ass that's not quite round, a soft pouch on my belly... I see so much, so much that never mattered before. But I pass over those words, because they're not new.

However, his confidence in his plans... That, I cannot ignore.

I believe there is nothing more dangerous than a powerful man riddled by delusions of grandeur that have seeped too deep into his brain. He's truly convinced that I will allow this wedding to go ahead, that this insane plan of his will have the end he envisions. This controlling behavior is being taken to a whole other level and the man he used to be has been completely replaced by the mad one next to me.

"You're completely delusional. You can't keep me locked in your house forever. Whatever plan you have… it's going to fizzle out. And when it does…" I trail off, that darkness that lives inside of me is just a bit denser. Subdued fury lives there, and for these last three days, I've worked so fucking hard to be rational, when all I've wanted to do is slit his throat, cut his head off, and shove it on a spike on his front lawn.

That's another piece of my imagination that puts a smile on my face.

"*Our*, not mine—*our* house." A tinge of exasperation touches the tone of his voice, and I can't help but roll my eyes. The next second, a feral sound comes from him, a strange sort of growl, making me stiffen in my chair. That noise matches the madness in his glare.

"You're such an ungrateful little bitch, aren't you?! That fucking roll in your eyes will end up getting stuck to the back of your head if you don't cut this bullshit. There's only so much patience one can have." The flare of his nostrils and the look in his beaded eyes make me swallow my disgust.

"Language, Ryan," his mother calmly scolds.

I turn to her at the other end of the table, watching as she slides another piece of chicken into her mouth. *Language…* that's what she's worried about. Not the fact that her son has kidnapped a woman, the same one he is forcing to marry him, whilst bringing whores into her home. Fucking language.

I stop myself just as my eyes begin their all too familiar roll.

"I'll speak exactly how I please in *my* house, mother," he spits as he cuts into that piece of meat as though it wronged him.

I forget; we're in *his* house now. In *his* lavish dining room, having dinner with his mother for the third night in a row. The mother he allows to still live in *his* house. It hasn't belonged to his mother since the moment the dirt covered his father's body.

I hold my fingers crossed that he'll get pulled away with "business" and he'll leave me alone. Maybe tonight I'll manage to sleep.

I can practically feel the bags under my eyes without touching them, my eyelids already heavy and it's barely seven o'clock. But I can't let this fatigue get me. Not until I'm sure he'll be out for the night.

I've been lucky the first two nights. He left just after dinner the first one and during it the second one. Two veins bulged dangerously in his temples as he took that phone call the second night, the sinew in his throat dangerously tense. I've never seen him quite like that before. Without a word he shoved me in the room he's been keeping me in, the only sounds coming from the slamming door and the click of the key as he locked me in. Somewhere deep inside I thought that whatever happened was some sort of distraction to get me out.

So I waited... I sat at the edge of the bed, in the light of the moon, staring at that door, for hours.

But no one came...

I never laid on the bed though, even as sleep threatened to take me, I couldn't allow that vulnerability.

The second night was the same. Only for a few minutes my eyes betrayed me, and I woke up just as my back hit the soft mattress. It was at that moment, when I shot up straight to my feet, that I realized just what this man does to me. What he's made of me... what he took away.

And as the second night passed, and no one came for me, I understood that I cannot wait for anyone to save me. I will always have to rely on myself. No one else. Because that was the only way to regain my strength in front of this man.

"I think everyone will have an early night tonight." Ryan looks straight into my eyes. "All of us."

"Fine by me." I place the cutlery on the plate and get up with a screech of the chair on the wood floor, his mother hissing at the sound. "Good night."

Just as I thought I was off the hook, the motherfucker speaks.

"I'll see you in a minute."

Something in the depths of my soul stiffens.

No fucking way.

The moment I'm out of view, I'm sprinting up the stairs, to my room, and bursting through the door on a strained breath, leaning against it as I shut it.

"Fuck!" I'm gasping, I don't linger. I walk to the other side of the dresser that sits against the wall, heels digging into the ground as I push the piece of furniture toward the door.

Only a soft knock interrupts me and it opens without warning.

I stiffen as my fucking heart gets lodged in my throat.

"I don't have much time." It's not Ryan… but his mother. I don't feel any relief though, just a different type of tension. "He just took a call."

I haven't moved yet. In this house, I always expect traps… and Mrs Holt is never a good sign of anything. Only, the woman holds a tray with a small porcelain cup of steaming water, a tea bag and teaspoon on the side, and hands them to me. I frown, my mind racing, and reluctantly take the tray and set it on the bed.

"I need more than tea, Mrs Holt." I hold her gaze in a tight grip. I don't want her to look away, I don't want her shrugging or brushing me off. "I need to get away from your fucking son! The man you raised into the savage he is." I nod suggestively toward the stairs.

She blinks rapidly, taking in the insult and my crude words, trying to look away. But submitting to another woman doesn't quite seem her nature.

"I… I didn't do this."

"Yeah. Just as my parents didn't raise me as cattle to take to the market and sell to the highest bidder. Pathetic… But then again, I guess they had no say on how my personality turned out. Your son, though… he's fucking certifiable."

She shakes her head, finally breaking eye contact, her eyebrows strained in a frown. She mumbles something under her breath, and the

269

woman I usually see at the other end of the dining room table flickers away.

"I don't know how… who… I don't know what happened to him." She sighs.

There's a tinge of defeat in her eyes. I'm not sure if it concerns her failed son, or her inability to stay strong in front of me.

Has she been holding on to hope?

Is she finally allowing herself to see the truth?

Sounds like me, not long ago.

"There's something wrong with him. I can't stop him." Her voice lowers.

"Oh, fucking hell. No shit! What tipped you off?" My voice rises with every word and the woman steps forward, eyes wide.

"Please…" she whispers. "He's only downstairs."

"Then tell me why you're here, and what your son really wants from me." I don't give a flying fuck about her regrets. This woman has never shown me an ounce of kindness all these years since I've known her.

"I'm not sure…"

"You're a bad liar." I step closer, right in her space, eye to eye. "What does your son want from me? I know his desire to take me as a wife has nothing to do with matters of the heart."

She turns her head, listening for any movement

or voices coming from downstairs.

"Some time ago, before my husband died, I found some files. Printed. I'm increasingly convinced that they did not belong to my husband," she whispers hesitantly, still listening beyond the walls of this room. "I couldn't look in great detail, but some of the files were quite complex in nature and others were documents."

"Okay, so how does this pertain to me?" I frown, crossing my arms.

"Because they all bore your family name. All your names… yours, your brother's, your mother's, your father's… they were all there. On bank statements, businesses, assets, contracts, deeds, birth and marriage certificates… everything."

"And you think Ryan was gathering all that information about us?"

She nods, her attention half on me, half out the open door.

"What use could he have with that?" I understand the business documents. If I would involve myself in a significant business deal with someone new… I would probably check them out as well. But… birth certificates?

"I don't know, but it was strange. All those documents in one place?"

"Like he's counting… assets," I mumble.

"And how to get to them," she continues.

Son of a bitch!

"Why should I believe any of this... Mrs Holt?" Her name drips from my tongue like tar.

She frowns. "I never liked you, Miss O'Rourke."

"My point exactly. Then why are you doing this?" I want to spit more comebacks at this woman, but her answer comes too quick.

"Because I was wrong."

My turn to frown.

"About you," she continues. "I was wrong about you. You saw the change in my son long before any of us did. I caught it far too late. And now... only blood binds us; and it's not thick enough anymore."

"I don't think you understand what you're saying."

"He needs to be stopped." She turns toward the open door. "Whoever that person is... it's not him."

"There might be only one way to stop him." Softness touches my voice this time around, this whole interaction feeling absolutely surreal.

Only the moment her eyes catch mine again, a different type of pain lives there. "I think he killed my husband."

My mouth drops at the same time as my arms fall to my sides.

Suddenly, heavy steps become a tad louder, and she walks out the door without another glance.

I'm left wondering what the fuck alternate

reality have I just fallen into, because I don't recognize whatever is happening around me right now.

Definitely surreal.

I shake my head and rush to close the door behind her, then turn my attention back to the large chest of drawers. The damn thing is heavy, but I plant my feet on the floor and with a deep screech, it finally moves. It only reaches the middle of the door, when a disturbing laughter echoes in the corridor behind it.

"Shit."

"You fool yourself thinking that a piece of furniture will keep me away from you. If I want you, I will get you!" The door bursts open, hitting the corner of the dresser that partially blocks it, and Ryan slips through. Two steps and my back hits the wall, his hand wrapped around my throat, the other one gripping my hip. "There is no escape from me. There will never be any escape for you. No matter where you go, no matter where you run, I will fucking hunt you. Those photos of you burying the man you killed will haunt you. The video I took as you stood and looked at his corpse, with no remorse in your eyes, will fucking haunt you. I can destroy you. And that alone strips you of that freedom."

The back of my tongue feels too big for my throat as his grip tightens, and that hand on my hip suddenly hits bare skin, sliding upwards under my shirt. I'm not sure how many muscles one has in their torso, but all of mine tighten to the point my lungs refuse to take in any air. I claw at that hand, pulling it away as fast as I can, but he goes back in, straight up to my bra covered breast, gripping it. A pained, strained scream escapes my throat, taking with it the last of the air I had in my lungs, and I can't force him off now... not when he holds me that way.

"This is mine too." The elastic of my bra scrapes my ribs as he grips the cup and yanks it down, pressing his hand over my bare breast. My brain is telling me to launch at him, to kick him in the balls, to do anything but stand here in his grip, allowing him to touch me this way, to force himself on me in this way. But my body isn't cooperating. I can't fucking explain it. It's like in the nightmares I have once in a while, where I'm getting attacked and I try to scream, but no words come out, not because I'm mute... but because I'm frozen. There's a disconnect between my brain and my nerves... and it happens when those beady, muddy eyes pin me the way they're doing now.

"It took a while to break you. But look at you now... it was fucking worth it." He grins and leans over, his lips almost on mine. But something inside of me breaks, the idea of his lips on mine so utterly repulsive that my knee suddenly connects with his groin before I've even finished thinking about doing it.

Only it wasn't hard enough to get him off me.

As he pulls back and that mad gaze hits me, I understand it was definitely hard enough to piss him off.

"Sir." A knock on the cracked open door interrupts us. "Your guest has arrived. Shall I bring her up?"

"Fucking lucky you are," he whispers to me. "Yes, Gordon, take her to my room."

"Will do, sir."

"Would you like to meet this one too? Maybe you should. Teach you a thing or two for when you're going to do your wifely duty."

"Fuck you." I'm seething. I swear it comes and goes at all the wrong moments. Never when I truly need it.

"Oh, you will. Not now, though..." He releases me and steps back, looking me up and down, the corner of his lips curved downwards, one eyebrow cocked. It's a look that makes me want to cover myself in baggy clothes and run.

He turns, walking back to the door, and pushes the chest of drawers back in its place.

"Stop moving my furniture around."

When he pulls open the door, a tall, slim woman

stops before it, hair so dark it looks like a starless sky and eyes a gray so bright, as the stars that fell off it. I'm surprised she's not afraid to make any movement in that dress. I would certainly be scared it would snap, but then again, it's short enough that it doesn't constrict her legs in any way. The deep red suits her, though.

"Hello, Raven," he greets her.

She catches my gaze for only a split second, but when she turns to Ryan, the most lascivious smile I've seen on a woman paints her lips. My eyebrows furrow, wondering whether her presence here is free of charge or not. But when Ryan's foot leaves my doorway, I don't linger on that thought and slam the door behind him.

Moments later, the lock clicks from the outside.

I cherish that lock.

Too bad I'm not the one with the key.

Twenty-one
MORRIGAN

THE DISTINCTIVE TURN OF THE DOORKNOB WAKES ME UP. Not a hard turn, not loud, only a faint click. I snap into a sitting position, the sheets gritty against my clenched fists, and wait, and my breath hitches when a soft knock sounds on the door. Just one. The next moment, a small white paper slides on the floor, stopping at the edge of the rug the bed sits on.

My eyes flicker between it and the door, my broken mind waiting for the trap to come, like the monster is under the bed and the moment my feet touch the ground, he'll grab them.

Nothing comes, only a barely audible sound of a door clicking in place.

Maybe a minute passes and muffled voices come through from the other side of the wall, in a tone of voice that makes my stomach tighten. I know what's coming. I heard it before I fell asleep, but at least the asshole didn't make me watch again.

I slowly step out of bed, trying not to make a sound, and grab the paper. Only it has a heaviness to it, and it's not a paper at all. It's an envelope. I discard its contents onto the bed, and the moment I see it, my gaze snaps back to the door. A fucking key!

Who…?

There are only a few people in this house at one time: two guards, Gordon, who's more of a coordinator, Ryan, and his mother; and none of them would have done this. As I pick it up, feeling the smooth texture of it, much lighter than a normal key as well, I think of the guest—*Raven*.

As I rub the key between my fingers, my gaze drifts out the window, to the dark clouds approaching fast, swallowing the puffy white ones until nothing is left of them.

Raven… Son of a bitch!

It hits fast and hard and somewhere in my chest, my heart rushes, beating a million miles per minute the moment I realize what's happening. It all clicks into place, just as I know this key will click easily in that door, even without trying it. The Serpent is certainly sneaky, and it makes one wonder if the purpose of The Sanctum's escort service is something else entirely.

I quickly change the blouse I fell asleep in, pulling a comfortable t-shirt over my head. I have no sneakers here, no comfortable shoes whatsoever, so barefoot it is.

The noises from behind the wall become strained. Moans... slapping of skin... and others I would rather ignore. And they increase in intensity—a perfect cover up.

I head to the door to try the key, grabbing the cold doorknob and twisting as gently as I can, waiting for a noise from the other side. I don't think any of the guards are up here. Ryan doesn't exactly run this house like a fortress, and tonight he might regret that. The key slides in with an ease that makes me wanna jump in excitement, and the moment I turn it and the lock clicks, a thunder rattles the windows.

I can't help but smile. It's like the gods are rooting for me. There's something about a summer storm that brings promises of delicious chaos and new beginnings. Fuck knows I need them both.

As I slowly open the door, the noises from next door are louder and I have to swallow down the only visceral sensation this man instills in me now... *sickness*. I have to focus. The corridor seems empty, so I slip out, closing the door behind me. But I won't lock it. I can't have him know I had a key; he can go ahead and think I learned how to pick locks or something.

The foyer is underneath me, and from there a grand staircase leads to a landing about halfway up, then splits into two smaller staircases that take a U-turn on either side, against the walls. I step closer to the handrail, looking down the main steps, which are dimly brightened by the moonlight from the landing windows. There's no one there. And I can't hear anything beyond the moans coming from Ryan's room at the end of the corridor, and the roaring thunder closing in.

I have to take a chance.

Turning to one of the staircases, I step down as carefully as I can, my attention on the ground floor that starts to peek through. There's no movement, but my heart beats like I'm running a marathon, muscles tense at the cusp of pain.

I reach the landing and stand against the wall, trying to hide from the moonlight as I look for movement, the ground floor much more visible now. I can only see the left-hand side of the foyer, and as I lean in, I catch a shadow disappearing toward the right. Somewhere in the distance, a doorknob clicks… then nothing. It might be the bathroom, since there's one around there, close to the kitchen.

I swallow my worries and rush down the steps, struggling to contain the elation the prospect of freedom brings. I can fucking taste it as my feet hit the marble floor and the front door is so goddamn clear in my sight, even when all the lights are off.

Suddenly, a doorknob clicks again and my head snaps toward the noise, but I only get to see a shadow, before something slaps over my mouth and an arm encircles both of mine, trapping them against my body. He slams me against his front, and just as I'm about to kick and scream, he pulls me under the staircase, against the back wall, covered by its shadow.

Fight-or-flight clouds my logic as I struggle against the man, but he presses his hand harder on my face, gripping my jaw, and holding me tight. The moment I feel his breath on the top of my ear, followed by the brush of his lips, something visceral erupts deep inside. That gesture throws me back in time, to a dingy bar at the edge of the city. Drunk, careless, surrounded by questionable people with bad intentions, dressed in ripped shorts that barely covered my ass and a flimsy t-shirt knotted under my breasts.

And when the wrong people noticed me, he came out of nowhere, wrapped his arm around my waist, pulled me against his front, and brushed his lips on the top of my ear, whispering…

"Reckless little Morri…"

I knew that voice, I knew that smell, but that

touch… that was new. I never felt it in that intimate way before. Because I belonged to someone else. But not anymore. He left me a broken mess, made me into a killer, and my recklessness turned dangerous. And that same recklessness brought me here… all alone… for his friend to find me.

Maddox.

Another soft blow of air brushes against my ear, down the side of my throat. My body relaxes, coming off that flight response, but the man doesn't let me go. His grip only loosens, enough that it allows my arms to bend, and I wrap my hands on his bare forearm that he holds against my chest. My breathing doesn't steady though, memories of that night… the dirty dancing… the sexual tension… they run rampant through my nerves. We didn't even kiss, yet even now I wish we would have. I wish we fucked. I wish I got my revenge. And I wish I got this angst out of my system. I wonder what he's thinking of as he holds me to him. How did he know I would recognize him?

Steps on the hard floor remind me of where I am and from within the shadows, I watch one of the guards passing through the foyer, toward the other side of the house. He's out of sight, but Maddox doesn't move, and I hear another set of steps coming from that direction, entering the foyer—the second guard.

Fuck.

I'm holding my breath, wary that he could hear even that, but the noises coming from upstairs rip through the house. My asshole *future husband* fucking Raven into oblivion. I can't help but feel for his mother. She's hearing all this shit, the disrespect. Music suddenly mixes with that bile-rising noise pollution and I can see the guard looking up to the second floor.

"Jesus Christ…" He shakes his head and disappears somewhere in front of the staircase, where we can't see him.

All we can do is wait calmly.

Only that calmness breaks, shattering into a crippling stillness the moment something in the darkness opposite us… moves. My feet dig into the floor, my body pushing against Maddox, as that darkness flows like smoke in our direction. But I seem to be the only panicked one.

Notes of bergamot and rich decadence slither through my senses when I take another slow breath, and as that shadow nears, and that scent becomes denser, cedar mixing in the fragrance, my heart stops.

Vincent-motherfucking-Sinclair.

The whole house is dipped in darkness, yet somehow his black eyes shine, thriving in the shadows he belongs in. The shadows he controls…

Another step and he's right in front of me, his body so close, yet not touching mine. I release one hand from Maddox's forearms and reach for him, fingers gripping the edge of a smooth, dense material. He doesn't move though, doesn't let himself be pulled in, shoulders straight, locked firm in an imposing stance.

Maddox slowly drops his hand from my mouth, brushing it over my shoulder, grazing my waist, pausing for a moment before it rests on my hip. Those memories rip through me once more, and even after all this time, that Bluesy dirty song we slow danced to that night floods my mind, and I squeeze his forearm involuntarily.

The Serpent reaches for me, placing his palm over my chest, right at the base of my throat, as the steps of the guard are heard yet again. Only they don't leave the room, they pace through it, filling me with adrenaline, with fear, desire, and a need for destruction. Of me, of him, of them... after the days I've had... I want to fucking burn this place to the ground! Only as the man continues to pace, my pulse rising with every step, The Serpent grips the base of my throat in his fingers, dragging them up until he holds me in his hand, and I realize I would like to burn first.

In a completely different way...

His grip is firm, possessive, and so goddamn

satisfying that my head drops against the body of the man holding me from behind. He tenses. I can feel the flex of his muscles, the soft hitch in his breath, the flinch in his bones. But he doesn't move.

As The Serpent grips my jaw, then slides that hand against my cheek, dragging his thumb over my lower lip, Maddox's fingers dig harder into my hip and goosebumps burst over my skin.

The guard's steps are closer, my nipples hardening against Maddox's forearm, and when his grip tightens on me, my gaze drifts into his. And right in that moment, when he looks down at me, The Serpent's thumb dips into my mouth, pressing on my tongue. Against the top of my ass, I feel a distinctive twitch, just as the man before me presses his body onto mine, trapping me. His darkness dips slowly over me, his breath touching my lips as his thumb slides out gently. Closer… I swallow the heaviness that sits in my chest, almost tasting the softness of his lips on mine, just as Maddox's hand slides slowly from my hip toward my lower belly, then movement in the corner of my eyes pulls my attention away.

Brief, silent chaos erupts.

The Serpent aims his free hand at the movement and a muffled *pop* startles me. He shifts in a split second, catching the man in his arms before he falls to the floor, pulling him in the shadow, just as the second guard steps back into the foyer, looking around for the disturbance. The Serpent moves out of the shadow, with a strange fluid elegance in his movements, one that has no business being there as he aims his gun at the man, trigger pulled before he can even open his mouth. He dips in just as the man threatens to hit the ground, lowering him slowly.

This is our moment.

Maddox releases me, but I linger a moment longer against him, my eyes on The Serpent that's turned to us. Only a moment... Just as tense. Just as suffocating. Only this suffocation is welcome. Craved. Needed.

They came for me.

The moment is broken when Vincent turns and moves away down the same corridor the last guard came from, and we follow.

"Shit." I couldn't stop that sharp whisper.

Both the men turn to me as I lift my foot off the ground, shaking the warm wetness from it as I realize what it is.

"Are you barefoot?" Maddox whispers, and I nod.

Before I can protest, he reaches down, sliding one arm against my back the other under my knees, lifting me to his chest. The Serpent doesn't move. His eyes turn to slits, narrowing on the man that holds me, his shoulders stiffer than usual, and I swear I feel that possessiveness in my bones as that gaze splits me. I bet Maddox can feel it too.

"We have to go," I whisper through gritted teeth.

The dark slits turn to me for a moment, before he shifts on his heels, and starts running through the corridors, as thunder fills the night. Holding on to Maddox, I will my gaze to stay away from his, the intimacy of the moment we shared seconds before leaving a lingering tension behind. I can feel it in the way he holds me, half avoiding to squeeze me too tight, to touch me in the wrong place, yet the tension in his thick muscles is unmissable.

The Bluesy tune lingers through my mind as well… and I still wonder if he remembers it too.

We turn on the corridor, through some smaller service rooms, and when The Serpent opens the last door, the whole sky explodes in electric white, a lightning zipping through the night sky, the magnitude of it faltering our steps. But we don't linger as the thunder splits the silence in its roaring boom, the rain suddenly crashing on us, heavy and dense.

We're slipping between the wall at the side of the house and some vegetation before stopping in front of absolutely nothing, a bare wall looking at me.

"What are we doing here?" I turn to Maddox.

He nods toward the wall, confused. "Escaping."

Of course. What did I expect? For them to have driven on the driveway?!

The Serpent jumps, grips the top of the wall and leaps in another impressively fluid movement, disappearing beyond it. Maddox then dips me to my feet, grips my waist, and lifts me until I can reach the wall and climb over it.

But when my feet touch the ground on the other side, and I turn, he's there, right in my space, looking down at me... the possessiveness in his eyes as clear as the lighting that burns the sky. And I can't stop myself, I can't do it... I don't want to.

He fucking came for me!

I rise on my tiptoes, grab his face in my hands, and when my lips crash on his, my world turns upside down. Because it feels right! As if it turned the right way around, and his intoxicating scent smells like home, so I kiss him again. And again! A second later, his arms take hold of me, and like a fucking python, they tighten around my body, taking my breath away.

He might as well keep it, because I think it always belonged to him.

"Come on." Maddox pulls us from this spell. I didn't even hear him jump over the wall.

It's such a surreal night, everything is happening so quick. Like a movie. Only I keep blinking and I'm in a different scene before I can settle in the previous one.

We reach a car and I climb into the back seat.

"Fuck!" The occupied driver's seat startles me.

"Good evening." Carter nods at me.

"You scared the hell out of me."

"Are you okay?" The Serpent climbs in after me and finally speaks.

"Yes."

"He didn't...? You're sure?" He's asking specific questions, without being specific at all.

"I'm okay. Raven... is yours?" I ask, looking between the men, Maddox now in the passenger seat.

"All ours. She did good, no?" Carter turns to me.

"Very good. Thank you." I smile gently, to each and every one of them, and they nod. None of them return the smile. "His mother came to me. She confirmed something I suspected—there's more to this than a sheer desire to marry me. Some time ago, she found paperwork, a lot of it, all about my family and I."

"What kind?" Carter looks at me from the central mirror, brows furrowed.

"Every single kind you can think of. Including birth and marriage certificates. Banks. Deeds. Everything." I hold his gaze for a second longer, stretching that silence. "One might think there are ulterior motives for a future spouse to hold so much information on their betrothed's family. I wouldn't mind getting my hands on it all."

"And we believe this woman?" Maddox asks.

"I've never cared enough to put stock in her words, but she is very rude in her sincerity. I doubt she would ever bother to be anything but honest. This time around, though... there was genuine fear in her bones. Before she had to run away from me, because Ryan was coming, she said something else." I take one deep breath, those words carrying consequences, potentially changing the whole game. "She suspects Ryan killed his father."

A synchronized sigh fills the car. One by one, the men turn, backs sinking into their seats as Carter turns the engine to life.

"I want to go back." Maddox doesn't turn as he speaks. "I want to find that paperwork."

"It's too risky. It's my ego here. None of that will help us in any way." I shake my head.

"We don't know... it might. And this storm is the perfect cover to roam through his house. We still have a little while before Raven is done with him." The Serpent pulls my attention to him. "Madds, go. But if the music stops, get the fuck out of there."

Maddox nods once and leaves the car. We're hidden well enough here, the headlights are turned off, even the thunder and heavy rain covers our engine, and all I can do is sink into this back seat, hoping to hell that he's not going to get caught in there...

I cannot help but feel as though these men are risking too much for me.

Twenty-two
VINCENT

WATCHING THE FIRE OF HER HAIR ON MY BLACK SHEETS, her freckled, soft skin tangled in them, the calm rise and fall of her chest, as she sleeps, brings a strange satisfaction, a calmness in my soul.

She holds the pillow under her head, and this peculiar sense of belonging takes over. I've been watching her for the last hour... when the sun was rising, the rays touched her, making her look like she's on fire, the shades of red matching hers. I've laid here, motionless, afraid that if I wake her, the spell will be broken and my Eve will disappear.

A soft moan escapes her lips, and she blinks slowly.

"Mmm..." She rubs her cheek on the pillow and finally opens her eyes. Smiling at first, then wider and wider, slight shock or panic in them when she realizes she's in bed with me.

"Good morning, Little Eve."

She lifts her head suddenly, looking around us, taking in the unfamiliar space, before she turns back at me.

"You're in my house."

I don't miss how her gaze softens for that split second before she catches herself.

"Um... how did I get here?"

"You fell asleep in the car. I brought you here, where you're safe."

"Okay... but how...?" Her gaze is mixed with worry, confusion, and comfort she tries to hide.

"You... you just didn't wake up. Madds picked you up, passed you to me, you... *nestled* into my shoulder, and I brought you in."

She just looks at me, blinking more times than necessary in these few seconds, before she slowly drops her head back onto the pillow.

"You could have taken me to Lulu," she all but whispers.

"No."

"You're not making the same mistake as Ryan, are you, Serpent?" She narrows her eyes on me.

"I want to keep you safe, that's all. And Loreley's would be a far too obvious place for you to escape to."

"Son of a bitch! He'll fucking hurt Lulu! He hates her! I have to go!" she rasps as she throws the sheets aside and sits up, just about to jump out of bed.

Before she can make the next move, I catch her and slam her back onto the bed. "She's safe, she's okay. We sent people to keep her safe. Nothing will happen to her."

"No, no, I don't…"

"I give you my word." My arm is wrapped around her ribs, pinning her to the bed, feeling her body slowly soften. Only that look in her eyes turns, darkening with a chilling edge.

"I've had your word before, Serpent." Her eyes narrow. "And in the end, it meant nothing." She pushes against the arm I've draped over her, but I don't waver.

Fuck… Sighing, I slide one leg over both of hers and hold her in place. I had to let her go once, and there's no way I'm doing it again.

"It meant everything, and that's why it hurt the way it did." I finally speak through her attempts to push me away, her body strong, yet not strong enough for my will. And at this point, when it comes to her, my will is unmoving.

"That's why it hurt *me*," she spits.

"It hurt me too, Morrigan!" At the sound of her name falling from my tongue, she falters, her brows furrow, the look in her eyes strained with broken emotions.

We call each other made up names. We call each other everything but who we are, because our names on our lips carry a weight of a love that never was, they carry promises and shattered dreams, and… they sound like hope.

And the hardest fucking thing in this world is allowing hope to brush your soul.

Yet here I am…

"Then… Then why did you do it?!" Her voice breaks for a moment, and somehow that makes me feel a little better.

"Because I had to."

How many times over the years have I imagined this exact moment?

How many times have I wished to find her, trap her beneath me, and tell her everything?

How many times have I almost risked it all and drove to her university?

How many times… have I been forced to give up on her, on us?

Too many. Far too many.

"Had to?! *Had* to?!"

With all her strength, she shoves me enough that she slips out of bed, so much rage in her eyes that it reminds me of the night Maddox and I caught her.

The night I knew she was mine.

I jump after her and close the distance between us.

"You *had* to leave me?!" She slams her hands against my bare chest, pushing me away. Only the woman is relentless! She tries to slap me, and I block her hand.

"You *had* to tell me that you didn't love me anymore?!" She pushes me once more.

"You didn't fucking love me!" Her rage is filled with anguish, but I need her to shut the fuck up.

I grab her and throw her on the bed before she even realizes what's happening.

"I never. Fucking. Stopped!" She stills, propped on her elbows, frowning. Her lips part, but she's finally speechless, and I feel... relief.

I know what I *had* to do to distance myself from her. I know how much it fucking hurt. Because no matter how brief it was, how inexperienced, how young we were, we recognized that our souls lived in the same shadows and found their matching darkness.

"Your father forced me. He blackmailed me," I finally admit.

"He... Wait, what?!" She slides up in bed, almost in a sitting position.

"You know very well how much the man didn't want me with you back then. It turns out that a cop friend of his found something. A mistake, the one and only that caught the eyes of the law. Your father gave me a choice… either break up with you, or Madds goes to jail for the rest of his life." Her eyes go wide at those words, and she clutches the sheets by her sides. "Countless times I thought of telling you about this, but I knew that there was no way we would be able to stay away from each other. We would have fucked up, we would have ruined it all, ruined Madds' life."

"Our love in exchange for his freedom…" She pulls her knees to her chest, wrapping her arms around them, as she turns her gaze toward the window.

A charged silence settles, questions lingering in the atmosphere, and for the first time in a very long time, I can't anticipate what happens next. Her lips are parted as she swallows dry sobs, gasping softly for air, her knuckles turning white from the tight grip.

She climbs out of bed once more, but this time, there's no rage… she holds her stomach as she takes tentative steps closer to the window, her breathing quickening.

Running my fingers through my hair, I have to force myself not to go to her. Not to pull her into my arms. Not to guide her in the direction I want her in.

Fuck!

I can't force her to believe me, to accept this… but goddamnit, how much I want to. I want to grab her delicate jaw in my large palm, wrap her fiery hair around my fist, and bend her into understanding, force her to accept everything I tell her with no questions asked.

Make her fucking want me!

Make her love me!

Make her fuck me!

But I'm no different from Holt if I do any of that.

Little Eve is mine, she always was. Through years and fucking years of this… building an empire with a lost empress, and now… she's back.

The smart thing is to keep a safe distance so the empress can take her throne by her own choice.

"Why now?" Her voice is smaller. "Why did you come back now?"

"The evidence is gone. The cop is under our control now. Madds is safe."

"And my father? After all of this, all he's done to Maddox… to us, you go into business with him?!" Her tone grows louder once again.

"I told you, Holt has something I want, and your father will most definitely suffer the consequences of his actions. There was never any question about that. I've envisioned the moment too many times during the years. Even if you and I weren't here right now… he would have still paid. If not for us, for Maddox."

"When did the evidence go away?"

I sigh. "About six or seven months ago."

In the reflection, I can see her eyes widening. She turns and looks over her shoulder for a few moments, before returning her gaze to the window.

"Six, seven months," she whispers.

"Mhm," I hum.

"My mother's party…"

Slowly, I close the distance between us, standing just behind her. I tower over her, but not by too much. Enough to see over her head, watch our reflections in the window, through the dense forest and cloudless sky.

"There were rumors about what your father and Holt wanted, sniffing around the docks, and what they wanted couldn't be done without the right connections. And The Sanctum has all the right connections. All we had to do was plant the seeds, and all of a sudden, all was forgotten, and we were invited to your mother's birthday party."

"Was it intentional? Your… timing?" She narrows her eyes.

"Yes." I don't miss a beat. "It took me too long. The longest it has ever taken me to do a job. I didn't care that you were spoken for. I needed to be around you… see if there was something there. And there was."

She shakes her head, but doesn't turn. "I stabbed you. How would you possibly believe there was?"

"Little Eve, I knew I had a chance the moment you pierced my chest. It was that look in your eyes… it wasn't of remorse, but passion so dark I could see your hurt, and your love too. You wanted to sink that blade deeper, but you knew you would feel that pain as well."

All I hear is her soft inhales and exhales. It makes my blood pressure rise. It's all come to this moment… and I can't bear the wait, the unknown.

"So what?" She finally speaks again. "You would have broken us up if all that went down wouldn't have happened?"

"I would be a liar if I say that I wouldn't have tried. I knew you were mine… I would have done my fucking best to make sure you knew that too. But, no, I wouldn't have broken you up unless that was what you wanted. I've hurt you enough…"

"You broke me. You hold a power over me that I cannot understand. And I fucking hate it. I hate how deep you can reach inside my soul, how many layers you can peel away and leave me but a shadow. I hate how long it took me to feel that I'm alive. I hate that I could never truly love again after you."

She whips around, pins me with her gaze, and suddenly I feel as though I'm smaller, weaker somehow.

"I still hate you... because you're the only one that saw exactly who I was, and pushed me further into that darkness. And then you left... and there was no one else like you."

"I never left." I'm finding it increasingly more difficult to stay leveled.

Tears fill her eyes, the green in her irises so fucking vivid it's like I'm lost in the forest outside of my window on a rainy afternoon.

"I had no choice, Morrigan... But I never actually left. I kept tabs, knew how your life was going, how smart you were becoming and how strong. Through gritted teeth and a broken heart, I was forced to watch you meet others, and eventually Holt... but I wanted to kill them all."

I fucking wanted to rip them apart, into small pieces, then drop them on her doorstep to show her what happens to the men that touch her. I wanted to fuck her in a sea of their broken limbs, desecrate their goddamn remains with our ecstasy.

I still do. Only Holt can fucking die whilst watching her take me on his future motherfucking grave.

Twenty-three
MORRIGAN

I DELIBERATELY HOLD MY BREATH AND FORCE MYSELF NOT to blink through the tears that I cannot seem to stop from flowing, just in case... just in case I miss any clue, any sign that he's lying.

Goddamnit... there's none. But he's The Serpent, cunning in more ways than most would know, that most would recognize. What the hell makes me think that I would recognize betrayal on his features?

I let go and blink once, pushing a steady stream of tears down my cheeks, my chest shaking, my hands painful from the tenseness in my fists, a deep pressure in my head. And the voice speaks inside of it...

You know you would have no trouble recognizing his

deceit… You saw it the night he left you. You knew he was lying.

I fucking did. I did. I don't know if he allowed me to see it, but I knew he was lying to me. I just didn't know about what. My insecurities about deserving him steered me from believing that he was lying about not loving me… I had no trouble believing that he didn't.

My fucking Serpent…

All this time, I've hated him. I killed because of how broken I was. I did so many stupid things. I almost did his friend too… Maddox. I always had a soft spot for that brutal man, that gentle beast that kept an eye on me, the reason Vincent and I never were.

I can't blame him. Any of them. I would have done exactly the same thing, not just for Lulu, but for Maddox too.

"So much time lost…" I whisper, unable to drop my gaze from those dark pits of his eyes.

"Yet no love was lost…" he whispers back on a long breath, with a warmth in his voice that spreads instant goosebumps on my skin, all from a shiver that starts in the center of my chest.

I shake my head gently as my bottom lip quivers. He cocks his head slightly, reaching over and brushing his thumb over my tears, before he swipes his tongue over it.

Then he dips in and I'm expecting a kiss to my lips, only he presses them to my cheeks instead, kissing away the tears that fell there. Microscopic currents he leaves behind, tiny electric shocks in the shape of his kisses, and he follows the trail down my face. When he reaches my jaw, a ticklish sensation explodes through me, my body shuddering, my hands grabbing onto his naked waist instinctively.

I could have sworn I heard a low moan somewhere deep in his chest at the same time I felt his muscles tense. He doesn't stop, though. He slides one hand into my hair, bending my head back, continuing to follow those stray tears, under my jaw, and down my neck, until there's nothing left.

Only my nails digging into his tight flesh. Fuck, he didn't look like this all those years ago, with defined muscles, wide shoulders, the kind of man you expect to do at least fifty laps a day in the Olympic pool. My fingers itch to explore, but I'm more intrigued by his own exploration.

As his grip on my hair tightens and my eyes close, he pulls back harder, and grabs my ass with his free hand, pressing my hips into his on a dragged groan. Mine or his, I'm not even sure. But his tongue swipes over my clavicle, up my neck, then down again, sinking his teeth where it meets the shoulder, the sharp pain pushing me even harder into him.

"Vincent…" A soft moan escapes through my

lips and every single muscle in his body tenses. My mind does too. I haven't called him that in years...

"Again!" he groans.

"...What...?" I open my eyes lazily, and the look that meets me is feral. Feral in a way that instantly makes my nipples hard, painful against even the loose fabric that covers them.

"Say. It. Again."

Oh... A smirk creeps onto my lips.

"Vincent..."

I have no idea how or when it happens; it's all a blur of movement as he all but roars and grips my ass, lifting me to him, and I'm slammed onto the soft bed. Climbing over me, my wrists become trapped in his grip high above my head, pushed hard into the mattress. His other hand cups my jaw, his index finger gently pulling my bottom lip down.

"Fuck... *Morrigan*." My name slips off his lips like honey. "It's kind of poetic, the sound of my name on your lips, the sound of yours on mine, isn't it? Yet it in a fucked up religious kind of way... you're still my Eve, and I'm still the serpent that pulled you to sin."

"The original sin... only I was always a sinner. You were just the devil who embraced me." I smile, grinding my hips up to meet his.

He drags that hand down my throat, to the neckline of my t-shirt, and in one rapid move, he rips it and I hold in a cry as the fabric grits my skin. Reaching the hem of my bra, he pulls it down, exposing my breast, and the moment the colder air brushes against that nipple, I can't help but moan.

"Always a heathen…" He dips down, capturing that peak between his teeth for a few moments, then sucks it to the point that pain seeps through and my back arches just as he releases. "…carrying a darkness that somehow found mine through the shadows. And it's never let me go."

"No love lost…" I whisper, my gaze fixed on his with an intensity I feel in my temples.

"None. Your darkness lives in my soul. You take it out and I won't be whole."

"I want to trust every word you say to me. I want to believe it all… and deep down I know I do. But there is a part of me that has fought this bond for all these years, the part that's been trained to protect me, which currently lives in disbelief. Almost as that teenager from long ago… the one that couldn't believe that you would look at me, that you would love me…"

He shakes his head slightly, swallowing, before he speaks. "Trust is earned and I'm going to take my time earning yours." He pauses, letting those words sink in. "But I saw you, Morrigan." He drags a finger over my breast, down my abdomen, dipping down on my belly, and I fight to focus on his words, rather than that electrifying sensation he leaves behind. "I saw you long before you think I did. I fought you, our connection... I fought the prospect of what we could be, because I didn't believe in it. I didn't want to, not after seeing what love does to people... But you, goddamnit, you wrapped so fucking hard around me, I couldn't shake you off even if I wanted to. My soul was yours, long before you actually became mine."

"Oh, Mr Sinclair, you definitely know the right words to say to get into a lady's panties." This moment feels too heavy with confessions, with these matters of the heart... I'm not used to it.

He narrows his eyes for a moment, and I swear he can read my mind.

"I'm already in your pants, Miss O'Rourke." He mirrors my grin at the same moment his hand grips my pussy and one finger pushes inside.

"Jesus... fuck!" I moan, my back arching once again, my core grinding on his hand involuntarily.

"It's the devil fucking you now, baby." He pulls that finger out and adds one more, slowly pumping in and out.

"Fuck..." I can't explain it. I've had men finger me before, I've done it myself... yet him, the way he spreads those fingers, the way he curls them, the way he pumps in hard, and drags out slowly... it drives me mad and makes me melt in ecstasy.

"What the hell, Serpent!" The asshole pulls out, completely.

"Oh, I'm Serpent again, then?" There's a cheekiness in his eyes that drives me crazy.

He lets go of me, unbuttons my jeans and pulls them down, leaving me covered only by a bra and a ripped t-shirt. But he solves that fast, ripping the rest of the fabric, before he undoes the bra and peels it off. I prop myself on my elbows to see him standing at the foot of the bed, staring at me with the sort of hunger that devours predators, with one eyebrow raised as his eyes drag up and down my body.

Shit... I don't have the confidence for this.

"Vincent... I..." I'm just about to reach for the sheet and pull it over myself.

"You're so goddamn perfect."

I smirk, my muscles relaxing a little, my plump flesh bursting in goosebumps.

He doesn't peel his eyes off me as he drops his pajama bottoms, and even though I've had him inside of me, the look of him naked in all his glory, standing before me, feels forbidden.

He's the work of art; long lean legs, that fucking V of muscles that join down low, and his cock. His damn cock, those soft veins, that glistening head, thick and beautiful. If you could ever call a cock beautiful, this would be it.

I finally drag my gaze over his abs, his broad

chest, and when I reach his eyes, his head is cocked, a knowing grin pulling at his lips.

"You seem to like what you see too."

"Couldn't say for certain." I feign ignorance. "At this distance, it's a bit blurry. I can't quite tell."

The laugh that follows, loud and deep, shaking his whole body as he presses a hand over his belly, spreads a sort of warmth through me that I haven't felt in a while—happiness.

He steps right to the edge of the bed, and I quickly flip over, no fucking around, my face up close and personal with that beautiful cock, and I don't drag it out… no… I wrap my hand around his length, and swallow him until he hits the back of my throat.

"Fucking hell, woman!" His legs shake, hands grab onto my hair, and I can't help but feel a little pride. I lift my eyes to him as I slowly slide my lips back to the tip of him and his gaze widens on me, his lips part, his chest rises and falls with staggered breaths.

I dip back in, sucking him until I'm choking, dragging my tongue as he hits the back of my throat and my spit falls down my chin, grabbing his balls and holding them tight to his body. Every choking sound I make, he matches with a groan, and as his grip on me tightens, he begins to thrust, and his ragged breaths just coax me on.

Fuck... there's nothing quite like subduing a man like this. Only I've never really had a man so ready to fall at my feet... and this Serpent looks as if he might soon.

All of a sudden, he pulls me back, forcing me to get up to my knees as my spit falls onto my breasts.

"I... I can't... Fuck! I may be The Serpent, but you're a goddamn devil woman with that tongue of yours!" he rasps, gripping my waist, and in one swift move, he lifts me and throws me on my back, grabbing my legs and pulling me to him until my ass is at the edge of the bed and he sinks to his knees between my legs.

"Vincent... just, just fuck me. Please!" I beg him because all I want right now is to feel the stretch of his cock in me.

"If my dick goes anywhere near you right now, I'm gonna come. And it's too fucking early for that." He doesn't waste another moment, his head disappearing between my legs, his tongue swiping right at my core, dipping inside my pussy, and I fall back on a sharp moan.

"That's it, my darling Eve." His tongue assaults me as he rubs my clit, over and over, until he presses his hand on my belly to stop me from squirming.

Then he switches, his fingers fucking me methodically, rubbing that delicious spot inside as he gently presses on my belly and I'm sure I'm going

310

to fucking implode.

He adds another finger, the stretch so fucking delicious, a satisfying fullness that makes me crawl back on the bed, makes me beg and shout, praying to the devil for more.

"Goddamnit, Serpent! Fuck me…"

But he doesn't listen. He presses his tongue hard on my clit, before sucking it slowly, my hips only held close to the bed by the fingers he hooks inside of me, the rhythm rising higher, the strokes deeper, the thrusts harder.

My whole body shudders, an orgasm that quite literally comes out of nowhere takes control of me and it explodes on such a high, I'm blind… Blind to the image of him crawling on top of me, deaf to the sound that makes my throat raw the moment his cock impales me, speechless to the amalgam of sensations and emotions I feel when I ride that orgasm as he thrusts into me.

It's painful and ecstatic all at the same time, and all I can do is ride it along… a slave to him. And goddamnit how amazing it is.

"Vincent…" I moan as I plant my feet onto the bed, knees bent, hips pushing into him.

"Fucking hell, Morrigan…" He reaches deeper somehow, stretching my pussy just at the edge of stinging, and when I lift my hands above my head, he takes the cue and traps my wrists, bracing himself on his other hand as he pistons into me with a raw force that brings me right to the fucking edge again.

I have no idea how much time passes, but his rhythm changes, his hips rolling into me, pulling out slowly and thrusting back in with force, and my mind is just... blank. No thoughts, no worries, no... nothing. Only this moment, only his body on top of mine, his skin touching mine, his cock inside of me... only me and him. Only us.

And just like that, with one more thrust, my pussy pulses too hard, gripping him as another orgasm shatters my body, and he drops on his forearms, braced on either side of my head, his eyes boring into mine as I scream his name. A guttural grunt vibrates from his chest and onto my lips, just as his cock begins jerking inside of me.

So much warmth fills me, his cum spreading, and thoughts of those implications, of us fucking raw, snake through my mind. Only there's no worry there, only acknowledgment. Any other man and I would have had a problem, yet him... somehow my subconscious trusts him.

"This..." he pants. "It's..."—he can't stop— "fuck. This was... Shit." He swipes a hand over his face.

I can't help it, I laugh, instantly feeling the need to run to the toilet as that warmth slowly comes out of me. Only his cock feels far too good where it is.

"You're gonna push me out, woman." He looks down between us. "Shit... I'm sorry, I got carried away."

"It's okay. We're safe, and I'm okay. Clean."

He shakes his head. "I'm never this stupid, but... Christ, fucking you bare is just..."

"I know." I really do know.

He dips in, pressing his lips onto mine, and this kiss has a touch of sentiment to it. Different, deeper, even though it's soft in its delivery. I grab his head in my hands and hold him here, hold him tight, because there's no way I'm letting him go. Not again.

Not *ever* again.

Twenty-four

MORRIGAN

THE SUN STREAMS THROUGH THE LARGE WINDOW, ITS rays warming us, and the only thing I can see is the tops of the trees. I have no idea where I am, where his house is, and I thought I would be much more worried. Maybe I'm stupid... maybe for the first time in a long time, I'm just going to allow myself to just... be.

His fingers run lazy circles on my hip, goosebumps spreading from that caress over the rest of me, and I nestle into his side a little closer. My head rests on that soft spot at the edge of his chest, one leg draped over his, and my hand is enjoying the slow beat of his heart.

Everything right here is a contrast of the life that exists beyond this sanctuary. The madness, the chaos, the pain, the deceit, it all lives somewhere far beyond these walls. And here, we are different. Here, we can be ourselves. He can be the one that softens when his eyes land on me, the one that cleans me up with a warm, wet washcloth after he fucked me into oblivion, the one that cuddles me when I'm spent. And I... I can be the one that, after all these years, can allow herself to hope. Hope that I can be by his side, that I can support him, that I can live the life I deserve, outside the constrictions and rules of my family, outside the ownership of my arranged marriage. Here, I can hope for freedom.

"I'm not sure why your organization is called The Sanctum... but this place, this moment, this feels like a sanctuary."

"It wasn't intentional." He shifts a little, sinking deeper into the pillow. "When we were kids, we found this beat up old tree house in this forest. We used to sneak up at night, or when things got bad, and hide there. It was our sanctuary... Later on, somehow, our name happened. It was always us; we always had our backs, we are each other's sanctuary too."

Fuck. There's beauty in that sadness, a purpose.

"When things got bad?" I pry, hoping I can get a better insight.

"Mhm... my father was... he was a mean motherfucker. I didn't care about how he treated me, but my mother, she went through a world of sorrow because of that son of a bitch. He was physical but not extreme, however there are other ways to abuse a person, and he mastered them all. She had no life, she wasn't allowed, she had no money, no friends, no job, no self-esteem, and toward the end... she had no will."

I stiffen, because all of that... it's the journey I'm on, and it hurts me, knowing that this man watched his mother go through that, and when he finally came back into my life, he found me in such a similar situation.

"I'm sorry... I didn't know about him. He wasn't around when we..."

"No. I chased him away when I was about sixteen. I grew, matured... got some balls, and the slithering devil in me grew as well."

"Has he come back since? Where is he now?"

"I'm not sure. But I think he believes I grew complacent, and I will have to get rid of him for good."

Does he mean...? "Kill him."

"Yes."

I nod against him. It should bother me, this blunt confession, yet I feel nothing. I would like to believe it's because I'm getting too used to being around him, The Sanctum, but in reality, it's the guilt about not feeling anything that's slowly dissipating.

"And the others?" I pry once again.

"They have their own stories… but they're their own to tell."

Of course… although I know a bit of Maddox's story. A bit, and yet it's still hard to stomach.

Maddox… fuck! The scene from last night springs to mind and I have no idea what to make of it now. No. No, I can't think of that now… *shit*.

"Eventually, we will have to go out there and face the world," I whisper, pressing my palm a little harder onto his chest, letting the beat of his heart pulse through my flesh, pushing those thoughts away.

"Eventually…"

I look up at him, his eyes closed, the sunlight making The Serpent look quite angelic. Black stubble covers his jaw, fading as it reaches his cheeks, his hair is wild around his face, and his thick black lashes somehow give him a strange innocence. He's a beautiful man, handsome in a way that makes you feel a little small when you're around him. But here, wrapped in my limbs, calm and serene, he looks like a completely different man—*my* man. And I certainly don't want anyone else to see this side of him.

"Where are we, Vincent?" He doesn't open his eyes, but he smiles. A glorious smile that crinkles the skin around his eyes, and fuck me with how breathtaking happiness looks on this man. And I put it there… *I put it there.*

"Home…"

That's it. One word. One word that holds implications of a future I stopped envisioning long ago. A future I craved and cried for. One I gave up on when the pain became too much. And one he gave up on too…

"Your home…" I need some reinforcement for my thoughts, a confirmation that I'm not jumping the gun.

"No." Opening his eyes, he turns his head to look down at me. "Just… home." He holds me there, his black eyes reminiscent of the moonless sky, yet somehow filled with the glimmer of stars.

He wraps his hand around my hip, giving it a quick squeeze, before reaching for my cheek and rubbing his thumb gently on my skin.

"It can be whatever you want it to be. It can be yours too…" he adds, and I'm searching for the right words that would fit this situation.

"And you think that, just like that, we're together. No questions asked?"

"I can think of a question to ask you…" My heart stops, and in my mind, I'm begging him to just keep talking. "But yes, just like that. You can hate me all you want, but your eyes don't lie, Little Eve. Now, a month from now, a year from now… no matter how long we wait, we will always end up right here. So, it might as well be now."

Well... *fuck.* Hard to argue with logic. But it's not really that easy...

"You would want that? For me to be here... live with you?" I narrow my eyes. The prospect... the idea feels insane, after all this time.

"I've lived too long without you, Morrigan. Having you in my bed when I go to sleep at night... it would be a privilege I've stopped dreaming of. But it is a privilege indeed, so I'll settle with simply knowing you're mine... and the rest can follow when you're ready."

I try to capture a change in tone, a hitch in his breath, pupils dilating, something to identify, not a lie, but insecurity. But there's none.

None at all, and I'm left staring at him, wondering how I've reached this point. And is it real?

"The night before Ryan took me to his house..."

"When we fucked against the window." He grins at me, and I slap at his chest. Playfully, because this comfort is just incredible.

"Yes..." I smile. "We were in my future apartment."

"Oh! I didn't realize. Loreley owns the building, right?"

"Yes, she lives on the top floor with Luke, and

she doesn't really want to rent the other two floors to anyone else. Not sure yet what she'll do with the first-floor apartment, though. Plus, since we own the club together, the proximity is quite nice, but most of all… I like it. I can see the sea from there, I love its old charm and character, and it's in an excellent location." I don't take my eyes off of him because I need to see how he truly feels about this.

"And it will give you the independence you deserve." The corner of his lips quirk gently and his eyes soften.

That's all I need from him…

"Yes." I smile back, and look toward the window, nestling just a bit deeper into him. Damn, this man is so good to cuddle.

And isn't that just surreal.

A small flock of birds suddenly flies away from the trees, pulling my attention to the window.

But really, where exactly are we?

I know there's pretty much just trees on this side of the house, but what about on the other sides? I reluctantly pull away from him and climb out, walking to the window.

It's only when I reach it that I realize I'm completely and utterly naked… yet comfortable. I could never do this around Ryan. He would condemn me since I'm too plump for his standards, but now… I'm smiling. The man watching from the bed right now makes me feel confident. I know if I turn, he'll be looking at me with hunger in his eyes. I shouldn't need a man reinforcing my comfort in my looks, but I guess emotional abuse does that to people.

"Are we at the edge of the forest?" I ask, noticing movement through the trees. Wait... "Is that a deer?!"

"Probably. There's a few around. Sometimes I see this stag, its antlers something out of a storybook. But no... we're not at the edge of the forest." His voice gets closer to me, until his warmth stands behind me. "We're pretty much in the middle of it."

I look over my shoulder and up at him, somehow struggling to believe him. The man looks like he belongs in the penthouse of the Rimbauer, the poshest apartment building in Queenscove. Yet he is here...

The forest stretches for miles. It's the only one at the edge of the city, I just never realized someone lived in it... I've walked through its trails many times, yet never even seen glimpses of a house.

Suddenly, a loud gurgle comes from my stomach, and I press my hand to it. When did I last eat a full meal? Being in Ryan's house made me feel sick enough that I haven't been able to eat properly.

"I think that's our cue to go downstairs." He rubs his hands on my upper arms and turns away from me.

I pull my gaze from the forest and swing around, stopping dead in my tracks when I catch how, one by one, his muscles ripple, with every step his legs tense, his ass a fucking sight for sore eyes, and his back... *damn*, his back. He walks toward the dressing room, and I finally move when he disappears inside, the mirage over.

"T-shirt or button-up?" he asks, as I finally follow him in.

"I'm going to live my cliché and choose the button-up please."

I don't miss the slight grin in his eyes. Am I missing something? Is shirt the right answer somehow?

He hands me a black one that I pull on as I walk over to my discarded jeans and panties, but I only put the panties on.

"I would argue that there's no need for them, but... who knows." I hear him behind me.

"Who knows? What do you mean?" I turn to him, watching as he pulls on a black t-shirt, over his black joggers, while heading out of the room.

As we walk down the floating wood staircase, I wonder how the hell this man carried me up these stairs last night. Opposite the stairs on the ground floor sits a beautifully carved wooden double door. I briefly glance to the left, noting the huge wood dining table sitting in front of the large windows at the front of the house, and when we turn to the right, I note the kitchen, made of dark, rough wood and black stone worktops, a large island in the middle.

But when I fully turn toward the back of the house, I stop dead in my tracks. Windows cover the whole length of it, only interrupted once every ten feet or so by thick wood pillars the same shade as the kitchen. It feels like I'm outside... and that view...

"Fuck..." My mouth drops, but I'm too caught in this view of the large deck with a dining and sitting area, all overlooking the dense, vast forest. Nothing else. Only green, vibrant forest.

"It's beautiful, isn't it?"

It is... I understand now, why he's here.

The soft sway of the leaf covered trees, the pale blue of the sky, the peacefulness...

Home...

Twenty-five

VINCENT

I LEFT HER WATCHING THE VIEW. I KNOW IT'S QUITE something. It's even more impressive when it rains. There used to be an old cabin here before, so all I had to do was tear that down. I didn't have to invade the forest much, since the plot was already cleared.

I turn the espresso machine on, then head to the fridge and pull out some breakfast ingredients, but when I turn around, she stands before the island, head cocked, eyes on me.

"What?" I stop in my tracks.

"You look… very domesticated. Unusual." She sits at the island, resting her forearms on it, still very focused on me.

"Unusual?" I drop everything on the worktop,

324

bringing over some eggs, veg, and some utensils and bowls. "Did you think I would be surrounded by servants?"

She pulls her shoulders back, her eyes widening slightly. "Not necessarily."

"I think my status in The Sanctum paints an interesting picture from the outside. Don't get me wrong, I like having staff dealing with shit I don't have time for. But I didn't grow up with a silver spoon in my mouth, and I need to stay grounded. Plus, I don't like people running around my house. This... well, this is my own sanctum. And there are guards roaming the grounds, but no, not my house."

"Sorry, I didn't mean to imply anything. I guess I've never thought of you in a house as inviting as this, just cooking and making coffee. I think... I think I've been surrounded by the wrong people." She turns her head toward the window, sighing as she intertwines her hands, clutching her fingers tight.

"There's no denying that. But... things will change. Soon. Very soon."

She turns back to me and smiles.

"So it's... only you here? All the time?" She raises an eyebrow, a knowing, questioning look in her eyes.

"Cheeky Little Eve. Why don't you just ask the questions you want answers to?"

"Maybe it's not my place to be that direct... I'm

trying to give you a chance to refuse to acknowledge the question, I guess." She grabs a small bowl, cracks a few eggs in, and begins whisking them.

"Not many people know of this place. The guys come here, and obviously the security team. My ex knows of it, but it's been a few years since, and... my mother, who comes fairly often. That's pretty much it." I shrug and go to make coffee and fry some bacon. I didn't miss the twinkle in her eyes when she saw it, nor the sound of her stomach. Did they starve her in the Holt house?

"Oh... your mother. June, right?"

I stop with the tongs midair and turn my head to her. "Yes. You remember..."

"Of course. I know I only met her once, but... that type of kindness stays with you. She lives in town, East Side, right?"

She's not wrong; my mom is a sweet woman, too sweet, too easy to take advantage of sometimes. Although the life she's led has slowly toughened her up. Not with the right people, though. With the right people, she's her normal self. Maddox considers her his mother too, and she's never called him anything but *son*.

"Not for a while. On this land, there used to be two dilapidated cabins which I tore down, one big one where I built this house, and a second hunting cabin about two miles south, where I built hers. I like keeping her close to me… safe," I explain.

"That's nice… I know you haven't had an easy life, but you have a loving family—your mom, The Sanctum. It's precious, you know." There's a sadness in her eyes that I wish I would be able to wipe away. I wish I could make things better for her, give her a new life, new memories… even new old ones.

I wish I could give it all to her.

"Could we eat outside, please?" There's a twinkle in her eyes as she points toward the deck, and I wonder if this is normal. For little things like that to pierce my darkness with rays of light.

I don't answer, I just grab the plates and head toward the back door, telling her how to open it and we settle outside in the crisp morning air. Not many words are needed, both content to be in each other's presence, the silence anything but awkward as we eat. Her eyes wander to the forest around us, to the birds that fly from tree to tree, the rustling of the leaves, and my eyes… they stay right on her. Observing silently every shift in her movement, that sparkle in her gaze when she notices something else to look at, the plump in her cheeks when she smiles, the soft wrinkles in her features. I take it all in, everything, even the way she delicately slides the food off the fork with her plush lips, the way stray strands of her brick red hair gently flow around her face in the forest breeze, the barely audible moan deep in her throat when she slides another piece of bacon into her mouth.

I'm mesmerized, trapped in this surreal image before me. Morrigan… my Eve, sitting on my deck, eating my food… enjoying my company.

"I'm not letting you go, Morrigan."

Her head whips to me, hair whirling over her face, and she quickly swipes it away, revealing the slight shock, laced with fear, in her eyes.

"I don't mean out of this house," I correct myself. "I mean you… us. You're mine. I don't fucking care how condescending and possessive that sounds, I genuinely don't give a shit. I will fight for you. I will fight to get you back. Unless you tell me right here, right now, that it will never be what I want it to be." I drop the knife and fork and stare at her, feeling the strain between my eyebrows, the shadows deepening over my eyes.

"What do you want it to be?" She narrows her eyes on me.

"Forever." I don't hesitate.

She nods slowly, pursing her lips, and the lack of a response brings a whole other level of anxiety. One that I don't remember ever feeling. I guess I've thought of this moment, the moment I revealed what happened all those years ago, that I still loved her, what I want from her, from us, and I've been aware of the fact that she could just reject me. Yet being faced with the prospect of it makes me realize that I haven't actually been fully conscious of the possibility of that rejection.

Was I too smug? Did I not trust that I would ever have this opportunity?

I can practically feel my heartbeat in the palms of my hands as they seem to dampen, and I shift in my chair.

"I can practically taste your nervousness, Serpent." Her gaze darkens, and as I take in the image of her and the one behind her, it hits me hard—the color of her eyes is the same as the forest that surrounds us. How interesting.

"I think you're imagining things, baby." I straighten slowly.

"Am I?" She drops her cutlery on the plate, pushing her chair back with a loud grind, and stalks toward me.

She brushes her hand over my chest, and I suppress a gasp. I know my heartbeat will betray me. She goes down my abdomen, reaching over my dick that's been half hard since she slid my shirt over her naked body, and gives it a hard squeeze that makes my toes curl. Then one more, before she rubs it gently, confusing me enough that the moment she throws her leg over the chair, I'm taken by surprise.

Her ass lands in my lap, my hands on her waist, her knees draped over the armrests, and she grinds slowly on me. I dig my heels into the floor and push, sliding my chair back enough that it gives her space, and my God, the smile she gives me is so fucking stunning as she watches me intently.

She reaches between us, sliding her hand under the hem of my joggers, pressing her palm on my cock before wrapping it around, rubbing slowly to the tip of me. *Fuck,* I have to keep my eyes from rolling to the back of my head as she pumps a few times, the feel of her on my cock just about too much to handle. I'm at the precipice of slamming her on the fucking table and driving into her, but it appears that she's the one that wants to do the fucking. And who the hell am I to say no to that.

"You're gonna fucking kill me, aren't you?" I ask as she shoves my joggers down, freeing me from them.

"You'll die a happy man then, no?" She grins as she presses my cock to her lace covered pussy, the grit of the fabric and the wetness of her so fucking enticing as she moves up and down.

"I don't know. Will I?" I cock an eyebrow and she licks the corner of her lips, challenging.

She releases me, my dick slapping against my abdomen, and she presses her pussy to it, rolling her hips as she grabs onto the back of my neck, back arching as she drops her head back and closes her eyes.

There's no shame, no inhibition, no restraint as she gets herself off on me, and Christ if that's not enough to push me over the edge. Using me for her own pleasure and I'm a willing participant at the cusp of begging her for more.

I don't though, no… instead, I dig my fingers into her waist, and push her harder against me, helping her grind until her moans echo through the forest, until I know the security detail that patrols my land can hear every note of it.

Just as her legs begin to shake, when I can feel the pulse of her cunt against me, she reaches between us and in one swift motion, she pulls her panties to the side and impales herself on me.

"Jesus fuck!" I can't help the scream that came out of me, almost covered by a delicious moan coming from her.

I think I will die a happy man.

One stroke and I'm balls deep as she unravels on me, shaking as she strangles my dick, and goddamnit, it's a view to behold.

"You're so fucking beautiful, all broken like that on my cock…"

When her pussy starts to calm, she moves again, rolling her hips slowly, until just the tip of me is inside of her, and it's a different type of ecstasy. Euphoric... I slide my hands under the shirt, one hand on her hip, the other on her breasts, and my head drops back, eyes closed as I savor the feel of her wrapped around my cock. Nice and slow, reveling in every drop of pleasure that connects us in this fucking peaceful moment.

"You're so damn handsome, all enthralled like that inside my cunt..."

I smirk as her rhythm quickens, and when I open my eyes, the intensity of her gaze on me makes my dick jerk inside of her. It draws out a violent moan from her lips, one that echoes a few times before the forest swallows it. I release her breast and clasp her throat in my hand, pulling her to me just as I push my ass up, my cock reaching much deeper inside of her at the same moment I press my lips to hers and she screams into my mouth.

"Fuck me, darling Eve, take everything!" I coax her on.

The rhythm takes another turn, as she slams onto me, and I push up into her.

"Make me come, goddamnit!" she almost yells the command at me, and I can't help but grin at the vixen. She always was wild, and even now, she doesn't cower from ordering the devil about.

I release her waist and reach between us, pressing two fingers on her clit, rubbing circles on it, watching how her lips part and her moans increase, and my fucking balls can't take it anymore. Wrapped tight around my cock, milking me hard, I try to pull myself together and hold on, but God-fucking-damnit, it's too much. I come so hard my balls hurt, my cock jerks, my abs tighten, and I fucking roar the moment she screams and shakes, coming with the same rhythm. I release her throat and she wraps her arms around me, holding on for dear life as she presses her head in the crook of my neck and I hug her to me.

Minutes…. Fucking minutes it takes just for her pussy to stop twitching around me and I can feel my cum slowly seeping out, only she couldn't care less.

She finally pulls away, just enough so she can see me, and she smiles—a glorious fucking smile that could move mountains and tame monsters.

There's a decadent innocence to it.

I want to keep it, preserve it until death comes and we get to continue our dance in the great beyond.

MORRIGAN

The humidity of our southern city somehow feels fresh against my skin here in the middle of the forest. We're in the same spot. I'm draped over him, and he holds me in his arms, one hand threaded through my hair in a tight grip. Yet... I can breathe, the air is lighter than it ever has been, I'm out in the open, yet I'm safe.

"I have men out here, baby. Men that might have just watched you ride me. They most definitely heard us." He talks softly in my ear, yet his words are wicked.

"Do you think we gave them a good show? Or should we try again for good measure?"

The rumble that shakes his chest as he forces himself not to laugh is endearing.

"I'm sorry, I keep forgetting you own a sex club now."

"You insult me, Sir. I own a fetish club." I pull away enough to look at him. "While sex might be happening, not everyone comes there for it. They come to satisfy needs beyond the actual sex." I dip in slowly, my gaze switching to his lips. "Cravings." I touch mine to his, brushing left to right. "Fulfill fantasies." Then I press against him, sinking my fingers through his hair, his stubble a delicious scrape against my face.

"My apologies, Miss." He speaks between kisses. "And do you fulfill any of your fantasies there?"

"I certainly fulfilled one a few weeks ago... never knew I wanted to be fingered by a stranger while watching another woman being fucked by a dildo and a man." His grip in my hair tightens and he pulls down, deepening the kiss as he leans slightly over me.

"Mmm…" he hums against me. "I had a similar experience. It never made sense to me why I had so much chemistry with that woman… why I wanted to taste her so badly… why I wanted to press her against that window and fuck her while everyone watched."

"Is that your fantasy, Serpent? Fuck me as everyone watches?" I lick his lips and pull on his hair just as he does.

"Oh, my Little Eve, I have many fantasies when it comes to you. And I could bet at least one of them we have in common." He jerks my head back and when I feel his lips on my throat, a shudder shakes me. "What fantasy fills that pretty little head of yours?" He licks me from the base of my neck to just under my ear.

"I don't know…" I'm lying. I definitely know.

"What makes that tight cunt of yours wet when you're alone at night?" He traps my earlobe between his teeth, biting just hard enough that my nipples perk up.

Oh, fuck!

"Dirty… filthy things."

"Filthy…" he whispers against my throat,

scraping his teeth down. "Who's doing these filthy things to you?"

"You..." I moan as the scrape of his teeth gets me fucking hot all over again, his cock half hard under me as well.

"I and... I alone?"

What?

"Yes."

"Are you sure about that?" His finger rips through my pussy, sinking so deep inside of me my body jerks up, but his hand in my hair holds me down.

"Fuck!" He adds another, as the heel of his palm rubs against my overly sensitive clit.

"Tell me... there's no one else under those stairs?" He finger fucks me so hard, my brain shuts down, my body limp, played like a violin by him. *Stairs...*

"Vincent, I..."

"Focus. Fantasies..." He pumps harder, rolling those fingers on that treacherous spot inside of me. "Who else is there when you fuck this pretty cunt of yours alone at night? Who else do you imagine?"

"I can't..."

"You can." He slams hard into me, his thumb now on my betraying clit, and I think I'm losing my mind.

"Maddox!" I cry as a shudder rips through me.

Definitely losing my mind. Did I just admit that to him?

But he adds one more finger, stretching me just a little harder, and I yelp.

"Your pussy would have to take more than just three fingers to accommodate him, filthy Little Eve." He bites into the side of my neck, his words sinking in at the same time. "He's a mean motherfucker. He would stretch that pussy so hard… but I would be right there with him."

"Vincent…"

"Yes, right here." He pulls his fingers just enough to reposition himself, and suddenly I can feel one pushing against that tight hole. But it's so wet from my pussy and his cum that was still inside of me, that it slides right in, and I don't bother to hold in the lust-filled cry that rips from my throat. It echoes through the forest. "I would fuck this tight little ass of yours, as he would rip through that pussy, and goddamnit… wouldn't that be fucking beautiful?"

He rolls those fingers with such skill that somehow I've fallen backwards, my back against the table, and his words… they fill me with the image of the man before me sharing me with the beast I've always craved. Vincent taking my ass… Maddox stretching my greedy pussy…

Jesus fuck!

The orgasm hits with that image front and

center, clawing its way through me so hard Vincent has to hold me, so I don't fall off of him, and it feels… it feels dirty. It shouldn't be as strong as it was… I shouldn't like this fantasy quite this much.

I'm wrapped in his arms and I'm not entirely sure when he pulled me there, but he holds me tight, running a hand through my hair. I move away just a bit and kiss his lips, lingering for a moment longer.

"Did you always know?" My voice is soft as I ask, and I have to force myself to look him in the eyes.

A smile touches them, and he nods. "The man never likes anyone. He's always liked you though, since the first moment he saw you break that guy's jaw."

"Vincent, no… not like that. No, not like you."

"I know, I know." He smiles. "He cares about you, he sees something in you he relates to. And it's that fascination that I always see in his eyes when he looks at you. You… well, I could always recognize lust in yours." His gaze darkens, the smile turning devious.

I'm not entirely sure how to respond to all of this, but all I can say is that this man never ceases to amaze me. This kind of freedom is so fucking refreshing.

Twenty-six
MORRIGAN

I MANAGED TO GET VINCENT OFF ME IN THE SHOWER AND proved that I could wash myself on my own, although he insisted he could do it so much better. He's somewhere in the bedroom as I dry myself, but all of a sudden, I hear a door close downstairs.

"Vin, sugar, are you in?"

My head whips to the bathroom door, heart lodges in my throat, and *"sugar"* opens the door, looking at me with interest.

"This feels like an ambush," I whisper. "Did you know she was coming?!"

"No idea. But sometimes she comes to bring dinner, because… well… she's a southern mother." He shrugs. "Your jeans are on the bed, along with your t-shirt, but you're welcome to keep my shirt

339

on." Those dimples make an appearance on his cheeks, "It looks good on you." And I just about melt, forgetting his mother is downstairs.

I quickly wipe the rest of my body, run back through the dressing room and to the bed, pulling on the jeans and his shirt as fast as I can. I tuck in the shirt so it's not too obvious, then try to make my hair presentable.

Oh fuck, no matter what, I still look like I just came out from his shower.

"Here goes nothing."

As I walk down the stairs, I can hear them talking in the kitchen, and my heart still hasn't come down from my throat.

"Just reheat it and it will be good as new." I finally see them, and the sight is such a contrast to The Serpent's image to the outside world. I can't quite fathom it's true. She's a short woman, a few inches shorter than me, with curly black hair, just like Vincent's, only dusted with grays, caught in a loose bun at the nape of her neck. She looks unnaturally sweet next to this man, in her flowery knee-length dress draping over her full hips, while... pinching her son's cheek.

When she turns and her gaze lands on me, she scrunches her eyebrows, takes a step forward, and cocks her head.

"Mamaw, this is…"

"Morrigan?! Morrigan O'Rourke, as I live and breathe!"

Ummm...

"Come here, sugar, let me look at you!"

"Hello, Ms Sinclair." I walk quickly to the woman that holds her arms open to me, too shocked to say more than that.

"Oh please, call me Mamaw June. Everyone does." She grabs me by the shoulders, holding me at arm's length, her smile so bright it could turn a sinner to a saint. "You're even more beautiful than I remember."

"I'm just surprised you remember me..."

"No one forgets a girl like you, honey." She draws me into her arms and squeezes me. It's warm. It smells of peach pie and a summer garden. She smells of love...

I hug her back, and only after she releases me do I remember her son is in here too. When I look at him, I can't quite pin the look in his eyes. Somewhere between surprise and disbelief.

"Come, eat, you look a bit too skinny." I burst into a full belly laugh as she pulls me along with her, toward the island, all too aware of my soft, plump body. She ignores me though, pulling out a casserole that instantly makes my stomach grumble with its smell alone, along with a basket of biscuits.

"I guess we're eating." Vincent sits next to me

341

and pulls a plate his mother sets on the island.

"We might have to go for a walk after this…" I'm not shy with the serving size, it truly does smell incredible, then I grab a couple of biscuits. "Damn, they're still warm." I whisper.

"There's pecan pie too." She points to a dish in the far corner of the kitchen.

"Definitely a walk."

"I'm gonna get out of your way because I had no idea he had a guest, but you have to come for tea soon!" She comes over and gives me one more warm hug, and my God, this woman feels so… homey. I almost forgot how sweet she is. I guess growing up with parents like mine, you forget how they're actually supposed to act.

"Thank you for the food! It smells so delicious!"

"My pleasure, sugar! Take care of yourselves." She walks out the door after kissing her son on the cheek, and I grab a spoonful of whatever she cooked, moaning like I just got fucked all over again.

I turn to Vincent, my cheeks full, chewing excitedly, but stop when I note his glaring eyes.

"Wut?" I mumble.

He shakes his head, biting his lip as those dimples threaten to brush his cheeks, and turns to his own plate.

Screw him, this food is more important right now.

And pecan pie!

"When are you going to tell me what the plan is?" I slide my feet into a pair of flip-flops that Vincent's mom left in his mudroom, definitely inappropriate for a forest walk, but I don't have anything else, and it's far too hot and sticky anyway, then follow him out the back door. We walk down the deck steps, through his back garden, toward a path I can see through the trees.

"A lot has happened, so it's probably the right time."

Now that I spoke with Lulu, my head has some clarity, because no matter Vincent's word… I needed to hear for myself that she's all good. She agreed that a couple of days in hiding might not be the worst idea. And she has his number if she needs to reach me.

The sun begins to set just as we enter the forest.

"I hope nothing has changed about my plan for Ryan. And at this point, I don't even fucking care if my father goes down with him."

He looks at me as we stroll side by side. I'm using this walk to get some distance, clear my head a bit. Being in that house with him will just drive us to fuck the whole time, and as much as I enjoy that,

I would like to also enjoy him beyond the feel of his gorgeous cock stretching me.

"I'm not going to lie, that's where this is headed."

My steps falter for a moment at his words, but I keep going as he takes in a deep, dragged breath.

He eases me in, telling me about Boseman, his connection with Ryan and the stupid shit he did. The threats on him and their business, failed attacks on them and even his mother, and it's all so frustrating. Even when I am not involved. I get it. I understand why the man needs to be found.

Then he tells me a story about the trafficking business my father is building with Ryan. About the drugs, the ammunition, about docks and transport, and the whole thing just baffles me.

I always made it my business to keep tabs on what my father was doing for work. More out of stubbornness, because that man's opinion of women is that we're not worth much more than cattle. The only difference would be that he expects women to always be made up and dressed to a certain standard. But since women have no place in business, and couldn't possibly understand it, both my mother and I were always kept in the dark. So I found my own way in. I had to. Something never really felt right with him and his organization. I knew they skirted at the edge of the law, but I couldn't see beyond that. And when I went to university, I couldn't keep a proper foot in, and I had no way of knowing if the man crossed the line into crime or if he was already there this whole time.

Is that really who he is? A man building his own organized crime empire?

Or is he just adding on?

The story crosses the line of insanity when Vincent tells me he traffics much more than that… and I can't help but wonder if my trust in this man that's supposed to help me take them down is blind. Children?! Really?! The man raised me!

I'm struggling to fathom it. Yet the events of the last few months certainly help make it more believable, especially where Ryan is involved.

"One of the girls we saved, she wants to stay here with her sister. We've kept everything under wraps, haven't alerted the police, kept it all between us, because neither Holt nor O'Rourke… sorry, Liam…" He skirts around that one, since we share that godforsaken last name. "… know who rescued all the people they trafficked. And we intend to keep it that way. Our cards will be laid out all at once. But we've managed to find the families for almost all the kids, with a few exceptions that have gone to a good children's home. We paid everyone off to ensure it's all kept under lock and key."

"How… how many were there?"

"One hundred and twenty-three."

I stop dead in my tracks, my hand on my stomach as I process those words, bile violently rising, burning my throat, and no matter how much I swallow, the image of all those faceless children, the horrible things they must have gone through… they're haunting.

"But I thought… I thought they only just started." My voice trembles.

"A few of them were Holt's doing before he joined forces with your father and had the access he has from the Ghost. Not many, though…"

We're on a wide path, maybe a road, and the moonlight hits us here, not a bright light, but enough that I can see the disdain in his eyes. Visceral disgust, his features heavy with everything he's been through since I've been kept at the Holt's house. The Sanctum organized pretty much a covert rescue operation in the span of three days. And it's those deep lines on his forehead, and that haunted look in his eyes, that drives me to believe the unthinkable—my father and my future ex are human traffickers. The scum of the fucking earth.

But one thing's for sure—the conflicted feelings that have plagued my violent need for retribution, are gone. Vengeance will be so much sweeter now.

We walked in silence for a while and I'm grateful for it. I needed to let the information sink in. To let the darkness that lurks in my soul feed on the horrors my vivid imagination cannot unsee, fuel for the revenge that will soon come.

"And there is a plan?" As the forest thickens and the moon glows brighter in the sky, the dust settles, and I can think with a clearer head.

"I need the information from Holt first, and we need to ensure he doesn't suspect our involvement in the break-ins. It's a massive financial loss for them. But also loss of trust with their *suppliers*. Rumor has it that they're quite… let's say angry."

I realize something, and I turn to him, grabbing his hand. "You kept him away from me. Indirectly, but all those nights he got pulled away because of phone calls. He left the manor, and I was… safe. My captivity and your rescue mission came at a most opportune time…" My eyes are fixed on him as we keep walking through the darkness. The fact that he and The Sanctum are the reason for my safety in there, even unintentionally, makes me feel something indescribable.

"It didn't feel like it from our side. Madds was worried that Holt was going to lash out at you… the outlet for the anger we were causing."

We stop in a clearing, my feet sore, since we've been walking for quite a while. But the smells of the forest, the crisp night, the starry sky… they make up for it.

"And you?" I turn, craning my neck to look into his dark eyes, and he faces me, his chest almost pressed to mine.

"Morrigan… when I look at you, I see something that most don't. I see exactly what you saw all those years ago in me. And I in you. A darkness that matches mine, the fury you subdue, and the resilience that makes you a survivor. I was terrified. Fucking riddled with guilt for what that asshole could be doing to you, and it would have been all my fault. Yet somehow I knew you would be okay. Even through my inability to help you, through the prospect that I could make things worse for you, I trusted in your strength. I trusted that you knew how to care for yourself. I had to trust that…" He shakes his head, eyes phasing out as his mind seems to go somewhere else, whispering a few more times, *"I had to trust that… I had to trust…"*

Fuck… I never expected this, any of this… his reaction to it all. His faith in me, the pain in him.

I grab his face, pulling him to me and out of that daze, and kiss him so hard that it hurts.

Because it hurts our souls too.

It hurts to know what could have been and how much he would have hated himself for it.

It hurts to know this man is exactly what my

348

soul needs—not the one to save me, but the one to help me save myself.

It hurts... seeing how much we have lost, but it's such a good hurt, knowing that we have found our way back now.

He presses a hand on the small of my back, the other on the back of my head, holding this kiss longer and longer, the feel of it penetrating my fucking soul, my heart aching for it to never end.

A gust of wind pulls us from the spell, bringing with it a humid scent that usually means rain through these parts. We both look up, but the skies are still clear. And then I skate my eyes around us, releasing him when I realize where we stand.

"The crossroads!" I exclaim.

"Did you really not know where you were that night?" A smirk pulls at his lips.

I shake my head, inhaling that scent of wildflowers. "I just took a turn and drove. I guess... it was meant to be in some way."

"I thought about that quite a lot. For a while, I was convinced it was intentional. I guess you're right, it was meant to be."

"So this is part of your land as well?"

"Yes, you missed the private property and private road sign that night..."

"So you really were just out for a run that night. Here I was thinking you were some creepy ass guy stalking through the forest."

"Well… just because it's my forest, it doesn't mean I'm not." He shrugs and I feel a rumble of laughter growing in my chest.

"You know, I'm still not sure what the price was for the deal I made with you."

"You sold your soul to me that night, right here, in this spot." He grips my waist, pulling me against his warm body. "Little by little… and you became mine. Such a beautiful, beautiful gift…" he murmurs.

"My soul is mine, Sir, thank you very much." I lift my nose and quirk my eyebrows as I regard him, palms pressed on his chest.

"Oh, my darling Eve, it's so very charming that you believe that." The grin he gives me, with those devious dimples, is devastating. Truly and utterly devastating.

He presses his lips onto mine, his arms wrapping me in a possessive hold, and I fear that my soul has been his long before we struck a deal at this very crossroads.

Twenty-seven

VINCENT

S HE TAPS HER FINGERS, ONE BY ONE, ON THE MARBLE TOP of the coffee table, making me a bit uneasy.

"And you're sure this plan will work?" Morrigan asks me for the second time, after I run through the details, most of which I've already discussed with the rest of The Sanctum. All but one—a backup plan that I had to discuss with her first. A crazy… fucking crazy backup plan.

"We've weighed as many risks as we could think of. We have them in a tight grip now. All of them," I confirm yet again.

"Sorry… I just don't want them to slip through the cracks. They have to pay. It's not just about me anymore." She sits back on the sofa, head falling against the edge as she rubs her palms over her beautiful face.

"They won't. The Sanctum is bigger than they think. It's bigger than you think as well. There is no chance for them now. You will certainly not marry that goddamn piece of shit, and all the children they have wronged will be avenged. You have my word on that."

She nods, seemingly satisfied with the reassurance, but I can still see the turmoil in her eyes. "Make the arrangements, then."

"It's all been arranged. One text to confirm your approval, and we're ready."

"Then I believe it's time for us to leave our sanctuary, Mr Sinclair."

Indeed, it is. I nod once, rising from the armchair, offering my hand to her. And she takes it with a smile on her face.

The evening offers the cover we need, and by the time the wheels of my Camaro hit the asphalt of Queenscove's downtown, it's just past nine. We're heading straight to Midnight to meet the others, along with Loreley. Morrigan demanded to see her in a safe environment.

She's safe at the moment. No one can see her through the tinted windows of my car, but I do worry that someone might spot us walking into Midnight. As secret as that bar is, The Sanctum is not the only one in this city with access to information. Our only advantage is the fact that as far as we know, neither O'Rourke nor Holt know that Morrigan has any involvement with us. It's never safe to assume, though.

The chirping startles Morrigan, who seemed to be trapped in deep thought. I pick it up from the center console, but the number on the screen gives me an unsettling feeling.

I think she catches onto it, an eyebrow cocked as I slide my finger on the screen.

"Everything o…" But I'm interrupted by angry and terrified cries. "What the fuck happened?! …"

"Vincent?!" Morrigan's eyes are wide as she clutches my thigh. Something in that gaze tells me she already knows who's distressed on the other end of the line.

"We're on our way! Stay away from it!" Fuck, fuck…. *Fuck!*

"What happened, Vincent?! Was that Lulu?!" She's turned in her chair now as I press the acceleration, weaving through traffic, ignoring the honking and red lights. I put an arm over her, pressing her onto the seat.

"Put your seatbelt on!" I rasp through the sound of the angry engine.

"Goddamnit, Serpent! What the fuck happened to Lulu?!" Oh, reckless Morrigan came to play. I can feel her fire touching me, her rage growing with every second that passes.

"Fuck." She's gonna hate me.

"We've passed Midnight." She turns her head, seeing our turn in the taillights, and when I make the next right turn, tires screeching on the asphalt, her ass sliding in the chair, I can feel her searing gaze on me. "Lulu. The apartments. The club."

I sigh, exhaling a breath that strains my throat, as I pull onto the street where all that she listed lies.

"The club is burning."

A gasp. No more. No other sound. And even the sear of her gaze turns cold.

I stop the car and look at her, only I meet her profile, stern, sharp, her chest rising and falling in controlled breaths. I'm used to her lashing out, screaming, raging, beating the shit out of people, but this... this is fucking terrifying, because it's a stage I've never seen her in.

We can see the lights of the fire truck coming from the back of the building where the parking lot for the club is. But I pulled in at the side of the building, since I don't want to risk being seen at the front, or the club's entrance. The moment the car doors open, we can smell it. Burnt wood and leather fills the air, but there are no flames out here. Maybe

354

it's a good sign.

We disappear in the shadows, quickly slipping through a side entrance that's fairly concealed, and once that door opens, the thick, choking smoke hits us first, and then the heat.

"Morrigan, you can't go in there!" I grab her forearm, pulling her back, but the woman shakes herself so hard, she escapes my grip, giving me a look of hurt that hits my soul.

"Don't fucking touch me," she seethes, then runs through the corridor.

I realize we walked in through the fire exit, ironically, and I follow her through the corridor that holds all the playrooms that luckily look intact.

"Nooooo!!!" Morrigan's cry splits the air, shattering some part of me that feels too much for her. Her pain too heavy. The flames have taken over the entire bar area, the storeroom in the back of it, and most of the stage and the seating area that surrounds it. Only the former has already been extinguished, black scorched wood and leather the only ones remaining.

"Ma'am, you have to leave right now!" A fireman grabs her upper arm just as I get to her. The moment he sees me, he freezes for a split second. "Please, it's not safe." Others are fighting the flames that engulf the bar area, the heat so strong, the smoke making us cough as it scorches our airways.

"For fuck's sake, woman! This is not the time nor the place, and Lulu is not here!!! Get the fuck out now!" I don't fucking play anymore. Gripping her upper arm, I pull her hard behind me, uncaring of the bruise I might leave on her flesh, of her protests, her screams behind me. I don't give a shit. I just need her safe!

We reach the foyer, but the smoke is still so damn thick and there's no one but firemen moving up and down the steps.

"They're in there." One of them points toward the service door that leads to the corridor Morrigan took me through before.

She rushes for the door, punching some keys on the number pad, but the electrics must be screwed because nothing happens, and she bangs her fists onto the door, screaming at it like it could magically open.

Only, it does.

One of my men opens it reluctantly, and his shoulders relax when he sees me, nodding as he steps to the side to let us in.

"It's open." He points to another door, and I don't have time to ask him any questions as Morrigan sprints to it and rips it open.

Fucking hell, this woman would just jump headfirst into any fucking situation.

I don't know what the hell awaits after that

door; she has no regard for her damn life. I follow her and end up in a small bar area, catching the moment Morrigan screams for Lulu, who is sitting at one of the tables.

"Are you okay?!" She holds her face in her hands, turning her to every side as she examines her, before padding her hands over her body.

"Morri! I'm okay!" She grabs onto her friend, her boyfriend reluctantly leaning in his chair, far away from them. Only when his eyes land on me, they widen for a moment too long.

Suddenly, Maddox and two of my men walk through the same door we came through and it's my turn to contain my surprise.

"What happened, Loreley?" I ask, stepping closer as I clasp Morrigan's shoulder. Only she shrugs it off, throwing me a look that very well spells *fuck off*.

"Ryan... We saw his men on the cameras. He watched as they ran out after setting the place on fire, then smiled at the camera." The disdain in her voice matches exactly what I'm feeling.

"Lulu... I'm so sorry. I'm so fucking sorry... I should have never kept you anywhere near me! This is all my fault. Goddamnit, it's all my fault!" Morrigan's voice breaks into painful sobs.

But her friend shakes her head, wrapping her arms around her. I step away, satisfied that I've

357

learned enough.

"Why are *you* here, brother?" I whisper as I retreat next to Maddox.

His lips part for a split second, his amber eyes darkening as they flicker toward the women.

"The men called me," he answers.

Right, and you came for... the men.

I hold his gaze for a moment longer, before returning my attention to the girls.

"I'm sorry. I'll get out of your hair... you don't fucking deserve this. I'll make up for it all, then... I'll be gone." Morrigan's pain roughens her voice. Or are the tears responsible?

"Don't be fucking stupid," Loreley rasps, rising to her feet. "You didn't do this, but that motherfucker that's forcing you to marry him did. And if you don't make him pay"—her golden eyes turn to me—"I sure fucking will."

I have a feeling that if I don't, she'll make me pay too. Loreley's family name carries weight as well. Her father rarely gets involved in shit around here. His business lies elsewhere, his money as well, and usually, if he does poke his nose around Queenscove... that means something is very, very wrong. And Mr Dietrich is one of our prized allies outside of our city.

"No, no, no. This, all of this, is on me! If I didn't let that asshole control me the way he has, turn into

358

this goddamn monster in front of my eyes, none of this... none of this would have happened! You don't fucking deserve this, Lulu!" She turns to me, and I'm taken aback the moment her palm whips my head so hard to the side, my neck aches. "And you!" Her fist almost connects with my face next, but I catch it just in time, her other fist hitting my chest. "You fucking promised she was safe!!! You fucking promised me!" Her voice booms through the foyer. Even the firemen that walked upstairs stop dead in their tracks, her tone grave, menacing and maniacal.

"Morri, it's not his fault." Loreley grips her shoulder to no avail.

"It is!!! You fucking promised! I believed you! She could have been there! Lulu could have been downstairs!!! She could have fucking died, Serpent!" I grip both her wrists, her heaving breaths so loud, she sounds like she might just jump at my throat. Tears spill over her plump cheeks, her green eyes so vivid right now, somehow emphasizing the pain, the fear she's feeling.

This is not the time to rationalize with her. That's not what she needs, but to let those demons out. All she can see right now is what could have been... how her best friend could have ended.

And I can't help but wonder... did Holt know Loreley wasn't in the club?

Twenty-eight
MORRIGAN

MY RAGE HAS SUBSIDED, IF ONLY FOR A FEW MOMENTS, enough to hear what the firemen that approach us have to say.

"It's all extinguished. But I hope you know insurance might not cover the damage. It was no accident, I'm afraid, but I believe you are already aware."

Lulu nods, gripping my hand.

"It didn't all burn out," he continues, and we let out a joint relieved sigh.

"There's plenty of damage, but some areas were untouched, thankfully. It looked like you have some floor fire barriers and most of them did their job. Please be careful going down there. The stairs are safe, but I cannot guarantee the whole ceiling or the floors are. Okay?"

"We have some hardhats upstairs, from the apartment renovation. I can bring them," Luke states, and Lulu nods to him.

"However," the fireman continues, "the car from the parking lot... I'm afraid that one is totalled."

"What car?" My eyes grow wider by the second as I take in the look of pity on Lulu's face.

"Your car, Morri... I'm sorry."

Only hours ago, I was in pure and total bliss, isolated from the world, from the reality of my situation, and it's hard not to think that this is some sort of punishment. I was finally living something I stopped dreaming about long ago. We were making plans, setting up contingencies, we were discussing my freedom and the rest of our lives. But as I look into those black eyes now, all I feel is fury. That type that will not push me to attack, but walk away disappointed... and never come back.

Shit... I fucking loved that car!

The firemen leave, and we're left alone.

"He probably thought that you came here after you escaped. Your car at the back confirmed it to him. Do you have any idea what he knew about the club?" My lips tighten into a thin line as The Serpent asks the question.

"Morri?" Maddox asks, a slight warning in his voice.

Fuck's sake!

"Whilst I was with him, he's never mentioned it. Anyone that wanted to know the information could easily find out it's Lulu's. It's a legal establishment after all," I comply. "However, when it comes to my involvement... only *you* knew." I narrow my eyes on The Serpent, my brain fighting to believe anything but the obvious conclusion.

He didn't miss the accusation, and I don't miss the hurt that suddenly appears in his eyes. It has to be him... or one of The Sanctum. There's no one else.

"Don't insult me." His words penetrate like the freezing cold in your bones, and they bend you in compliance. A talent few possess, but he's mastered.

At this moment in time... that's exactly what I wish to do—fucking insult him.

"Come on!" Lulu rasps, pulling my hand. "Let's see the damage."

"Let me go get some helmets." Luke steps away, but she stops him.

"Fuck the helmets. Get them later. I need you there with me," she pleads, and he looks at her, then at the door, lingering for a moment, fiddling with his fingers, as he turns back and comes to us. I can't blame him for being worried about safety.

"Here, I got some flashlights from the storeroom." Beau, one of our security guys, hands them to some of us, and carries on walking at the

362

front.

"They followed him, they knew he was in the bathroom," Lulu tells me as we go back to the foyer, the smoke almost cleared now, then follow him down the steps. "Watched him until he stepped away, and trapped him in there." I can't blame him... he didn't know to expect this.

As we walk down to our club that smells of wet ash and wood, the image before us is dire. Especially in the eerie light of the flashlights. With every step we take into the club, Lulu exhales little gasps, clutching her belly, her chest or her cheeks, pushing back little sobs.

We noticed everything in the back, starting from the corridor where the playrooms lie, is intact. Black from smoke, but intact.

But no matter what... we're closed for business. And fuck knows how I'm going to get the money to rebuild and start over. The bar was a fucking work of art, and the stage was perfect. The only place I felt truly and utterly comfortable dancing in public is decimated. Every single table and chair has to be thrown away, the floors need replacing, and...

"Watch out!" Hands wrap around my waist and chest from behind, and I'm whipped backwards just in time to witness one of the large light fixtures crash in the spot where I stood a second before.

I can feel The Serpent's heavy breaths against

my back, and I would shrug him off if he wasn't holding me so tight.

He may have just saved me, but it doesn't negate the promise he almost failed to keep, or the fact that… he may be the reason this happened in the first place. I shake away from his grip and turn, reaching for Lulu.

"We'll be okay, Lu, we'll rebuild. We'll come back… I'm so sorry… So sorry." I rub her arm, looking up at her sweet smile. Even through all of this, she's still smiling at me. I don't fucking deserve it.

"It's not your fault, Morri. This is not on you."

From her left, where Luke stands, his arm around her waist, holding her tight to him, I hear a hitched breath. Only I could have sworn it sounded more like a scoff. I turn my gaze to him, and he quickly looks away.

"What are *they* doing here." He's not bothering at all to hide his distaste as he points his head at Vincent, Maddox, and his men. Only he wasn't as quiet as he thought.

"We're here because we are in business with Mr O'Rourke and Mr Holt. And we"—Maddox steps up, closer to us, the red glare from the emergency lighting making him look more menacing than usual—"always keep an eye on the people we associate with."

"And you just… happen to be in the area?" he continues.

"Luke, for God's sake, stop it! If it wasn't for them noticing the smoke, this whole place, this whole building, would have been up in flames. We would have lost everything!" She skirts around the subject, since she knows very well of the detail The Sanctum put on her, but I know she kept everything to do with them to herself. Luke is not aware of *my* connection to The Serpent.

"I'll go see if the firemen are still outside and find out what the protocol is here, since this was no accident." He purses his lips, clearly not happy with the response, but his eyes are on me the whole time.

Lulu may not be blaming me, but Luke definitely is.

"Alright." She nods reluctantly and pulls away from us, walking over to the burnt-out bar as he leaves.

The moment he reaches the stairs, Vincent nods at one of his men and he quickly makes his way upstairs as well. After all, we need someone to make sure there will not be a second attempt at our lives while we're here.

"I'm not sure what to do here…" Lulu turns to us.

"We'll figure it out. We'll talk to the insurance company and convince them to cover us." I move around the broken light fixture, my feet slushing in the wetness left after the firemen put out the fire.

"I'm not sure about that," Vincent chimes in. "Even though it wasn't your doing, considering it was criminal, the insurance company will launch a full-on investigation with the police. It could be a long time until this is sorted, as they need to prove it wasn't one of you that did it."

"Fuck..." I swipe a palm over my face, wondering how I'm going to make this work. "That will open a whole can of worms. And delay things." I spent pretty much every penny I had on this. Nowadays I'm not exactly making money, since I've been unable to work. I'm fucked... and she's fucked too just because of me.

For the first time today, Lulu cries. Not hard, not loud, but a few whimpers escape and tears fall, and she wipes them quickly, like she has no right to break down. Most of her inheritance went into restructuring the building, renovating her apartment, starting the renovations on mine, and the club. It was too early to get any profit from the club, as it will take a long time for that. Whatever money she has left, or profit from the small bar at the front, is not going to reach very far into renovating this place.

I wrap my arm around her shoulder and pull her to me, powerless to make her feel better.

Silence falls upon the charred remnants of the main room of the club.

"The Sanctum will invest." Maddox's rough voice booms through the dark space and my gaze instantly goes between him and Vincent. I can tell Vincent is taken by surprise by the statement, but he composed himself quickly enough, watching his friend. "We'll front you the money, and assist you in the renovations to ensure everything is done properly and in a timely manner, so you can reopen quickly."

"Don't be mad!" Lulu exclaims. "You're asking us to be in business with The Sanctum?! No. This is Morrigan's and my business, no one else's. Not even Luke is involved in this!"

"We don't want to be partners. Return the investment when the money comes in and you are able to do so, and we'll be out of your hair. No commission, no partnership." Maddox is now a few steps away, only his eyes are fixed on Lulu, not on us, just her.

"So you can come and claim some sort of interest on me? I know how you lot work, racketeering and all that shit. Nah, I'd rather step on my pride and ask my father." Jesus, she's feisty, but in front of Maddox? That's a bit risky.

My whole body freezes the moment I hear a smirk from Vincent's direction. I look at him and he bites his lips, trying to keep serious, but his eyes fail him. He's fucking laughing!

"Sugar, you don't seem like the type of woman that believes rumors that fly around. We don't deal with racketeering." Maddox smirks too, and even through the red emergency light, I swear I can see Lulu's cheeks reddening further. And it doesn't look like embarrassment. But then she hisses, she actually hisses at the man.

"I am not. Your. *Sugar!*"

Maddox smiles, then turns his gaze to me.

"What do you think?"

"Lulu and I will discuss it and we'll let you know. Thank you for the offer, Maddox. Should we get out of here before the ceiling collapses on us?"

"We should," Vincent speaks. "We'll leave the detail. They'll stick to staying out of sight, but we cannot risk Holt or O'Rourke finding out we're... too close."

"We have to meet Holt anyway. I believe he may have what we're looking for now and it's time to pay up on our investment." Maddox gives us another look, then turns to Vincent.

"Perfect timing. We have to see if he says anything about this." Vincent points around, stopping at me.

"What if he knows of us? Or what if he has surveillance to see if I was going to return here? It

368

could have all just been a ploy to draw me out... What if he sees you guys leave or..." Fuck! I was expecting some things to go wrong. But this... this was definitely not on that list.

"We'll keep to the story we told Loreley's boyfriend. After all, we did not get where we are today without knowing absolutely all that moves around the people we associate with, and your father knows this. I'll go out the way I came. I'll talk to you later." He comes close to me, and I know he can see my apprehension.

I hold his gaze, wishing he would just go, because my mind is a mangled mess and I'm not sure if he's the right one to trust right now.

"Morrigan, he will pay for this. They will *all* pay for this. Of that, I can assure you." With those last words, he twists on his heels and leaves, the others in tow.

"We need a drink." Lulu takes my hand and pulls me away from the chaos that surrounds us.

I guess we'll deal with the cleanup later.

Twenty-nine

VINCENT

"So, why did you say you were so adamant on finding this Boseman character?" Holt asks after we go through brief pleasantries. We met in a parking lot downtown, a random spot that's actually not random at all. It's one of our many public spots under surveillance.

"We didn't." Finn squashes his curiosity then and there.

"Right." He warily looks between all of us. "Well, if you're looking for him, then I'm just glad I didn't end up getting into business with the man."

"What did he offer?" I ask.

Holt looks at me for a moment too long. Just when I think he won't answer, he opens his mouth.

"Too many terms and conditions. We didn't like

either."

I nod. I would say that it sounds like him, but in truth, I have no goddamn clue what he sounds like now. The man I remember wouldn't have a leg to stand on in front of the elite of this city. Not to mention me, or The Sanctum. He's changed, stupid as always, since he's gone after my family, my Sanctum, and my goddamn fucking territory, but he's definitely changed. Otherwise, he couldn't have had business connections with the likes of Holt and O'Rourke.

But his balls are growing bigger than his brain is, our little spies talking of takeover and infiltration into business he has no place in. But *he wants* a place. So we need to find him and eliminate him before his claws dig too deep and leave a mark.

"Do you have something for us?" Carter asks, ending the pleasantries. I welcome his lack of patience, as we need to move this along.

"The bastard was hard to find." Holt nods, grabbing an envelope one of his men gives him, then hands it over to me.

I pull it open, inspecting its contents: an address and a name. *Jackson Davenport.* I raise an eyebrow at Holt.

"That's the name he's living under." He preempts my question.

"Interesting choice." It's hard to keep from

rolling my eyes. Jackson fucking Davenport?! Good ol' Lester Boseman chose a pretty fancy name there, and it matches none of the man he actually is.

Carter reads the name and looks at me with a stern expression, on the brink of a scoff, before he slides the envelope in his inner pocket.

"Posh, I know. I guess it bodes well if you want to go into business with the right crowd. Some years ago, my own pops pulled the same stunt. He needed a pseudonym for a certain… shell corporation and gave himself a high society name to fit in with the investors he was chasing." Holt scoffs as he slides his hands in his pockets. "Turns out that most people don't give a shit what name you go by."

His pops… my mind goes into overdrive at the choice of words and story that Holt decided to share. But I keep my face straight, resisting the urge to look at the others. This changes everything, and I can't wait to find out if the others caught onto it.

"Names don't cover sins," I respond, feeling that spark that threatens to reach my eyes. Adrenaline, enthusiasm, I don't know what it is, but I need to get the hell out of here now. "Pleasure doing business with you."

"Have a good night." He nods, his eyes swiping over us all.

We turn on our heels and head to our cars. Madds came in his, Finn and Carter together, and

I'm alone in mine, but we're not going to the same place, and I need to talk to them about this meeting.

Madds is about to go pick up two lovely ladies and bring them to the man waiting patiently in the basement of our safe-house, and we're all dying to hear what the hell he has to say. Only the ladies have no idea what's coming, and their reaction will definitely determine if the plan Morrigan and I discussed earlier is still going to happen. As it stands... I doubt it will. The woman seems convinced that I told Holt about her involvement in the club and it fucking hurts. Does she really think that I would double cross her like that? That I would cheat her in this way with the man I'm trying to save her from?

Fuck!

Can I blame her, though? When your parents pretty much end up selling you off to the man you're trying to escape, just to enable some fucked up business transaction... trusting others is difficult, especially the man that left you all those years before.

"Finally!" All the cars start moving away, and we head toward the safe-house, Madds rushing in the other direction. I don't know how else we'll be hit, if we will, but I just hope no one will be following him.

Damn, this whole night took such a fucking turn.

"You better have a good fucking explanation for why we were practically dragged here by this neanderthal, Serpent!" It's Loreley's melodic voice that splits our ears as she shouts from the bottom of her lungs the moment her and Morrigan enter the concrete corridor, at the other end from where Finn and I wait.

She walks with such determination in her step, making her look as imposing as us. A businesswoman. Fearless.

Morrigan, on the other hand, her furious eyes pin me down, her hands rolling into fists repeatedly, and she looks as if she's about to charge at me.

"Dragging me like that and bringing us into this damn bunker! Luke is gonna be worried!" Loreley keeps shouting as they get closer.

"Oh, I very much doubt that." Finn smirks next to me.

"What?!" She quickens her step. "What the fuck did you do to him?! Is this your goddamn ploy? Your way of convincing us to take your money and bring us into some shady fucking business?!" Madds slips by Morrigan and catches Loreley by the upper arms, just as she's about to lunge at Finn.

"I swear to God, you brute, if you don't let me

go right now, I'll chop your dick off!" She shakes her body as she tries to get a good look at the man that's a head taller than her, and I have to give it to her… she has balls.

The scar that sweeps down from his forehead to his cheek, just about missing his eye, gives his powerful and grave look a menacing touch. Not that he needs it. His six-foot-five frame, wide and packed with fighting muscles, would be enough, especially since he never smiles for the sake of pleasantries. He scares the living daylight out of most people just by leaning his head in the right direction. Yet Loreley doesn't seem to flinch around him.

"Luke is here." Finn pauses as he squeezes the door handle. "But he has nothing to do with our proposal for Metamorphosis. On the contrary…" He slowly opens the door.

"…the contrary?" Morrigan has been quiet up until now, and I have to give it to her, I was expecting her to lash out since her eyes landed on me. I guess her recklessness chooses its battles after all.

"Luke!" Loreley screams as she passes us by.

"What the fuck did you do, Serpent?" Morrigan stops by me, her voice low but rough, only her head turned to me, her lips in a straight line, eyebrows furrowed. She doesn't linger, but steps into the room, taking in the image before her: Luke with a bleeding nose and a bloody, swollen eye, tied to the

375

chair in the middle of the sterile room, Carter quietly watching him from afar.

"Baby, untie me! Get me out of here!" he pleads with his girl. "This is all your fault, bitch!" he spits at Morrigan that just walked into the room. "You fucking ruined everything for Loreley!"

Morrigan doesn't respond, but I don't miss the flinch of the muscles on her back.

"How about we tell these lovely ladies what you graciously told us after only two punches? What do you say?" Finn walks around to the table and grabs Luke's phone. "Or better yet, let's start with the phone call you made when you were *going to talk to the firemen.*"

"Baby, don't listen to them. They're all lies! They're trying to get to you, get in the middle of us!" he begs, pathetic desperation clear in his eyes. Does he really think Loreley is that stupid?

"Let him the hell out of these ties!" She swings around, heaving as she looks at Finn.

"Give us a moment, and then you can decide for yourself what you want to do." Finn brings out the phone and stands next to the chair.

"Start explaining, Finn. I'm losing my damn patience here." Morrigan is behind her friend, a shield protecting her from us.

"When darling Luke over here went upstairs to supposedly talk to the firemen, he actually went

376

to make a phone call," he responds, a wicked smile pulling at his lips, but it's doused in cunning anger.

"We sent our man upstairs, if you remember," I take over, "and when we left, we found him, held tight by our men, as he was spouting useless protests. And that is when we were told that when our man followed him, Luke said these particular words on the call: *There's something you need to know, Morrigan came back, but she's…* And that was the moment our man took the phone away."

"And I'm supposed to believe your man?! Surely you must have more than that to go on! It means nothing!" Loreley whips her head around, her eyes shooting daggers at me, and Morrigan follows.

"Finn, give Morrigan the phone," I tell him.

She takes it away, confused.

"Check the number. Call it if you wish…"

She waves in front of Luke's face to unlock it, then checks the call list. Her eyes go wide the next moment, but she's staring right at Loreley. Frozen. Unable to tell her that the one that actually betrayed her, the one whose fault it is for losing what she loved, is the one that sleeps in her bed.

"Morri….?" Loreley's voice is meek, begging almost, pleading that the reality she sees plastered all over her best friend's expression is not the same one we presented to her. She pulls the phone out of her hands and looks for herself. "The timestamp…

377

Morri, whose number is this…"

"Answer me!" she rasps when the response doesn't come.

"It's Ryan's number…" It's almost as if she's afraid to speak the words that spell betrayal.

We all watch as the soft, broken look on Loreley's pale features morphs until they settle on one vicious emotion: anger. By the time she turns to her boyfriend, she's red in the face, a deep crease between her eyebrows, lips tight, and with that phone in hand, she smashes her man right across his jaw, whipping his head to the side with enough force that we hear the crack of the phone screen.

Morrigan goes to pull her away, but I grab her hand and shake my head at her. We'll stop her if it goes too far, but for now… Loreley needs this. She looks at me, emotions clear in her eyes, but it's not the time or place to talk about this. Sure… I would like an apology for her belief that I would betray her in such a way, but then again… the man Loreley has been living with for quite some time has done exactly that. The ball most definitely isn't in our court tonight.

"Why, you goddamn son of a bitch?! You motherfucker!!!" The crack of his nose echoes through the concrete room, as Loreley smashes her fist right in the middle of his face. "Answer me!" She goes again, sinking her fist in his stomach as he spits

378

blood on his t-shirt.

"For you!!! For us! Because I fucking love you!" he shouts as his bloody nose drips into his mouth.

"What?!" she yells, but we're all confused at this point.

"I wanted that bitch out of our lives!" he spits toward Morrigan. "I fucking hated you since the moment we met. I knew you would get in our way. Too many fucking opinions, too much advice, too much influence you have on Loreley! We would have been more if it wasn't for you, always in the fucking way, always around, now in business together, living under my goddamn roof, spending our money!"

"*My* roof! *My* goddamn money! Not yours, *mine*!" Loreley pulls his attention back to her. "You're telling me you did this because you were jealous of my relationship with my friend?"

"I loathe her! She's a horrible influence, always pulling you down, pulling you into her fucking drama, her issues, and now with the goddamn Sanctum, out of all things?! I wanted to make it look like you lost everything because of her. I wanted you to see what I see and drop her. Send her fucking packing! Away from us! Away from you. You don't need friends! You have me! You don't need anyone else to get in our way! I want it to be us two, just us, forever!!!"

379

At this point, we're all a bit flabbergasted, watching the ramblings of this man that has a few too many control issues, and they're not even the good ones. Fair enough, I would be wary of who Morrigan associates with, but... this is weird.

"That's it... you wanted Morrigan out of my life, *our* life, and your solution was to tell the man forcing her to marry him, the one who abuses her, the one that fucking kidnapped her in front of my eyes, that she's in business with me?! Then you wanted to ruin things further by telling him that she's involved with the only people that can help her out of it."

Luke's gaze becomes clearer as his eyes widen, the realization that he fucked up only now dawning on him... yet he still seems to have some hope in there as he begins to plead with her. Only Loreley falls into a frenzy of punches, slaps, and kicks, probably hurting herself more than him, and just as I'm about to jump in, Madds closes the distance between them, wraps his arms around her and pulls her away even as she kicks and screams.

"What do you want us to do with him?" I ask Loreley.

"Oh, I know what I would fucking do to him!" Finn pulls a gun and sticks the end of the barrel to Luke's temple, who just freezes in place. He's not from our world, so he doesn't fully grasp our ways. I'm sure he's never even seen a gun before, let alone felt the cold metal of the barrel against his skin.

"No!" she shouts. "I want him to pay, but no death. Please, no death!"

"Thank you, my love, then..."

"Don't you fucking dare call me that! You will go as far away as possible from me, from us." She reaches for Morri's hand, and she quickly grabs it. "You will never contact me, never fucking think of me, never dare step foot even in the neighboring towns! If you do, The Sanctum will be the least of your problems. You will disappear from my life, unless you wish to disappear altogether." And with that, she turns on her heels and leaves the room, Morrigan pulling out of my grasp and following her out.

"Do not let him go until we tell you." I look at my men, as Finn, Carter, and Madds follow the girls out of the room. "When our plan has ended, throw his ass as far away from this town as possible. Got it?" They all nod and I walk out after the others.

He's a liability, and we can't risk him going to Holt or O'Rourke before we get to them. And goddamnit, my hands are itching to get to Holt. The gun straps next to my ribs vibrate against my muscles, begging me to just go now and blow his fucking brains out.

Only I can't. He's my only in, because if the address he gave me for Boseman is a trap, which I suspect it is, I have to keep him alive until Boseman is found; and dead. Although I suspect I may have to fight with Morrigan over who gets to end Holt.

A smirk pulls at my lips... it sounds like a good fight to have.

MORRIGAN

We're in this small room at the end of the corridor, my arm wrapped around Lulu's shoulder as I watch the man I felt betrayed by walk in. I was almost convinced it was him, and the part that wasn't sure was merely hoping that it wasn't true.

I went to the worst-case scenario in two seconds flat, and as his obsidian eyes fall on me, I'm not sure how to apologize.

I realize that it's not because I can't find the words, but because I fear that it will not be the only time something will happen and I will automatically throw the blame on him because of past events.

Do I not trust him?

Do I not believe in him?

Because if that is the case, maybe our involvement should end the moment the pact is fulfilled.

"Morrigan..." He speaks first, that deep voice penetrating my soul, a shiver passing through me.

There's a warmth in him that seems to show only for me, one that exists beyond those straight lips and grave gaze. He didn't lash out. He didn't even get angry as I accused him of betraying me to the one man I hate most in this world. He simply waited until he could make it right… Just like he did for all these years, he waited until his friend was safe.

"I think Lulu and I need to go." I finally speak. The plan will go ahead, but my mind… my heart… I need to get away, get a bit of distance to clear my head. But most of all, I need to be there for Lulu.

"Will I see you the day after tomorrow?" I can just about hear a hint of uncertainty in his voice. Or is it fear? It does something to me.

"Eleven." I nod, then turn to Maddox. "Will you pick us up about half an hour before, please?"

"As soon as I find out what you're talking about, sure."

Oh… they will, all of them, soon enough, and I reckon they're all going to call us crazy, Lulu in the lead.

We're nestling on her comfy sofa, in what has suddenly become just *her* apartment, no longer shared with anyone, sipping some hot chamomile tea. It calms the nerves, like her grandma taught her.

Maybe it's an old wives' tale, but it does feel like it's working.

"Not gonna lie, Lu, I'm not even sure what to say… I'm responsible."

"Why?" She scrunches her eyebrows at me. "Look, the man is clearly insane. I just…" She huffs and rolls her eyes. "There were red flags, I'm not gonna lie. But I ignored them because it was never something too crazy, too deep, or too concerning."

"I can't believe he hated me that much." I never thought anyone could. I've never done anything to him.

"Did you ever see anything that could indicate… this?"

"Well… sort of. I knew he didn't like me pretty much from the start. But it wasn't me he needed to like, it was you. So I just got over the weird things he sometimes did or said. However, I've never seen anything to indicate this level of madness."

"It's funny, isn't it?" She smirks and it's the first hint of a smile I've seen on her face since the club was on fire. "We both ended up with such insane men, obsessive, completely off their rockers."

I chuckle at the realization.

"I always knew we had similar taste in men, but this is a bit over the top." It turns into a full belly laugh. I wonder how fucking mad *I* look right now.

Lu joins me, and we laugh our asses off at the terrible situation we've gotten ourselves into. How the fuck did it happen?! One crazier than the other, and here I thought getting involved with The Sanctum was the worst thing I could do.

How fucking wrong I was.

"How do you really feel?" I ask her once we calm down.

"I'm not sure. I think if it was a normal breakup, or at least a normal betrayal, I would have a harder time. But this... it's so fucking surreal that I have no reason to have a broken heart. I'm just angry." She finishes her tea and sets the mug on the table. "It was getting rocky with him, you know? It wasn't the same for me... he was becoming a bit too possessive, a bit too controlling. I don't know if it was because of the club, but he always wanted to have eyes on me, see where I was, who I was with. And that spark just wasn't there anymore."

"I think that in your subconscious you did add two and two together, all those red flags. I'm pissed off it reached this point where he had to burn down our club to fuel his delusion, but I'm glad you're rid of him." I'm relieved. I never liked the guy. Not just for her, I just never liked him.

She pulls the throw from the back of the sofa and drapes it over herself.

"What about you, canoodling with a mafia boss?" She winks at me, and I can feel a blush creeping over my cheeks.

"He's not a *mafia* boss. Also… I don't think he's the boss at all. The Sanctum… it's peculiar."

"Honey, you can call it whatever you want, a syndicate, organized crime, it all amounts to the same underworld." She shakes her head at me and rolls her eyes.

"You should know." My gaze darkens and she stills for only a moment. The name Dietrich is spoken in hush tones in some parts of this country, and no matter how much she was allowed to do her own thing, Lulu is very much aware of her family's… *heritage*.

"Don't make me tap into my roots and smack you, woman!"

"Fine, fine! I'm actually worried I fucked it all up.. I thought it was him. I feel like shit."

"He didn't seem upset in the least when we left." She shrugs. "What was he saying about the day after tomorrow, by the way?"

"About that…"

I settle in and brace myself to tell her what happened at Vincent's house, some of it anyway, but more importantly… the crazy plan we have.

This should be interesting.

"He asked me if I would like to go have dinner with him. At his place." I set my phone on the island.

"Someone's impatient." She flashes her eyebrows suggestively. "You gonna go?"

"I don't want to leave you." We woke up this morning feeling a bit lighter. We talked, we planned, we talked some more. It's been a pretty damn good day so far.

A long time has passed since I've been able to just be with her, no Luke. And last night she reacted surprisingly well to the plan Vincent and I devised, at least after the initial shock. Apprehensive about it, sure, but, well... I needed that, not her approval necessarily, but she's my Lu, I needed her to know before I dove headfirst into it. She reacted even better to the dirty little tidbits I shared, like the fucking fantastic sex.

"Oh please. I'll be fine. Someone from The Sanctum is lurking in the shadows watching over me. And to be honest... I wouldn't mind a little alone time. I have to get used to it anyway."

"Are you gonna break while I'm gone? Will I come back and find you crying in that big bathtub of yours?"

"Yeah, tears of joy!" She raises her eyebrow in

that *obvious* way. "Nah, seriously now, you know me, I might cry a little, get this frustration out, but to be honest, I'm more susceptible to going back to Luke and killing the motherfucker. Now that the shock has passed, the Dietrich part of me is fighting to come to the surface."

Yeah, I was a little surprised that she stopped Finn from taking it too far down in the basement, but… she does still have her moral compass. Unlike me.

"Go! Seriously! Enjoy that hunky man of yours, and I'm gonna enjoy a bottle of wine on my own."

"Okay… I will. I'll let him know to send someone for me. I love you, you know."

She hugs me and smacks my ass on the way to the bedroom, knowing full well I have to wear some of her clothes, since I have none.

"I know… after all, what's not to love."

"Epitome of modesty." I roll my eyes and laugh.

Thirty
MORRIGAN

I ARRIVED BACK AT VINCENT'S HOUSE, AND I ALMOST skipped on my way up the steps. But I was so fucking apprehensive as well.

Only the man welcomed me with a cheeky smile on his face. No sign of upset, of anger, nothing. Though he is The Serpent, expecting him not to know how to hide his emotions would truly be ridiculous.

"So, did you enjoy your dinner?" he asks as I dab my napkin around my mouth, careful not to smudge the deep red lipstick I'm wearing. I've grown used to checking it delicately in the reflection of knives during meals. After all, it is my signature color.

"Delicious. And highly intriguing, which is why I have trouble believing you prepared it." Oysters were the appetizer, and it was such a delightful surprise. Then, what seemed to be an intricate pasta dish that left me utterly confused. I have no idea how to make that.

"You were there when I finished making it!" He laughs at me, but I don't miss the way his gaze darkens, like he's ready to flip me over his knee and spank me into obedience.

"Hey, I only saw you stirring a pot. I don't know how those ingredients got in there."

He rolls his eyes and I have to bite my lips. He was the perfect gentleman tonight, but the night is young, and I'm hoping he won't be such a gentleman after dinner. We're at the dining table, sitting on opposite sides, unable to touch, barely reaching to cheer our wine glasses. My skin itches for him.

It's been goddamn hard.

It's been harder finding the right time for that apology I really need to make.

"Vincent… about what happened." I can't wait any longer.

The man places his napkin on the table, settling back into his chair, one eyebrow raised.

"I was wrong, thinking that you were the one that betrayed me… I was wrong. I'm not gonna lie, it was a peculiar instinct, an involuntary reaction driven by the past. You dropped me… just like that. My brain is fully aware of the reason why you had to, but my heart is taking a little while to catch up.

Because, no matter what… it still broke. And after all of that, all I had was my family and their *endearing* qualities that are bound to leave scars when it comes to trust. Then it was all topped by Ryan…" Shit, this is less coherent than I thought it would be. "I know, I know you're not any of them. I know… Fuck, I'm sorry."

He straightens, dropping his elbows on the table and intertwining his fingers. Only I can't read his expression. I feel as though I'm looking at The Serpent now, not Vincent.

"I really am, I didn't want to believe it, but… I hope I can make it up to you," I continue.

Suddenly, a wicked smile tugs on his lips, and he quickly glances at the time on his wristwatch. "I think you can."

He pushes his chair back, rising elegantly, rounding the table, and stopping behind me. I have no idea what's happening, but the moment his hand touches my almost bare shoulder, swiping to the front of my throat, I don't fucking care. That touch is electric, doing something to me I can't quite explain. Hypnotic and so utterly soothing. He applies a little pressure, tipping my head back, then the man dips in and kisses me on a ragged inhale, turning me into a puddle.

"Come, Little Eve." He offers me his hand, and I take it willingly, following him toward the stairs.

He guides me up and turns me as we head to the bedroom I'm comfortably familiar with now. But he stops me in the open doorway. "I want to see the heathen in you tonight."

He swipes his hand, pushing my hair off my shoulder, and when his lips touch me there, my head falls back against him.

"And I want you to trust me."

I begin to turn to him, but he stops me, and I see something dark before the light goes out. Then a piece of soft fabric covers my eyes. I touch the material—some sort of silk.

"Trust me." He stops me once again from turning, and I drop my hands from the covering. I'm both intrigued and a bit frightened.

"Is there any point in asking what you plan on doing to me?" I ask as he gently pushes me into the room.

"With you, little one, what I plan to do *with* you. I may have taken your sight, but you will be a willing participant."

I may be scared, but it doesn't trump the excitement of the unknown. And it kind of sounds like he forgave me for yesterday.

His hand runs over the middle of my back, and I hear the delicate zipper of the dress as he drags it down, then swipes the straps off my shoulders. He tugs on it, over my breasts, over the full hips it pauses on, and eventually it falls to the floor.

Then there's nothing. Dragged out moments of silence. I can't even hear his breathing. My arms are suddenly too heavy at my sides, and I fist my hands, resisting the urge to lift them and cover myself.

"I'll never tire of looking at you… I almost don't want to do it for too long because I still want to discover new things about you later."

"Vincent…"

"Take your panties off," he interrupts.

I do as I'm told, hooking the sides on my thumbs, dragging them down as slowly as I can, bending over at the hips as I step out of them. I can hear his heavy breaths now, and fuck if they don't sound like music to my ears.

He presses his hand on my back when I get up, pushing me slowly until my legs hit the upholstered bed.

"Climb up. On your forearms and knees."

Again, I do as I'm told, and when I reach the position, I feel so utterly exposed, my ass up in the air, my pussy on full display.

"So *fucking* beautiful, Morrigan."

I can feel him behind me, not touching, but somehow his energy is there, his eyes traveling down my body, and my back arches on a shiver.

When his finger touches me, swiping through my pussy that's already wet just from the intrigue of it all, I dig my hands into the sheets, fisting the fabric. He dips in on one long stroke, two fingers making me moan, going straight to that spot that makes my legs shake. He curls those digits until the sounds coming from my pussy are the only music in this space. As he pushes one more in, I throw my head back, the delicious stretch so goddamn exhilarating, sending another shiver through my whole body, my nipples perking against the lace of my bra.

Then he pulls out without warning, making me whimper. Only, my protests are replaced by moans the moment the bed dips and his tongue swipes through me. And by God, this man could make me come just with his tongue. He licks me, sucks me, eats me fucking whole and I just want to lay down on a fucking platter for him.

He swipes that tongue from my pussy to my ass, sending yet another shudder through my body, that tight hole tensing further at the feel of him there.

"This will be mine tonight, Little Eve. I'm gonna fuck you until you scream, and when you do, I'll fuck you even harder."

At that declaration, my pussy tightens around nothing but air, and I can feel it… the wetness slowly dripping down my thighs.

"Look at you, so fucking ready, aren't you?"

Then he leaves me. But I don't move.

I hear some shuffling behind me, and the

distinctive sound of a metal clasp, then nothing.

Suddenly, one hand grips my ass cheek, his cock presses against my entrance, and just like that… on one long, deliciously painful stroke, he drives home, and my head whips back on a wicked cry.

"Never has anything felt quite this way. Never." He pulls out until just the tip of him is in me, and I squeeze around it, reveling in the groan that shakes his chest.

"Fuck me, Serpent, fuck me until I won't know my own name!"

"You better fucking remember mine."

My back arches when he fists my hair, at the same time he slams into me with too much force and somehow not enough.

He goes at me like a wild animal, and I need it. I need to feel him everywhere, I need to hurt, I need to cry, I need everything!

Gripping my chin, he dips his thumb into my mouth, and I suck on it, rolling my tongue around, before he pulls it out. As his rhythm slows, I flinch when he pushes that digit against my ass, but he goes slow, until the discomfort, the tension, it's all so arousing.

He keeps fucking me, moving in and out of my ass, and when he releases my hair and brings his other thumb to my mouth, I know what's coming.

"That's it… you look so damn pretty with my

fingers stretching this tight hole."

Not sure if I feel pretty, but I sure do feel goddamn good. My moans are getting hungrier and hungrier, demanding more, because having him fill me this way is a whole different type of ecstasy. I bring my fingers to my clit, pressing against it as he drives into me and mere seconds pass before I'm screaming like a little whore, coming on his cock and the delicious feel of him in my ass.

I collapse on the bed as he pulls out of me, but he barely gives me any time to breathe before he climbs behind me.

"Come to me." He pulls me onto his body, my back to his front, dragging his hands all over my flesh, kneading and rubbing as I relax deeper into his body. "I'm nowhere near done with you," he whispers.

My eyes would dart open, but I'm blindfolded and it makes no difference.

"On your knees, Little Eve, straddle me."

"You're gonna kill me tonight, aren't you?" I laugh.

"Hopefully not. I need you."

I laugh, but I'm interrupted by the sound of something squirting.

"Is that…?"

It is. I can hear it as he rubs it on his cock, and then the cold feel of that lube on my ass. I relax as he dips inside again, and damn that feels so damn good. Only I know what's coming, and I can't help being a little apprehensive about his thick cock. I don't have time to linger on that thought though, as he pulls out and grips my waist, guiding me until my ass is higher, right where he wants me. And where I crave to be. He releases me, and suddenly I can feel the tip of him against my ass, but I appreciate the position. I can take my time. As I press down, there's a different type of pleasure that stems from this. The lube makes it easier, and I'm probably not halfway in when I realize the pain is just as pleasurable, so I press harder, drawing on it, reveling in the curses that come from the man beneath me.

"It's too much…" I moan.

"Oh, you can take it."

"I didn't say I couldn't." I smirk, and he groans beneath me just as my ass hits his hips. I'm so fucking full. Deliciously so.

He pulls me against him, and I prop on my elbows as much as I can on either side of him, pulling my legs from under me, planting my feet next to his thighs, so I can still hold myself up. I roll my hips onto him, slower, adjusting to the fullness of him, moaning harder as the rhythm quickens. He grips my waist, holding me up, and starts moving, faster, harder, and there's no pain, no discomfort, just a delicious tightness.

"Do you trust me?" His tone startles me from this reverie. It's wicked, but firm, and I feel all too aware. My skin sizzles, my nipples perking up under the lace of my bra.

"Y… yes."

"I would never do anything you don't want to. You know that." His tone softens just enough to comfort me.

"I do."

Then I hear steps on the wooden floor, and I stiffen. Vincent doesn't. He carries on, and my ass suddenly hurts.

"Relax, Little Eve."

I trust him… right? I do… he wouldn't…

The bed dips and I know without a shadow of a doubt that not only are we not alone in the room, but I'm also not even sure we were at all this whole time. And now, we're not alone in bed either.

I lift one leg, instinctively trying to close them, but Vincent widens his, blocking me.

"Trust me."

I'm not sure how his words work, how they affect me, but they sink in immediately. And as they do, that second person comes so close I can feel their body heat. When a calloused hand presses against the base of my throat, it startles me.

But that touch… that scent… I recognize them.

"She's beautiful, isn't she?" Vincent asks.

"Goddamn gorgeous."

Maddox.

It's fucking Maddox.

Between my spread legs.

Looking at my dripping pussy.

While Vincent fucks me in the ass, and I swallow my moans.

And there's no denying where this is headed.

He drags that hand from my throat, down between my breasts, so slow, taking his time exploring me, and when it reaches just above my pussy, he stops.

"This is the moment where you tell me to fuck off. And I'll go."

My lips part ever so slightly, my mind muddled by the cock that's making me feel too good, by the fantasies that live in my head, the cravings I've always had for this man... the fear of having two at the same time, the implications of it. Yet I can't do it... I can't say no. I can't tell him to go away. I want this, so fucking much, especially now when I can see it's such a clear possibility.

"Stay," I whisper, and he doesn't spare a second. Just like that, his fingers slip inside my pussy and on a loud moan, my head falls back against Vincent's shoulder.

They move in and out of me almost at the same time, and I'm not entirely sure how I'm supposed to stay sane as Maddox spreads those digits every time he almost pulls out. Then a third one goes in, and I'm lost. He pumps in, a wicked sting as he stretches me, and at this point, I'm the one rolling my hips onto them.

Fuck!

Those digits leave me on a low groan and all movement stops. Vincent holds me still, and something else presses against my pussy. Maddox's cock is just about to impale me, and it feels much, much thicker than anything that has ever been inside me. Suddenly, Vincent's words about three fingers not being enough run through my head.

He slowly pushes inside, and the burn begins, the stretch already too much, yet somehow not enough.

It's surreal… I can't believe this is happening.

"Take it off," I rasp.

"Take what off?" Vincent asks.

"The blindfold."

I feel the brush of the fabric against my face and when I open my eyes, blinking a couple of times, he's there—Maddox, his intense honey eyes on me, guiding his impossibly large, condom covered cock inside of me. He's fucking beautiful.

A small grin tugs at the corner of my lips. It mirrors in his eyes, yet the man still looks feral. And I'm a little scared. And a lot more desperate for more.

"Lift your legs." His words come across more as growls, and I do as told, settling my weight on my elbows and Vincent's hands on my waist, as Maddox wraps his hand around my thigh and pulls it to his chest.

He pushes that scary cock of his farther inside of me and I'm not entirely sure if I begin to disassociate, but the fullness... fucking hell... the fullness... the stretch... it's a bundle of pain, pleasure, torment, and ecstasy. Then he's all in, and I'm sure he's rearranged an organ or two on his way there. The feel of both of them inside of me is nothing like what I expected. I can feel them against each other, but I can't quite understand how.

The moment Maddox begins to move, I don't care how.

"Jesus Christ..." I moan and he takes that as his cue. They both do, and suddenly they move. Almost at the same time, and my mouth falls open as the strain and euphoria spread like lightning through my body.

Maddox tightens his hold on my leg as his thrusts quicken, on the same rhythm as Vincent's. The moans that echo through the room are wild, their pace primal. The feel of them almost rubbing against each other is surreal, and so fucking hot.

They thrust harder into me. One grunts, the other one growls, and I'm just the little toy between

401

them taking everything they've got. And by God, they have a lot to give.

"I would have never thought…" The man above me speaks through heaving breaths.

"Me neither," I moan.

I drop my head against Vincent's shoulder, turning to him. His wicked grin tugs at one corner, and I press my lips to his. Somehow that coaxes them both on and they fuck me harder, thrusting as I almost scream into Vincent's mouth, but the man dips his tongue in and feeds on each sharp note.

I want this moment to last for days, the euphoria of it, but I can feel those electric threads pulling at me from both ends. I can feel them wrap around my core, around my ass, and I break the kiss, my eyes fixed on Maddox, and the man somehow knows.

He reaches between us, and the moment his fingers begin rubbing against my clit, I shoot up, propping myself up on my hands, closer to the man before me. His head drops, our foreheads almost touching, our gazes so fucking transfixed, the magnitude of this moment too much.

Too fucking much!

"Oh my Gooood!!!"

My cries fill the room as my whole body begins to shake, my pussy and ass convulsing violently around the men that stretch me. Their groans and growls follow my cries, and as Vincent pulls me against his front, Maddox's grip on my thigh becomes bruising, and they both begin to twitch as they sink deep inside of me.

I don't know who comes first, but the feel of those jerks against one another while I'm riding this incredible high can't even be matched by fantasies. I revel in each and every one of them, concentrating on every single pulse, every sensation, every breath, every groan and grunt... I focus on it all, because I know this will never happen again.

I don't think I would even want it to.

It was goddamn perfect in each and every fucking way!

"Thank you... thank you..." I whisper, heaving.

When I finally open my eyes, the men begin to pull out of me. I look between them, and they both have a mirroring crooked smile on their lips, and I can't help but laugh.

What the hell just happened?!

Thirty-one
MORRIGAN

THE ATMOSPHERE TODAY HAS BEEN PECULIAR, NOT because it was strange or bad, but because it wasn't any of that at all. Vincent's plan has been set in motion, and somehow the entire day flowed like a strange, beautiful dream. I'm sitting at Lulu's kitchen island, looking out the window, through the row of buildings, at the sea, wondering when the next step will be.

Ryan is bound to make his move, and since we returned from Vincent's house, we've been on edge. He has made no attempt to contact me. He is still, as far as we know, unaware of my connection to The Sanctum, but he knows I am here, at Lulu's. I insisted for her to stay away, stay at Vincent's place, or anywhere else with The Sanctum until it's all finished, but in true Lulu fashion… she wants to be in the middle of it all. With her friend.

I love her, but she's just as careless as I am, only in different ways.

It's the middle of the afternoon, and I'm not sure if it's in my mind, but it feels as if the world has gone silent. Eerie and disturbing.

Suddenly, my phone rings, vibrating loudly on the marble countertop, startling me almost off the barstool.

"Fuck me…" Lulu rubs her forehead as I shake my head at her. She feels it too…

"Yes?" I answer.

"I'm going to Midnight soon. I can send someone to pick you up if you will feel safer there. The guys are already there." Vincent's voice eases me.

"It's not a good idea. If he's going to make a move, the last place I should be is at Midnight. And you know this…"

He sighs on the other line. "I do know it… I just can not seem to be able to wrap my head around putting you in harm's way intentionally. I feel like you're the bait… and this is a huge mistake."

"Serpent, it's unlike you to be… shall I say, insecure?"

"Never!" he scoffs. "Maybe… Fuck." He pauses long enough that it brings a strange, giddy smile to my lips. "I just got you back, Morrigan. If something happens, if I lose you..."

"Got me back? I don't think we established anything, dear Sir. You're getting a bit ahead of yourself there." I can't help but laugh, as much as I know I'm full of shit.

"You're mine, Morrigan O'Rourke. You're mine whether your mind can wrap around that fact or not. Your soul knows it's mine, your heart has always been mine, and eventually... you will realize it too. And no matter what, you will still end up here, with your hand on the scar you left on the skin above my heart, and your lips on mine. Maybe then you will realize that I've always been yours too..."

A loud bang startles me, and I briefly pull the phone away from my ear, looking confused between it and Lulu, as she pushes away from the countertop and rushes to me.

"Vincent?! Vincent?! Goddamnit, answer me!"

Another sharp bang echoes through the already loud commotion on the other line, and my shouts are relentless as I fucking plead for a reply. Any reply!

"Goddamnit, Serpent!!! Say something!!!"

Then the line goes dead, and the panic sets in.

Deep into my bones, seeping into my marrow.

Flooding my bloodstream.

And when regret joins in... I break.

Never have I ever felt the paralyzing fear that splits me now. I call him over and over again, yet it goes straight to voicemail.

Now I'm shouting from the depths of my lungs at my phone as I wait for Maddox to answer the fucking call, and as I hear a sound that's just a bit different than the normal ringing, I just start talking.

"Something's wrong! Go to Vincent! There were two bangs! I couldn't hear him anymore! Go the fuck now!!!"

"Morrigan, what are you talking about?!" His deep, gravelly voice just doesn't seem urgent enough!

"Goddamnit, Maddox! I was on the phone with Vincent! It went dead!"

This time, he doesn't linger. He starts shouting at the group, ordering at whoever else is there with them. Chaos suddenly erupting on this side of the call.

"We'll send someone for you!"

"I'm okay! Just go to him! Grab everyone, damnit!!!"

Madds hangs up and I pace through the open plan space, back and forth, threading my fingers through my hair as I force myself to cope with this helplessness. Even Lulu has no words for this. She stares at me with a worried gaze, yet I'm not sure if it's for me or him… or us.

What if…

No, no, no. He's fine. He is fine!

He's The—motherfucking—Serpent! He is fine! No one can touch him!

But what if…

No!

Tears fall from my eyes as I chase away those devastating thoughts. The sneaky ones that force me to realize that my fear of losing him, when I didn't even acknowledge that I am his during this conversation, trumps that mighty question I haven't answered to myself about trust. It fucking squashes it to the ground! Because I can build that fucking trust, I can kill my insecurities and find out who *this* man is, not the one I knew so long ago.

But my heart… my heart already bleeds for him in the most decadent, unhealthy kind of love. I'm his, no matter what. I am his and he is mine.

And I didn't get to tell him that…

Too much time passes, yet I know it's not a lot at all. Not even enough for the guys to drive from Midnight to Vincent's house in the woods. It is still too long. I've kept calling, but that goddamn voicemail was the only sound at the other end, gritty and irritating, and it took everything in me not to smash this phone on the ground.

"It will be okay. You'll see, everything will be

okay."

I shake my head at Lulu's words, wiping the tears off my cheeks and eyes.

"Fuck… Luke was right. You should not be friends with me. I should be thousands of miles away from you, on the other side of the damn globe, because you do not deserve this. Look at me! I'm a fucking mess! And you're getting dragged into this bullshit! Fuck… if you get hurt because of me…" I slap my palms on the windowsill, somehow searching for an answer in the faint shades of burnt orange that start appearing in the sky, as all that fear, panic, and anger mix in this explosive feeling.

"What will you do?" My soul leaves my body as the sound of that voice slices through my eardrum. I turn around slowly as a shiver shakes my flesh, like I'm afraid I'm going to spook him and he'll make the wrong move if I turn too fast.

There he is, Ryan Holt, in the middle of Lulu's apartment, one arm wrapped around her from behind, the other holding a knife to her throat, as three of his men stand tall and firm behind him.

"Let her go." I'm trapped. We're trapped. The detail The Sanctum had on us probably went to Vincent.

"Where would the fun in that be?" The grin that lifts the corners of his lips and eyes is disturbing.

"Drop the knife, Ryan." I heard somewhere that

409

attackers respond favorably when you use their names. It reaches them at a deeper level for some reason, like you're reminding them that they are still a person.

"But it would sink so beautifully into her soft skin." He makes a face, like puppy eyes on a rabid dog.

"And if it does, you will never have me. I'll remove myself from this plane, if one hair on her head is broken. Let. Her. Go." I squeeze my fists as I will myself to keep my tone even. For Lulu's sake.

He narrows his eyes ever so slightly as his features become more serious.

"If anyone gets the privilege of removing you from this earth, dear fiancée, it is me, and me alone."

"Try me." My foot lands on the floor with a determined, loud thud as I step toward him. I may have become a different person recently, obedient and low key afraid of the man that threatens to kill my best friend, but the thought of Lulu being involved in this has brought a whole other type of courage to rise within me. Even if my insides are shaking.

It's strange, how one person could have this invisible hold on you, even when they are not touching you. It's as if my soul knows the consequences of his madness, and it tied itself together, just so he can't do it himself. Only that rope is loosening… and at the risk of becoming a noose, I will stand up to him.

Cocking his head slightly, he regards me with a bit more seriousness in his features. He begins pulling the knife away, only, just at the last moment, Lulu hisses and a red line appears in the trail of the blade. The motherfucker cut her!

"Oh, I'm sorry, did I nick you?" He feigns distress, but that mad smirk lives happily on his face, as he pushes Lulu away.

I catch her, checking her neck. It's a cut, but it's not too deep.

"I'm so sorry…" I plead.

"Come! I spared her life, now come, before I change my mind!" His hand is outstretched, waiting impatiently for me.

"Don't, Morri, please don't!" Lulu begs, holding my wrist as I move toward the man that is to be my husband. The one that only plans to keep me until my family fortune is his…

"I have to. I can risk myself, but not you, Lulu… never you."

I'm yanked away, while Lulu's screams echo through my mind, mixing with the bangs I heard on Vincent's call. I wonder if any other devastating sounds will be added onto that by the end of this day.

A day that started in such a surprisingly

wonderful way, after an absolutely insane night…

I sat in the backseat of Ryan's Mercedes, unable to control the tears that fell freely from my eyes. Vincent's last words on the phone ran on a loop in my head, until my chest hurt too much to contain myself. I've clutched my hands together so tight, my nails drew blood from my palm, my shoulders cramp from the tenseness, and on the inside… I feel empty. Numb. Broken.

I had him… for a moment, a split moment, I had him. He was mine. He came back to me. Even when I didn't want him, he came back to me.

There's an aching pressure in my chest, causing tears to fall in waves. The stone walls of the back room of the church absorb my whimpers, my pain filling this room that should be filled with happy memories, with a sorrow that only seems to grow.

I opened a dam… and I cannot seem to stop it.

"She is my sister! You will let me in now, or I'll make sure that old mausoleum at the back will have a new inhabitant!" Cillian's voice sounds from the other side of the heavy wooden door, which separates this room from the corridor that leads to the main room of the old church.

The wood creaks as one of the doors opens, and

412

I quickly swipe a sleeve over my eyes, getting up from the chair to go to the window.

I don't think my brother has seen me cry since I was seven. I fractured my wrist punching one of my father's friends who told me that since I'm a girl, I should smile more, otherwise boys won't like me. I've rarely heard him laugh the way he did that day, not at me, or at me being hurt, but... my reaction. There was pride in that laugh, and it was the only thing that encouraged me to be brave in the emergency room. My parents didn't come... they had company.

I don't know what happened to us. To him.

"How are you, Morri?" I don't quite recognize the tone of his voice. There's a level of care in there that I'm not sure if I should take as manipulation.

"Peachy, brother."

I don't turn as I hear him walk away from me. What is he doing?

I peek to my right and he's inside the small bathroom at the end of the room, signaling me to come in. I narrow my eyes at him, and finally make a move when he rolls his eyes at me. When I walk in, he turns on the tap to the max, and comes closer. Not touching, though. My brother never really touches anyone, for that matter.

"He has not been found at the house," he whispers as my eyes widen, my heart beginning to

413

race.

"What? What the hell are you talking about?" I almost rasp at him.

"I've spoken with his friend," he cuts me off, whispering again and signaling me to do the same. "I gave him an address for the man that is responsible. He might be there."

Vincent... he's talking about Vincent and Maddox. I clutch the shirt over my heart, somehow more at ease than I was thirty seconds ago. If he wasn't at the house, maybe... *fuck*... maybe he's not gone. However...

"Why are you telling *me* this, brother?"

He blinks, once... twice... three times, then sighs, hidden pain in those light blue eyes. "Because I know that when I abandoned you... you found help elsewhere. Plus, the friend told me to let you know. I put two and two together."

I felt utterly betrayed by my brother; no matter our distance, we had only each other... and then I had only myself. He has barely been present in this affair, never really lending a hand apart from some fleeting words of encouragement. And suddenly, he's helping The Sanctum.

"You really aren't aligned with... them"—I nod toward the door—"are you?!"

He shakes his head once, his eyes fixed on mine.

"I was never given any reasons not to trust Dad.

Not until... recently." He seems to drift to a dark place in his mind. "Only the man knows too much about me. Controls too much. And my *army* is not big enough to take Ryan, to ensure that Dad doesn't find someone else to continue the same sickening business. So I reached out to... one of the ones *you* associate with now."

"Did you?! When?!" Vincent didn't tell me any of this.

"A few days ago, after some of Dad's and Ryan's affairs started crumbling. Just after, I planned to come and break you out, only to find out that you were already out. We met, and I was told they were waiting for the last of the group to discuss. Only he was... unavailable." There's a tinge of a smile at the corner of his mouth, and I could have sworn I felt the rush of a blush on my cheeks.

"You wanted to save me..."

"Too late, it seems. And you had to rely on someone else..."

An uncomfortable silence falls between us. I cannot blame him, yet he is not without fault either.

"Why didn't you run away?" He finally breaks that silence.

"Like you, brother, the man controls too much... he held too many things against me. Including you."

"Me?!"

I nod. "If I was to suddenly disappear from his

415

life, he would kill you all; you, Mother, Father...
Lulu. But as you can imagine, at this point I don't
care much about Mother or Father."

"Jesus Christ! We're the reason you're caught in
this bullshit?! My God, Morrigan! You should have
said something! We could have gotten you out of
this!"

I smirk and shake my head. "I tried speaking
with Father once, and all I got was a hard slap
across the face. Plus... it's not just that. Ryan holds
something on me, something that could land me in
jail for a very, very long time."

Cillian furrows his eyebrows.

"Do I dare ask?"

"If I ever end up getting out of this situation"—I
wave around me—"maybe I'll tell you. Although...
the fewer people who know, the better. However,
what are you going to do now that you know all of
this?"

"The problem is that the most recent events
have pulled all resources away to find the missing
man. I'm unsure when my backup returns. But rest
assured, sister, one way or another, you will escape
this."

Suddenly, a hard knock sounds on the door
and my body goes stiff, but Cillian runs out of the
bathroom to check it out.

Mrs Holt appears in the door frame, sighing

with such sadness in her eyes and I can't help but match it.

"I thought you got out..." She walks toward me, stopping a foot away. "I was told to come help you get ready for... the ceremony." Those words seem to hurt her. I've never seen Mrs Holt quite like this, but I guess once you crack the door open, letting some feelings out, it's hard to close it.

"I thought so too..." My mind drifts to the night I escaped. Or better yet, when I was helped to escape... Maddox and Vincent under the stairs come into my mind, yet it's only Vincent that I see vividly.

And I may never get to see him again.

Thirty-two
MORRIGAN

T HE WOMAN LOOKING BACK AT ME IN THE MIRROR, covered in the hideous, sparkly, princess style wedding dress, looks nothing like me. Like it's someone else's reflection. She's living a nightmare. Her green irises shine too bright from dried tears, her eyes so red and swollen that even the rushed bridal makeup doesn't succeed to mask it.

Mrs Holt left my wavy red hair loose, only pulling together two thick strands from my temples, braiding them at the back and fixing a long, thin veil into it with a sparkly comb.

The hair… it's the only thing I like.

"You look beautiful," she all but whispers, and I look at her reflection, standing behind me. We haven't spoken a word since the moment she walked into this room. Until now. Nothing would have been appropriate for the situation, the atmosphere too tense, sad and somber.

I still have trouble believing this is the same woman I met years ago. It seems like whoever she used to be has slowly died, as the belief that her son killed her husband has strengthened.

I want to answer her, be polite, but... the will doesn't come.

This whole time I spent with her in here, getting ready for this ridiculous affair, I've dissociated deeply, caught somewhere in the recent memories made at Vincent's house. In his bed, between his sheets, in his shower... in the woods, where it all began for the last time.

A tear forms and falls too fast for me to blink it away, and I watch in the mirror as it pulls with it some of the makeup that covers my face. I don't bother fixing it. Mrs Holt doesn't either. She simply puts her head down and turns away.

This day would have gone to plan if Vincent wasn't missing... or potentially dead. Not anymore... There's no one else to save me now.

Even the anger is gone and all that's left behind is this... hollowness.

Only it can't truly be called hollow if anguish and grief reside there.

I hold on to some twisted hope that the pact

we made must be fulfilled… through some hellish intervention, he must keep his word.

He cannot break the covenant.

He cannot…

A familiar burn begins in my eyes, straining in the middle of my chest, my breathing staggers, and I have to turn and brace myself on the back of the chair that sits in front of the window. I wrap one arm around my middle, my head down as I will myself to calm, because I know that what would come otherwise… will be almost impossible to stop. I cannot break, even if he will not save me, if he will never return… I cannot break. Eventually, I will save myself. When I've devised a plan that won't land me dead or in jail, I will find my freedom.

I've been through worse.

Have you?

I take a deep breath, ignoring that voice that leaves behind doubt and insecurities.

A knock on the door startles me, but I only lift my head to look out the window at the burnished sky bathing the world in shades of fire.

Too bad it's not all up in flames…

"It's about to start," Mrs Holt announces.

The end of my life—that was the knock that signaled it. Only it seems to have switched on something inside of me. Anger… fear and hopelessness. Like a flood, it pours inside of me,

420

filling every vein and nerve with this dangerous concoction that spikes my adrenaline. Through heaving breaths, I finally move and stand straight, turning to Mrs Holt, who now stands closer to the door.

I shake my head frantically, taking a step back.

"We must go," she pleads, more with her eyes than her voice.

But I can't, I can't go, not to him, not ever! I keep shaking my head as the knock sounds on the door yet again.

"Go away!" I finally shout, but I can't seem to fully recognize that voice.

The knock is harsher, rattling the hinges, the door shaking, and even as I watch it, I still flinch at the sight.

When the door opens with a loud bang, swinging so far, it hits the wall, Mrs Holt almost falls to the floor as she jumps out of the way. The guard that stands in the door frame holds an arrogant look in his eyes. I recognize him—he was at Holt's house when I escaped... when Vincent and Maddox helped me escape. He obviously isn't pleased with me; he most likely suffered some consequences for my actions.

Good.

"It's time. Mr Holt is waiting." There's exasperation in his tone, and I can't imagine why.

It's not him waiting at the damn altar.

"No." I stand firm, looking him straight in the eyes.

"There is no time. Move. Now!" He steps closer, and he's only a couple of steps away when my ass hits the desk and I brace myself on it.

He sighs and comes straight into my face, rolling his eyes at me as he grips my left arm, yanking me away. Only I grab onto the desk, plant my feet onto the floor, and pull back as hard as I can, yelling at him to *fuck off*! I grip harder onto the desk, reaching farther back as I try to force myself out of his hold. But my hand slides through a stack of papers, and I'm just about to lose my grip, when something smooth and cold grazes my hand. I grab onto the thin, long metal, and with the adrenaline growing a little higher, I stomp my heel onto his foot, watching as he stumbles back, just about yelping in pain.

"You fucking bitch!" he rasps as he regains his balance.

In the next instant, he closes the distance between us, bringing one hand toward my throat, and I knock it off before it touches me, but I'm not fast enough to catch the other one. He wraps it around, holding tight as he steps back and pulls me toward him, and I push onto his chest, trying to force him away. Only the fucking wall of a man doesn't move! I bang my fist against his body, wherever I can reach in this angry and panicked state, and he doesn't even flinch!

"Stop fucking fighting!" He loosens his grip, using it to guide me toward the door, the darkened corridor that takes us to the main room of the church, seemingly lengthening before my eyes and only one expression comes to mind as I look at the abyss of it—dead man walking. My electric chair, my noose, my damn lethal injection stands beyond it.

And I'm not. Fucking. Ready!

As the man that holds me in his grip is about to take me through, I strengthen my hold around the metal object I'm clasping, hoping it has a sharp fucking end, just as I swing my arm up, jamming it straight into the side of his throat. He gasps like a fish on land as he releases me, the shock so beautifully clear on his face. The moment I pull away from him, I take that metal with me, sliding it out of his flesh.

And crimson becomes my new favorite color.

It sprays like a damn garden hose out of his throat, on the sweet notes of Mrs Holt's screams, splashing all over my hair, my face, and as the man collapses onto his knees, it paints a morbidly beautiful, abstract painting all over my pristine white dress.

When he collapses onto the floor, gasping one last time for air as I take a step back away from his body, I realize… I'm smiling.

The pool of blood beneath him is not large, most of it having soaked into the many layers of my dress, and I wonder… should this bother me? Should I be disgusted? Run and hide and freak out that I just killed *another* man?

Maybe it should.

Yet as I step over his body, watching the door at the end of the corridor swing open and two more men walk through, I realize I feel nothing for him. No guilt. No terror. No fear. That numbness inside of me, the one filled with anguish and grief, revels in the ruthless, careless rage that took over. It feeds on it, because feeling even the most damaging of emotions is better than feeling nothing at all.

Tucking what appears to be a letter opener somewhere in the folds of my dress, I walk straight toward the men that entered the corridor, but I don't care about them. Somewhere in this rage, I found the courage to take this whole thing head on. I have nothing else to lose.

Nothing at all.

They might see that in my eyes, or maybe it's the blood on my dress, or the splatter that stains my freshly made-up face, that makes them pause and look at me with apprehension. They even make room, pressing against the walls as I stalk between them, toward the room where the man I loathe waits at the altar.

I bask in the drama, pulling open that door into the small foyer where my father gasps loudly as he waits to walk me down the aisle. I confidently move past him, glancing at every single person that just stood up in the pews of the church, all gasping or gaping in shock and confusion, and I fucking smile at each and every one of them.

There aren't many anyway. My mother, my brother, and maybe a dozen other people I don't recognize. I doubt they're friends, maybe guards.

The man in question stands at the altar, trying but failing to contain his astounded expression, falling into displeasure. The priest, a step behind him, is completely pale as he takes me in, and I kind of feel for him. I know him; he's a good man, and I know he was forced into this situation just as I was. Only he doesn't look like he just slaughtered something—I do. Yet again that thought widens the smile that pulls at my lips.

I don't falter in my steps as I head straight for Ryan, standing next to him, my eyes fixed on the priest, who flinches, forcing his gaze to return to his bible, even as it flickers between the book and my bloody dress.

"What the fuck did you do?" I hear his gritty voice next to me, and with a serene feeling settling deep in my chest, I turn my head to him.

"The man you sent after me, he spilled." I smile

and turn my attention back to the priest, who closes his mouth just as I look at him, his eyes wide enough that I'm sure it hurts.

"You killed him?!" Ryan doesn't sound happy with my reply.

"Oh no… he died all on his own." I pause for a few seconds, then turn completely toward him. "Is there a problem?" I grab onto the sides of my dress, lifting it ever so slightly, and look down at it. "I think this looks rather pretty, better than it did when I first put it on."

My theatrics are fueled further as I begin to twirl on the gasps that sound from the pews. I stop, facing Ryan, who seems to have taken a step back, a slightly disgusted look on his face.

"Stop it!" he rasps between gritted teeth.

"Wait a second. Did you think that I would make this easy for you? You goddamn gaslighting, abusive piece of shit. You thought that you would force me into marriage as a price for some deal you made with my degenerate father, kidnap me, then burn down my fucking house and business, put my best friend in danger, and I would just roll over and ask for more? I am done, darling fiancé. You've put me down long enough, and the funny thing is… when one realizes that there's nothing left to lose… all bets are off." I take a small step toward him, feeling the madness that seeps out of my gaze. "And they are definitely off. If I have to go into this, I'm going in all guns blazing."

All of a sudden, the heavy double doors of the church burst open, bright light floods the space, and I get to witness the most beautiful sight, one that makes me want to jump in joy.

As one man is thrown in and slides across the stone floor halfway down the aisle, the only thing I can call the others are warriors at the end of a battle. Dirty, bloody, their steps heavy and assured as they follow the injured man that curls into himself, moaning.

They command the room into stunned silence, some of the witnesses dropping their gazes to the floor, wishing they would suddenly be invisible, as they stop in the middle of the aisle, right where the broken man is lying, their attention right on us. They look vicious, yet with an eerie calmness in their bones, their confidence profoundly boosted by whatever trials they've just been through.

Only the man whose terrifying gaze is fixed on me has no business looking that fucking attractive covered in bruises and blood.

I greet him with a calm, sweet smile on my lips. "Hi."

Thirty-three
VINCENT

"H<small>I</small>," I <small>GREET HER BACK, AND HER SMILE WIDENS IN</small> an impossible happiness that I put there. I would crumble to the fucking ground and kiss her feet if that son of a bitch wasn't standing next to her right now. If none of them were standing around us right now.

The moment my gaze fell on the bloody princess standing in front of that altar, the shade of red I saw before my eyes was more visceral than the one that stained her skin and dress. In that moment, all I wanted was to put a bullet in every single person who simply stood there, watching her agony. My fucking Eve... he hurt her. They fucking hurt her!

Only the reckless woman looked at me like I hung the fucking moon the second I burst through those doors. A beautiful sparkle filled her eyes, and suddenly the blood splattered over her freckled skin, looked goddamn gorgeous on her. It belonged in her chaos, because that smile when she greeted me, the way she carried herself covered in that crimson, told me what I needed to know—none of it was her blood, but she definitely was the cause of it.

My crazy, beautiful Eve.

The whole room is silent, apart from the moans of the piece of crap lying on the floor before us, who now tries to get up on his feet. As my gaze moves to Holt, I cock my head and wait for him to understand who he's looking at.

"What is the meaning of this?!" It's O'Rourke that gets up first, feigning some sort of confusion in this situation.

"We were hurt we were not invited to this... happy affair. So we decided to invite ourselves. With the help of Holt's friend over here." I hear Finn behind me.

"What are you talking about? Who is that man?" O'Rourke continues.

"Oh, I'm sorry, the bruises on his face might confuse you. This is Jackson Davenport," I say with a posh transatlantic accent. "Better known as the piece of trash Lester Boseman, Ryan Holt's best man. We thought you might need him at the wedding, so we brought him to you."

I don't miss the way Ryan fidgets slightly, and if I were him, knowing what he knows, I would too.

"You might be confused, Mr O'Rourke. You thought you were Holt's partner, but I hate to be the bearer of bad news, you're just the bank account. Nothing more, nothing less." I kick Boseman and slide him farther onto the floor, so I can move a tad closer, but also because I really fucking enjoy hearing him moan in pain.

"I don't know what you think you know, Serpent, but you need to leave right now. This is a private family event and business will be discussed another time." Holt's tactful approach puts a tinge of a smile on my face.

Interesting. Are we trying to diffuse the tension and avoid the crash and burn of his whole plan with pleasantries?

"Who said anything about business? I enjoy a good event, a good party, and I would very much like to bear witness to the fall of the O'Rourke family. Or the attempt at that anyway." I swipe my gaze over the people sitting in the pew to my right, pausing a little longer on Cillian, the man to whom apparently I owe a debt now.

"What are you talking about? The O'Rourke's will never fall!"

"Holt, care to explain your cunning plan to your business partner? Or shall I do it for you... starting

430

with him?" I grab Boseman by the hair and lift the lump of meat enough so he can look in the direction of the family.

"You need to get out of here, right now, Serpent!" Holt seethes. "Take them out! Now!" He waves at three of his men, ordering them in our direction, and they comply.

One by one, they rush around the pews, down the aisle, toward us.

And one by one, they fall to the ground on the distinctive silencer pop of Carter's gun, and the screams and gasps of the other two women present.

I cock my head at the man holding *my* woman by the arm. "You must have more than that up your sleeve… right? Or was all your security based solely on Boseman's people? Your daddy really left you high and dry, didn't he?" I can't help but laugh. "In hindsight, mine wasn't much better. I do regret not stomping on the back of his head when I made him bite that curb before I chased him out of town."

His eyes twitch, he wants to look away, but I have this strange gift that's part of why people fear me so. I can hold them here, dangerously enthralled in my gaze, until I know their bones shake with fear, until what I have to say is etched in them.

"You're going to go to jail! All of you! I'm calling the police, right now!" O'Rourke's wife shouts, fear and desperation in her voice.

431

I ignore the woman and continue, pent-up frustration for the man making me speak faster and faster. "In our last conversation, you slipped, threw a breadcrumb at us, and I love breadcrumbs. I use them, put them in my little dish, gather extra bits to go with it, and make something delicious. Like finding out why you know who Boseman is to me; not just *how* you found out, but *why*. Making that comparison to your own father in our discussion made me wonder, are you closer to Boseman than you made it out to be? Was all your bullshit about taking months to track him down, just that... bullshit? Turns out it was. You tried to play The Sanctum, play me. And, motherfucker, you thought we wouldn't find out he's been your partner for a while?! Overconfidence has to be supported by some intelligent actions, by brains, and here you are, thinking you can slap some shiny, new gloves on, walk into the ring, and think you can box?!"

"Jesus, how do you even make this stuff up? You have an overactive imagination." Holt laughs, a proper belly laugh, and I can see for myself a glimpse into her relationship with him. Gaslighting should be this man's nickname.

"Am I imagining what is happening at this moment in this church? Am I imagining your empty bank accounts that only see action when Boseman transfers money into them from one of his shady ones? The debt collectors threatening to break your bones? Or the containers of people we opened in the docks? Or the warehouses and houses you filled with them? Since I'm not imagining all of that... I don't believe I'm imagining you bringing Boseman back into town."

"But then again... we did gain something out of this. Didn't we, brother?" I look at Madds, who's a step behind me to my left. I can see the suggestive smirk in his eyes.

We certainly did.

I turn and my gaze falls straight on my prize, the one I would do this all over again for. I would fucking invent a deal, invent a crime, invent a fucking war, if it would mean that I could end up in a situation where she would come to me for a covenant that brings us back together all over again.

"Oh yes. Too bad we gained this cunning motherfucker's return along with it. Desperate idiot. You see, O'Rourke, Mr Holt over there killed his father because he didn't like how he handled business anymore, didn't like the control or the fact that he wasn't as involved as he believed he should be. And when he was gone, he discovered that his daddy not only left them penniless, but in a mountain of questionable debt."

I can slowly see some wheels turning in his eyes. He doesn't try to speak over me anymore, and even his wife is slightly stopped in her tracks with the phone in her hand as they try to make sense of it all.

"Holt is your fifty-fifty business partner in name only… Your financial partner, in your lovely drug, ammunition, and child trafficking business, is him." I lift Boseman by the head a little higher, enjoying the hiss of pain.

"You better tell me right now if that's true, boy!" O'Rourke snaps the phone out of his wife's hand and turns to Holt. She barely notices, her wide eyes fixed on me, like it hurt to hear aloud exactly what her husband does now.

"He's trying to fuck up our plans! It's not true! You know very well who Boseman is, my own business partner, which makes him our associate. Everything else has nothing to do with you!" Holt is shaking slightly as he tries to control his anger. Or his madness. They both peek through, though.

"Is he really?! Because he seems to know an awful lot about our business, and the way you're sweating right now doesn't give me much fucking confidence!" O'Rourke grips the back of the pew in front of him, the wood creaking under his hands.

Holt rolls his eyes, and sighs loudly, a finality in the way that air leaves his mouth.

"Useless sack of shit! You were supposed to kill him!" He cracks, a crazed look developing in his eyes, and his growing rage is directed at the man kneeling in front of me. "All you wanted all this time was to destroy The Serpent. You put our whole operation in danger because of your obsession with him! And now that you finally had the green light and the perfect opportunity… you fucked up!"

"Because the boy he last saw when he was sixteen is not the man he found in my house today. As I am sure you know by now, Mr O'Rourke, Lester Boseman is my darling father, but since him and my mother were never married, she was free to give me her family name, of which, as you can imagine, I'm very thankful for. You both have a lot in common." I look down at Boseman, pulling him back by the hair, until he can look into my eyes. "Only I'm done with you now."

I grab his head with both hands, as his eyes widen with terror, and in one swift, violent move, I twist so hard and far, that the man goes completely limp in my hands on a blood curdling crack that echoes through the church. He falls to the floor with a loud thump.

Finally…

An eerie, calm silence descends in my mind. Like a door I closed on a chaos I could never truly escape.

I'm definitely not the boy I used to be, because that boy knew what had to be done, but he just didn't have it in him to do it. I did, and damn if it doesn't feel good seeing his fucking lifeless body sprawled at my feet.

"What did you do?!" Holt rages, taking one step forward and dragging Morrigan with him, as he gapes at the body of the man who was helping him build an empire to get his fortune back.

"You should understand. After all, you did the same to your father, and you plan for another." I step over the corpse and stop next to the pew before the one the O'Rourke's are sitting in, and give him a suggestive, fleeting look.

"None of this concerned you! None of it! My wedding, my goddamn business, none of this had anything to do with you! You gave me what I asked for and I did the same for you, no matter who Boseman is... was to me or anyone else. You wanted him, and I gave him to you. Anything else didn't affect you! Now get the fuck out!" The man is in stitches, and I understand in a way. He doesn't see the whole board, and there's a whole game being played on the rest of it.

"Who said that I'm actually here for you?" I cock my head and let those words sink in as both Holt and O'Rourke look between each other, confused.

Thirty-four
MORRIGAN

I SHOULD HAVE SCREAMED, REACTED IN SOME WAY WHEN Boseman hit the floor—but I didn't even flinch. Instead… I can't help the smile that spreads over my lips and the shiver that runs down my spine.

Me, The Serpent is here for *me!*

I'm not sure why, but I feel like that teenager from years ago, the one that turned into a puddle and got butterflies in her stomach when Vincent Sinclair swiped a lock of hair from her cheek and tucked it behind her ear, before he even spoke two words to her. I want to run to him, jump into his arms, and claim him in the middle of this goddamn church! He locks his eyes with mine and I swear he looks as if he wants to do the exact same thing.

I'm enjoying this show though, all these

revelations, all these confessions. It's like watching a fucked up reality show on TV, only I'm in the center of the action. Might as well add some fuel to the fire.

"So many people in this room had… or have"—I grin at my father, looking him dead in the eyes, as everyone turns to me—"a pitiful excuse for a father. Two of them are dead. I wonder what will happen with the third. Tsk tsk tsk…"

"So, are *you* going to do it?! You're going to get rid of me, girl?!" He laughs loudly, mocking me in an attempt to put me down as he always does. Only it's the first time he's done it with an audience larger than my mother, and I stand my ground.

"You stupid, ignorant old man. You always act as if you're the most knowledgeable in the room, yet you missed the fact that the sociopath you're forcing me to marry played you! You're his damn piggybank! Our whole family is!" Ryan forces me in front of him, violently attempting to cover my mouth as I push him away. "And you stooped so fucking low for him. I mean, you were already scum in my eyes, but now… you're child trafficking scum!" With every word, my voice rises to a loud, gravelly note, and I bite Ryan's hand away when he tries to cover my mouth again. He grips my throat instead, holding me tight enough that he can keep me from moving away from him.

I don't miss Vincent's eyes moving between his

438

hand and face with such a vicious look in them, *I'm fucking shaking.*

"Oh, you ungrateful little bitch!" My father pushes my mother against the pew, trying to make his way out, toward me, when suddenly, he stops dead in his tracks.

"I think not." Only three little words my brother speaks as he presses a gun against the back of father's head.

"Cillian? What are you doing, son?" His voice shakes ever so slightly.

He doesn't reply right away. He looks between Vincent and I, then cocks the gun, our father flinching against it.

"I believe asking for gratitude from the daughter you are selling to a man that plans to wipe your entire family off the face of the fucking earth, starting with you, feels a tad idiotic. Don't you think?" Father shakes with fury at those words, but he's flinching because the betrayal is so thick... his daughter, his son, his business partner.

He has no one else to trust. Yes, he has his wife, but she doesn't mean anything to him. She's not a bargaining chip or a business deal.

"You've done some really terrible things, Father, and I'm tempted to let Ryan put the beginning of his plan in action, so it saves me from doing it."

"Cillian!" mother gasps and covers her mouth.

"It's true, you know," he continues and I can't help but smile, "the business partner you're selling your daughter to plans to kill you, then mother, then me, to ensure everything the family owns goes to her. Then he plans to kill her too, wiping our name off the face of the earth and taking all that we own for himself, to regain the fortune his father lost."

"That's enough! Stop getting your nose in business you don't understand. Fucking paranoid woman..." Ryan's hand wraps just a bit tighter around my throat, and I catch Vincent take a short step forward. But I quirk my lip at him. I want to be here next to Ryan, because when the time comes, when the ball drops... the motherfucker is mine!

"Is it all true?" After an awkward pause, my father asks Ryan. "Was that your end goal? To kill me for my money?"

"Isn't it obvious?! They're working with each other, inventing insane scenarios so they can get Morrigan out of this wedding. We made a deal; your daughter is mine, and our business is ours. It can't be undone. Not now, not when my other business partner is... out. Not when I know what I know about you, and your involvements in such... heinous activities." I can feel Ryan fidgeting behind me, switching his weight from one leg to the other, yet he still manages a maniacal laugh that shakes his chest.

"You son of a bitch!" my father snaps, truly snaps, raging at the man whose hand is now tightening a bit too much around my throat. "I'm fucking saving you from bankruptcy. I let you into my fucking house, gave you my fucking daughter, and blackmail is my thanks?! You ungrateful, entitled piece of crap, I'm going to end you!"

"Oh no, Father. *You* don't get to end him. Nor do you get to judge him, not after all you've done." I ignore his comment about *giving me* away. He stops his rant and looks at me with such disgust.

"And you do? Your dear father might not know what you've done, but I do." Ryan pulls me to his right, by the throat, turning me so I can look at him when he throws his threats at me.

"You dare threaten me too? Don't worry, *darling*, after tonight, none of it will matter." I smirk at him, no fucking tinge of pain when he squeezes me a little tighter as he grits his exposed teeth. "My sins are nothing in comparison, and tonight, you will both pay for yours."

"I've been lenient with you. I've given you freedom and allowed you more than I should have. You're fucking taking advantage of me now, and I'm losing my goddamn patience. We're getting this pitiful excuse of a wedding done now!" He rolls his eyes at me, the exasperated expression appearing more desperate than he thinks.

441

"Lenient? Since the moment you took your father out of the picture, you've fallen into a pit of madness, slowly shutting down the person you were when we started going out. You're a goddamn sociopath and I've been wondering if you've actually always been one, but you were just hiding the signs because of your father." I pause for a moment, drawing in a breath. "There will be no other vows tonight, apart from this one... I vow that you will not be leaving this church with your soul still in your body, and your body won't go past the old graveyard behind it. It's my vow to you too... Father." I slide my gaze to the man that stands between the pews. My brother behind him, but the gun is no longer aimed at his head. It's in his hand still, though.

Ryan tries to pull me to him yet again, heaving as he grabs me with the other hand, but he stops the moment Vincent's voice fills the church with blood curdling menace.

"I wouldn't do that if I was you!" I look toward the man I love and freeze when I see all of The Sanctum, including some of their guys in the back, have guns aimed right at us. Ryan stills for a moment, and when he tries to step sideways, behind me, the cocking of Vincent's gun echoing gently through the stone-walled church, makes him rethink the move.

"I should have sent Severin to jail all those years ago. And you too, Serpent. Then maybe I wouldn't have had to deal with this goddamn charade now!" my father rasps.

Maddox steps right next to Vincent at the sound of his last name, his eyes dead-set on his friend, the questions so vivid in them. Yet he doesn't say a thing.

I'm angry for him; he has no clue.

I can feel the pulse speeding under my skin, pins and needles spreading in a discomfort that makes me want to rage! Memories from that time flooding me! All the anger, all the confusion, the regret... the goddamn heartbreak!

"There are many sins for which you will pay tonight, Father, and don't you think that taking Vincent away from me by blackmailing him is not one of them." I can almost feel the mania in the strain of my eyes.

I'm done with this. I'm done with the fucking chatter. I'm done with my father, with Ryan, I'm done with it all.

"Wait. How the hell does she know that I threatened to send Severin to jail? I know for a fact she wasn't aware then." My father turns to Vincent, and I love the grin that quirks his devious lips.

"Because I told her." He looks at Ryan and that grin has a destructive confidence in it. "When we helped her escape your house, and brought her into mine, where we stayed... for days." He finishes that sentence in an almost lewd tone.

"You… you and The Serpent?!?!" Ryan hisses at me, and I can't help the beautifully wide smile that forms on my face. "That's it!!! I'm fucking done with this insolence! Father, get us fucking married, right now!" He tries to turn me toward the priest, who seems to have taken a few steps back from the altar, keeping his distance.

"No!" I hear my brother shout in the next moment.

"Don't worry Cillian," Vincent speaks, calm and collected. "He can't marry them, not legally anyway."

"What the hell do you mean?" My father takes a step forward past my mother, just as my brother aims his gun back at his head.

Vincent smiles a devastating smile at me.

"She's already married."

"To me," Vincent adds.

The collective gasps are positively exhilarating. They're not of congratulatory joy, they are pure, delicious shock.

"As of this morning, Vincent *The Serpent* Sinclair is my husband." I let that sink in for a moment. I'm a sucker for that dramatic effect. "It was a

444

beautiful ceremony. After all your effort, Father, after all you've done, we still ended up together. You blackmailed him away from me, forced him to leave me to protect our friend, and then"—I laugh—"all these years later, it was you who brought us back together. I guess in a cynical kind of way, we have you to thank for it."

"You whore!" Ryan rasps, giving me a look that used to infuse me with terror.

Only it doesn't have the same effect on me now. I simply use it as kindling on my fire, and I want to make him burn.

"Says the man who forced me to watch as he fucked another woman?" I don't miss the outraged gasp from one of the women in this room. "Spare me the righteous bullshit. This was our back-up plan. If something went wrong and he was unable to get to me before you said *I do,* at least on paper it wouldn't be legal. Your whole plan, your only plan, is ruined. Considering what happened tonight, I'm going to say it was a great one."

"You're a disgrace to this family!" My mother shouts from the pews, as my father suddenly charges out into the aisle, stopping in the middle of it and looking straight at me.

"I knew you were a lost cause, always so rebellious, always so insolent, but I never thought you would do something like this behind mine and your mother's backs! You ruined everything, as you've done since the moment you were born." My father perches himself on that high horse and it almost makes me laugh. But when he reaches inside his coat and aims his hand right at me, I realize I'm staring at the barrel of a gun. Maybe a second passes, and a loud pop splits my eardrums, the sound bouncing off the walls of the church, blood splattering all over me, adding to the carnage that already paints my face and dress.

I catch the moment of disbelief in his eyes, that very moment just before the light goes out, when realization strikes… and then he's gone. Smashing down onto his knees first, then falling face down onto the floor, on a loud crack as his head makes contact.

A blood-curdling shriek makes me roll my head in discomfort, as my mother launches herself on top of my father's lifeless body, and I can't help but wonder… even now, as the man that oppressed her for so long is gone, even now she sees loss, not freedom. *Jesus…*

As her screams still fill me with exasperation, she reaches somewhere under my father's body, and when she pulls her hand out, that gun is yet again aimed right at me. My muscles stiffen.

I expected this from Father, but not from her. Not my own mother.

When another pop makes my body flinch, the bottom of my dress gets splattered with yet another shade of red. Then my mother falls face first over her husband.

Somewhere in the back of my eyes, I can feel a subtle burn as I watch her body limp. Did I have hope? Did I think that without my father, she would be a different woman? The one she suppressed during the years she spent under his iron fist? Did I think that she would finally… love me?

I did… *she was my mother.*

My gaze flickers to my brother, whose gun is no longer aimed at anyone. He looks up at me, and we stare at each other for a few moments… It hurts, it hurts that it had to come to this, that we were nothing to the people that birthed us. It hurts that nothing could be done, that they didn't love us, even though, somewhere deep down, we still loved them.

I have no idea who shot them both. Was it the same person? Or was one shot by one, the other by another? Do I want to know? Does it matter?

It does… and eventually, I will find out.

Somewhere next to me, I see movement in the corner of my eye, and I realize there is only one man left in this massacre.

Slowly turning, I swipe my gaze from my parents' dead bodies, to the man I blame for most of this. I take a small step forward.

"What now, *darling*? Your plan is ruined. You have no money, no life, no one that cares. You'll lose your house, your cars, racketeers are on your tail… you're done." I take yet another step forward, but this time, he takes the same step back. "Almost."

"I'm going to make you pay for this!" He grabs my arm, his fingers digging hard into my bicep. "For destroying my life, starting with the first ever moment I laid eyes on you!" Before the sentence is finished, his mouth still open, I pull out the letter opener, and with a hard swing upwards, I sink it into his flesh, into those muscles that fill the hollow space inside his mandible, where it connects with the throat. His mouth falls open with shock, and I can see the sharp metal inside it. It pierced his tongue and hit the top of his mouth, blood pouring out of it with a speed I didn't quite expect.

For those few moments, the shock that keeps him from reacting to the pain is utterly satisfying. I was expecting screams, begging, swearing, lunging at me, but for those few moments, it's silent.

Then chaos descends, as he pulls me toward him, his hand still gripping my upper arm, and I pull the metal out of his mouth, just before he manages to. When his hand reaches for the letter opener, I knee the bastard in the balls, and the moment he instinctively bends over, I grab him by the bow tie, hold him tight, and sink the motherfucking metal

448

straight into his left ear as hard and fast as I can.

The screams that follow are so visceral, I would feel sorry for him if this wasn't exactly what the asshole deserves. Only he doesn't fucking die! My breathing quickens, my whole body is taken over by this raging heat and I lunge back at the metal. I push his hands away as he tries to pull it out, so I can pry it out myself and shove it in all over again.

He needs to fucking die already!

But an arm wraps around me, pulling me back against a warm body that smells of enticing bergamot, and he holds me so close, so tight, in such comfort. My lungs seem to slow down their effort, smothering whatever fire started inside of me. Then another arm extends on the other side of me, a gun aimed at the man that writhes in pain in front of us, and my fidgeting stops.

The end is in sight.

I sigh and sink back into the man that keeps me safe.

"End it." Two words I speak, and the pop of the silenced gun sounds like sharp metal on metal, sinking through molasses.

Just like that... it's all over.

He falls at our feet, limp... blood puddles underneath his head, spreading further and further.

I hear voices around me, orders, instructions... there's movement too. Only I'm stuck here, watching

449

him, unable to pry my eyes away, just in case… just in case he somehow gets up.

Just in case I'm imagining it. Dreaming it. Hallucinating… Just in case it isn't over.

"Come on, Little Eve. Let's go."

"What if…?"

"It's over. He's gone. They all are. Just as I promised you." Vincent pulls me away gently, and my body complies, yet even as I move, my eyes are still stuck on the limp man.

Blackness fills my vision, blocking my view of him, then two warm hands grip the sides of my face and guide my head up. The most beautiful, dark and vicious black eyes meet me, carrying more emotion than I thought possible.

"It's all done, Morrigan. All done." He presses his lips to mine, hard and possessive, holding me there for a moment longer than needed, and when he breaks away, there is something in his eyes I cannot quite place.

Is it relief?

Thirty-five
VINCENT

FOR THE FIRST TIME IN WEEKS... MONTHS... MAYBE EVEN years, I wake up and the world isn't spinning aimlessly. The dust settled, the woman that's haunted my dreams for far too long, wrapped tight in my arms.

I brought her to my home last night. Mamaw June was in the house, riddled with worry. She stopped in front of me, red eyes still wet with tears, and couldn't bring herself to come too close. Instead, she took Morrigan by the shoulders, looked her over, and pulled her to her chest, hugging her so tight, until Morrigan broke down. They stood there as she finished crying, and I felt completely helpless. And in awe. I'm used to reckless Eve, I'm used to her anger, her violence, her outbursts, her sassiness...

but seeing this vulnerability, after the actual victory, it shows her in such a different light. A different type of strength.

Mamaw June made sure we ate, then in her true fashion, quite literally sent us to shower and to bed before she left. Like we were nothing but children... not two grown ass adults that pretty much came from battle. Morrigan still carried blood on her face, even though we tried to wash it off in the back room of the church, as our men were cleaning everything up, along with the clean-up team we sent for. We left everything in order for Father Brown, but nothing can scrub off those memories from his mind. Safe to say... I don't think we're ever going to be welcome in church.

Before Mamaw left, she stopped in the doorway of my house, turned slowly, and looked at me with such pain and relief in her eyes that I actually felt sorry for the life I pulled her into.

"I can't ask you to stop this, to choose a different path anymore. This is it for you, I understand that, but... I'm proud of you. I'm sorry you had to do it, but I am proud of you." I was expecting the first part of that, but not the second. *"You did all of this for her, you did it for her life, for love, you did it to save her... and I know you did it for me too. You used that darkness that dominates you for selfless reasons."* She finally hugged me after this. She wrapped her arms tight around me, my aching

452

muscles hurting so bad, but I couldn't tell her that. She thought I was dead…

Just as Morrigan did.

When I went upstairs, I found Morrigan standing in front of the shower, still dressed, just looking at it. I'm not sure it truly hit her that it's over. Truly over. That she is free. She played her part in her life so well, put up a wall so high and thick, pushed through the shit her family put her through, then her boyfriend. Even in university… she just pretended that all is well and that a different life wasn't actually waiting for her when she returned. And now, for the first time ever… she is truly free.

I undressed her whilst she watched me, her eyes never leaving me. Then I undressed myself as the room was steaming up, pulling her with me under the spray. I washed her, then washed myself, and just as I was about to get out and take her with me, she wrapped her arms around my waist, pressed her head on my chest, and… just held me. Nothing more, nothing less, she just held me…

I thought that it was only her that needed this intimacy, this comfort. As she squeezed just a little bit tighter, memories of the day started flooding me, and one by one, the attack inside my house, the gunfire… struck unconscious and taken to Boseman's safe-house… they weighed me down. I got out, but not unscathed, I'm a bit broken, bruised,

I'm pretty sure I have a few fractured ribs, but I got out, because all I could think of when I was tied to that fucking chair, was Morrigan. I didn't wait for all those years just so it could end in a few hours. Then the church... Boseman finally dead, her family, Holt... It didn't just end for her. This was the end of a large chapter of my life as well. This wasn't just her revenge, it was mine too.

So we just held each other, under the warm spray of the shower, waiting as it washed away some of our sins, some of our sorrows. I think it worked. We fell asleep instantly after we got out, naked, skin still damp, glistening in the moonlight streaming through the floor-to-ceiling windows.

As I watch the sun streaming in now, it really does feel as though it's the first day of the rest of my life. And I can't fucking wait to live it.

"Mmm..." she moans softly, rubbing her cheek on that soft spot between my chest and shoulder. When she opens her eyes and finds me looking straight at her, she stops mid inhale, the seconds that pass feeling more like time itself standing still.

Suddenly, filled with desperation, she grabs me by the hair, tugging at me to get closer and meet her lips. She presses them so hard against mine, until they ache against my teeth, but I don't stop her. She only releases me for a split second before she dives back in, kissing me hard and fast, pulling at my hair,

454

making my scalp ache.

Yet I can't help but smile through those urgent kisses.

When she finally releases me, I realize she's smiling too.

My Little Eve.

"It's over... isn't it?"

"It is. You're free to do... everything." I rub a thumb over her smile, because I forgot how beautiful the genuine one looks on her. When I run my fingers through her red locks, she hums gently and pulls herself to my lips again.

"Can I start by doing you?" she whispers against me, and the laughter that bursts out of me gains me a hard slap on my chest.

"Maybe not, then." She tries to pull away from me, but in one swift move, I yank her whole body on top of mine, and she scrambles to prop herself up and straddle me.

"Oh no, don't you dare. You already offered. You can't take it back."

"Watch me." She purses her lips.

"Oh, Little Eve, I am going to watch you... as you take it, take me." I grab her by the throat and pull her to me, shutting her up with a deep kiss, forcing my tongue into her mouth, battling her own, before she finally melts into me. Her small hands grip my throat, tightening, taking my breath away as her hips grind over mine, her pussy getting wetter against my growing erection.

Grabbing her ass cheek, I press her harder against me as I push my hips up, and swallow the sharp moan that escapes her. *Fuck...* she sounds so goddamn beautiful when she's filled with ecstasy.

I slide my hand between her ass cheeks, past her ass, down to her tight, wet cunt, and when I slide two fingers inside of her, her back arches and she whips her head back on a loud moan, breaking our kiss, her tits pushing into my face.

"So goddamn beautiful!" I lick my lips as I watch her roll her body on top of me, and when her eyes drop down to look into mine, the flames of fucking Hell itself stare back at me.

"Fuck me, Serpent." That smile spells motherfucking menace, and the Morrigan I know, the one she never lets out enough, comes to play.

I pull my fingers out of her, grip my cock, guiding the head to the wet center of her, and I'm barely there, when in one long stroke, she drops down the length of me, balls fucking deep.

"Goddamnit!" I release her throat, grabbing her ass as my own back arches, pushing myself so fucking deep inside of her, I think I saw Hell, Heaven, and goddamn-fucking Valhalla, all rolled into one.

She doesn't waste time lifting her ass and

dropping down hard on me again, and all I can do is hold on to her hips as she leans back, propping herself on my thighs, her head fallen back, her long hair tickling my skin. Then she fucks me so hard, the only way I can describe it is her using me to get off. She fucking uses me for her own pleasure, rolling her hips in all and every direction it suits her, and I'm just enjoying the fucking ride.

And what a ride it is.

Her moans fill my bedroom, a sinful song along with the slapping of our skin, her cunt so damn tight against me, especially when she does that wicked thing where she squeezes as she lifts herself up, and my tip is the only part of me inside of her.

My fingers bruise her hips, but somehow, as my grip gets tighter, her movements are more vicious, her moans louder, her cunt tighter. And as her heaving breaths show exhaustion, I reach over and grab a fistful of hair, pull her to my chest, grip her ass cheek, and bury so hard and deep into her, she screams and sinks her teeth into my shoulder.

"Mooore…" she moans as she drags her tongue over the edge of my ear.

So I give her more, not fast, but hard, long strokes as I piston into her, pulling her head back, swiping my tongue over her exposed throat, as I release her ass and slide my hand between us. The moment I reach that sensitive skin that covers her clit and press hard on her, she shakes. Not in an orgasm, but with the realization that she's so terribly close.

And so am I.

My balls draw up. The only thing keeping me from spilling inside of her at this very moment is the fact that I have to get her there first. Although her pussy is so goddamn wet... I'm not going to last much longer.

I rub two fingers against her clit in fast, small circles, enjoying the way she squeezes her eyes shut, biting her lip as she swallows a long cry, and when her legs begin to shake and her pussy spasms around me, I'm at my wit's fucking end.

I come at the same time she falls on top of me, crying in ecstasy against my chest, my cock jerking inside of her.

"Fucking hell, woman..."

"Aha... fuck..."

Our loud, heaving breaths work in unison as we come down from that high, and even though I know we need to move at some point to clean up, I could just lie like this forever. Her soft body on top of mine, skin against skin, our hearts beating too fast, too hard, too loud... *fuck*.

This is it for me, isn't it?

MORRIGAN

"What now, Vincent?"

We cleaned up, pulled some t-shirts over our bodies, and now we lie here on the bed again, yet for me it feels like a strange limbo. We're… married. I'm married… only it wasn't for the right reasons, was it?

"Now, I think we should go get some food," he replies, and I narrow my eyes.

"That's not what I meant." I shake my head at him. "I know it was your idea for us to marry, just as a precaution in case something happened and ruined our plan. But… you can get out of it now."

He regards me for a few moments, blinking rapidly as he quite visibly gathers his thoughts. I could have sworn a tinge of regret flashed over his expression. But I blinked and it wasn't there anymore. Did I imagine it?

He was forced into this, just as I was. Only I don't…

"We can get an annulment," he interrupts my thoughts. "I told you, Morrigan, you're free now. Free to make your own choices, build your own path outside anyone's control, and I will not stop you."

"Really? You wouldn't stop me or protest if I told you right now that I want an annulment? You wouldn't be angry, or hurt, or upset? It wouldn't affect you in the slightest?" I'm struggling to rein back my disappointment in his response.

"I wouldn't stop you, wouldn't be angry, or hurt, and if I would be upset, I definitely wouldn't tell you. Us getting married was about your protection, just another union forced on yourself because of circumstance. There's too much fire in you, and it was never given enough oxygen to burn at its true potential. I definitely will not be the one to hold you back, if that's what you wish."

He sighs, shaking his head, and the expression in his eyes shifts all at once, a veil that falls, uncovering truths, desires, fears…

"But I can't lie and say I wouldn't be affected. I want you, Morrigan. I want you by my side now and for the rest of time. I want a life with you. You're the Eve to my Serpent. Everything I forced myself not to dream of all those years ago, *that's* what I want. I want to be the first thing you see in the morning and the last thing you see at night. I want you in every way possible."

He swipes a hand over his face and yet again he sighs.

"I just… I want you so much it fucking hurts. But this is not about what I want, it's about you. I will never be the same as the men we killed for your freedom. No matter how much I would love to tie you to my bed and never ever let you go, I will never do that unless it's your wish."

He looks at me like we're two universes that have finally collided after a millennia of trying to find each other. Lovers who had to travel through time until they found the right one where they were supposed to be together.

There isn't just love in those eyes. There is an obsession that eats at him, because he has to subdue it like a caged beast. And I cannot do anything but admire how much he forces that just for me. To give me space, to let me grow and be whoever I need to be. He holds back out of fucking respect, and there's no way I would need anything more than that from the man I love.

"However"—he stops my train of thought yet again—"don't mistake my respect for lack of passion. Because I will do everything in my power to make you mine. I would go through what we've been through all over again if I had to, because we belong together, and I know you know that too. You are meant to be my wife and I your husband, and I will wait for you to find the person you're supposed to be, but make no mistake, Little Eve, my ring will still end up on your finger. No matter how much you will delay it… I am yours, and you are mine."

I cock my head slightly, lifting one eyebrow as I look at the man that was always meant to be mine.

I'm not sure if he caught on to the slight insecurity in his speech, no matter how confident he is… there is a tinge of fear that I will reject him, that I will ask for that annulment. One corner of my lips quirks up, and he narrows his eyes in slight confusion, like a man feeling mocked, and I can't help but release the smile I've held back, because he is so fucking right… he *is* mine and I am his. We're restarting our journey somewhere in the middle, but it's exactly where I need to be.

"You're mine, Vincent."

"Till death do us part?" He smiles, sweet and devastating at the same time.

"Till death do us part."

THE END

I hope you enjoyed Morrigan and Vincent's story
in Reckless Covenant.

Are you looking for something darker to read?
Check out My Kind of Monster
by scanning the QR code!

Also by THE AUTHOR

My Kind of Monster:
a Dark Contemporary Romance

Even in Death:
a Romantic Horror Novella

Blissful Perdition:
a Lesbian Romance Short Story

Vows and Vendettas:
a Dark Mafia Romance Anthology

About
THE AUTHOR

Lilith Roman is a romance author who lives with her husband and fluffy bear-dog in the UK, where she writes contemporary and paranormal stories laced with a little danger, intense passion, and dark themes, that always end in a Happily Ever After. She's far too passionate about chocolate, cursing, and steamy books, and her love for horror movies convinced her that even the monster under the bed needs a love story.

Sign up for her newsletter to be notified about releases, books going on sale, events and other news!

CONNECT WITH ME

lilithromanauthor.com
lil@lilithromanauthor.com

Thank You
ACKNOWLEDGMENTS

I tend to babble, so I'll try to keep this short.

I have to start with my husband… I love you, even more now when I see how supportive you are, even when I'm constantly absent and tired. Thank you for grounding me when it becomes too much and I'm ready to throw in the towel.

To J Rose, I still don't remember how you came into my life, but I hope you never leave. Still waiting to be seduced though.

To Mackenzie, my editor, you're my no 1 cheerleader and I'm not quite sure if I would still be sane without you.

To May, thank you for casting an eye last minute on this story. I'm always scared when you read my stories, but I love your brain, your input, and you.

Dani, thank you so much for including me in this collection, it's such a brilliant concept and I'm so grateful that I got to be part of it.

Finally, to all of you... my Sirens, my Jackdaws, bookstagrammers, bloggers, booktokers, all of you who wanted to help me read or promote this book. Thank you from the bottom of my heart!

Love,
Lilith

Made in the USA
Las Vegas, NV
26 June 2023

73888386R00277